SWITCHER

Brian White

Once When All Was Quiet

Worlds torn asunder by flurries of light,
As minds begin to be;
Twisted and formed to survive the fight,
But who holds the key?

This book is dedicated to
my lovely wife of over thirty years, Marcia

Foreword

Shortly after the terrorist attack on New York and the Pentagon, I watched all developments carefully as did nearly everyone else I'm sure. One night I saw a news report about the plight of women in Afghanistan. What particularly bothered me was a scene in which a woman was marched into the soccer stadium in Kabul amidst a crowd of cheering men, forced to her knees, and then shot in the back of her head. Her crime was refusing to wear the traditional burka.

That was when the idea for SWITCHER came to me. It was more in the form of questions. "What if a woman is thrust into an impossible situation involving several men much larger who had dire plans for her? What if her only defenses were guile and strong will?"

The answers came as quickly as the questions. It took time to transfer them from my mental notepad to actual paper. SWITCHER was born, written to show the women of the world who are treated as property they can overcome anything. That is the motivation behind the story. I hope you enjoy it.

Spook

Forgetful sleep
Sickest of kin;
Models thy keep
To rise again.

CHAPTER 1

July 17, Burksdale Memorial Hospital Maternity Ward, 22 years ago

Nurse Ashley took a few moments to calm her nerves before opening the waiting room door. She feigned a slight smile while looking among the occupants. "Mr. Jackson, Doctor Abelson needs to see you."

Televised forecasts for scattered afternoon thunderstorms replaced various conversations. Most in the room were grateful their names weren't called, that prior notifications were congratulatory gender announcements. Fear replaced excitement for the recipient of her message. As he closed his cell phone, his hands began shaking. "Why?" He asked. "What's wrong?"

Ashley's smile grew. "The doctor will explain everything, but let me ease your mind. Both your wife and child are recovering nicely."

A large sigh slipped out of his mouth. "Is it a boy? When can I see him?"

She struggled to remain calm while answering. "It's a girl. You can see her soon but I need to take you to the doctor first; if you'll please come with me?"

This is a huge disappointment for him. He is Brent Jackson, owner of Jackson Realty in need of an heir. His requirements are for a son which he'd hoped would be his first-born. A girl just won't do. Observations have shown females don't have the mettle needed for this brutal line of work. She'd ruin everything he'd worked so hard to build. Well he'll just have to start over. Let Paula have the girl and he'll set about prepping his son for life. When he took one step toward her, that smile fluctuated just enough for him to see. It caused him to stop and summarize a reason for her odd behavior. "Is she retarded; my daughter?"

Plans for leaving the girl as a ward of the state began forming until the nurse shook her head. "Not as far as we can tell Mr. Jackson. She's a healthy, beautiful baby."

Jackson resumed walking until he was facing the nurse less than six inches away. The nurse's smile remained constant even under close scrutiny. "I can see you're not going to give any answers," he said. "Lead on so I can get this over. I have a son to make."

Ashley blinked like something smacked her forehead. Jackson's brows knitted together, head tilted slightly, and started to speak just as she turned to walk down the hall. His apprehension compounded tenfold when she said "Doctor Abelson is waiting for you."

To Jackson, this silent march toward points unknown had the feel of going to a morgue for body identification. Dozens of dreadful possibilities ran amok in his mind, blurring his ability to think straight. His heartbeat accelerated when the nurse stopped in front of a closed door. One quiet knock from her hand preceded her turning the knob.

A balding middle-aged man seated behind a desk was quietly talking into a tape recorder until he saw them. The sorrowful expression on his face made Jackson want to take back the pregnancy. His head nodded to the nurse, and then looked at Jackson. "Please come in," he said.

Fear slowly changed to anger as Jackson finally processed what little information the nurse supplied. His wife and girl were okay which means all this death-watch attitude was for something else. Time was too precious a commodity to waste, yet these clowns seem determined to keep him as long as possible. Abelson rose but remained behind the desk like Jackson did while firing a useless employee. This further enraged Jackson as he pushed past the nurse. The door closed once he was clear. Before the doctor could speak, Jackson rushed across the plush carpet to stand with his belly against the desk, hands balled into fists. "Okay I've had it with all the spooky crap. You have two minutes to tell me why I'm here instead of beside my wife or I start ripping apart your walls!"

Abelson's expression remained unchanged even though Jackson towered over him by a foot. Slowly Abelson's hand came out indicating for Jackson to take a seat which was ignored. "Mr. Jackson,

I'm sure you know by now both your wife and daughter are doing just fine, and I do apologize for the way this must have appeared to you. There were complications during the delivery that gave us a pretty good scare, but our skilled staff was able to save them both."

That sounded extremely evasive to Jackson, like a cover-up of some kind. His mind began formulating theories of surgical errors as he menacingly leaned closer. "Go on," Jackson said.

Slowly Abelson sat down, his chair sliding away a few inches. His cowardly retreat nearly made Jackson hop over the desk.

"Even with today's medicine, we don't hold all the answers. Have you ever heard of Placenta Percreta?"

The fear began returning as Jackson receded from the desk. "No."

It felt like the floor was about to fall out from under Jackson's feet, but he managed to remain standing close to the desk. Abelson's face softened slightly as he opened a drawer to retrieve a pamphlet. "Your wife had an unusual development during labor extremely similar to Placenta Percreta" he said. "I could go into the details if you like, but it's summarized in the pamphlet. Even with her regularly scheduled prenatal visits it remained undetected. If this affliction is permitted to advance into a natural birth, there is almost always a high fatality factor."

"But you said they're doing fine."

Abelson smiled as he handed the pamphlet to Jackson, which pictured a smiling mother in bed holding her newborn. Jackson accepted the document without looking away as the doctor spoke. "It was a combination of ability and a little good luck that enabled us to save their lives. Your wife is currently undergoing treatment and appears to be responding well. You should be able to see her in a few hours. Your baby is in perfect health though. Would you care to see her now?"

Relief washed over Jackson as he chuckled silently a few times and stepped away. Those actions seemed to lighten Abelson's mood as well. "Maybe in a minute," Jackson said. "Tell me; how long do I have to wait before I can make my son?"

The ambiance seemed to change instantly. Abelson's face darkened. "I'm afraid your wife can't bear any more children. Keep in mind she almost *died* today!"

Jackson's teeth ground together, his jaw locked, muscles tensed, and eyes narrowed to tiny slits as he allowed the pamphlet to slip through his fingers. "You mean you sterilized her?"

As Abelson started shaking his head, Jackson turned to walk toward the door. "Mr. Jackson, we did all we could to save your wife."

Out of fear of what he'd do if he looked back, Jackson yanked the door open and stepped into the hall. Sounds of a chair quickly rolling across carpeting reached his ears just before he pulled the door shut so violently, three hospital attendants looked at him. One nasty glare at each person sent their eyes searching elsewhere. Abelson wisely chose not to follow or it was a good bet he'd wind up a customer in his own establishment. Jackson stomped down the hall heading toward an exit.

Once outside, Jackson began vocally commiserating. "What good is a girl to me? I need a son, not a sniveling playing-with-dolls fantasizing-about-Prince-Charming daughter."

A man helping his very pregnant wife to the door gave wide berth to Jackson as they passed. Jackson almost warned him off, but decided not to waste the time. Why should he be the only one to suffer from this institution's incompetence? He resumed walking, misery filling his mind once he reached the car. "My company's future is doomed. I won't adopt anyone else's trash, and a girl would destroy Jackson Realty. If I divorce Paula, she might find the courage to take half of everything. Oh God I'm trapped."

As he placed the key in the lock, enragement returned. His thoughts reverted toward the medical incompetence that led to this debacle. Heat instantly rose from the interior once the door opened, which seemed an extension of Jackson's fury. His jaw tensed as he literally fell onto the seat. "I'm going to make that holier-than-thou doctor pay through his teeth for what he did. And God keep that little girl out of my sight. Every time I look at her it'll remind me of this day!"

CHAPTER 2

Tuesday May 12th, Jackson Residence, Present Day

At last I'm free from that tyrant. It's time to put this horror behind and get on with my life. My plans are irrevocably in motion, but mom keeps following me around like a sorrowful puppy worried expression included. As I made one final glance toward the stairs, she placed her hand on my shoulder. "You can't leave like this," she said.

Defiant victory forged a smile as I pulled free. "Watch me."

My big suitcases were in the car. I merely wanted to make certain nothing I might need was left. Now that I'm satisfied there's no reason to wait, I turned to step into the pre-dawn morning. She pushed past me down the porch steps and stood blocking my way. "Your father has forbidden you from leaving. If you go, he'll disown you!"

That was the final insult. Rather than walk past her, I placed my hands on my hips and glared. "You honestly think I care? He's never acknowledged *anything* I've done." A chuckle snuck out. "He's not even here to see me off. The high and mighty Brent Jackson conveniently needed to be elsewhere after escalating his threats for the past three days. You quietly sat through it as usual. When are you going to realize he's a manipulating bastard who uses you any way he can?"

Her mouth opened and then closed, eyes dropping to the sidewalk. Birds chirping in trees sounded like a sad lullaby to this ending.

She wasn't the one constantly punishing me, nor was she always putting me down. However she allowed me to rot under his hateful ways meaning it's time to go.

"Look, I'll call when I'm settled," I said.

A single tear ran down her cheek when I brushed by her. "Joyce," she said.

That stopped my progression but did not grab my eyes. "Please don't go."

In spite of the true regret in her voice, there was no way I could continue living under dad's terms. If I tried explaining it again, she'd only become more upset. Rather than risk turning sorrow into anger, I faced her and quickly kissed her cheek. Before she could pull me into a hug, I stepped out of reach to continue toward my car.

Sunlight broke over the horizon when I climbed inside, forcing me to lower the visor while lifting my spirits. Mom stood in front of the porch, chest heaving from apparent sobs as I started the car. Without hesitation I pulled away.

Once I was on the Interstate, all traces of sadness evaporated. I felt free and realized this must be how criminals feel when they're paroled. While singing the songs from the radio station, I continued heading east into my future.

Since that nightmare at my sixteenth birthday party, I'd been quietly saving and planning for this day. Dad had no idea how much money I'd tucked away and truly believed his final threat of cancelling my charge cards would force me to reconsider. If he noticed I'd never used them, he never let on.

Yesterday I closed my accounts, pulling out enough money to live comfortably anywhere I choose until finding a teaching job. My grades were superb. With a Master's Degree in Education, I should have no problem locating a school near the beach. But first I want and more importantly need a soothing vacation to clear my mind.

Fourteen hours into my journey, it occurred to me that if I continue heading to the ocean there could be a problem finding a room for the night. I was already in North Carolina's mountains, far enough to feel safe from probing parents. The exit sign said food and rooms were just ahead, so why not sleep in a small town tonight and start fresh in the morning?

A quarter mile off the ramp stood a quaint little country hotel which looked empty. Had it not been for the light shining through windows in the office, I would've thought the place closed. That sense of adventure escalated as I pulled into the lot.

Nobody was in the office. It took three dings of the bell to bring a bored-looking teenager forward. Just in case my father tried calling in some favors from his more influential acquaintances, I signed-in under a false name. The clerk didn't even look at the register, just handed me a key with the instructions to clear out by ten tomorrow. Then he walked back to wherever he'd been.

Hunger made an audible complaint as soon as I stepped to the lot. That would have been terribly embarrassing had it happened with the teen listening. Rather than inspect my room, I turned the car around and headed out looking for the food promised on the highway sign.

About two miles past the hotel, a garish neon sign lit up the sky claiming fine beer and quality foods. Since I'd traveled this narrow highway without seeing another vehicle, I decided there'd been enough adventure for one day and pulled off the road. It was then I noticed only two other cars were parked. Granted this is a Tuesday night, but don't these people do anything during the week?

Soothingly cool night air rushed in when my door opened, but as soon as I stepped onto the lot a sense of foreboding came over me. One quick check of the surroundings proved nothing sinister was afoot. It must be tiredness making me jittery. Even though there was no reason to feel threatened, I quickened my pace until I opened the door. A song asking if it was my body, or something I might be was playing on the jukebox. The tune brought back memories of college and how one of my friends dated a guy who loved that musician.

Two male heads looked at me as I entered. One was manning the cash register near the door and the other was seated at the bar. It appeared no one else was inside. The cash register guy took my order for white wine as I selected a table. Once he'd stepped behind the bar, the other guy rose to walk toward me. He appeared to be in his forties and was eying me like a piece of meat. Involuntary shudders coursed through me as I looked away. Approaching footsteps halted a few feet to my left. "Good evening Miss. My name is John; and you are-?"

"Tired."

A deep breath escaped from him, causing me to look his direction. The expression on his face bordered on hilarity like he was surprised to be rejected by someone half his age. Though it took a great deal of effort at concealing my true feelings, I forced an apologetic expression while drawing my own deep breath.

The employee returned with my wine and a menu, interrupting my planned talk while placing both on the table by reaching around John. When the bartender tried getting a good look at him, he oddly turned away but remained where he was.

The employee left. John stayed. To get rid of him I said "Look, I'm sorry. It's just I've been driving all day and have a long way to go tomorrow. All I want to do is eat and get some sleep. I'm really not in the mood for company."

Though his face appeared hurt, his eyes almost looked elated. Then he shrugged his shoulders and looked at the bar. "Suit yourself; but if you change your mind, I'll be over there."

I monitored John's retreat as he walked away. Then he settled on a stool spinning so his back was toward me. Relief over his acceptance of my request permitted me to peruse the menu. The employee returned as soon as I closed it, taking my order. Murmuring came from the bar, grabbing my attention once the employee left.

John was talking on his cell phone, apparently carrying on a business discussion based on the bits and pieces I overheard. His concentration remained focused on the back wall, reassuring lost interest in me so I could have the first sip of my drink. Soon all thoughts of his attempt to join me became irrelevant as I relished my first night of absolute freedom.

Five minutes later my food was placed before me. Never in my life has a chef's salad looked so appetizing. With great zest I consumed every morsel, basking in the liberty of adulthood. John walked by as I sipped the last of my wine, paying his tab and leaving. It relieved me to see him go.

One stop in the Ladies' Room suddenly became a necessity. It could have waited, but I felt better giving a little more time between John's departure and mine.

After I paid the bill and stepped through the door, I noticed both cars present when I pulled up were still here. My rational mind said John was simply walking home while my creative side screamed run. Another quick scope of the area showed nothing out of the ordinary, but I still hurried my pace. Just when I reached my car door, tires screeching from the road rushed into the lot. A black van pulled between the bar and me, slowing when it was two feet away. The sliding door yanked open before the vehicle stopped. Panic filled me as I desperately opened my purse in search of keys. Footsteps hitting the pavement started to draw my attention, but a cloth with an oily smell was placed over my face blocking the view. Everything started becoming fuzzy; almost surrealistic like a dream. All fear melted away as I relaxed into oblivion.

CHAPTER 3

Oh my head; I haven't felt this bad in a very long time. My entire body aches. How'd I hurt my left shoulder? Why can't I move? The last thing I remember is; oh God!

As I slowly opened my eyes, one stark light bulb directly over my head forced me to squint. My arms and legs are tied to a bed; dear lord I'm naked!

Don't panic Joyce; no one is here. If they raped me, when I get out there's going to be hell to pay. God just the thought of it makes me feel filthy. Okay calm down. I have to put it out of my mind and keep focused, but where am I?

This room looks like a small concrete shed of some sort. All I need do is quietly work the ropes loose and run out the door. Someone is bound to either see me or hear my calls. Yes that'll do it, don't give in to rising hysteria. Oh no I hear movement on the other side. Someone's turning the knob. The door opened, a shadow appeared in the threshold. "My how I enjoy the view," a male said. Then he stepped across the threshold, rapidly changing from a shadow to a man. John from the bar was lewdly staring at me. I knew it.

"Let me go you filthy pervert," I said.

His eyebrows shot up as a smile formed. Slowly his eyes walked across my flesh making me cringe while he reached behind to remove a cell phone. After leisurely lifting it to his face, he pressed a button on the side. "She's awake," he said.

My eyes went past him to glance through the open door. Outside looks like a crude gymnasium with an empty table set close to the entrance, and the far wall is lined with what appears to be switches. He stepped in front of the view while casually strolling toward me, causing me to close my eyes.

So now he's going to do it. I will survive this atrocity and make that bastard burn! When the mattress went down close to my right side, I cautiously looked at him. His smile was tremendous just watching me. "Feel like some company now, little Miss Tired?"

In answer to his question, I yanked violently against my bonds while glaring at him. Since my legs are tied together, when he goes to change that I'll kick him into a girl. "You keep away from me or you'll be painfully sorry!"

While shaking his head and making ticking sounds with his tongue, he glanced at the ceiling briefly before looking at me. "Out of all our acquisitions, none have ever shown the bravado you have, Joyce," he said.

All struggles halted as my mouth fell open. He smiled. Quickly I realized he learned my name from searching my pocketbook. Then my mouth shut while his hand threateningly rose in the air. I will not give him the pleasure of seeing me cringe.

While leisurely placing his hand on my belly, he said "I find it utterly amazing that you, in such a vulnerable position, can have the courage to talk to talk like that. All those before you were pleading by now. My, oh my, it's going to such a joy breaking you." His finger tracing a line down my belly momentarily made me concentrate on his intent. When it reached below my navel, I saw he'd shaved me. Oh this bastard is going to pay. Once he saw I'd noticed, he removed his hand. If he thinks this will break me, he's in for one huge surprise. He slowly returned his eyes to my face. "You really are a pretty little thing, even if you don't recognize your own beauty."

Where is he going with this? What's happening here?

"Oh don't look like that my lovely. We know all about you. For instance, we know you recently graduated from college with a Master's in Education and a minor's in History, but let's go a little further back, shall we? You were born in Burksdale Oklahoma to Brent and Paula Jackson. You were not happy there, possibly as the result of some kind of abuse, left without divulging your plans, and simply wanted to disappear. Tell me Joyce, was it your mother or father who abused you?"

Don't let him get to you. "Go to hell."

The sound of a heavy door opening into a cavernous room echoed through the doorway. John glanced in that direction before returning his attention to me. "Looks like the party's about to begin," he said.

"A little word of advice; try curbing that vulgar tongue of yours. The others aren't as forgiving as I."

Numerous footfalls slapping across a hard floor reached my ears moments before four men entered. John rose from the bed walking to them. One man seemed to stand out from the rest. He looked to be in his fifties, stood six inches above John, and had a slight pot belly. When he moved toward me, John fell behind. "I think some introductions are in order," he said. "My name is Earl, but you can call me master."

Chuckles broke out following his asinine statement. He'd better not put any money on that. "Over there, I believe you already know Hank."

I should have known a coward who sneaks up behind women wouldn't use his real name. Earl turned from me to focus on Hank.

"She truly is amazing," he said. "Mark, would you and Fred bring the chest in here?"

A man about my age and another closer to Hank's walked out. That left an oriental man whose age is early thirties standing in the entrance. Earl seemed to stare at him, which caused him to look uncomfortable. That's very interesting.

Shaking his head while facing me, he said "Watch out for Fred. He's as horny as an oyster-eating eighteen year-old in the girl's locker room. Just so you know; he's the older of the two."

Now I know four names with faces, assuming they're genuine. Earl glanced at Hank. "I've never seen such behavior," he said; "not even a silent whimper. Fugi, fetch the printout."

The oriental guy seemed relieved as he turned to leave. What kind of nationality does that name indicate? Slowly Earl returned his attention to me. Something in his eyes made me shiver. That created one of the most evil smiles I've ever seen. "Now that's better," he said. "It's time for you to learn why we brought you here."

Mark and Fred entered the room carrying a wooden foot locker. Earl glanced at them before looking back at me. "You are about to undertake a wondrous adventure," he said, bringing laughter from Fred. "In spite of what you may think, we have absolutely no intentions of raping you." His hand gently cupped my breast causing me to grimace. He released me saying "I'm going to let that rude incident slide since you're new. From this moment forward, you will do exactly what we say until such time as someone buys you."

18

My eyes popped open to a smiling Earl. Did I hear him right? Footsteps coming from the other room did not detract my attention. His head nodded twice, simply staring at me until Fugi walked up and handed him a stack of print-outs on old-style continuous computer paper. Fugi glanced at me with an almost sadness in his eyes.

"The official auction doesn't begin for three weeks," Earl said, "but there's already been an incredible interest in the pictures we sent to our wealthier clientele. Even the sheik responded! I haven't been this excited since my first successful transfer!"

He raised the stack over his head and allowed it to unfold to the floor. Then he turned it so I could see names and questions regarding my availability date. This can't be real; he's made it up just to frighten me. "You're going to pay for this, all of you," I said while scanning the room.

Slowly Earl's hand descended, allowing the papers to fall from his grip. The smile left his face as he stared at me with those evil eyes. Only this time I glared back. "I can see we need to begin the lessons," he said while snapping his fingers twice.

Fugi stepped forward, handing over a small device that looked like a garage door opener. Rather than leave, Fugi's face seemed to change into an expression of fury. Before Earl could say another word, Fugi grabbed my breast. Paralyzing agony immediately racked through me.

Breath froze in my throat while every nerve on my neck and breast burned. I can't move or see; Oh God I'm going to die! My ears feel ready to burst. Suddenly air rushed out in a scream. Gasps followed; the pain is subsiding. Gradually I became aware of laughter. Fugi was picking himself from the floor. Earl casually looked from me to Fugi and asked "How many times I got to tell you? Don't handle the merchandise!"

Trembling reduced to where I could think straight. What just happened? That couldn't have been from his vile touch. Fugi scurried to the doorway looking at the floor. Earl started shaking his head while facing me. "That was far more powerful than intended I'm sure," he said. "My assistant created an electrical ground doing what he shouldn't have."

With my nerves slowly settling, I looked away from Earl toward Fugi. He appeared nervous, like a cat searching for an opening. A tap on my shoulder returned my attention to Earl. "Chances are you probably haven't felt the little necklace you're wearing due to being all woozy from our pick-up methods, or Chloroform as it's more commonly termed. I call it a shock collar. What you experienced was the stun setting made worse by an idiot's hand. Here's the thing Joyce; it's modified to be deadly if certain events transpire. For instance, this remote will either incapacitate or kill depending on the button pushed, and hidden activator sensors over this doorframe and scattered through the halls are true marvels. Should you wander within two feet of the door or slip by us, you won't believe the pain. Then you die."

His eyes wandering to the small section of concrete over the door encouraged mine to search as well. No differences were noticed. He returned looking at me, causing me to look at him. "Two feet; take it to heart. There is no escape. Your old life is over. The sooner you accept that, the easier it'll be."

A nod of his head brought Mark and Fred close to the bed carrying the chest. "You're official designation from this day on is BL Seven Forty-Two or simply Seven forty-two," he said. "The sting on your left shoulder I know you feel is your brand."

He paused long enough for me to quickly twist my left arm. A horrid mark was burned into me just as he said. Oh my God, these bastards marred me. Ooh! My teeth gnashed as I glared at him.

"Don't chip a tooth," he said, "it'll lower the value. Oh, before I forget; should you pull on the collar or try to remove it in any way, well, it has a defense mechanism that'll ultimately trigger the deadly part."

Thumping from the chest being placed on the floor interrupted Earl. Fred removed a large key ring, loudly clinking keys in the process, unlocked the latch, and faced us with a bored expression. Earl shook his head as he returned his attention to me.

"Good help is so hard to find these days. Now where was I? Oh yes the brand. We collect, retrain, and dispose of all hair colors. I never discriminate."

Hank chuckled, bringing a smile to Earl. "The BL portion stands for your hair color of course. You are a true blonde, the most gorgeous one I've ever seen but I'm getting off-track. We tend to rotate inventory based on last obtained. What I mean is the most recent *successful* transfer had red hair."

20

Does he truly expect me to believe this tripe? There's no way he could do what he claims and remain free. What are their real motives? Shuffling feet brought my attention to Fugi, who looked afraid. Earl quickly glanced at him before resuming his talk. "I won't go into what happened with our last acquisition; suffice it to say you're the seven hundred forty-second blonde we've liberated from the burdens of free will."

Fred snorted, bringing both of our attentions. He was grinning and obscenely staring at my body, while Mark had a longing in his eyes looking at my face. I have to put aside my utter contempt and find a way to use their perverted cravings against them.

"I can almost read your mind, seven forty-two," Earl said. "You have plotting for escape written all over those luscious features. Let me clue you in on how safe it to think along those lines. Just because we've branded over twenty-two hundred people, not all made it to auction day."

As if on cue, Mark and Fred lifted the case to hold over me. Oh God what's in there? "You see in addition to other things I run a dog food exporting company, so can easily dispose of a, shall I say, defective product. But before I do-;" they opened the case and began tilting it toward me, "we have a little fun. Welcome to Hell!"

Stenches of rotting meat made me cough. The case began dropping its grisly contents on my belly. Human fingers, toes, and a wide assortment of parts in various stages of decay slapped my flesh. Horror forced all control to flee into an insane netherworld of denial. Four smiling faces seemingly took on qualities of demons, moving my mind dangerously close to insanity. Screams from my soul pierced the air until rescuing blackness engulfed my mind.

CHAPTER 4

Oh God please let this darkness mean this is a nightmare. Wake me up. I'm ready for it to end.

One tremendous yank against the ropes bore serious pain, proving this was real. The light was off. That means unless those monsters enjoy lurking about in the dark, which I wouldn't put past them, I'm alone. Now I can think without interruption.

Their ghastly chest proves at least part of what they said is true, but I must force the horror of it out of my mind or I'm doomed. I have no choice but to assume everything else he alleged will happen unless I stop it.

Earl mentioned three weeks. The way he said it makes me think that's true. I really don't believe they're planning to rape and murder me. Fiends with that in mind would derive greater pleasure in torturing victims to death, or at least would've sexually assaulted me by now. No he has another agenda. It doesn't matter if he's managed to sell one person or a thousand. I have to believe he knows ruthless people experienced in the subjugation of others. If his clientele weren't fully capable of picking up where he left off, they'd all be in jail. That leaves three weeks to find a way out. It would be best to turn them against each other. Let me think about my options.

Hank is a company man all the way. He was the only one to make Earl smile. That might indicate he's second in command and could have dreams of running the show. Hey, that could work. If I can get him alone, maybe I can convince him he needs to act on it thus creating enough confusion for me to slip by. Next I need a conspirator waiting to usher me through.

Fred scares me. The way he stared at me makes me think if we were alone he would rape me and then walk away. I have to list him with Earl and leave him out of my plans.

Something is already amiss with Fugi. He looked like he expected the others to kill him at any moment. If I can get him alone, maybe we can plan our escape together. Wait a minute; that kind of thinking could prove disastrous. I must not let my guard down for an instant. If he was in trouble, reporting my scheme might be viewed as a way to get in good with Earl. For the time being, I'll watch him closely.

Mark is a mystery. His eyes say he's different than the rest. It was almost like he wanted to get me alone so we could talk. I hate the thought of him being interested but I must not permit personal disgust to interfere. Perhaps if I pretend to like him, he'll help once war has erupted. When we're safely away, he'll see the real me turn on him.

Okay that means Hank and Mark are my best choices, but I have to proceed carefully. If the opportunity presents itself, I'd like to start with Hank. The way he acted in the bar tells me he has a huge ego and would take little prodding. When he's begun creating trouble, I'll call on Mark. Until then it's time to put on a performance better than any I've done before. If I could fool my father, I can certainly trick these bastards.

Now let me start planning for the contingency that Earl misled me. I cannot permit any surprises to alter my self-control. It's imperative they-.

Something's moving on the bed. God these bastards are sick. What are they up to now? It feels like someone is running his fingers quickly across the mattress just to frighten me. How he knew I was awake is beyond me. I will not give in to fear.

Wait, that's not a human hand. Hands don't have whiskers. Oh God some creature is rushing up my belly to my neck.

Before I could scream, a tug on the collar initiated thousands of tiny lights flooding my sight as the breath stuck in my throat. Acid poured from my neck down and up, cooking my scalp; boiling my spine. Oh God the agony; I can't stand it!

Through my fevered mind it looked like a brighter light came on as the fire was subsiding. Breath was able to be drawn while my nerves slowly calmed. When my sight cleared, I saw Hank standing in the doorway lowering his remote.

"That's it," he said. "I've asked Mark over and over to keep his pets contained. The little bastard must've snuck in here while we were cleaning you up. Just once I wish Earl would listen to me and get rid of the whole lot." His expression darkened. "If you want to avoid serious pain, you'll forget this ever happened."

Please give me strength to clear my head. This may be my only opportunity. My throat was slightly constricted, making my voice hoarse. "I'm not going to say anything about this. It wasn't your fault and I don't want you to get into trouble. Thank you for saving my life."

His head nodded as he started to turn. One quick glance beyond him showed nobody standing in the door. Plus his threat of retribution should I speak of this informs me no one else was close enough to see. We are alone. Okay here goes. "I'm sorry for the way I treated you at the bar."

That slowly turned him back toward me, a puzzled expression on his face.

"Big strong men turn me on. Now that I've had the chance to really look you over, I, well, I hope I'm not too forward saying this, but I like what I see."

A smile grew on his face as he started walking to me. It took all of my willpower to appear as what I hope to be seductive. He stopped moving once he arrived next to my face. "Go on," he said.

Leisurely I allowed my eyes to wander his body, stopping briefly at his knees. Then I casually reversed direction until I was staring at his face. He appeared ready to explode with excitement. "It's obvious *you* are the one who does all the careful planning, yet you aren't given proper credit."

He sat on the bed tilting his head sideways. "Now why would you say that?"

While licking my lips sensuously, I smiled. "The way you acted in the bar, like a general calling for his troops. At first I thought you were the leader until Earl entered the room." A frown grew on my face for added emphasis. "You backed away. I realized it could have been a misunderstanding until you mentioned Earl not listening to you, like he's in charge. His ignorance nearly killed me. Have you ever asked yourself what they'd do without you?"

His eyebrows rose while straightening his head. "Are you suggesting I leave?"

My head shook a few times before settling on his eyes. "It was a rhetorical question. Whatever you decide to do is up to you. What I meant is; could the others survive without you?"

A look of deep consideration narrowed his eyes while looking at the wall on my other side. "I don't think so."

Nodding my head moved the mattress enough to regain his attention. "I believe you. You're the one who deserves to be in charge here. Why for someone with your brains, it shouldn't be a problem seizing the right moment."

Those eyebrows shot up again. "You're talking about mutiny."

All I did was nod my head. His eyes narrowed as he looked at the pillow over my scalp. "In order for me to succeed," he said, "I'll need someone watching my back. If I were to release you, could I trust you to help?"

Focus on calm Joyce; I have to proceed carefully or he won't believe any of this. "You really don't need me; I'd only get in the way. But to answer your question it would be an honor to do whatever you say."

In a blur his hand smashed the pillow close to my scalp, grabbing a handful of hair and yanking. His free hand pushed on my shoulder keeping me immobile. Agony instantly filled my eyes with tears. "I'm sorry for whatever I did," I said.

"Not half as sorry as you'll be if you try that stunt again you stupid idiot!"

His pulling intensified; feeling like the skin was ripping from my skull. Whimpering snuck out. My neck was being pulled at an angle from my shoulders. "Oh God please stop. You're killing me!"

"No I'm not, but the others will."

Relief flooded my body when his hand slammed the pillow, releasing his grips in the process. As I blinked to clear the tears from my eyes, he rose and stomped three steps away. "Did any of what Earl said sink into that blonde brain?" He asked. "They will *kill* you at the slightest sign of resistance! Don't you at least remember the chest? Are you that anxious to contribute?"

Watery eyes kept him a vague shape. Oh God I have to forget the pain and not lose control. Think carefully and calmly. "No sir; I'm truly sorry-"

"SHUT-, UP!"

My mouth closed. Sight was finally cleared. His hands clasped behind his back, a look of sympathy crossing his face. That angered me but I maintained my apologetic expression. His head shook a few times while walking to the top of the bed where I couldn't see. "I'm going to let you in on a little secret very few before you have known. With every new acquisition we form a betting pool. It's mandatory at a thousand dollars per bet. Your odds are bleak, seven forty-two. Earl has bet we'll have to kill you in two weeks, Fugi said you won't last through tomorrow, Fred's bet he'll finally get his chance with you next week, while Mark is slightly more optimistic in betting you'll last all though the training and then have to be put down. I'm the only one who bet you'll live until someone else takes possession. Would you care to know why?"

Oh my God this is insanity. Stay cool. It's my only hope now. "Yes sir."

Angry footsteps slapping concrete preceded his returning to where I could see. Fury on his face made me cringe. "It's because I have to cover all bets! Since I found you, it's my responsibility to keep you alive until you're out of here! From this day forward, you will only speak when told to do so, walk when we say walk, jump, smile, frown, everything. You will obey without hesitation! Failure to do so will lead to the *direst* of consequences! Is there ANY part of that you don't understand?"

"No sir."

As he stared into my eyes, the rage changed back to sympathy. All my strength was used to appear regretful. Then he shook his head again while turning toward the door. After covering half the distance, he stopped and faced me saying "I now feel the need to tell you this. It just might save your life. I must say I am astonished at how calm you've remained, and that should have been my first warning. You see, everything Earl told you is true. We have obtained over twenty-two hundred people during the last twelve years, but not all of them were successful sales. That chest is only partial proof of what I'm saying."

His eyes dropped to the floor briefly before looking at me. "Your hotel room was properly checked out of, your clothes burned. That thing you called a car is being chopped into pieces as I speak, and your cash has been evenly divided. There is no place for you to go. No one knows where you are so no one will rescue you. You have no hope of escape. That collar will bring you down if you stray. Your very life

26

depends on accepting this."

While studying my eyes closely, his head shook a few times. Even though I wanted to spit at his false concern for my safety, I hid those emotions behind a facade of surrender. "They say the eyes are the windows to the soul, and they're right," he said. "Everyone we killed had a fire burning just behind their pupils. Our successful transfers lost it long before this point. In spite of everything you've been through including this talk, you still have that fire seven forty-two. If you wish to remain alive, extinguish it. Believe me when I say the others are looking for reasons to end you. And, if you ever try another stunt like this again, I will kill you myself. Lost money aside, I'd rather have someone trainable over a hopeless cause. Your time to choose is now; live or die? I'll leave you to consider the prospects."

Just before turning away, he glanced toward the left side of my head. I cringed as he quickly walked to that side reaching for me. He lifted a dead rat next to me. A scream stated to build but a warning glance from him quelled it. Slowly he backed to the door, silently stepping through without taking his eyes off me, shook his head a few more times, and quietly shut it. The sound of the latch clicking echoed with the intensity of a gunshot, his words piercing me like a bullet.

Everything I own is gone; that much is certain. What I saw tumbling out of that terrible chest proves they've been around for awhile, yet there's not even a hint they exist in any news sources. Somehow they're able to yank people off the streets without anyone noticing. Now I believe that list Earl showed me is genuine; they have an established line of clientele apparently capable of keeping their victims quiet. People simply disappear.

Oh how I wish I'd confided in Mary. Even she thinks I wanted to vanish and doesn't know where I was going or when I was to arrive. In all probability my mail to the Burksdale Police will be delivered tomorrow, assuming this is still Tuesday. That notarized letter was designed to inform the cops I'm not missing but moving to another city, so anything my father might say could be ignored. No one has a clue what's happened to me. I am totally on my own.

Tears streamed down my cheeks. These bastards are experienced in seeing all possible tricks or they would've been shut down. Chances are no matter what I try; someone tried it before and failed. What should I do, what can I do? Is this it; am I finished?

Silent sobs gave way to heaving wails. Bleak possibilities filled my head with images of great suffering. Oh what is to become of me? Walls blurred under tear-filled eyes. In my solitude I despaired.

Like the rising sun changes the gloom of night into the assurance of a fresh day, comfort crept forward from the deepest recesses of my mind. Many of the tight spots I'd faced and defeated returned to the front of my thoughts, rebuilding strength. Dread was replaced with new hope. I must not give up. I have to fight. These bastards think they know me but they haven't a clue. I've lived through hell and survived and will do it again. I am Joyce Allison Jackson and by God I will get free!

For now I'll play like I've given up. That fire Hank spoke of will be placed beneath a shade. Earl said the auction is three weeks away, which indicates they need that much time to arrange it. If I act like a good girl, they'll untie me. Once that happens I'll watch them closely while appearing like a beaten person. Sooner or later their guard will drop and I'll be left alone. When that happens I'll be ready.

Wait a minute; trying to rush past those monsters could kill me. I need an escape plan to get past their defenses. Though I don't know if there are sensors in the walls as claimed, I do know their remote controls are a danger. Somehow I must find a way to eliminate it. If I could get my hands on one, I'll be able to study it and see. There has to be a way to remove this blasted collar. Okay that's the first order of business. Take a remote when no one is watching but I can't wait too long. If three days pass without the opportunity presenting itself, I'll start charming Mark. He's the best hope I have.

Hank is a waste of time. I realize that now. However something in Mark's eyes tells me I might be able to reach him as long as I don't underestimate his loyalties. Hank was my fact-finding mission. A little more subtlety is required. Now they're all going to see how I fooled my father for twenty-two years.

The rattling doorknob immediately brought a change to my face. It's time to begin. As the door swung open, I stared at the ceiling like I'd surrendered. Even when this horrible odor that made me think of someone who hadn't bathed in two weeks assaulted my nose, I ignored it. "I'm glad to see you're taking my warning to heart," Hank said.

Slowly and without changing my expression, I turned my head to the doorway. That terrible smell was under a large covered dish he was holding. A huge smile was on his face as he sauntered into the room.

"By now your body has had the time to remove the knock-out toxins and can handle solid food," he said. "This is an old family recipe chock-full of all the nutrients you're going to need. We wouldn't want you fainting during your training, now would we?"

As I blankly looked at him, his expression changing to anger informed me he expected an answer. "No sir."

His eyes narrowed while scrutinizing my reactions closely. The vacant expression remained on my face, which finally relaxed his harsh appearance. With his smile returning, he sat on the mattress and removed the cover. Considering how little effort it took for me to calm his suspicions, it shows these guys are going to be easier to fool than my father. "It smells worse than it tastes," he said.

Maintaining my blank expression took a great deal of energy when I glanced at the plate. Small bits of what looked like meat were nestled in brownish red gravy. Lord I hope he's not kidding about the taste. It smells like filthy socks.

Mark entered the room holding a small bottle of water. The sight of it made my throat ache for liquid refreshment. Is any of this safe?

Why go to this trouble if they wanted poison me? That talk about clientele and auctions leads me to assume they want me alive. In order for that, I have to eat and drink. They know tampering with the food would result in my refusing to eat later. It's safe. I really have no choice other than eat this slop because I need my strength.

For a few moments Mark looked at me, and then placed the bottle on the floor next to Hank. He glanced at my face again just before turning to leave. His expression was almost sorrowful, which is intriguing. Could he regret my being held like this? It may be time to expedite my seduction of Mark.

Hank speared a small hunk of meat asking "Are you hungry?"

I was until that aroma floated in here. "Yes sir."

The smile on his face grew like a mother feeding her young child. My expression remained blank, even when he brought the fork close to my nose. "Don't breathe the steam and it'll taste better," he said. "Like I said, this is an old family recipe that has everything you're going to need."

At least he told the truth. When I held my breath, the food didn't taste bad at all. This meat is something new. There's some sort of sweetness. Suddenly my stomach growled, bringing a bigger smile from him. "Yes seven forty-two; all of this nutritious food is for you."

After a while, the flavor grew on me and it was really doing the trick. Once I started eating I realized how hungry I was. In very little time the plate was cleaned and the final bit of water drained. Then he lifted the plate from the mattress, picked the water bottle off the floor, rose, and stared at me with a terrible smile. His face looked like something out of a nightmare. It took all of my willpower to gaze back like I didn't worry about his horrifying change. Please let this be a sick joke.

"That's a good girl; you cleaned the plate faster than most. Can you feel it yet? A little sugar goes a long way in concealing the rancid taste, wouldn't you say?"

Oh dear God what is he talking about? What did he put in that meat? All control fled as I stared at him in shock. "My but you are an excellent actress. I have to give you credit. I really believed your expression would remain unchanged like you no longer cared. Man, am I glad I'm wrong. It wouldn't be as much fun watching you while I explain our techniques."

Slowly he turned to walk toward the door. When he neared it, he quickly spun around startling me. "Everyone, and I do mean everyone, thinks Earl is insane with all the preposterous claims he makes. How in the world could he possibly sell over two thousand people without getting caught; they think. Then they start scheming, convincing themselves how they're going to be the ones to blow the whistle. Oh, and let's not forget his cavalier attitude about saying our real first names; some of our more strong-willed cut through the humiliation to really pay attention. Did you think it was out of arrogance that he talked like it didn't matter?"

That bastard drugged me. If he thinks I'll forget any of this, he's terribly mistaken. My teeth gritted together, looking at him in pure fury. "Ah good; now comes the anger;" he said. "Our most intelligent acquisitions realize we don't want them dead, only changed. And I can tell by your face you know this, but also believe whatever we do will fail. Well guess what? You're so very wrong!"

His head nodded twice as a few chuckles escaped. That wicked smile seemed to intensify while my thoughts turned toward finding a way to hurt him. "Your expression is *priceless*. I never tire of doing this. You see we have an association with this doctor who's not your average run-of-the-mill physician. He's working on some kind of serum to reverse aging, a natural interest to him since he's also the finest plastic surgeon I've seen, but I'm getting off-base. During the course of his research, he created a drug that literally reverses minds to pre-birth." Another chuckle escaped. "It hasn't been touched by the FDA but we like it anyway. Along with its obvious advantages there are severe dangers as well. Without the proper follow-up care, anyone receiving this drug would literally lose the ability to think, move, eat, drink; basically stay alive. And for the effects to meet our needs, it must be taken with food thus insuring complete absorption. In order to succeed we lead our inductees into believing our methods only involve intimidation so they'll eat the special food. Guess what again? It's in your tummy rapidly breaking down. Congratulations, seven forty-two; your treatment has been administered flawlessly. Soon you won't know who you are, where you are, or what to do. That's where we help out in case you didn't know."

"You bastard!"

More chuckles responded as he simply smiled at me. "Enjoy your final moments of rage," he said. "They'll soon be over. Your old life is officially erased, seven forty-two. Welcome to the world of commodities. I'd love to watch the transition but alas, duty calls. We'll see you in about fifteen minutes or so, not that you'll remember."

Chills coursed down my body as he leisurely stepped through the entrance. My limbs started trembling as he faced me while slowly closing the door. A whistle could be heard just before it latched, and then the light went out.

I've got to get this stuff out of my body. Come on think; what kind of meat was that any way? Oh my God, I just ate a rat. That bastard served me filthy vermin. Concentrate, I ate a rat; come on stomach I ate a disgusting rat. Get rid of it.

It's no good. I was so hungry my body refuses to reject it no matter what I think. Oh no, I believe the drug is starting to work. I will not give in.

Eleven times eleven is one hundred twenty-one. Fourteen times fourteen is-, is-.

Concentrate; Although Christopher Columbus was credited with being the first European to discover the Bahamas, there is growing evidence to support the theory that Norwegians first made the discovery centuries- centuries-.

I can beat this; focus on calm. Our country was formed when laws were imposed without-;

SWITCHER

Stay with it; the world isn't spinning. It's all in my head. I am Joyce Allison Jackson, born in Burksdale on July-; I am Joyce Allison-, I am Joyce-, I-; I-; I? Who am I?

CHAPTER 5

It doesn't matter. Everything is slipping away. Whatever was bothering me is gone. I'm so content and relaxed. Oh this feels wonderful.

Look; the dark is bright now. People are rolling a strange looking thin screen on four long legs. Aw it looks like a swing-set frame. It's almost as tall as they are. Now they're placing it over my head. Oh good; they tilted the screen so it's blocking the bright light. Do they want to play games?

"Can you hear me?"

Is that voice talking to me? "Who are you?" I asked.

"God," it responded. "Do you understand?"

Is that really God? He's fat, balding, and wearing a dirty tee-shirt. I always thought he'd be older and wiser-looking.

"Look at the screen and answer me," he said. "Do you understand?"

His voice sounds impatient. I've displeased God. Quickly doing as he said, I stared at the screen answering "Yes, am I dead?"

Fire immediately burst into being. Oh please make it stop. "You have angered me," God said. "You will only answer my questions with yes or no. Do you understand?"

The fire is raging, reaching for me. I must do as he says or I'll burn. Panic forced my head to start shaking in denial. "Yes."

Suddenly the fire snuffed out, beautiful swirling colors replacing it. They're so pretty; thank you God. "The fire is gone, but I can bring it back if you disobey," he said. "Concentrate on the colors. Look at them closely. Do you see a door?"

A door; I must find a door. All I see are colors spinning quickly and-, wait. There it is. I see a door in the middle of the patterns. "Yes."

"On this side you see an exact copy of you named Joyce. Do you understand?"

Part of me pulled away, walking to stand close to the door. "Yes."

"You have pleased me. The door is opening. Do you see this?"

I'm so happy God is pleased. Wait, I see the door slowly opening. It isn't wide enough for me to look through. "Yes."

"Very good; now on the other side you will see a new-born girl. The infant's name is BL Seven forty-two. Can you see her?"

As the door opened further, I saw a tiny baby girl floating amidst the colors. Aw she's crying. Should I tell God? No, I'm sure he already knows and will take care of it.

"Answer me," God said.

His voice sounded angry. While trembling I said "yes".

Terror brought forth whimpers while I waited for eternal damnation. "I will not punish you as long as you do what I say."

Relief instantly soothed my fears. "The door is your mind," he said. "Joyce and the baby are two halves of the same person. You are an outside observer of both halves. Do you understand?"

"Yes."

Slowly the baby began moving toward Joyce.

"For now Joyce and the baby will remain separate," he said. "The door will stay open. You are to place all of this in the deepest part of your mind and forget about it while you're awake. Do you understand?"

The screen flickered briefly. Was that some kind of message? "Answer me," he said.

"Yes."

All movement halted; the baby remained where she was just watching Joyce.

"You will not remember what happened after you ate your last meal. You will eat all food placed before you. Starvation is a sin. Do you understand?"

"Yes."

Suddenly the pattern began rotating rapidly. It's moving so quickly my eyes hurt. Black dots have formed spiraling lines going the opposite direction. "Watch the screen," he said. "When you dream of actual events from your past, you are to forget them after you awaken. Do you understand?"

"Yes."

It started spinning faster. "Repeat your last commandment," he said.

After clearing my throat, I obeyed. "Watch the screen. When you dream of actual events from your past, you are to forget them when you awaken. Do you understand?"

Even though I did my best to mimic God's voice, chuckling seems to indicate otherwise. "And he said you were quick-witted," God said. "One final commandment for now; you will see a great terror. Watch the screen closely."

Snakes began sprouting out of the center of the colors, looking at me with flickering tongues. Please make them go away. "Snakes are your worst fear," he said. "They are very intelligent and hunt for you when you disobey. They will kill you if they find you. The mere mention of the name snake will freeze you in your tracks. You will remember your great fear of snakes from this time forward. Do you understand?"

Now the colors were completely blocked by slithering snakes. There are hundreds, no thousands of them squirming in all directions. Oh no they see me. They're coming for me. "Yes."

I can't move; they'll kill me. Oh please I'm sorry. Make them go away.

The colors are back, all snakes have left; thank you God. "Sleep," he said. "Forget all dreams."

Pounding of footsteps toward the stairs indicated mom's continued impatience. "Aren't you ready yet Joyce?" She said. "Your guests will be here any minute!"

Why is she pressuring me like this? A girl turns sixteen once, and he said he'd be here. Surely if people arrive early she can entertain them until I'm ready. I have to look my very best. "I'll be down soon."

An exasperated grunt responded. That's all right. At least I can concentrate again. Oh Paul; I pray you feel the same about me as I do you.

We met in the mall. I was with Mary killing time when this cute guy with blond hair, green eyes, and incredible body started following us. At first I was frightened until he introduced himself. His soft voice melted away all fears.

He's eighteen, out of school and has a job at a gas station. His eyes sparkled when he looked at me. My knees grew weak watching him. It was hard to think straight. Mary noticed the connection and carefully guided us to a table in the food mart. Before we were seated, she said there was an errand she needed to run and left. Once we were alone, we learned a great deal about each other.

Although he lives with his parents, he's saving up for an apartment. There's almost enough money set aside but he needs a little more time. I mentioned my savings and how unhappy I was with my father, that I'd like to live with him. At first he seemed interested until he learned I was fifteen. Then everything seemed to grow cold. It wasn't until I told him my birthday was coming in a couple months before he smiled again. Since then we've been talking on the phone almost daily. Yesterday he promised he'd be here today.

"*JOYCE!*" Mom shouted. "If you're not down here in five minutes, I'm bringing your guests up to your room!"

Have people started arriving? I didn't hear the door.

Mom really went to a lot of trouble. Mysterious trucks started pulling up front this morning as she rushed me upstairs. When I tried sneaking a peek, it was like she knew ahead of time and caught me before I could look into the basement. Even though I acted upset, I still smiled when she wasn't watching. Sometimes she's the best. If it weren't for her, I'd be insane by now.

Dad is a different story. His despicable treatment of me instilled great hatred years ago. Why he can't stand me is a mystery but I won't let it bother me today. Thank heavens he can't be here. Okay I hope I'm ready.

Tromping downstairs soothed no one. My stomach felt queasy from excitement and mom looked enraged. "You know that's not a good color for your face," I said. "Maybe you should remove some of that blush?"

For a moment I thought she was going to swat me, until her head started shaking as she looked me up and down. Then a smile grew and tears formed. "You are a vision," she said. "My princess has grown into a beautiful young lady."

This was rapidly becoming one of those embarrassingly mushy moments where others would see and it would haunt me forever. "Thanks mom, but don't get all bleary-eyed. People might talk."

Chuckling broke out just as the doorbell rang. Thankfully mom turned to enter the kitchen when I opened the door. Mary was standing outside holding a large gift. "Am I the first?" She said.

That's so typical of Mary. Not any kind of greeting, only concern about missing everyone else's arrival. It's like she didn't want people to see how she enters. We've been best friends for as long as I remember and do everything together, yet that quirk of hers has always puzzled me. "Not this time," I said.

She appeared absolutely hurt with her eyes dropping to the door stoop. "Who beat me here?"

"Me."

Her eyelids narrowed, jaw tightened, lips frowned, all while slowly facing me. "I was going to say happy birthday but forget it you smart-aleck!"

Then she gritted her teeth in a snarl while preparing to throw the package at me as I stood still looking innocent. An animalistic grunt from her was all I could take. Laughter followed as she feigned insult, until finally giving in herself. As she stepped inside giggling, mom glanced around the corner. Once we gained control, she said "Hello Mrs. Jackson."

A mysterious smile formed on mom's face as she entered the living room saying "Hi Mary. Why don't the two of you go downstairs?"

That was an oddly short welcome from mom. What did those trucks bring here? Mary and I exchanged glances before looking at her. Mom's smile seemed to grow waiting for her response. "Sure," Mary said.

Nervous excitement built as Mary handed the gift to me, I thanked her, and we marched toward the kitchen stairs leading to the basement. Mom stepped aside allowing us quick passage to the doorway. Pink lights could be seen emanating from inside the family room at the bottom, making our journey down that much more intriguing. Once we reached the floor, my breath was taken away. "Oh wow," Mary said.

It immediately stood out; a two and a half foot tall ice Swan perfectly formed and crystal clear. The thick wings were raised like it was in flight, with feathers on both sides of the body shaped to form the number sixteen. A pink light beneath the stand illuminated the entire sculpture, refracting from the tips like rainbows all over the room.

A fountain was gently spraying fruit punch eight inches into the air next to the swan. Vases of flowers adorned the long table which held a banner reading Happy Sixteenth Birthday Joyce! Beside the punchbowl rested a yellow three-tiered cake with white doves adorning all sections on the side, and large confectionary red flowers on top. Colorful floating balloons were tied to the legs, and long thin pink streamers crisscrossed the ceiling. My sight blurred, stunned into immobility. "Happy birthday sweetheart," mom said.

She was directly behind me. Somehow she'd crept silently downstairs to remain on the next-to-last step. Even the creaking eighth step didn't betray her descent. As I turned to her, the most loving smile was on her face watching me. "Mom, I-;" words failed. I simply stared at her.

Tears formed in her eyes. "Don't get all blustery," she said, "people might talk."

Two chuckles escaped from me while I stood almost still, my head involuntarily shaking from side to side. Mary retrieved the gift, walking into the room to place it by the table. She was the only person outside of the family to know how hard my life had been, and wanted to give us a little privacy.

For the first time in my life I felt magical. Mom stepped to the floor, her arms outstretched. I rushed into her embrace, relishing the moment of unconditional love. Then she backed away, looking at me with warmth in her eyes. "Your other guests will start arriving soon," she said. "I better go wait for them. Stay down here and enjoy, my love. This is your special day."

No sooner had she climbed five steps, the doorbell rang. Mary walked to me while mom hurried away. "Come on, kiddo," she said. "Let's go count the roses."

My legs felt rubbery, almost numb. Mary slipped her arm through mine, guiding us into the room. It was like I floated through air moving into this wonderland designed just for me. Babbling from the punch bowl added an exotic touch, like this truly was a faraway land where everything was happy and beautiful.

People started arriving, wishing me well while commenting on how incredible the room looked. Though I think I responded intelligently, this whole event still held the surrealistic quality of a dream. Talk was continual as I shifted from friend to friend, until Paul entered the room. That made this day complete. His arrival hushed gossip and chatter as eyes carefully watched him searching the room. Then he spied me. A smile grew on his face. My heart was pounding, butterflies tickling my tummy as he came right to me without detour. Those piercing green eyes made me blush, forcing me to look at my shoes. "Happy birthday Joyce," he said. "This is quite a celebration."

His compliments returned my attention. "Thank you."

Mary managed to herd folks away from us, granting a little isolation. Paul smiled looking at me, placing his arm across my shoulder taking me as far from the others as possible. Once I was in the corner facing him, he placed his arms against the walls on both sides protecting me. "I'd like to take you out sometime," he said.

Had he asked me to, I'd have left the party right then. "Okay."

Time seemed to stand still as he moved close to my face. Talk that moments before competed with our conversation now sounded like it was miles away. His hand left the wall, moving to my chin. The touch sent electrical charges coursing through me when he lifted it. Then it happened.

Loud angry shouting came from upstairs, silencing everyone in the room. My father's voice rang out, enraged over something mom had done. Heavy footsteps stomping the floor directly over head shook the streamers, bringing worried expressions to all in attendance. "What's going on?" Paul asked.

Oh God why couldn't he have just stayed away a little longer? Faces looking around the room eventually settled on me. More shouts from above made me wish the Earth would swallow me. "My father is home. Obviously he's mad over something."

That fairy-tale feeling of before came crashing down from the heavy weight of reality. Happy carefree talk became whispered conspiracies as my guests grouped in threes while nodding heads and glancing my way. Paul's eyes widened as he turned away from me, nervously watching the steps. He didn't have to wait long. Thundering stomps rapidly descended the stairwell until dad stared at the many cringing faces. Slowly he scanned the room, looking over the many until he saw me close to Paul. With unbridled fury in his eyes, dad quickly crossed the room until he was glaring at Paul. My fears over what was about to happen formed a pleading expression as the two of them faced each other. "Who are you?" Dad asked.

Paul quickly brushed his right hand against the side of his jeans before lifting it in a gesture of friendship, a smile on his face. "I'm

Paul sir; Paul Youngblood."

Dad briefly gazed at the outstretched hand like it was diseased before narrowing his eyes to frown at Paul. "I've seen you somewhere," dad said. "I never forget a face. Ah, you work at the gas station my company uses which means you're over eighteen. You'll have to leave immediately."

The smile instantly vanished from Paul's face as his mouth dropped open and arm lowered. My eyes went wild with anger as I stepped between the two, squaring off with dad. "*What*?" I asked. "You don't even know him! Can't I at least have one moment of happiness?"

Guests quietly began leaving, sneaking up the steps as fast as possible. Dad ignored me, reaching out to take Paul by the arm. "If you value your job, you'll go right now," dad said.

Blood built inside my ears. I felt in danger of exploding from pure fury. Moving in front of him I said "How dare you. This is the final straw. I'm going to live with him. What do you think about that?"

Rather than acknowledge I was even there, dad made a clicking sound with his tongue while continuing their march. It forced me to walk backwards. "Contributing to the delinquency of a minor carries a stiff jail sentence in these parts," he said. "I know the mayor and police chief personally. So tell me Paul, is what she just said true?"

By this time we'd reached the steps; Paul literally trembling. When his head started shaking, my heart sank. "No sir," he said. "I have no idea why she said that."

A magnanimous smile formed on dad's face as he released Paul's arm and patted his back. Shock froze all my movement as I watched this horror conclude. "I suspected as much," dad said. "Tell you what Paul, you leave now and never contact Joyce again in any way, well; then we'll let this remain the figment of a girl's fantasizing imagination. Let me find out otherwise, a pretty boy like you better learn how to shower with your back against the wall. Believe me when I say I can make it happen."

Tears filled my eyes, running down my cheeks watching Paul dash up the stairs. Everyone else had left; the cake uncut. "Why," I asked. "Why did you do this?"

When the front door slammed shut, he faced me with a victorious smile. "I knew nothing about this little waste of cash until one of my employees came up to offer her best wishes for you today. When I asked how she knew, she said one of her friend's daughters was invited to the party. A quick on-line scan of my account showed an enormous amount of payments made using the debit card. Had it not been for that little heads-up, I may not have caught it since your mother *used* to balance the check book. Do you have any idea how angry I get when my money is squandered on frivolous things?"

My head started shaking, mouth dropped open as I stared momentarily at him in complete astonishment. Memories of how happy he became every time he upset me flashed in my mind; prompting me to focus on the calming technique I developed just to rob his pleasure. While closing my mouth I moved past him to the stairs. "Where do you think you're going?" He said.

Fear from what I'd say or do kept me quiet. This seemed to transfer rage from me to him, which brought an unseen smile to my face as I continued climbing. "Yes, please run away," he said. "Then I can hunt you down, have an excuse to put you in reform school AND lock your boyfriend up for years!"

When I arrived at the kitchen, I noticed that, too, was empty. Mom had again left me to fend for myself. As I turned the corner to head to my room, I manipulated grief into scheming.

I won't leave, not yet. First I want to make absolutely certain I can take care of myself. That requires a solid education. For now I'll do exactly what he says without backtalk. Even when he has his mood swings, blaming me for things I didn't do, I'll apologize and promise never to do it again. Yes I'll put on an acting performance worthy of an award. Then when the time is right, I'll find a way to publicly embarrass him just like he did to me today. After I leave this hell, I'm never coming back.

Once I reached the bedroom hallway, weeping could be heard coming from mom's room. That angered me. Look at how she's cowering in there, broken. Never will I allow any man to treat me the way she-

----

"Seven forty-two; oh seven forty-two, this is your wake up call. We have one *hell* of a day planned for you!"

CHAPTER 6

Wow I'm exhausted, must've been a bad night's sleep. Wait a minute; oh God-

"Seven forty-two, you've gotten ripe over the last couple of days. It's time for your shower."

I've been here two days? Slowly I faced the door. Hank was standing in the threshold, holding a large towel in one hand and what looked like women's underwear in the other. When he stepped into the room, Mark entered carrying a card table with Fred close behind hauling a fold-up metal chair. What's going on?

While Hank stood like he was supervising, Fred and Mark went about placing the table and chair with almost military precision. Shivers ran along my spine as I realized they must've perfected it over time. When they finished, Fred stared briefly at me while Mark turned to leave. Hank cleared his throat as an apparent signal to Fred, who quickly left closing the door on his way out.

"Orders from the top," Hank said. "From this moment on, you are to be clothed. I must say there's been a lot of activity pertaining to you, but I'll save the good news for after breakfast. Now I want you to get dressed and come with me."

My arms and legs are tied. How does this genius think I can perform that miracle? Silently he placed the clothing on the table and walked around the bed untying me. Again experience was displayed in how he remained out of range of my legs.

Backing to the door, he said "This one time I'm going to be compassionate. Get off the bed slowly and let feeling return to your hands and feet; then dress."

When he reached the door, he turned around. I can't believe it, now's my chance. In order to facilitate the blood flowing quickly, I started flexing my feet in all directions as I quietly moved across the mattress. Please God, don't let this bed squeak. When I touched the floor, icy-cold concrete nearly made me gasp. Slowly I grabbed the towel with both hands, twisting it into a rope, and began stalking his back.

"If you're planning on trying something naughty let me remind you of the sensors and where I'm standing," he said.

That warning gave me pause but only for an instant. If I rush him, my momentum will carry me into him. Past experience with this blasted collar lets me know for at least two seconds I have motor control. I'll grab his neck with the towel, shocking the both of us. By all I cherish, I'll cling to him with my teeth if necessary. It'll force the others to disarm it, and as long as I hang on they can't use their remotes. Then I'll threaten to strangle him unless they set me free. As I drew within jumping distance he calmly said "There's one more thing you need to know. Snakes are in the drain pipes all through our building. They're attracted to loud noises like a struggle."

My heart started pounding; breathing accelerated. The towel slipped through my fingers. I hate snakes! Oh no I'm too far from the bed to jump off the floor. Exhales became whimpers as terror stopped all movement. God if I stir they'll hear me!

"It'll be all right," he said. "Just dress quietly and they won't come. Let me know when you're ready."

"I-; can't-."

Casually he turned bearing a friendly smile. "I'm going to let that unauthorized talk slide as well," he said. "Our tracking sensors showed all snakes resting at the other end. There's been no reason for them to move. Try to relax. As long as you do what we say, we'll protect you."

They're not here. Oh thank heavens they're sleeping. As Hank looked away, I tip-toed to the table and lifted the two items of clothing. It's not underwear. He brought a bikini swimsuit. Once I was dressed, I lifted the towel from the floor and remained still. "I'm ready."

Although I just learned this place is infested with horrible snakes, it doesn't change much in regards to my escape. He told me all I need to know, be quiet when I make my move. That way they won't realize anything's; wait. What an idiot I've been.

Forget the remote. He had a cell phone. It was on his back waist when I first woke up but I don't see it now. They obviously keep them somewhere close-by. I need to find it.

Without warning he lifted his remote. Oh God I did what he said and he couldn't have guessed what I was thinking. Why is he punishing me? As I tensed for agony, he pressed a button, and then opened the door. Nothing happened. Isn't that interesting?

"To answer your unasked question," he said, "I just disarmed the collar but did not unlock it. If you try pulling it off, it'll rearm in a most uncomfortable fashion. Now you can step through the door and come with me."

At last I have a chance; these guys look out of shape. I can probably run faster than any of them. I'll ram into him, grab the remote as he struggles to keep balanced, and take off. His trusting of my being broken is going to be their undoing.

Once he stepped past the door, Fred pointing his remote entered my sight. Luckily I was able to contain my surprise and appear docile. Sooner or later they're going to lower their guard. I'll be waiting. Hank turned to his left clearing the way for me to leave.

The room outside is enormous, bigger than a high-ceilinged gymnasium. Four closed steel doors identical to the one holding me captive are on the same wall as my cell; electrical switches, knobs, and levers are on the opposite wall. On the right are five pull-down metal tables. A large steel door in the center of the wall we're walking toward is the only detraction from painted bricks. This must be some kind of converted warehouse. Whoever set this up is well-financed.

Fred fell in behind as we silently continued walking to the larger door. Hank fished a big key-ring from his pocket when we neared it, paused long enough to search the keys, and then placed one in the lock. It swung outward with a hissing sound like it was breaking an air-tight seal.

On the other side was a darker-lit hallway running a hundred feet. Mark was facing us at the far end, his back against a closed steel door similar to the one we just stepped through. Three drain covers equally spaced apart lined the concrete floor. Five doors were on the same side as my room, four were steel but the one in the middle was wood. On the opposite side one large steel overhead door reminding me of a two-car garage was located halfway down, with another standard wooden door near the end. I'll bet that door Mark is protecting leads outside.

Our destination appears to be the middle wooden door on the same side as my cell. Hank's key-ring made another tinkling appearance, until he located the right key to pull the door open. Blackness seemed to swallow the dim lighting creating a sense of dread nearly betraying me. I must focus on calm. It's my only hope. He casually reached around the side, moved his hand around briefly before an audible click sounded and bright green illumination flooded outward.

"There's an eight-inch drop," Hank said. "Watch your step. I want you to take care of all business, and then thoroughly shower. We'll be back in fifteen minutes."

A pinch from Fred startled me, bringing a glare from Hank. "Don't do that," Hank said. "You'll bruise the merchandise."

"She ain't going to be marred," Fred said. "If you tell I'll deny it. It's just I can't help myself. She's the most gorgeous piece I've ever seen!"

Hank's chest puffed out like a proud poppa. A slight smile grew on his face, instilling a powerful desire for me to scratch it off. Rather than act on those feelings, I buried them and entered the room.

Large shiny green tiles met my feet with icy awareness. The room is covered with them, giving this place an eerie green glow. It's the size of a locker room shower. Four showerheads adorned the far wall, with two commodes lining the one to the left. I don't want to think about why I'm only now feeling nature's urge. Three clothes hooks on the right wall supported a towel, robe, and another two-piece swimsuit, while a small plastic tub containing soap, shampoo, and various other hygiene items sat on the floor under them. This can't be a warehouse. It must be a refurbished school.

"Fifteen minutes," Hank said while pushing the door closed. "You'll regret making us wait."

Fear of being shocked while standing on a wet floor hastened me. In less than fifteen minutes I was finished, dressed in the new suit with the robe covering it, and waiting close to the door. Just a few moments passed before it opened, making me think they'd been watching. Hank looked in, an ingratiating smile on his face. "You've done well," he said. "Now it's breakfast time, or maybe dinner depending on which side of the door you stand."

Is my timing that far off? It feels like early morning but without windows I have no idea. In spite of the chuckles when I climbed out, I was able to conceal my confusion. A blanket of indifference

45

enshrouded my true feelings while I waited for Hank to lead us away.

Our return trip was uneventful until we entered the big room. I can't be certain, but I think someone is whimpering behind one of the closed doors. Oh my God they've struck again. "Move it," Fred said as he pushed my shoulder.

That abrupt shove startled me into Hank, who faced me with a glare. "Do I need to train you how to walk?" He asked.

To argue the point would be meaningless and detrimental to my plan, so I looked at him with an apologetic face. Slowly the anger faded as he shook his head a few times while turning around. That little pause gave me enough time to confirm. There was definitely someone in the room closest to the main door. I could hear movement coming from inside.

Steaming food was waiting for me. Either Earl or Fugi, probably Fugi, must've placed it on the table just before we entered the big room, and then went elsewhere. Perhaps it was his moving around inside the closed cell I heard before. I hope so. The thought of another captive here gives me shivers. Hank removed the remote from his pocket after I stepped across the threshold. His shadow betrayed it. Before I could turn, an audible click was heard. "Okay twinkle-toes; your collar is activated and you know what that means," he said. "Eat all the food quickly. You don't want the snakes to smell it or they'll come."

Fred snickered as I quickly scanned the room. Oh God; are they here? "Relax seven forty-two," Hank said. "They won't come unless the food is here for awhile. Hurry up and eat. In a half-hour we have a pleasant surprise for you!"

He closed the door, leaving me on my own. There are no snakes I could see, and he did promise protection as long as I do what he says. But if they come how will he know? Shock collar or no shock collar, I'm screaming loudly for help. As for the so-called pleasant surprise, I'll deal when the time comes.

To avoid the possibility of being heard by the slithering monsters I tip-toed across the floor. Once I reached the table, the same pile of meat I ate before was looking at me. Something inside my head was trying to get my attention, almost like a whisper or warning. This place must really be getting to me; now I'm hearing ghosts.

For minutes I stared at the food, that near-audible ghost seemingly taking on substantial form. Then I remembered a lesson I was taught in bible school about starving myself being a sin; or was that church? It doesn't matter. I'm very hungry.

This doesn't taste as sweet as before, but it's still an odd pink meat. The flavor is unlike anything I've had. It also has a strange texture, kind of soft like liver. They must have tenderized it tremendously making it easy to eat. As I speared the last piece, a loud bang outside the door startled me jostling it off the fork and under the bed. That's going to bring the snakes guaranteed. I have to get it.

Sounds of the doorknob turning entered the room when I lifted the bedspread. An electrical outlet and cable hook-up were just underneath, but I can't see the meat. Wait a minute; why are these outlets hidden in here? They look like something for a television or computer. Images of spinning colors played in my mind. It makes no sense.

"GET AWAY FROM THERE," Hank said.

"But I-"

Hundreds of matches ignited around my throat. Words froze, I toppled over. Contact with the floor created new points of agony like bees stinging. Then it ended. Before I could catch my breath, two strong arms yanked me from the floor. "Don't you EVER talk without permission again," he said.

He's got to be told no matter what. Shivers ran down my spine thinking about snakes coming for that piece of meat and then waiting for more. As I drew a breath to speak, he shoved me away and pulled out the remote. A snarl formed on his face as his teeth gritted together and murder rose in his eyes. "I'VE HAD IT WITH YOU," he said. "IF YOU SAY ONE WORD, JUST ONE LITTLE PEEP, I'LL KILL YOU NOW AND APOLOGIZE LATER!"

Before I could react, he rushed forward to grab my arm. Then he pulled me out of the room so quickly I nearly fell. It took four steps for me to straighten and look ahead.

A three and a half foot tall pillory had been placed in the middle of the room perpendicular to the main door, obviously our destination. Worries over dropped food fell to the back of my mind as I began thinking of reasons why we were heading toward it. Earl and Fugi were standing on both sides of it, moving out of the way when we arrived. Hank pulled the robe off, which I permitted without resistance.

Rough-hewn openings had been cut out for the head and arms. Loose splinters appeared a real threat for any type of movement. Hank positioned me so I was facing the switches, and Fugi stepped forward to open the top half. Oh God what now?

If I tried anything, they'd know I haven't surrendered. All I can do is play along and hope what Earl said about their wanting me alive is true. The height forced me to bend. Fugi lowered the top, locking it in place with a flimsy latch. Even though I might be able to break it away, damage from the splinters would be extensive. Earl walked to face me smiling like he was about to deliver terrific news as Fugi backed up.

"Never in the twelve year history of my company has there been such an interest," he said. "My account is literally flooded with requests. Normally I'd just forget about them and hold firm, but something inside told me to do this."

He drew a deep breath, exhaling while looking at the ceiling like he was grateful. His attention drifted to me as he said "My dear, you are the cause of an unprecedented event. There's been such a large demand to confirm you really exist that I gave in. Obviously it was only a day's notice, but quite a few took me up on it. Some are already here with more arriving every minute."

Oh dear lord; I hope he's not saying what I think. Calm; keep calm no matter what. It's my only hope. "Though it's way too early for any of them to take possession, still they come," he said. "This will have the same hands-off rules that apply during standard auctions, but if I were you, I'd expect some pretty close examinations. You will not speak to anyone. You will not move should someone look in a place that makes you uncomfortable, and you will stare unemotionally at the floor no matter what you see. Any infraction will be dealt with quickly and decisively. Do you understand?"

Chills ran down my spine. His question sounds frighteningly familiar; why? "Yes," I said.

More shivers traced my back as he smiled. That expression looked like something out of a horror movie. "Later I'll tell you who I really am," he said, "but for now I must play host. Try to keep absolutely still. Those splinters can be a real bitch!"

Like an excited child who's been given permission to play with a new toy, Earl spun and nearly danced out of the room. If he thinks this indignity will break me, he's in for one huge surprise. It's almost like old times. My father tried to humiliate me in countless ways, which failed simply because I can picture myself in a different setting. From what I've read it could be a form of meditation. I don't know and don't really care. It works. Now these clowns are going to experience one of my many tricks.

Hank and Fugi remained at my sides, not moving even after soft classical music began drifting through the room. That's strange. I didn't notice any speakers. Now I hear people talking. Stay calm; focus on another place.

Dozens of men and women entered carrying mixed drinks, laughing and talking like this was a grand party. Soon they were around me. All I could see were pants and skirt hems moving in an almost blur. Excited chatter blended together, forming a sound I imagined to be wind though tree leaves. Some bent down to look at my face, which I envisioned as floating clouds. Finally all but one pulled back, his legs remaining in front of me, his voice proved it to be Earl. "As you've just seen, she's no computer-generated trick. Our training has just begun so I can't hold the sale today."

Numerous sounds of disappointment responded; followed by the shadow of Earl's raising arms.

"Folks; folks please," he said. "You know my guarantee. Rather than let her go as is, I'm going to make her my crown jewel. For now I must ask you to be patient."

A snicker came from him as he turned briefly toward me before facing the crowd. "After all, isn't she worth the wait?"

Voices began sounding angry, numerous questions being shouted. One that seemed to gain momentum also held my attention; when? Earl's hands rose again, prompting them to quiet down. "The official date has not yet been decided. You will be notified through the standard channels with ample time to prepare. To give you an approximate time, we're looking at about two and a half weeks."

Angry shouts responded. Oh no, this feels like a riot in the making. Two more shadows moving close to my front quieted the crowd. "Closed bids will be accepted immediately," Earl said. "Now if you'll come with me, I'll treat you to a fine dinner."

Arguments rang out. Suddenly a pair of pants ran around the side quickly grabbing the bottom of my suit. Fugi was immediately gone from sight. A loud thump, a moan, and then a man falling to the side with his eyes closed became visible. Fugi dropped on his haunches to check his neck for a pulse. That action halted all noise as he looked at Earl and nodded his head. Then he glanced at me with a strange, almost sorrowful expression before quickly rising.

"Take that man off the greeting card list," Earl said, creating scattered chuckles. "If there are no further questions, our meal awaits."

Fugi moved directly in front of me as Earl guided all strangers out. With no one really watching me, I moved my head just enough to look at the people wandering away. There must be at least fifty following Earl. This is just unreal. Are there really that many degenerates around? Surely at least one is an undercover agent waiting for the right time to break this slave ring apart.

Once everyone had cleared out, Hank and Mark grabbed the downed man's arms and began pulling him toward the door. Fred waited a few minutes before darting behind me. When they stepped out of the room and the steel door closed, a quick yank had my bottoms down. Oh God here it comes; rape. I don't know if I'm strong enough for this.

A stinging slap against my butt pushed me forward, driving splinters into my wrists and neck. Agony from a dozen spikes drawing deep blood forced a pained cry. Tears formed in the corners of my eyes. I gritted my teeth in an effort of regaining control. Fugi spun around. "Knock it off," Fugi said.

Another hit drove me further, bringing out a scream. Oh God I'm losing my mind. "What are you gonna do, tough guy?" Fred asked. "Use your kung-fu shit on me? Well give it your best shot because I ain't stopping."

He smacked me so hard my entire back began throbbing. Blood dripped to the floor. Everything started spinning. "I don't want to fight you," Fugi said, "but you know the rules. If you don't stop I *will* put you down."

Another agonizing slap was delivered as Fred said "All talk and no action. You may have been courted by Earl long ago, but those days are over. It's your word against mine. Who do you think they're going to believe, little lost man?"

Slowly Fugi began moving to the side. "Me," he said. "They know as well as I how perverted you are. Step away from her. This is your final warning."

Through my fevered brain this confrontation grabbed my attention. It cut past the throbbing to modestly calm me.

Is this some kind of civil war I'm witnessing? Could I turn Fugi into an ally? He bears close watching for now. Keys being placed in the lock precipitated Fred's quick departure from behind me. Fred was halfway across the room when the door opened.

"Look at what he did," Fred said while pointing at me.

Hank and Mark entered, both looking first at Fred, and then me.

"You son of a bitch," Fugi said. "You planned this whole thing out."

Mark ran across the room, unlocking the pillory. As he carefully raised the top, some of the splinters pulled free. It stung like a swarm of enraged wasps. Tears ran down my cheeks as I grimaced. Then he gently helped me out, pained movement making me whimper. God my wrists have so many pieces of wood I can't move my hands. As I began carefully pulling out slivers with stiff arms, Mark dropped to his haunches to pull my suit up. Throbbing diminished enough for me to glance at him out of gratitude.

"Out, both of you," Hank said. "This is my find and I'll be damned if I'm going to let anyone kill my bonus. We'll sort this through later. Go tend to Mathews. He's prepped for a reminding finale."

That last sentence chilled me. He must be referring to the guy they just hauled away. Even though Mathews was a son of a bitch just for being here, he might be in for an experience no one deserved. Hank's order sounded like a decree of terrible fate.

For a moment it looked like Fred was going to argue, but a stare from Hank quelled it. It would seem my opinion about Hank's role as second in command is correct. Fugi calmly walked toward the door unafraid of Fred. Hank watched them leave, and then came to me. "Can you walk?" He asked.

"Yes," I said and instantly regretted it.

The muscles in my neck shifted under the collar, driving some of the splinters deeper. My assessment was wrong. When I took that first step, my body movements brought intense agony that caused me to swoon. Hands immediately grabbed my shoulders. Hank held me steady with a concerned expression as he examined my neck, while Mark started cursing Fred under his breath. Then we started moving slowly to the room. Both gently helped me sit on the bed. Hank turned to leave but Mark moved within inches of my neck. "Hold off on the collar a few minutes," Mark said. "She still has splinters near it."

A grunt came from Hank. "So?' He asked. "I looked; none are close enough to pose a risk. Let her get them out herself."

Mark turned away, straightening his posture as he faced Hank. "Will you just give us a few minutes?" He asked. "With my help we'll be done in no time."

One loud chuckle came from Hank as he smiled and slowly shook his head. "Fred was right," Hank said. "You do have an infatuation with her. That's bad beans bro'. It'll get you in trouble. Better to walk away and let her fend for herself."

This was becoming very interesting. Mark shook his head while looking at me. "There's no reason why she should struggle needlessly because of Fred's stupidity," he said. "Leave the collar off a few, all right?"

Hank sighed deeply. "All right lover-boy," he said. "Just hurry it up. You don't want Earl to see you mothering her."

That warning meant something. He froze all movement standing to the side watching me. A sudden jab of pain reminded me why this argument began, pulling my eyes to my wrists. Several larger pieces were close together on my left, which I carefully began tugging. Then a quick yank on my neck surprised a gasp out of me as I looked at Mark dropping a large splinter. His eyes were warm and kind while reaching for another one, showing a slight smile as he glanced at me.

CHAPTER 7

Ten minutes after Mark convinced Hank to hold off activating the collar, he tugged the last splinter from my neck. Specks of clotting blood dotted both wrists like macabre freckles, and I can only guess my neck looks as bad. Before they left, he waited in an almost chivalrous manner until I'd removed the last sliver. Now that I'm alone it's time to evaluate what just happened.

As Fugi checked the man he knocked out, his expression toward me seemed apologetic. That isn't the first time he's appeared sad or concerned. Fred towers over him by at least a foot yet didn't fight during their confrontation, lending credence to what he said about Fugi's battle skills. He would make a powerful ally, but the one nagging fact that can't be ignored is why he's here. Surely if he's as skilled as Fred's cowering indicates, he could leave anytime. Something obviously holds him, and that something might be strong enough for him to ignore my proposals for an insurrection. At this time it's best to stay away from him. I only hope if things start going badly when I make my move, he'll look the other way.

Mark is an entirely different matter. He appears close to Hank which means they trust each other. Since Hank was cautioning him about his so-called infatuation over me, it's a safe assumption he's never acted like this before. That element of inexperience is on my side. He will be my target.

The first order of business is to separate him from the rest. It won't be easy since Hank is probably watching me closely. Perhaps with subtle hints and casual smiles I can plant the urge for him to make it happen. May God forgive me; I'll most likely have to seduce him a number of times. Then when he's not expecting it, I'll remove his remote and keys to hide under the mattress as a last resort. He might decide to help if he thinks I'm in love and want to be with him. His getting me out is the best scenario. That would be quiet and not draw the snakes' attention.

Snakes; in all the confusion I nearly forgot about them. Oh God that piece of meat must surely have brought them. They might still be in here.

Panic set in, my legs instantly off the floor. Although the room was silent that didn't mean a thing. They're sneaky. No way can I remain in this room without knowing if the snakes have come and gone or waiting for the right time to strike. I must force myself to check. If I see even the slightest *hint* of reptilian eyes staring back, I'll scream loudly enough to bring someone running. My heart began pounding as I rolled to the side and began tugging the blanket upward. When it was bunched on the mattress, I carefully leaned over the edge.

It's still there. The meat is right where it fell. This makes no sense. Hank said if food was left around for awhile, the snakes would smell it and come. They couldn't have missed it since the meat has been sitting for over an hour almost on top of the drain. Granted it could mean they just haven't smelled it but I don't think so. Fred's chuckling after Hank warned me suggests it's a lie. Snakes are not in the pipes. If snakes aren't in this building; what about the sensors over the door? No dimples in the paint, flaws in the brick, or irregularities in the ceiling can be seen.

I have to know. It would be nice to stand next to the door holding the chair ready to hit the first person who enters when everything else is set. If sensors turn out to be another lie, I'll keep that knowledge to myself and act like I believe they're real. Then when the time is right, I'll catch someone by surprise. Okay here goes.

Even though I know snakes aren't here, the thought of them still gives me shivers. Forget about them and focus. There are no sensors and I'm going to prove it.

Moving to within a few feet of the door was easy. Then my mind demanded I pause. Before advancing I looked closely at all areas around the door. Nothing stood out, even in the frame and floor. It has to be safe. Since Hank might check in on me at any moment, I need to do this now. One-; two; three!

I broke into a run toward the door. Sight failed, I was on fire. It felt like acid eating through my neck to boil my blood as I fell forward.

My body slammed into the door forcing a tumble backwards. Contact with the floor felt like hitting a bed of nails. Lights began dimming; pressure in my head felt like it was going to explode. As fast as it began, agonies ended. Am I dead?

Dizziness prevented me from moving too much, but I was able to look toward the door and see Mark lowering his remote. Footsteps echoing inside the big room indicated at least two other people were running. Hank and Fred skidded to a stop behind Mark.

"What'd you do to her?" Hank asked.

Through my fuzzy eyesight I saw Mark shake his head while looking at Hank. "Take a look at where she is," he said. "She ran the door. Had I not been close enough to hear the impact or if she'd dropped inside the red zone, we'd be cleaning up a mess right now."

Pure fury was in Hank's eyes as he slowly looked at me. When he started moving, Mark stepped in front. "Remember your bonus," Mark said. "Calm down and don't do anything you'll later regret."

Hank looked past Mark still glaring at me, his eyes like two flamethrowers roasting my face. "You have one chance to stay alive," Hank said. "Convince me this wasn't an escape attempt."

My mind was still spinning and body tingling, making it nearly impossible to think. Then an idea seemed to come from somewhere else. Slowly I pushed myself up using my hands, staying seated on the floor. "I," I said but was so garbled I needed to clear my throat a few times. "I saw a snake."

Trembles ran through my body at the mere mention of a snake. To add emphasis, I quickly looked behind and pointed toward the floor beneath the bed. "It was there oh God make it go away!"

Movement was heard as Fred pushed between Mark and Hank. "Bull shit," he said. "You're lying and I'll prove it!"

Lord I hope Mark turned off the collar. I have to take the chance. If I can reach him, this might work out better than I'd thought.

Fred quickly marched to the side of the bed I pointed and grabbed the overhanging cover. When he began lifting it, I sprang to my feet running directly into Mark where I gripped him, shaking terribly. He placed his arms over my back in a hug.

"See," Fred said, "no snakes. Now I can have some serious fun with that fluff!"

Mark began rubbing my back in a soothing manner, while Hank's movements out of the corner of my eye grabbed my attention. His lids squinted as he ducked down slightly. Then he raised his arm, pointing at a spot under the bed. "What's that?" He asked.

A terrified whimper from me followed as I tightly shut my eyes and buried my face in Mark's chest. He started patting my back while saying calming things. Based on the sounds I heard, Fred moved in response to Hank's question. "It's a piece of meat for God's sake," Fred said. "You're not buying into this are you?"

"Seven forty-two," Hank said, "is that what you were looking for earlier?"

With Mark still holding me in a protective fashion, I slowly nodded my head. "Yes," I said. "It fell off my fork. You said food left in my room would attract snakes. I couldn't reach it before, and when I checked a few minutes ago-, oh God those eyes! Get it away! Get it away!"

Patting my back softly, Mark said "It's okay. They're gone now."

Shoes loudly slapping concrete indicated Fred was approaching. Rather than look at him, I kept my eyes tightly closed while gripping Mark tighter around his waist. Footsteps stopped very close to me. "I don't believe this," Fred said. "You two goons are the most gullible imbeciles I've ever known! Let's see what Earl thinks!"

As he pushed between Hank and Mark, our balance was thrown off. We nearly tumbled sideways, which caused my hands to inadvertently grip his butt. A quiet sigh escaped from him, almost a moan of pleasure.

Though what just happened was completely repulsive to me, I quickly returned my hands to their original position and looked apologetically at Mark. He was struggling to maintain a calm appearance under Hank's stare, but just underneath I could see a spark of desire. After turning my face to where Hank couldn't see, I smiled before closing my eyes to lean contently against his chest. His heart was pounding so fiercely it was nearly pushing my face away.

"All snakes are gone seven forty-two," Hank said. "They won't return. Fred has the food and they're following him. It's time for you to step back. If something spooks you again, call for us. Don't ever run at the door."

For a few moments I remained hugging him. Then as I began pulling my arms away, I brushed his fanny with the arm Hank couldn't see. Granted it's a calculated risk, but I have to make sure he wants more. On my fifth step into the room, an audible click sounded. Hank was lowering his remote when I faced them, while Mark was staring at me with a slight smile. Now I wait for him to make his move.

The door was closed. Eventually boredom set in which prompted me to lie down. Fatigue from not sleeping well slammed into me. I rested for awhile, and then closed my eyes. Before I dozed, keys being placed in the lock brought me alert as the door opened. It wasn't Mark as I'd thought. Earl stepped inside, closing the door. "I trust you've found your accommodations satisfactory Joyce," he said. "It's time we got to know each other better. Tell me a little about yourself."

This is not good. He suspects I'm plotting against him. My only prayer is to stay calm while feigning ignorance. "I don't understand," I said.

A smile grew on his face as he nodded twice, and then walked to the chair. His eyes never left me as he pulled the seat away from the table to sit down. It felt like his piercing stare was cutting though my body to probe the secrets of my soul. "Not bad acting," he said, "not bad at all. You understood the question all right, but will only answer with what you think I want to hear. Since I really don't have time to waste on learning what I already know, I'll cut to the chase. I understand there was a slight mishap a short while ago. You interrupted a filet mignon meal with that stunt."

Focus; he's trying to trap me. All he's following is a gut feeling exactly like my father did when he thought I was plotting. I tricked dad then, and I'll fool this bastard now. His smile didn't fade while I blankly stared at him; those eyes continued their intense study until his head shook a few times before he drew a deep breath and exhaled saying "You *are* quite a find. Had anyone else tested the sensors they'd be dog food by now. Your little story might have fooled some but not me. I have an understanding about you Joyce. Would you care to know why I can make such a bold claim?"

Rather than look uninterested, I formed a perplexed expression as I slightly tilted my head. It took great willpower for me to maintain control over the two emotions rampaging through; fear from where this was heading and mirth about his feelings on knowing the real me. In silence I waited.

"Afraid to talk, huh," he said. "I tend to have that effect on people. You see I didn't always run a successful transfer business. Oh no; up until about fifteen years ago, folks called me The Eraser. I was a problem-solver for the person with enough money. If someone bothered someone else and they contracted with me, well, the troublemaker would soon die. Yes my dear that's right. I killed for money. Only I believed in doing things differently than others in my profession. Not only would I eliminate the source of trouble, I'd also eliminate the body. Folks would vanish, my customers had a problem removed, and dogs ate well. If you count me, three out of four were winners! So how could he do that without getting caught, I imagine you're thinking. Since I hate seeing beautiful ladies needlessly taxing their minds, I won't keep you in suspense."

One of the most patronizing smiles formed nearly bringing a reaction from me. It helped me overcome the revulsion I felt at how he talked about murder with such a casual tone. Oh how I wanted to slap that arrogant expression off. His expression eased into something sinister, bringing goose bumps to my back. "It all begins with homework," he said. "People who needed my services first contacted my associate. That way if it turned out to be a trap, when I struck they'd never see it coming. Only once did a set-up almost succeed, but that's not important for tonight's campfire tale. By understanding the habits and patterns of not only my marks but also my clients, I was able to precisely choose when to literally take-out one or the other. Hollywood glamorizes what I did, making it look like a guy in a suit wearing a Fedora hat hiding in bushes. Though I found it mildly amusing, it was as far from me as you can get. They always died. I'm still here."

I really wanted to say for now when he paused, but held my tongue. He rose from the chair, walked to the door, opened it to look out, nodded his head, and then closed it to face me. What is going on?

"Oh sure I had crude beginnings," he said. "My first kill came when I was thirteen. A schoolmate turned me in for cheating on a test, which brought real wrath of God punishment from my alcoholic father. It was then I decided to even the score. I began following the little snit without his realizing it. Then one sunny spring afternoon, with birds chirping in trees and bees buzzing wildflowers, I struck."

This intermission looked more like he was recalling a fond memory. His cold way of talking about an apparent killing of a young boy chilled me to the core. "He was alone in the woods just goofing off. My only weapon was an eight-inch pocket knife which proved more than adequate. I always kept the blade nice and sharp to state an incidental footnote. Anyway, he was looking under a rotting log as I crept up behind him, quietly opened the knife, and plunged it into the back of his skull right-, here."

He turned his head briefly, pointing at the soft spot where the neck ends and head begins. "You see I'd done my anatomy homework just for him," he said. "I knew if I cut down deep enough in that place, he would lose mobility without dying right away. Ah the look on his face as he fell is something I'll cherish forever!"

Concentrate on calm. Don't let those shivers become visible. "The first thing I did was tear his shirt into strips for gags to shut him the hell up. Then I pulled off his pants and used them as a loose bandage around his neck. A trail of blood might draw curiosity-seekers you understand. Once I was satisfied his pants would soak it all up without coming loose, I grabbed his ankles and pulled him deeper into the woods." A chuckle escaped. "I wasn't too careful about where I walked either. Now I knew abandoned coal mines were nearby, but once word got out about his disappearance that would be the first place searched. I headed away from them, not really sure what to do. Then the answer appeared in front of me. A huge anthill with swarming red ants was practically asking to be fed. Nature can be kind at times, don't you agree?"

My control is fading. This monster is sick. His smile is on the verge of making me nauseous. I must not permit this to alter my appearance. "I finished stripping him, removing his pants bandage as well. Then I carefully stepped over the hill but used him to knock it over, making sure he was setting squarely on top of the opening. His eyes immediately went wild with fear. The ants soon covered him until he looked like he was wearing red shimmering beads. They were so pissed at having their home toppled I got stung quite a few times removing the gag. Two options went through my mind while watching them crawl into his ears and on his eyelids; kill him now just to be safe or leave him to a slow death. I decided on the latter which turned out to be the right vengeful choice. It took over a month for them to find his skeleton which they identified using dental records. Since the flesh wound I inflicted had been hungrily removed by then, they assumed he fell on top of the hill and hit his head which knocked him out. Newspaper reports stated ants swarmed him before he regained consciousness, and his clothes had been taken by wild animals for nests. It was the perfect crime that laid the foundation for my future, one that I improved to the point I took all bodies with me after a hit.

Sometimes they were still alive, and that's where you come into play my lovely."

Oh my God what does that mean? The most terrifying smile appeared as he opened the door without looking. Fred and Hank were standing just outside staring at me.

"Have you ever heard the term under-reacting?" He asked. "By now you should at least look disgusted, yet here you are calmly staring at me waiting for more. I've seen it all Joyce. People plead, bargain, threaten, swear allegiance, or say I made a mistake just to save their lives. Every once in a while I got someone who faked being dead. Subtle signs gave them away. Sometimes it was a slightly changed facial expression like a frown when moments before it wasn't there. Other times it was one that should have changed yet didn't, like when I closed their eyes and moved the head, the eyes remain closed when they should have reopened. You, fall into the closed-eye category and must now be punished."

Earl raised his remote and gave it a hard push, and then the other two ran in the room on both sides of the bed pulling me across the mattress to the floor. So this is it; they're going to kill me. I haven't a chance as long as these two have such a tight grip, but once it's relaxed I'll make them wish they'd never seen me.

They hauled me through the door so quickly I was literally dragged. A wooden chair with handcuffs attached to both sides of the seat back, and two more cuffs on both front legs was our destination. Earl was jogging beside us, his remote constantly pointed at me. In a blur of motion that made me dizzy, I was in the seat with my wrists locked at my sides. Before I could regain myself, both ankles were secured. Then they backed off, giving Earl enough room to drop on his haunches and look me in the eye.

"You're far too valuable to kill," he said, "and I certainly don't want to risk damaging that luscious skin. That means you get one free pass but ONE ONLY! If you ever blatantly disobey us again, this will be you."

As if on cue, the main door opened. Mark and Fugi entered pulling two ropes over their shoulders tied to a naked man's ankles three feet behind them. He was on his belly, hogtied with ankles at opposing angles so his knees were apart, gagged, and struggling against his bonds. Fred ran out of the room snickering as Mark and Fugi stopped fifteen feet in front of me. The man looked at me in such fear it cut to my soul. All I could do was blankly stare at him or my safety would be jeopardized. Fugi's expression was unreadable, while Mark almost appeared sorrowful. Oh no; what are they going to do?

Fred answered my mental question by returning with that hideous chest, really struggling against the weight. Mark turned to help him gently place it on the floor. Fugi moved away from them heading in my direction.

"Just to make sure no further infractions are possible," Earl said, "I'll be replacing Hank as your trainer for now."

Hank moved toward the bound man, apparently unbothered by what Earl said about being replaced. I followed his departure with my eyes, which brought my attention to the wedding ring on the bound man's finger. He has a wife, maybe children who'll never see him again if this continues. Sadness filled me as I looked pleadingly at Earl.

"There, that's better," Earl said. "You just might learn something that'll keep you breathing. But to make sure you fully appreciate the lesson you are about to see, I want you to know this. We were planning on converting him into BK seven forty-three. That all changed when my dinner was interrupted. His death is on your shoulders."

The man's eyes went wild with panic, intensifying his efforts at breaking thick rope without success. His grunts and muffled screams intensified when Mark, Fred, and Hank started circling him like predators searching for a tender spot. I can't just sit here and watch. "Please don't do this," I said. "He has a wife. If you let him go, I'll do whatever you say."

Earl's eyebrows shot up as he stared at me in utter surprise; Fugi's head twitched slightly. "I'm not going to shock you for such a gallant gesture toward a stranger, but you already broke the rules by talking," Earl said. "How in the world can I believe you'll do as we say when you *constantly* break the rules?"

Dread grew in my soul watching Earl casually face the three and nod his head. Fred kicked him in the side, spinning him slightly while bringing forth muted moans. Hank grabbed the hair on top of his head, violently tugging him away from me.

"YOU FILTHY BASTARDS," I shouted "STOP THIS INSANITY!"

A short burst of electricity shot through my neck, tensing already stressed muscles to the point of bruising. Tears momentarily clouded my vision. When it improved, Earl was shaking his head looking at me. "You did it again," he said. "I guess some people are slow learners."

Before my eyes had cleared, someone had kicked him, turning the poor fellow to where his knees were pointed toward me. Hank casually reached into his front jeans pocket to retrieve a long pocket knife. "A man after my own heart," Earl said. "Watch what happens next."

Bile rose from my belly to my throat threatening to continue outward. Hank leisurely held the knife in front of the man's face, and then snapped it open. A nasty blade with the cutting edge serrated in the middle gleamed in the bright room light while Hank slowly turned it for all to see. Horrified begs for mercy broke through the gag as Hank snatched his left ring finger, positioning the blade just below the ring.

"Uh oh," Earl said, "looks like the bum is filing for divorce."

When Hank began pushing the knife down, I closed my eyes and turned away. Another short burst of electricity surprised them open. A continual stream of garbled pleas filled the room, sickening me into closing them again. Earl grabbed my chin, forcibly turning my head to face the madness. "You will watch this or I'll replace him with you!"

It felt like the ground was shifting under my feet making me dizzy. By the time Earl moved out of the way, Hank was already holding his grisly prize in the air. The man was making grunts more animal than human while yanking so hard on the ropes; blisters large enough to be seen from this distance began forming. Then Hank started whistling as he turned toward the chest, happily relinquishing the knife to Fred. My God these diseased monsters must be stopped.

"Now it gets interesting," Earl said. "Fred is a firm believer in animal control. Even money says he goes for the neuter."

Earl's face changed while watching me. It became a demonic visage from hell; his eyes almost glowing. Wooziness started overtaking me, causing my head to involuntarily move. One long howl of terror rose from the man when Fred reached between his thighs.

"Told you," Earl said just as sweet unconsciousness released me from this nightmare.

A sharp, pungent aroma snapped me awake. The first sight I saw was Earl pulling a smelling salt container away from my face, while hands holding me steady belonged to Fugi. Everyone else was gone, including the man.

"I decided to be magnanimous and let you sleep through the preliminaries," Earl said. "My point has been made."

Loud mechanical humming sounded from outside the closed main door, vibrating the floor so violently it ran from my feet to my shoulders. Earl glanced toward the door briefly before looking at me. "My own design," he said. "It's really a carry-over from my former occupation."

Rapid thumping joined the hum, sounding like several dozen hammers quickly striking thick metal in an alternating fashion. "What I didn't tell you before was how my nickname of The Eraser truly came into being. I only hinted about it. Normally I don't go into such detail, but for you I'm making an exception."

The humming suddenly sounded strained like it was struggling with something heavy. "Like I said before, most who do what I did consider a contract completed after their target was dead; not me."

Screams muffled by the door entered the room while the humming continued and the thumping sounded different, like it was now smacking something soft. Bile burned the back of my throat just thinking about the possibilities. "I have this arrangement with an importer in South America who accepts my shipments of dog food without question."

His shrieks became more intense like he was in horrible pain. "Of course I add other fillers, but the main ingredient is human meat and byproducts."

One impossibly loud screech was heard, followed only by the noise of a working machine. Chills coursed through as I stared at him in shock. He evilly smiled in return. "Before meat can be shaped into chunks and roasted to a dry meal, it must be turned to mush. My machine really isn't that portable with all the chopping blades and pounding mallets, but it can be hidden when not in use. You should feel honored. Other than my associates here, you are the only *living* person to know my grinder exists."

God I'm going to get sick. A violent rush from my stomach to my throat forced me to clamp my mouth shut, making my cheeks expand before I could contain it. Then the door opened, intensifying the sound of the grinder tenfold. It became deafening, almost distracting my attention away from the hypodermic needle Hank was holding.

"Oh, before I forget, I have a little memento for you," Earl said.

SWITCHER

Inside his palm rested the bloody wedding ring worn by their victim. I stared at it, my body trembling as insanity threatened to seize reality. Chugging sounds from the hall seemed to ease slightly like the machine was finalizing its gruesome job. My head began swaying, yet the ring held me mesmerized. A sharp sting to my hip broke the hold as I looked at Hank withdrawing a needle. Instantaneous unconsciousness ended this horror.

CHAPTER 8

Wow this is fun. I'm going for a walk with people. No, wait; I'm being carried. Or is it both? Who cares? I feel great. And look; an open doorway is coming at us. I didn't know they could move. Whoops; it got us. Uh oh; now a bed is moving toward us. Aw I really don't want to lie down. Let's go for another walk.

"You will stay where you are."

That voice sounds like, oh yes. It's God. I better do what he says or he'll get angry. Oh goodie; here come more people pushing that strange screen. I like company. Are we going to watch a movie?

"Before we begin," God said. "You will tell me about your escape plan."

What does he mean? I don't want to leave. Oh, he means the other me. Why is that important? "Tell me," he angrily said.

Four horrifying snakes dropped on the mattress slithering blindly around. My body locked in terror, breathing became difficult. I can't move. They'll see me. Oh God please take them away. Four more flew through the air to land on my legs. "The snakes will keep coming until you tell me," God said.

My breathing changed to rapid short pants watching the hideous things crawling all over. Those terrible monsters are going to kill me. "Please, make them go away," I said.

They began writhing into frenzy, bumping into my arms and neck. Horror focused all attention on the monsters, making it nearly impossible to think.

"If I remove the snakes, will you tell me the truth?"

"Yes, yes; please, take them away! Take them away!"

All slithering ceased just when God's angels appeared, removing them from me. Oh thank you! "Just as I called them away, I can send them forth again," God said. "Always keep that in mind. Tell me about your escape plan."

Relief bathed over me like a soothing creek until God's warning sank in. Terror returned, forcing me to look at him pleadingly. If I don't tell him, the snakes will get me. "The other Joyce was planning to escape. She wanted to seduce Mark and fool him into helping her, or at least steal his keys and remote."

Shifting sounds like feet being moved were heard coming away from God, but I couldn't dare look away. "Does the other Joyce love Mark?" God asked.

My head began shaking, "no."

God smiled knowingly, briefly glancing at something behind me before looking at me again. "Does she even like him?"

I must answer or the snakes will come back. "No; she despises him."

His smile broadened as he again looked to my back, and then returned his eyes to me. Good, that happy smile means I've pleased him. "What would she say if I told you Mark loves her?" God asked.

Her revulsion rose through foggy barriers to reach me. My face frowned into a disgusted appearance. More shuffling sounds came from behind, followed by a bang like something was hit.

"It sickens her. He is a diseased fiend who must be stopped. She saw he had feelings for her but hid her loathing to use him. When she was safe she'd turn him in."

Loud footsteps smacking concrete seemed to indicate someone was angrily leaving. When I looked at the door, two angels were moving the screen toward me.

"The other Joyce is quite an actress in a dangerous play," God said. "You will let her know about this discussion when she awakens, and how Earl will always find out if she tries something else. There is no escape."

As God has commanded, I must obey. When I fearfully nodded, an angel stepped in front moving the screen into position. Once it was tilted facing me, the angel moved away. Suddenly beautiful colors began swirling, drawing my undivided attention.

"Watch the colors," God said. "Do you see the door we spoke of last time?"

Gradually the opened door grew out of nothingness, a tiny baby girl floating on the other side and a duplicate of me walked toward her. "Yes."

Suddenly the colors began gently spinning in the opposite direction. "Do you see the baby BL seven forty-two?" God asked.

Aw, the poor thing is crying again. "Yes."

She reached for me, making my heart ache to go soothe her. "Now she's aging," God said. "She's a three year-old toddler. Do you understand?"

Her arms and legs stretched while the crying stopped. A little girl stood in the doorway, looking confused and lost. "Yes."

"Look at the other person," God said. "Do you see Joyce Jackson?"

It was like the girl floated away as the other Joyce faced me. "Yes."

She can't move and looks so sad. I wish I could help her feel as good as me.

"All of the life experiences are contained inside Joyce, not BL seven forty-two. The young girl has an empty mind. Do you understand?"

"Yes."

The screen flickered briefly. What was that?

"Very good," he said. "For now, you will only see Joyce standing in the door. BL seven forty-two is hidden behind her. Do you understand?"

All at once the screen started pulsating as it slowly turned. "Yes."

"Good," he said. "When you wake up, you will not remember anything other than telling Earl about the escape plan *and* what I'm about to say. Is the other Joyce afraid of insects?"

My brows knitted together. Why does he want to know that?

"Answer me," he angrily said.

Flames instantly erupted, consuming all colors. Oh please make it stop. "She doesn't like them, but isn't afraid."

All fire went out, replaced with colors spinning much faster than before. "This commandment will be deeply planted into the other Joyce's conscious mind. She will believe all insects terrify her, much more than snakes. They will swarm over her biting and stinging. They will eat her alive if they find her. Do you understand?"

Bugs of many types came crawling out of the center, swarming until the screen was covered with them. Some had stingers, others large clicking mandibles.

"You will answer me immediately," he said.

Horrified shivering escalated to jostle the mattress when all insects stopped moving to look at me. Terror nearly locked my throat. "Yes," I said.

Just like the fire, all bugs vanished. Oh thank you! God is all-powerful. "Very good," he said. "To reinforce what was commanded before, you will not remember any dreams. Do you understand?"

"Yes," I said.

"Sleep now."

Bright early May sunshine heated my black cap and gown this Saturday morn to the point I wished the ceremony would end. After four grueling years of heavy class loads, coupled with May semesters and summer schools throughout, my degree is in hand. I had accomplished what others take five years to do. At least this scholastic environment was a marvelous change from life under dad's cruel watch.

A Master's Degree in Education with a Minor's in History should safely see me away from him. My moment of vengeance is so close I can't stand sitting here listening to the mayor congratulating us. In a way I'm insulted that the best the president of Whitmore University could do for a commencement speaker is a local political windbag. Talk about dry and boring, this joker could put an insomniac out in ten minutes flat.

Finally he finished, the loud clapping probably a show of thankfulness for his stepping down. Two more speeches to go, and then I'll have my temporary certificate. Once I'm relocated, I'll let the dean of student affairs know my new address so they'll be able to correctly send my official diploma. Graduating third in my class means I don't give speeches in front of the student body, but boy do I have one prepared for later.

I didn't know with any certainty dad would be here. He missed my high school graduation as well as last year's service for my Bachelor's Degree. It wasn't until last night I got the call from mom telling me not only were they going to make the three-hour drive, but many of our family would be here as well. Not that I'm untouched by this show of family support, but I am surprised at their interest. For me it's like the universe has finally set things up in my favor, granting me this opportunity to right a horrible wrong.

Money buys many things including blind eyes. Whenever an extended family gathering took place, everyone thought of me as the child born into a life of luxury. Dad's insults, temper flare-ups, and astonishing punishments seemed to be missed even when it happened as they watched. Well today they're going to observe a reversal of humiliation. Then in three days, I'll be away from his miserable self-serving ego forever.

With a final congratulation from Dean Jefferson, the graduation ceremony concluded amidst cheers. That was when it truly hit. My home for so long is no more. The dorm room I held now belongs to younger students. Professors, classrooms, the library, even the dining hall, were not a part of my life any more. Parties, dates, movies, and concerts will become memories to cherish forever.

If I don't stop thinking like this, I'll start crying. My car is packed. All that's left is to find my family for the really big speech. Wait, there's mom waving at me. Dad is next to her looking like he had a wonderful nap. That figures. Ah, here they come now, pushing through the crowd. "Joyce I'm so proud of you," mom said, "graduating third in your class!"

Her impact nearly sent the both of us to the ground. Had it not been for our mutual hug, it might've turned out embarrassingly. "Thanks mom; so how was the trip?"

This is happening exactly as I planned so long ago. I'll continue playing the good little girl until I exact my vengeance. As I looked from my proud mother to my somewhat bored father, his shoulders shrugged. Mom and I disengaged watching him. "It was a pain in the rump," he said. "I wish you'd listened to me and attended Burksdale College instead of this God-forsaken money pit! The very least you could have done was finish first, not come in third place."

My father; the football hero who injured his knee in college is criticizing my accomplishments when the only requirements he needed for graduation was to read the letter on his jacket. That's him all the way, and with mom allowing that insensitive remark to go unchallenged, that's her as well. Had it not been for Uncle Phil convincing him that my attending school away from home would mature me faster and better prepare me for the future, I would have commuted the entire time. Chances are had that happened; my plan to leave would have been executed prematurely. For that I owe him, but now I mirrored dad's reaction to my question by shrugging. His head shook as he turned away. "We'll talk about where you're going to live after lunch," he said. "I'm starved. Since we arrived early, I took the liberty of reserving a chunk of Paschal's Steakhouse off the highway exit. You know the place?"

When he said we'd talk about where I'm going to live, it took great willpower not to laugh. Instead I smiled sweetly at him. "Yes."

His head nodded once, and then he looked at mom. "Then you can meet us there," he said. "Come on Paula; if we don't get going, the rest of the family will run up one hell of a bill!"

Mom looked from the ground to see me smiling. It seemed to relax her. If she could catch a glimpse of the raging mental war I was battling just to hold it, she probably would have wept. He turned to walk away, not even looking to see if mom was with him. As was always the case, she followed two steps behind.

All the goodbyes were said last night. Friends I made while attending school are now with family. Crowds are dispersing, heading to various celebrations I'm sure, only they're leaving together. Here I am alone watching the backs of my parents grow smaller as they continue walking away. In a bizarre smattering of irony, this left-alone symbolism defines my past. Now that my future is assured, I can truly enjoy my smile thinking how soon I'll be the one with the shrinking back.

Traffic was unreal. It took almost thirty minutes just to get off campus, and then the fun really began. Every traffic signal in the city of Mayden became a test of patience. Out of state vehicle license plates sitting through two, three, and sometimes four cycles proved this rustic little town was ill-prepared for the annual onslaught of collegiate graduation. None that I saw were local, like the townies went into hiding until this blew over. One hour after I opened my super-heated over-packed car to squeeze in, I realized those locals were the truly learned. Finally the Interstate ramp loomed ahead and just before it sat the restaurant. Cars packed the parking lot in the same manner as every other eating establishment on the way here. Lots of money was changing hands today.

People crowding the entrance lobby turned out to be my family. Numerous congratulations were offered. Even though I thanked their show of support, my mind was concentrating on my upcoming surprise. I haven't been this excited since the night before I left for college.

Commotion from the cashier's location silenced the crowd, drawing our attention. Dad was arguing over something, no doubt the reason behind this lobby back-up. Based on the bits and pieces overheard, his reservation had been cancelled due to tardiness. A suit-wearing man approached in an attempt at quelling the disturbance. The man and my father walked out of earshot, but body language indicated dad was not pleased. Most might have surrendered and changed plans, but not my father. He only accepts victory and finds the right verbal threats to use in his battles. Such must've been the case. Five minutes into it the man's shoulders slumped. He nodded his head twice, raised his hand to call forth employees from other locations, and walked into the dining area. Four male workers were soon following his footsteps.

Family chatter slowly resumed. Dad remained where he was, his back to us and hands on hips. That stance made me think of a school disciplinarian overseeing disruptive students writing out the one-hundred sentences on the blackboard punishment, nearly making me laugh.

Sounds of heavy tables dragged across wood planked flooring rose above the din of people eating. Eyes began drifting toward the apparent struggle like they expected to see customers running out brushing sawdust from their shoulders. Clacking plates coupled with tinkling silverware made me think they were setting the table in the dishwashing area for convenience. Then all grew eerily quiet.

Customers already seated were able to observe the monumental rearranging that took place, while we in the lobby couldn't. Conversations that moments before mingled together ceased as attention drifted to this small army called my family. Expressions ranged from the mildly curious to absolutely shocked. I was convinced if we screamed one word in unison, at least three ladies would faint into their food. Finally the head-waiter, manager, or whatever the guy in the suit was called, put in an appearance where we could see and motioned with a finger for us to follow. It took two glances to make certain his gesture wasn't insulting.

Moving in the indicated direction was both comical and frightening. People pulled their plates away from the aisle as if they expected one of us to sample the cuisine at their expense, while others showed visible hostility at our passing like they were ticked at having their meal interrupted. I was mostly concerned about what would happen if someone up front tripped backwards. As tightly packed as we were; that accident might create a chain reaction of domino-like tumbling strong enough to knock out a wall. Five minutes and about three-dozen angry stares later, we were seated scanning menus which permitted me to gaze at the miracle that is now our setting.

It looked like the manager opened a previously closed section for us. That or another reservation was cancelled and we were placed in their stead. I can come up with no further explanation as to how such a huge part of this busy establishment was so quickly arranged to accommodate our gathering of sixty.

Two long tables were perfectly lined up to the outer edges of a small one like an open ended rectangle. White cloth table covers adorned the tops, separating us from all the other guests eating on plain wood. Chairs were situated on both sides of the long ones, with my father, mother, and me alone at the top. Menus, silverware, napkins, and water glasses were carefully placed in front of each seat. Nobody was crowded, able to casually study the menu without bumping elbows. Two waiters methodically worked their way through until the last order was taken. When they left, my father tapped his glass with the knife to grab everyone's attention. A few taps later, our party was quiet and he got to his feet. "Folks," dad said, "thanks for making the trip to this dust-mote in the middle of nowhere. As you know, we are celebrating the end of a serious drain to my savings account, Joyce's graduation."

A few chuckles sounded, bringing a smile to his face. Oh I can hardly wait for my turn. "Not all of the blame for dragging us away from civilization rests with Joyce. There is a brother of mine who deserves the proper gratitude as well."

Uncle Phil held up his water glass, smiling like he'd won the office pool. Laughter and a smattering of applause followed until he returned the glass. Dad's attention shifted to me. "But now it's done," he said. "Goofing off in school for a meaningless degree is over. Monday comes in two days. You start paying me back. I've even opened a new secretarial position just for you. Welcome to the real world, sweetie!"

Though the laughter and applause that followed indicates they believed his entire speech was sarcastic, I knew the only sarcasm was his last word. Even his smile toward me looked more out of self-satisfaction than happiness.

"Thank you," he said, "now we can eat if the help here remembers how to cook."

Before he sat down, cries for me to speak rang out. Dad started shaking his head while holding up his arms to quiet the rising throng. "She's not one for public speaking," he said. "I'm sure she'd like to offer her thanks for your being here as well. Isn't that right Joyce?"

My time has finally come. Even though his question to me was more of a command, I smiled grandly while pushing my chair away from the table. Applause sounded when I rose, but dad looked irritated. That's a healthy beginning. "First off, I'd like to tell all employees of this lovely establishment I appreciate the amazing effort you exerted in preparing this place on short notice, and how much I've enjoyed living in Mayden the last four years. Your town is beautiful and people friendly. I hold many fond memories to cherish forever. It truly became a home to me that I hate leaving. Please keep this in mind when you handle my iced tea."

Laughter rang out as dad took his seat slightly red in the face. "I would like to thank you all for being here," I said. "To see so many warm and loving faces truly makes me feel wonderful."

Cheers sounded as dad closely watched me. His face showed a combination of concern and impatience. "My journey to this point began years ago. You could even say it started when I was punished at the tender age of six. Do you remember that night when you taught me about the frailty of plastic dolls, dad?"

The vein on his left temple began expanding like it did when he was getting mad. Other than that, no movement came from our party. Tension mounted as dad stared at me, silence seeming to descend over the entire steakhouse. "Forgot about it huh?" I asked. "That's okay; it haunted my young mind for months and is forever on my mental notepad. Oh, let's not overlook the basement storage room. You know; the one with a crack somewhere that let water and bugs in, but the tight seal on the room's door kept them from the rest of the house. I learned a lot about overcoming my fear of dark places when you locked me in there for hours."

Gasps followed, with a few heads shaking denial. Uncle Phil watched me closely, a frown on his face. But it was dad's reaction that most others were observing. His eyes were wild with unbridled fury. "My plans solidified after my sixteenth birthday party where you grew enraged over the money you said was wasted on me. You *must* remember that, when you chased all my friends away and threatened to have a boy arrested simply for being there. It took months before I could overcome the humiliation you rained on me." A chuckle slipped out. "That wasn't exactly an extravaganza for the social registers, was it daddy dear?"

"That's enough," he said, his face bright red with anger.

As I smiled at him, my head started nodding. "It's funny you should say that, because those were the exact words I quietly whispered over the years. So many memories, so little time left; which brings me to my final point."

Wood dragging across wood nearly echoed through the quiet restaurant when dad slid his chair back. Even patrons not part of this family were watching with rapt attention. As he rose to tower over me, I decided to change a few things. "Graduation day is an ending that heralds a new beginning. What we call life should never be spent living in fear. We have the privilege, no, the obligation to choose our own paths. No one should be allowed to intimidate or subjugate another regardless of motive or strength. Cowards taunt the weaker, control is their goal. Only through other's surrender do they maintain the illusion of power. Never be afraid to speak your mind. We must stand firm against all oppression or our lives will always be hollow."

Dad was trapped. He didn't know what to do or say that wouldn't make him look bad. He only held a small portion of my stare. Mom was looking at her plate with tears in her eyes. My message has been heard. Now I hope it does some good. "I am about to embark on a grand adventure," I said, "one that will take me far from here. This coming Tuesday I leave behind my old life in search of a better one. My heart will be my guide, my meaningless degree my ticket. This is exciting for me, and I'm so very happy you're here to share it. Thank you."

Mom's head jerked to stare at me. Dad quietly sat down, his eyes betraying a scheming mind. Not a single person responded to my ending as I also took my seat.

Gradually talk from other tables resumed while our party was stunned silent. Waiters began delivering food, but it was as if all appetites had been lost. No one lifted a fork or glass. All eyes were switching between dad and me like they couldn't comprehend why I'm walking away from so much money, and what he did to make me choose to leave. That's their problem; like dad said it's done.

When my food arrived, I dug in with the zest of a starving woman. Eventually dad started laughing, building into a full-blown guffaw. It caused me to place my fork down thinking he'd finally lost the last bit of his sanity.

"You've had your fun," he said. "Now it's my turn. If you leave Burksdale, don't ever come back. You will no longer be part of my family."

Three chuckles came from me as I lifted the fork. "Took you this long to come up with such an impotent threat? You've never treated me like a part of your family. As far as I'm concerned, you are no longer a part of mine."

"You are not leaving-"

A door violently opened startling me awake.
"Get up you bitch! We have a score to settle!"

CHAPTER 9

Foggy remnants of sleep instantly fled as I focused on Mark in the doorway, his remote aimed at me. Dear God, they injected me with some kind of drug that forced me to tell them everything. "I'm not going to say this again," he said. "Get that lying, conniving ass out of bed or I'll kill you on your back."

My mind rapidly searched for something to disarm this situation, but nothing came forward. Then I noticed he was alone. These actions might not be sanctioned by Earl. Either this was a frightful test or he was acting impulsively. If it's the latter, he'd face an almost certain death sentence should he proceed, yet he doesn't seem worried. As I climbed off the mattress to face him, I silently prayed for the first choice.

A wicked smile grew as he said "I want to watch you squirm like the maggot you are. We'll start off slowly just so you enjoy the full spectrum of that collar. Do you have any last words before we begin?"

He wants me to beg for mercy. I will not give him the satisfaction. "No."

At this point my escape plans were back to the beginning. Since they have drugs capable of forcing me to tell them anything, perhaps death would be a welcome release. His eyes grew wild, jaw tightened, and he lifted the remote a little higher. My eyes looked at his in defiance. Then his hand lowered. "This would be too easy," he said. "You deserve something much more lingering for playing with a man's heart. See you soon, lover."

Before he could turn away, the main door opened with an echo in the outer chamber. From a distance Fred said "WHAT THE *HELL* ARE YOU DOING?"

Based on the sound of his steps, he was practically running toward us. Mark leisurely glanced in that direction before looking back at me. "Just having a little farewell talk with my former would-be girlfriend," he said.

"You didn't-?" Fred asked just as he reached my door. An expression of relief formed on his face when he saw me standing. A plate of food in his hands prevented him from wrestling Mark's remote away. He jogged in the room, putting the food down and then reaching in his back pocket for a small bottle of water that he tossed on the table. "Eat," he said. Then he quickly faced Mark "Have you dropped off the sanity-plank? You know Earl told you to stay away from her. If he catches you here, he'll use you for target practice!"

An eerily peaceful smile grew on Mark's face when he looked at Fred. "Everything's cool; I needed closure, that's all."

"Yeah? Well that remote in your hand doesn't close garage doors, you know!"

Mark laughed while putting the device in his back pocket. "For me it did," he said while turning away.

Fred began walking out of the room shaking his head while ignoring how close I was to him. The thought of rushing him came to mind, but with Mark nearby I knew it would fail. I'm not ready for suicide.

When the door closed and my nerves slightly settled, I looked at the meat. A compulsion from deep inside drove me to the table. In spite of the adrenaline still pumping through, hunger seemed to take over my thoughts. It demanded I clean the plate, which I did without hesitation. Once the last of the water was drained, my mind cleared enough for me to analyze what just transpired.

It seems Fred, Mark, and Hank, are close. Fred showed genuine concern over Mark getting caught by Earl, and Hank mentioned something about the danger of Earl seeing him help me. There has to be a way I can use that fear of Earl to my advantage.

Mark is a danger. His show of composure may fool the others, but I saw the fury beneath the calm. Sooner or later he's going to snap. When that happens, I pray someone else will be close. I wonder what would happen if I told Earl what Mark said.

That's it! I'll start turning Earl against the others one at a time. Earl obviously places some value in keeping me alive or he wouldn't have told Mark to stay away. He just might take preemptive measures to protect me if he feels a grave risk exists. At the very least his wrath will cause confusion and fear among them, much more so than now. That could give me the opportunity to slip past them. In order to succeed, I still have to act frightened and plead for his protection. Even if they use those drugs again, Mark's anger is real and I know it. In fact I'd bet money they'd try to stop Earl from asking me any questions. No matter what other plans I divulge, Mark's threat will be disclosed.

The rattling doorknob immediately grabbed my attention. If that's Mark coming to finish the job, I'll scream so loudly they'll hear me on the street. Once the door was opened, Hank holding a closed box looked both ways before sliding it across the floor.

"You just aren't worth it," he said. "Everyone's gone nuts over you. I'm sorry I found you. I need your solemn word. You lie to me and I will hunt you down. If I help you get the hell out of here, will you swear not to tell anyone about us?"

He's got to be kidding if he thinks I believe any of this. "What do you mean?"

Nervously looking toward the main outside chamber door, he said "Look you ditzy blonde, I don't have a lot of time. Here're clothes and a cell phone. Don't use the phone now or Earl would pick it up. We'd both be dead before you finished pushing the third button. Wait until you're far from here before calling. Change quickly. We have to move while they're occupied."

This has gone far enough. He's seriously underestimating me if he thinks I'll fall for this trap. While I remained seated, I crossed my arms and stared at him. "Why would you do this?"

A deep sigh escaped as he stared at me impatiently. "Simply put Earl won't let me kill you but he's ready to kill Mark because of you. We've been friends for many years and I *don't* want to lose him. I want you out of the picture. If you turned up dead, Mark would be shot as the prime suspect. If you simply vanish, Mark would be in the clear since he's being monitored as much as possible. There's no way he could haul you out of the building without being seen. Earl would probably blame Fugi but that's okay. Now for God's sake move it."

His remote appeared as he clicked a button. No shock followed, making me grow more curious by the moment. Then he stepped clear of the doorway, granting me a small amount of privacy. One thing is for certain, he seems anxious.

Had he closed the door, I might suspect a boxed bomb or some other booby-trap. Yet it's ajar and I can hear him nervously pacing the floor which lends a slight amount of credence to what he said. On the flip side, he didn't remove the collar, only disarmed it I think. Well whatever he's up to will be answered once I check out that box.

Slowly I approached it, kicking it with my toe. It moved without any resistance. The contents are light like clothing and a phone are all that's inside. Then I gripped the top to pull open.

My lord, there's the cell phone he talked about. It's powered up and resting on a gray outfit, just sitting there waiting to end this nightmare. Tears welled in my eyes as I began to reach for it. Then the material under the phone moved with my hands inches away. A huge cockroach climbed from under the gray blouse, its horrid antennas moving constantly while it climbed on the phone.

Breath froze in my throat as I stared at it. More of the beasts appeared, dozens of them scurrying to the edges climbing out. My heart felt like it was going to explode when they reached the floor heading for me.

Panic hit; I screamed while running away. The bed is my only hope. In three long strides I was standing on the mattress, staring at them aimlessly wandering around.

"BOO," Hank said leaning across the doorframe, making me jump. His face broke into a large smile as he entered the room. "I guess you don't want to leave, huh?" He asked while lifting the box.

When he held it up, more roaches fell to the floor before he closed the lid. How can he even touch that thing? With the box under one arm, he walked to the bed and grabbed my arm. "You'll have to wait outside until the exterminators arrive," he said.

With one monumental yank, I was off the bed in the midst of those scurrying horrors. He hauled me across the floor, my eyes wide and watching the rear. Breath froze in my throat, my heart beating so hard it felt ready to explode; then something odd started happening. Just before we left the room, three of the monsters flipped on their backs like they were dead. More showed signs of dying. How is that possible?

Hank was dragging me so quickly I couldn't gain my balance. In little time I was seated in that chair with the cuffs, Hank already locking the arm he'd grabbed. He moved behind the seat, quickly locking my other wrist. "We've prepared entertainment just for you," he said. Then he grabbed my ankles from beneath the seat and locked them. While rising he said "I'll go see if the popcorn's ready."

Everything happened so fast I didn't have time to think. Why did he do what he just did? It's obvious he played off my grave fear of insects, but for what gain; a sick joke? And how did he know I wouldn't just reach for the phone anyway?

That thought made me shiver. Somehow he knew. The drug made me tell him.

Before he left the chamber, a whirring noise over his head caused me to look up. Two long cables with manacles on the end were lowering from the ceiling, looking like hungry claws reaching for him. When I looked to the wall opposite my room, Fred was carefully watching the progress of the wires while working a switch. What is happening?

Hank left through the main door moments before the cell door closest to it opened. That's where I'd heard whimpering earlier. I thought it was the man they killed, but the sounds indicate someone else had been in there all along. Earl wearing a jacket was the first to exit the room, brutally pulling the arm of a beautiful redhead wearing the same color clothing that was in Hank's box. Her eyes appeared defeated offering no resistance, yet Earl was obviously getting pleasure from hurting her.

There was no longer a reason for me to conceal my true feelings. Since Fred was in the room while Hank did his bug-bomb joke, they were all in on it. Anger seethed when Mark appeared stretching her arm away from Earl like she was a wishbone. "It must make you feel like real men torturing helpless women," I said.

Earl looked at me, eyebrows rising. Then he continued tugging the girl toward the hanging manacles.

From somewhere deep inside my mind, a festering rage took root. Watching those two monsters pull her across the floor like a toy made a mental commitment grow. Escape wasn't enough; I want to personally hurt them. Somehow I'll find a way to make them wish they'd never seen my face.

Fugi entered the room carrying a pistol. Oh dear God they're going to shoot her. Even though she saw his entry, she offered no struggle as they locked her arms over her head with the manacles. "I'll see you bastards burn!" I said. "Do this and I swear you'll regret it!"

A nod from Earl to Fred precipitated a short intensive shock that caused me to clinch my fists. Hank returned without the bug box, walking across the chamber to stand next to me. Mark moved to my other side. Fugi and Earl marched away from her, stopping about five feet in front of me. Their position was obviously preplanned since I could see the girl with ease. A blank look was on her face as she stared at the floor. "R six ninety-eight," Earl said. He waited for her to look at him. "You have been returned and rated defective. By decree of document one-nine-three-three, you will be replaced within five months, your services to be terminated immediately."

My mouth dropped open, eyes widening in shock. Her expression remained unchanged like she didn't understand what was about to happen. Fugi lifted the revolver to Earl when I gave a monumental yank against all bonds drawing their attention. Seething fury clouded my mind as I clinched my teeth to focus on Earl. A snarl formed on my face, my nostrils flaring from enraged breathing. "You'd better kill me next," I said. "As God is my witness, I won't rest until you're gone!"

Earl held up his hand, apparently warding off any form of punishment. "I'll think about it," he said while turning his back.

Fugi looked at me a little longer, his mind apparently mulling things over. I stared at him with a pleading on my face. Then his eyes grew cold as he again held the gun out for Earl. "NO, you bastards!"

Hank placed one hand over my mouth, the other one behind my head. It effectively muffled my shouts, while his experience at this sort of thing prevented me from biting him.

"Is that the right pistol?" Earl asked.

"Yes," Fugi said, "taken from the Meadows exhibit like you wanted."

What does that mean; Meadows exhibit? It must be important because an evil smile grew on Earl's face. "Excellent," he said. "That gun is designed to fire special splintering bullets that enter but don't exit, making it a clean but painful kill. I have so few of them and don't wish to waste a new one on trash. Tell you what old chum, you do it."

A look of surprise formed on Fugi's face, his eyes blinking twice. Mark started moving toward Fugi's side away from Earl. Fred entered my line of sight, assuming a position that created a triangle surrounding Fugi. "It's not what I do," Fugi said.

Earl slowly backed away. "It is now," he said. "For three years you've tagged along without carrying your weight. Today that changes. You have a choice to make; shoot her or me. It's the only way you're leaving this room."

The girl watched this drama with impassive eyes like she didn't care. What's wrong with her? To me this was becoming exciting. Fugi snapped the gun from butt-first to a firing position like a real pro. Then he pointed it toward the floor. "I don't kill in cold blood," he said. "Since you knew this before I sided with you, and you now feel it isn't enough, I'm terminating our original deal. If you try stopping me or tracking me later, you will become the reason I do kill."

A heavy sigh escaped from Earl as he slowly shook his head. Hank released me, moving in a circling motion to get behind Fugi. Earl continued backing away, but the other three started closing in. "I had such high hopes for you," Earl said, "but you've been one high disappointment. The original BL seven forty-two proved it. Tell me Fugi, if you don't kill in cold blood why'd you kill her?"

Even though Fugi was cut-off from an easy escape, he calmly held the gun at his side while focusing on Earl. This is a far cry from the frightened man I first saw. "You know as well as I she went mad," Fugi said.

Mental images of another human being who was contented at one time then subjected to this brutality fertilized the rage-root. They drove her insane and act like it is just part of the day. Earl smiled, only it looked more like the satisfied expression of an executioner watching the head fall off. "What you're saying is you only kill if it's necessary or in mercy; bull shit! But you're partially right; our deal is off. The rest, however, remains to be seen."

Fugi pointed the gun at Earl while slowly backing to the door. Hank paced his steps, not closing in but remaining between Fugi and his destination. "I don't want it to end like this, but I will shoot if any of you get in my way," Fugi said. "Stand clear of the door."

Earl laughed with cackles straight out of hell. Chills coursed down my spine listening to it. When he stopped, his eyes were evil with anticipation. "Surely you don't believe I'd conduct this test with a working gun? Go ahead, pull the trigger. It'll save us a lot of time."

While Fugi continued backing, his expression changed to grim determination. Earl casually reached behind to bring out a strange gun. Its handle was too wide for his hand to completely grip, which made Fugi frown. Then Fugi leapt doing an overhead somersault just as a burst of compressed air exploded. A dart seemingly appeared on the back of his left calf while he was landing to face Hank. His eyes stared in disbelief at it, dropping the gun. He stumbled forward feebly reaching for the tiny arrow. Hank moved away, observing Fugi softly moan once and then topple sideways. Rather than catch him, Hank permitted him to hit the floor with a thud. Three muscle spasms indicated a painful reaction to the drug, followed by unconsciousness coupled with rhythmic breathing

"Shall I fire it up?" Fred asked.

Once the four standing men reached the unmoving Fugi, Earl shook his head. My eyes widened as I realized he was asking about the grinder.

"No," Earl said. "I have something more interesting in mind. He cost us money two weeks ago. I think it only fair he replaces it. We're going to need Doc."

He grinned at Hank. "Contact the Japanese consortiums when we're finished here. Tell them we may have a new female porn star and will know for certain in two days. If they're interested, they can have first crack at her in a month, pardon the pun."

Raucous laughter resounded through the room, Fugi remained absolutely still. Then Hank turned to calmly open the main door, Fred and Mark walked past Fugi to release the girl, and Earl casually strolled to me. Hank stepped out of view, the girl was soon in her room with the door closed, and Mark and Fred now approached Fugi. Earl stood silently nearby overseeing the other two grab Fugi by the ankles to pull him toward the cells like garbage to a dumpster. This callused treatment of an associate stunned me.

"It's a shame, really," Earl said. "Without a doubt he was the best at using his hands and feet for weapons."

Their progress halted in front of the cell furthest from the main entrance. Fred fished out his keys, searching briefly before placing one in the lock and opening the door to drag Fugi inside. "He started going soft several months ago," Earl said. "Not that he was ever a valuable asset other than crowd-control. Something about his martial arts training prevented him from doing any real nasty work I suspect. But it'll soon be forgotten as he becomes a she to please millions of fans; which brings me to you, my beautiful cash-roll."

My eyes widened watching Earl, who smiled gently while looking at the room holding Fugi. Sounds of tearing cloth could be heard, followed by more laughing. Earl's head began shaking as he looked at me.

"Boys will be boys," he said. "It doesn't matter who's naked, they like to play."

Goose-bumps grew on my arms as I closed my eyes in utter contempt. His unspoken meaning was understood. What did those bastards do to me when I was out?

"Oh well, back to you," he said which immediately opened my eyes.

The soft, almost fatherly smile was still on his face. Then he clasped his hands behind his back, turning from me. "I'm sure you were told at least part of this before your first treatment but don't remember. You're so special I'm going to tell you everything, even the parts you were instructed to forget."

He paused without looking at me, letting those words sink in. What does he mean I was instructed to forget? It makes no sense. This must be another sick joke.

"About fifteen years ago, I met the most remarkable man I've ever seen. Back in those days I was still The Eraser. Anyway, he contacted Hank, saying something about an associate of his causing troubles. That guy had to go. Do you remember what I told you before about doing my homework?"

As he slowly faced me, I nodded my head once. A feeling of grave peril much worse than any I'd experienced before started growing. "Good, I don't have to repeat myself. It took some time for me to uncover who Doc really was, even with my extensive network that would make any law enforcement agency envious. His incredible security measures told me either he was a trap or had something big enough to warrant serious hiding. My curiosity grew by the hour. When I finally uncovered his legitimate needs, I made him an offer. You see he's a plastic surgeon specializing in trans-sexual cases, but his real interest lies in finding a serum to control the aging process. Just think of the possibilities, eternal youth in our lifetime. That isn't what excited me. His reason for contacting Hank came as the result of a major serum set-back that kept killing his animal subjects. The drugs have an element that reverses brains to a pre-birth level. That means his animals literally forget how to eat and drink due to the not yet fully formed higher brain cells. They'd die unless hooked to life-support. And if the brain-killer was taken out of the serum or weakened, the subjects suffered fatal aneurisms. It was perplexing Doc, but angering his aide who demanded all work cease immediately. That's when my negotiations began."

Fred stepped out of Fugi's room, followed by Mark who pushed the door shut. Their footsteps briefly interrupted Earl as he glanced that way. His nod served as a signal to them. The drug he used to uncover my escape plan; is that what's he's so excited about? If so it doesn't work. I know exactly who I am but he thinks otherwise; good. He patiently waited for the others to arrive before returning his attention to me. "Where was I? Oh yes, the negotiations. Unlike most in my former profession I have an ability to see the big picture. Time was ticking and I knew someday I'd be the one shot. Rather than continue taking out other people's trash until I died, I wanted to venture in a new direction. It was damn perplexing since I didn't know what route to take, until Doc called. The simple fact he had results of subjects dying from the serum without the brain portion let me know he could remove it. I came up with a revolutionary idea. On a bright chilly March morning, I broke my golden rule to meet a customer."

His smile was now like a person recalling the fond memory of a friend. It silently spoke volumes about Doc's character. He's as cold-blooded as Earl, possibly worse. "We reached an agreement in less than five minutes. I take care of Doc's problem and supply him with human test subjects, and he provides me with the brain-killer as well as use of his surgical talents. Once his trouble was erased, I got to work on a new career."

My eyes opened wide as I realized where this was heading. As if on cue Hank stepped into the chamber holding a hypodermic needle filled with a yellow solution. Earl's smile became pure evil watching my expression. "God I love this part," he said. "The look on your face is legendary! But if I relish in the moment any longer, I'm liable to forget something. What fun would that be?"

The two of them smiled at each other, and then at me. Both appeared extremely entertained which enraged me. I will fight this to the end. "Human trafficking isn't a new concept nor is it dead. However running a market of that type in this country is next to impossible. The fundamental flaw is the human psyche, always desiring freedom. Even intimidation will eventually fail. All it takes is one person to escape and there goes the neighborhood. My dream was to find a way to eradicate that desire, and *then* sell them to the super-rich. You'd be astonished at how many folks with overflowing accounts exist in the world, and shocked at how deranged some can be. Anyway, for three years we experimented with the right level of medication. Chilean dogs ate well during that spree. Finally we discovered quite by accident," he held up his index finger, "it must be delivered in three watered-down treatments, the first in food. That way your brain cells have a chance to gradually absorb the recombinant nucleic acids without complete cellular meltdown. While you're in the euphoric state of brain regeneration, we plant hypnotic seeds paving the way for future treatments. It also causes fatigue due to the serious trauma your central nervous system endures, which you've amazingly overcome. I am impressed. Now here's the real kicker cutie-pie; I bet it seems like a few days have passed since you first opened your eyes. Guess what? Your first meal was yesterday morning."

He laughed a few times, holding up his arm to ward off Hank's approach. What he just said can't be. "A little sleep followed by a hearty meal and you're ready for the next dose. That's right; you ate the treated breakfast yesterday, lunch today, and now a midnight snack. The longest amount of time needed between doses is after the first because we have to make sure all treated food is digested. Injections only require half the recovery wait. Too much brain-killer too soon, the name becomes painfully obvious. To expedite the drug's absorption before the next dose, we stimulate our guests' metabolism in numerous ways involving fear and anger. Of course we've never held a sales presentation or killed to accomplish the task, but for you Joyce nothing's too good."

Fred laughed, drawing Earl's attention momentarily. "A scant few have bad reactions to the personality assassination, requiring us to administer tests that weed out those who can't adjust. I mean we hardly ever fail, but if you look at six ninety-eight, you'll see how once in awhile we turn out a dud. The first test always involves snakes. We plant an unshakeable terror that freezes movement at the mere mention of one. Then if behavior remains unchanged except for that glaring difference, we know the candidate could probably handle our modifications and move on to the second treatment. You passed it with flying colors by the way. Just in case that fear already existed, we find something for the second test the inductee isn't afraid of like frogs, birds, mice, or in your case, insects. Then we put out irresistible bait. If we succeed, you live. Had you overcome the terror to grab the phone, any button pushed would've activated the kill setting of your collar. Thank you so much for being alive."

My head started shaking denial as Hank held the needle in the air, tapping the glass container and then squirting a tiny amount into the air. "Goodbye Joyce Allison Jackson, hello BL seven forty-two," Earl said.

"Don't-; don't-; don't-; don't-"

Time seemed to slow, the rapid pounding of my heart all I could hear. Hank's arm formed a rear tracer of light while inching the needle toward me. Ghostly images of my mother, father, Mary, Katie, teachers, professors, and others involved in my life materialized behind Hank when he reached my arm. Mom started crying when a sharp sting made me squint. Dad shook his head in scowling judgment watching Hank remove the needle. Mary waved goodbye, and then melted away. Katie looked at the floor where fog began rising. Soon the mist covered everyone other than my parents. Dad mouthed the words you deserve this, while mom wept. Then they disappeared in the fog. Peace filled my soul when all concerns vanished, too. This is such a wonderful place. I've found my true home.

CHAPTER 10

Nothingness exists; wait, swirling colors of the rainbow are filling the void with beautiful patterns. How wonderful it is watching them dance. "You will see a stream of light running from your head to the door," a voice said. "Do you understand?"

That voice; it's the voice of God. I must do as he says but I only see colors. "No."

Heavy breathing followed along with sounds of moving feet. The colors disappeared; darkness took its place for a moment before the colors returned. Red, green, blue, yellow, and violet once again twirled into a whirlpool, but nothing else was seen. "We're too late," another voice said. "She's gone."

Footsteps moving toward me sounded just before my shoulders were grabbed. "Listen to me," God said; "concentrate on my voice. Let it pull you back to our previous meeting. There is a door in the colors. Do you see it?"

Shapes shifted, making different designs of many things. Snakes, bugs, fire, but no door. "No."

Powerful hands shook my shoulders, making my wrists drag against something holding them at my sides. "Concentrate on the middle spot in the colors," God said. "It is a door. It is your door. Can you see it?"

The spot in the middle is not changing. "No."

I was shaken hard enough to slam my back against something hard. A face with strange, constantly changing features appeared in front, carefully looking at me. It exhaled slowly while shaking like in denial. "It's over," a third voice said. "There's no salvaging her now. Do we terminate?"

My shoulders were released, silence ensued. The colors continued swirling, changing flows and speeds. Something different is happening. Wait, there in the middle. I see a door. Light is flowing from the center of my forehead, gently bathing it in white. "Yes," I said.

Three heavy exhales responded. "I am pleased," God said. "You will hold onto that door with all your strength. Do you understand?"

I must do as God says. "Yes."

"The door is open now. You will see Joyce Jackson moving to the other side. Do you see her?"

Slowly the door opened. A woman identical to me appeared, walking through the doorway. It is the other Joyce. She's avoiding the light coming from me, a frightened expression formed as she covers her face with her hands. "Yes."

"Now you will reach into her mind and take out knowledge of language, hygiene, anatomy, fear of snakes and insects, and respect for others. It will be kept between you two for future use. You will leave her knowledge about life experiences, self-preservation, inhibitions, judgments, and intelligence. Do you understand?"

Her arms fell motionless to her sides. My light reached her head, causing her eyes to close. A golden ball of energy rose from her mind following the light. It stopped midway between us. "Yes."

"Joyce Jackson is aging five years per second. Do you understand?"

She started becoming old rapidly. Soon her hair turned gray and stringy, her face wrinkled, back arched. "Yes."

"The part of her mind you hold remains unchanged," God said; "now Joyce Jackson is dead, along with the part of her mind still inside her. Do you understand?"

Her eyes shut as she toppled to the side. "Yes."

"She is in a deep closed grave covered with snakes and insects," God said. "The snakes and insects guard that side. Do you see this?"

Ground started shifting beneath Joyce, opening a dark pit that she toppled into. Then it started filling in until a smooth surface appeared. Snakes slithered across the top, insects flying near the door but not crossing the threshold. "Yes."

"Now you see three year old BL seven forty-two standing in the doorway," God said. "Your light is touching her head. Do you understand?"

Rising from the door jamb emerged this small child terribly frightened of the snakes and insects. Even though the light coming from me now protects her head, she's still screaming madly. "Yes."

"You will place the memories from Joyce Jackson in her mind. Do you understand?"

Her cries stopped as she concentrated on my light stream. The golden ball of energy descended our link, gently entering her head. "Yes."

"Now the toddler is six years old," God said. "Do you understand?"

Immediately her arms and legs grew slightly, her face becoming larger. "Yes."

"You are an empty vessel that will do whatever is commanded without thought or hesitation. Your only wish is to please. Do you understand?"

Earth on the other side of the door shifted, like someone was trying to dig out of a hole. Snakes and insects began moving toward it. Then the colors started spiraling out of control, hurting my eyes. I must answer God no matter what. "Yes."

"Now BL seven forty-two and you will merge," God said. "You will respond to her name, use her memories, but she will not talk or think. She will cease to exist after you completely absorb her. Do you understand?"

I began moving toward her as she started toward me. We met, holding each other tightly. Then she painlessly entered my stomach and chest, her head finally reaching mine. A rush of memories followed, making me feel dizzy. "Yes."

"The door has closed," God said. "It has switched to a dot in the colors. Do you understand?"

Snakes slithering across the ground became difficult to see as the door gradually closed. Then it shrank until it was just a tiny spot in the center of the colors. "Yes."

Insects crawled out of the middle moving across the colors in great swarms. Please make them go away.

"The dot no longer exists," God said, "only insects. If you ever try to find this place again, insects will hurt you. Always remember your terrible fear of insects. You are now and have always been BL seven forty-two, but you will answer to seven forty-two. What is your only wish?"

A smile grew on my face. "I only wish to please," I said.

All insects vanished; the colors started spinning in reverse. The screen flickered once. I think that was a message of some kind.

"While you sleep, dreams of the dead Joyce Jackson's life will be shown to you. These are lies. Joyce Allison Jackson never existed. For the rest of your life you are to ignore them. Failure to comply will result in your death. Do you understand?"

"Yes," I said.

"Sleep now."

I knew it. Ten minutes have passed with no sign of those three bullies. What a bunch of cowards. Although I think they're loud-mouthed idiots, Mary is absolutely terrified strongly tugging my arm. "Why are you moving so slowly?" She asked. "You heard them say they were going to kill us this afternoon!"

Every since fifth grade began, Ben Kensington, David Palmer, and Sean Carter have been after us. I don't understand why they pick on me in particular and Mary because of our friendship, but I've had it.

Reasoning didn't work. When I finally said I only want to be left alone, it was like a joke to them. They laughed and said they were going to get me. For over two months Mary and I had been running home not knowing if they were serious. It's gone on long enough; this morning when they started taunting me I told them to back off or else. That was when Mary almost fainted, and they said we were dead.

"They've threatened us every afternoon," I said. "Let's see if they mean it."

Her mouth fell open in shock. Then she began pulling my arm harder. "Do you want to get hurt?" She asked. "What's wrong with you?"

That question brought back memories of last night's talk with dad. For no good reason, he decided I was wasting too much time. I am to come straight home after school, have mom call him when I did, and start on my homework immediately. When I was finished I could watch television but not play outside. He said it was because the first report card showed all grades to be excellent but not enough teacher-comments. Genuine perfection brings forth more than standardized marks, and until he was satisfied I was grounded on school days. "I just want to enjoy being outside a little longer," I said. "When I go into my house, I won't be allowed to leave until tomorrow."

Though her expression changed to one of sympathy, her tugging did not diminish. "I'm sorry Joyce, but at least you'll be able to come out tomorrow. If those boys catch us, they might hurt us to where we won't be able to come out at all. Now let's go before it's-; oh no. Here they come."

She'd been facing me, her eyes nervously shifting between my face and what was behind me. Then her expression changed to one of horror as her attention set on something over my shoulder. My heart accelerated as I turned to look. There they were running at us quickly. "They're going to catch us," she said, "run!"

As she released my arm and rushed away, I calmly faced their direction and began walking toward them.

"WHAT ARE YOU DOING?" Mary shouted.

Adrenaline was pumping through my veins, giving me strength I didn't know existed. My casual walk in the boys' direction slowed their speed but did not turn them around. "Go home," I said. "I'll put a stop to this."

Taunting laughter could be heard from them, Mary's feet noisily slapping asphalt now sounding like something far away. Even though my instincts were screaming for me to flee, I forced myself to casually walk into their midst. They surrounded me, circling just like the Indians around wagon trains I'd seen on my favorite TV show. When I tried walking through them, Ben, the biggest of the lot, pushed me back. "Don't touch me," I said.

A sneer grew on his face as he slowly reached his hand toward me. Then he poked his finger against my shoulder, quickly withdrawing with a look of disgust replacing the arrogance. "Cooties," he said. "Now I have to wash my hand."

The others laughed, I calmly looked at Ben. "It's about time you washed," I said.

Laughter instantly ceased, Ben obviously angered by my outward lack of fear. "I don't want any trouble," I said. "Leave us alone and we'll leave you alone. What have we done to you?"

"The rich kid wants to know what she's done," Ben said.

What does that mean? I'm not rich. His companions started making cooing sounds like they felt sorry for me. "Here's what you've done to us," Ben said. "Your dad fired my dad. Now we're poor and you're going to pay!"

This can't be real. Why is he angry with me over something my father did? "I'm sorry that happened," I said, "but it has nothing to do with me. Stop threatening us over something my father did."

Ben's face darkened as he nodded his head once. David and Sean each grabbed my arms, holding me tightly in their grip as I struggled. "Oh it's more than a threat," he said.

"Let me go."

My struggles intensified to no avail. They held my arms tightly to my sides. Ben started looking me over, making me feel sick to my stomach. "Hey Bennie," David said. "I wonder what color underwear she has on?"

David's hand grabbed the bottom of my skirt. Ben watched these actions with a growing smile. "Let's find out," Ben said.

A raging fire erupted in my mind as David started lifting. Fury built to the point I was breathing heavily. Then Sean's grip weakened. "Guys, I don't think this is a good idea," he said.

Ben looked at Sean, a sneer forming. "What's the matter Sean-ie," Ben asked; "you chicken?"

I was bigger than David and Sean. The only reason Ben was larger than me was because he'd been held back two grades. If I can break free, I can probably beat the two holding me. Then I'll focus on Ben. David halted his movement briefly, long enough for me to move. Sean created confusion and doubt which caused David to relax his hold.

In one monumental yank, I was free from both boys' grips. My skirt hem ripped slightly as I spun on David to mightily kick at his hand. He tried moving out of the way, but it wasn't fast enough. My foot landed solidly between his legs, lifting him slightly off the road while bringing a pained expression to his face. He moaned while grabbing the area of contact, toppling to the street doubled-up. That's very interesting. "Now you're really going to pay," Ben said. "Grab her Sean!"

David was still lying in the road, obviously in great pain. My eyes focused on Sean, who appeared nervous. The sound of footsteps softly moving reached my ears, prompting a snarl to form. Ben was trying to sneak behind me. I spun around while backing to where I could see them both. "Would you give me a hand here?" Ben asked.

Sean's head started shaking as he turned his back. "No," he said, "this is wrong. Leave her alone."

Groans from David drew Sean close. Once arriving Sean leaned over to look at his face. I moved to a position where I could keep an eye on him while concentrating on Ben. Out of the corner of my eye I saw Mary running across the front yard of the nearest house. "Hey you big jerk," she said; "looking for me?"

His eyes became surprised, almost afraid. A slight smile grew on my face as I took two steps toward him. Mary reached the ditch, jumping across with ease.

"SEAN," he said. "Get over here!"

Mary scrambled on the road, moving behind Ben but keeping at a safe distance. Sean rose to his full height remaining near David. "I'm leaving," he said. "You're on your own."

David slowly moved, getting on his knees while still holding himself. Then he began retching like he was nauseous. Sean ignored us, turning his complete attention to David.

"Here's the deal," I said. "I'm sorry about your father but I had nothing to do with it. If you leave now and never bother us again, I won't tell people how you were afraid to come after me. If you want to fight, bring it on."

This was a calculated risk. When Ben didn't rush me before, I had the feeling he was really a coward. Just in case, I started loosening my legs by making small kicking motions.

Sean spoke quietly to David, talking too softly for me to hear. He helped David to his feet, and they started walking away. David had a terrible limp, barely able to move. Ben observed their departure with growing anger. "Get back here," he said. "This isn't over!"

Neither one responded, continuing their walk down the road. When I looked at the tear in my favorite skirt, it did something to me. Anger over the senselessness of it all started seething rage to form. It wasn't David's fault as much as Ben. My eyes became wild, teeth clinched together in a scowl, and then I inhaled as I charged forward loudly shouting. Mary watched closely, frozen from apparent shock. Ben immediately moved out of the way, trying to run around me which I matched perfectly. I tripped him, bringing him down on the street so hard it must've cut his hands. He started crying like a baby, giving me a strange sense of satisfaction when I closed in. "Leave us alone or I'll really hurt you," I said.

One more glance at my skirt clouded my better judgment. Fury took over as I walked behind his huddled mass, grabbed the shirt out of his rear waist, and ripped it halfway up his back. Mary laughed so hard it made Ben crawl away in shame.

"Come on champ," she said, "let's go home."

Just to make certain this wasn't a trick, I watched until Ben climbed to his feet and walk away, head lowered. Righteous victory created a sly smile as I faced Mary. "I don't think they'll bother us again," I said.

She snarled "if they do-," while swinging her fists wildly.

The sheer comical appearance of her make-believe fighting made me snicker, until it broke into full-blown laughter. She lowered her hands to laugh with me until we both calmed. Our journey home was completed in silent companionship, the sun feeling warmer, the sky looking prettier.

Homework was relatively light. In less than two hours I was done and watching television downstairs. Halfway through my favorite show, the kitchen door opened unexpectedly early. Dad was home. A few loud indecipherable words were spoken before he started thundering down the basement steps. My heart raced hearing the heaviness of his stomps. When he cleared the last one, he walked to the TV without looking at me to turn it off. His attention remained set on the blank TV. "I got a phone call about an hour ago," he said. "Do you know anyone with the last name Kensington?"

Slowly he faced me, anger tensing all his muscles. The thought of lying came to mind but it would only lead to more trouble. "Yes; Ben Kensington goes to my school. He's been picking on Mary and me for months!"

His head shook in agreement. "And did you fight with this Ben Kensington today?"

I felt like the one who started it based on his tone. "He attacked me. I only-"

"That's enough! Whatever the reasons he had I'm sure were valid. You're going to pay for his shirt and apologize."

My mouth dropped open in shock. Then I quickly rose from the chair to lift the torn hem where he could see. "They did this first. And the reason he came after me-"

"Go to your room. You're grounded for a month with no TV."

Tears formed in my eyes, blurring his image to where I couldn't recognize it. "But-"

"Two months then; I will not have my daughter fighting no matter the reason. That's boy stuff, something you couldn't hope to understand. Go cry in your room. It sickens me to watch."

This is unbelievable. He doesn't care to learn the truth. It's like he enjoys punishing me by always looking for reasons. I know better than to argue, he would make the grounding longer. Why does he hate me so much? What did I do to deserve this?

Silently I slumped toward the stairs feeling unjustly convicted. While I climbed the steps, sadness changed to anger until halfway up. Then it became determination.

There are two kinds of truth, the absolute and the partial. Since he only seems interested in the partial from others, that's all I give him and pretend to be unaware of anything else. The next time we have a confrontation, I'll stay calm and act surprised asking questions to find out what he knows. Then I'll respond accordingly. I won't lie but I will omit. If he finds out about the rest I'll say-

----

"Wakie wakie sunshine; we have a glorious day in store for you!"

CHAPTER 11

Cloudy remnants of sleep gradually evaporated as I opened my eyes. A huge yawn escaped, followed by some stretching. My arms and legs are sore. Why is that?

"Sleep well gorgeous?" A man holding a tray of food in the doorway asked.

Confusion forced a perplexed expression on my face. "I only wish to please, but may I ask a question?"

The man entered, walking to the table next to my bed. "Ask away detective."

Now I'm more confused. "I only wish to please, but what did you mean detective? What is-?"

"Just ask your question!"

He sounded mad. This is not what I must do. When he placed the tray on the table, I smiled at him. "I'm sorry; I didn't mean to make you angry. Please tell me who you are."

His head began shaking in disgust as he turned toward the door. "I hate this part. I really wish Earl would just pump your ass full of that shit rather than three now, wait a week, three more, wait a week, and then two for shits and giggles. To hell with brain damage, when they look as sweet as you no one cares about the mind! Listen up you blank bimbo; I am Fred, your God."

As he began stomping out of the room, sadness filled me. "I'm sorry Fred my God."

That stopped him, slowly turning to face me with a smile growing. That's wonderful; I've made him feel better. "To help make your job a little easier," he said, "I'll tell you the next person to enter is called Hank's fly is open. Repeat his name."

97

Great joy; he's happy and I can make the next one happy by knowing his name. "Hank's fly is open?"

"Yes; very good," he said. "Now to please him, you have to shout his name and then point at him while grinning. Have you got all that?"

Oh this is fantastic. He said I was very good. I won't let him down. "Yes I've got it Fred my God."

They certainly have strange names around here, no numbers at all. At least he's happy. The smile on his face as he walked out proved it.

Odors from the food on the table made my stomach growl. I'm hungry. One more yawn, and I sprang out of bed to sit at the table. There's water in this strange bottle, but no opening. How am I supposed to drink?

"Thought I'd check in on you this morning," a voice said from the door.

A huge smile formed on my face as I placed the bottle down and took a deep breath. "Hello, HANK'S FLY IS OPEN."

His face reddened and changed to confused shock as he looked to his left, right, and then the front of his pants. Laughter from two people erupted behind him as I lifted my hand and pointed, grinning. He appeared annoyed as he stepped into the room, closing the door. "Juvenile delinquents," he said. "Who put you up to this?"

My arm dropped. This didn't make him happy. I have failed. "I'm sorry. I only wish to please. Fred my God told me that would make you happy."

"He-; who-; *what?*" He asked. "This is why Mark usually greets our new guests. My name is Hank and his is not Fred my God. It's only Fred."

I'm so confused. "Only Fred and you are Hank?"

Hank nodded his head, making me feel better.

"Only Fred is the one who told me."

For a couple of seconds Hank just blinked at me. Then a frown formed. "I need a vacation," he said. "His name is Fred."

Oh no he's upset with me. A pout formed.

"It's okay seven forty-two," he said. "I know it isn't your fault."

That's wonderful; he's not mad. "I'm really here to tell you someone's coming to see you," he said. "You won't have time to eat all your meal, but if you hurry you can at least have some of it."

Someone's coming to see me. That's great. But he said I have to hurry, if only I could get this bottle open. "I only wish to please, but could you help me open this?"

As I lifted the bottle, a smile crossed his face. "Simply twist the top off," he said.

He said to twist the top off. That must mean the top half. Okay I'll do it.

Holding the bottom half in my left hand, I gripped the top using my right. Then I tried twisting it, but nothing's happening. He'll be upset if I don't do this right. Maybe if I put a little more strength, it'll open. Oh my hands are becoming slippery but I can't stop trying.

Hank walked deeper into the room, coming at me just when my right hand slipped to the pointed top. It spun off, squirting water all over the front of his pants. Wetness darkened the crotch, moving down both legs. He quickly pulled out the front. "YOU IDIOT! Look what you've done! Oh shit, it's spreading! DAMN I can feel it trickling down my legs. Now my socks are getting soaked!"

Tears instantly filled my eyes. He's very mad at me. "I only wish to please. I'm sorry."

Slowly he looked from his pants toward me. Pure rage was in his eyes, making me whimper. "Oh no you're not. Somehow you knew I wouldn't have time to change. You did this on purpose!"

A knock on the door preceded its opening as I was shaking my head. Fred and three other men entered, one carried a medical bag. Before Hank could turn away, Fred glanced at his pants and started laughing and pointing. "Looks like you zipped up too soon."

The youngest man just stared at me, Fred started slapping his sides; Hank's face turned bright red again, while one of the older men looked at Fred. "Are you quite finished?" He asked.

Fred nodded his head while wiping tears from his eyes. A few chuckles followed before he finally grew quiet. Then the older man faced me. "I think some introductions are in order," he said. "I'm Earl, that's Mark," he pointed at the man staring at me, "I believe you already know Hank and the laughing hyena we call Fred. Now let me introduce you to one of my closest friends Doc. Say hello, seven forty-two.

Earl smiled while Doc looked closely at my eyes. "I only wish to please. Hello, seven forty-two."

When Fred snickered, Earl glared at him ending it, and then looked at Doc. "My crowning glory," Earl said. "We nearly lost her due to incompetence," he glanced at Mark who stared at the floor, "but

I was able to save the day. Of course she's raw material until we begin the second phase early next week. You're more than welcome to sit in."

Doc's head began shaking as he studied my eyes. "Something's not right," he said. "Look at her eyes. You'd better let me take her."

Mark's head snapped up. Earl formed a surprised expression as he placed his hands on his hips. "You old dog you," Earl said. "I didn't know you like your women in this condition."

Fred chuckled three times, but Doc remained serious. "I know my drugs," he said. "She's showing signs of resistance. I'd like to closely examine her."

"You and about a million other men," Earl said.

Hank looked proudly at me, Earl appeared amused, but Doc continued staring at my eyes. "I'm serious," Doc said. "This is dangerous. She needs to be expunged after I've finished the dissection."

Fred glanced at Doc before settling on me, an expression of concern. Mark seemed shocked, Hank looked upset, but Earl remained calm as he placed his hand on Doc's shoulder. "Relax, will you?" Earl asked. "Everything's cool. We have it all under control."

A frown formed on Doc's face as he placed his bag on my bed. "You called me here to operate on Fugi," he said. "If you want me to proceed, kill her now."

No one moved for a few moments. Then Earl lowered his head and sighed. Hank stepped between Earl and me. "You're not considering what he said?" Hank asked.

Earl slowly shook his head. "It's the lesser of two evils. Give me your remote."

They are talking about me. Why does Doc want to kill me? Have I made him angry? Hank stared at Earl for a few moments before reaching in his back pocket for a small object. Earl accepted it, walking past Hank to stand directly in front of me. "Seven forty-two," Earl said. "Do you know what it means to die?"

All eyes were on me, Hank's especially saddened. "I only wish to please, yes."

"Tell me," Earl said.

Why is everyone so upset? There must be a way to make them happy again. "I only wish to please; it means to stop living."

Earl nodded in agreement, glanced at Doc, and then back at me.

"Do you want to die?"

If I did, that would leave them sad. "I only wish to please, no."

"Why not?"

Doc moved to where he could see my eyes better. "I only wish to please, which I wouldn't be able to do any more."

His eyebrows shot up as he again glanced at Doc. Then he held out a small box for me to take. "Do you know what this is?"

It looks vaguely familiar but I'm not sure. "I only wish to please, no; I'm sorry."

Hank moved close, drawing Earl's attention briefly before he focused back on me. "You are to stop saying I only wish to please," he said. "It won't matter much longer. This is called a remote. I want you to take it and press the second button from the top. That will kill you and please me. Do you understand?"

Chills coursed down my back after he asked that. Why would it bother me so much? It doesn't matter. He looks sad and if I press the button, he'll be happy again. "Yes," I said while accepting the remote.

It fits nicely in my hand. There are four buttons on it, and which one is right? As I turned it over in my hand, the strange writing on the back showed the top. Everyone backed away from me as I placed my finger on the button. "Push it," Earl said.

A smile grew on my face as I looked across the room, and then pushed the button. Electrical shocks froze the breath in my throat; the remote tumbled to the floor. My neck is burning, body locked in place. Every nerve in my body painfully twitched. It feels like my hair is on fire. Agonizing spasms racked my arms, crawling like stinging red ants to my legs. Lighting began dimming, and then I was better. Am I dead?

"You've just witnessed our quality assurance test," Earl said. "Had she delayed pushing the button, Fred would've killed her instead of saving her. Normally we do it two days after the third dose to allow recovery time, but since you were so concerned I decided to up the time table. Now are you satisfied?"

Fred was lowering his remote while Doc moved in for a closer look. My muscles were calming. I was able to wait for further instructions.

"And you're absolutely certain she knew nothing about that device and how it works before you handed it to her?" Doc asked.

Earl laughed lightly, placing his hand on Doc's shoulder to draw him away. "This is the first time she's seen the front," Earl said, "but she's felt what it can do. Had the first drug set not worked properly, she would've searched the remote for a way out instead of obeying. As I said, you're more than welcome to attend any of our training sessions. Just let me know in advance. Heck, I'll even arrange a special showing for you."

"Don't lower your guard with her," Doc said. "I'm telling you she could be trouble. Something in her eyes bothers me."

More laughing from Earl followed as he glanced at Fred. A nod was exchanged between the two of them before Earl looked at me, and then Doc. "She's bothered a whole lot of people on the internet," Earl said. "You know our security measures are impossible to beat. If you're right and she manages to slip by, what's she going to do other than die? Relax, leave her to me. Now we have your patient sedated in room five. He's never really been happy as a man. It's time to change that."

Fred grinned evilly at Doc. Hank left the room, lifting his pants to flap them slightly while stepping out of view. Doc turned his back to me, the bag still on the bed.

"I really wish you'd reconsider," Doc said. "I've known Fugi since his days with Guardia. He single-handedly brought down the Daindridge house, and look what he did for you. He's second only to you in assassinations. You're ending a powerful ally."

Earl's head nodded a few times, an expression of sadness forming. "I'm well aware of his legendary past," Earl said, "including the treaty he forced Pinkerton into. Don't forget I was there. But that was years ago."

With Doc watching closely, Earl clasped his hands behind his back and walked toward the door, facing us when he was within two feet. "He's gone soft," he said. "It's like he's reluctant to do what needs to be done. I've given him many chances, but now it's dangerous. Our production has slowed because I have to watch him closely."

A deep breath was drawn before Earl exhaled while continuing. "Over the last few months he's shown signs of regret. It culminated late last week when he killed one of our initiates. Granted she was no longer fit for general consumption, but there are hunt clubs who pay dearly for human prey. With the right programming she could have given them a memorable experience. He took it on himself to judge that wrong, and I suspect he's now feeling the same about my entire operation. To give you a better understanding about the seriousness here, last night he threatened us with a gun. Had I not shot hit him with a tranquilizer dart and he got away, what do you think his next target would be? I can no longer trust him; neither can you."

Doc's head started shaking as it slumped forward looking at the floor. "That's too bad," Doc said, "but why not just kill him?"

Earl smiled while walking toward Doc causing Doc to lift his head. "You told me the last time we talked you needed a woman in her forties for your experiment. Once Fugi has been, well, changed, the testosterone production will cease and she'll meet those requirements; right?"

No response. Doc silently stared at Earl. "I take that as a yes," Earl said. "You sounded excited like you were on the verge of a breakthrough. Now is your chance to see. If you're successful, I'm going to recoup the money lost due to his impulsiveness. If you're not, the body is here for disposal. Doesn't that make sense all the way around?"

Slowly Doc's head started nodding, bringing a huge smile to Earl's face. "I may have isolated the chromosomal imbalance that attacks neurons in the female brain," Doc said. "Fugi should have complete recall of his past if I'm right. That's what concerns me. If he's as dangerous as you say, why run the risk of his wrath?"

Earl glanced at me. "You mean her wrath," he said. "That's not a concern. You take care of the body; I'll take care of the mind. All you need for reassurance is to look at my seated beauty there. She held a Master's Degree before I worked my magic."

Is he talking about me? Why does he think I'm holding anything? A quick glance proved my hands are empty. Before I could ask, Doc looked at me on the floor, a smile growing. Okay they're happy; no need for me to do a thing. "You've convinced me," Doc said. "Now I need something different from you in return. How soon can you leave?"

"It shouldn't be much longer," Earl said. "What do you need?"

Doc looked toward Earl. "Most test subjects you've been supplying have been female," Doc said. "Though it has helped me to the point where I am now, testosterone production still acts like an antigen toward stimulated organ rejuvenation, especially at the neural sub-cellular level. As you know it's been one setback after another and I must redirect attention. For that I require four male specimens of varying ages; the oldest no more than forty with the youngest at six. Whatever else you can get will be acceptable, but they should be preteens if at all possible. Will that be a problem?"

Earl's eyes indicated deep thought. "It'll take extra planning due to the accelerated missing person's report," he said, "but I'll get Hank on it. Consider it done."

"Outstanding," Doc said. "Take me to my patient. Now it's time for me to work my magic."

CHAPTER 12

It's been hours since everyone left. Why am I still alone? Did I make them mad? Earl told me to sit in my seat and finish eating, but the plate has been cleaned for so long the gravy is crusty. Finally I hear voices outside my room. Oh good, the door is opening.

"Hello seven forty-two," Earl said; "miss me?"

A smile is on his face, but I'm not sure how to answer. "I'm sorry, I don't understand."

His head nodded as he entered the room and shut the door. Then he looked at me, his smile getting larger. "Nor should you understand. It's absolutely all right. Doc is finishing with my next prize which looks to be a roaring success, so I'm going to spend a little quality time with you while I can."

He sat on the bed facing me, his head shaking while smiling. Does that mean he's happy or sad? "You have no idea how excited I am about you," he said. "Bids higher than *any* before have started flying in, and we're weeks away from the official date. In order to celebrate, I'm going to take better care of you starting with a new room."

Suddenly his face darkened, looking angry. How can I make him feel better? "I want you to listen very carefully to what I'm going to say," he said. "If Mark weren't such a vital part of my team, he'd be on a cot next to Fugi right now. He knows I need him, but he also knows I will kill if he does something stupid. Still he acts insane whenever your name is mentioned, and I fear for your safety. Hank and Fred keep an eye on him when I'm busy, but if he gets near you, I want you to cry out as loudly as you can. That will please me."

At last, a way to please him; I smiled and nodded my head. It almost made him smile; great! "Much as I hate this part, I have to make Fred your guardian," he said. "I need Hank for our next outing and Mark is unstable, which leaves the thief in charge of the open safe. You have nothing to fear from Fred other than his, shall I say, twisted fantasies. I swear that guy would screw the hole in a hornet's nest if he had a long enough ladder. Should he touch you below the neck, it would please me for you to tell him I said stop, and then tell me about it. Can you do all that for me?"

Two ways to make him happy; this is far better than I'd hoped. "Yes, I can do all that."

His face finally broke into a big smile as he reached behind to remove his remote. One audible click sounded while he rose to his feet. "Come with me. It's time to check out your new digs."

Whatever digs are makes no difference; he's pleased with me. As I pushed away from the table, he turned to walk toward the door and opened it. Once he was outside the room, he motioned with his hand for me to come. After I arrived in front of him, he turned to walk next door. Then he opened it and stepped to the side.

A much larger bed was the first thing I noticed. Then I saw the sink, toilet, and table with chair. Fresh fruit in a basket rested in the center of the table, plus a complete outfit hung on a hook near the back. This is absolutely fantastic; all these wonderful things just for me. He smiled watching my reaction. "It's safer for you here," he said. "There are no surprises around the doorway. Go ahead, it's all right."

The food I'd eaten before no longer filled me. Just the sight of that fruit sent me into a frenzy of desire. My mouth watered as I stepped across the threshold, heading straight for the table. An audible click coming from the doorway momentarily captured my attention as I watched Earl lowering his remote. Then he pushed the door shut, leaving me to my own temptations.

Delicious fragrances of bananas, oranges, and apples filled the air in an almost taunting manner. Growling from my stomach caused trembling in my hands as I plucked a green grape to toss in my mouth. Sweet juices flowed over my tongue, sending me into a paradisiacal fantasy of colorful pastures and warm breezes.

Time lost all meaning as I delved ecstatically into a flavorful orgy of decadent gorging. Once half the basket was gone I felt queasy, returning a half-eaten peach to the basket. The bed seemed to call my name. Drowsiness brought forth a yawn, moving me to climb on the mattress and close my eyes. Eventually I found that perfect spot to completely relax, gently drifting asleep when the door yanked open. It startled me alert, bringing me up to look at Fred appearing upset.

"Earl wants you washed but he won't let me do it," he said. "DAMN IT why was I given the short straw? Get your ass out of bed! Babe, you need a shower."

He's mad. There must be something I can do to change that, but I don't know exactly what he means. "I'm sorry," I said, "I don't understand what you meant by short straw. Is there something I can do to make it long?"

His frown changed into a smile as he leaned against the doorway. "You bet your bikini bottoms there's something you can do to make it long, but it'll have to wait. In the mean time grab your clothes from the hook and let's go; chop-chop!"

Now I'm confused. As I quickly looked the room over, Fred shifted his feet loudly which caused me to look at him. "Ain't no gold other than what's on the bed," he said. "What the hell are you looking for?"

"I'm sorry, but I can't seem to find the chop you want me to chop."

For a few seconds he stared at me, blinking his eyes. Then an angered expression crossed his face. "Are you being sarcastic with me?"

Oh no; now he's mad. "If it would please you, I'll be sarcastic. Please tell me how."

With a disgusted expression on his face, he stormed into the room, grabbed the clothes from the hook, and threw them over my head where they covered my face. "I haven't got time for this shit," he said. "There are things I want to do. Get out of bed now!"

The tone of his voice motivated me to jump off the mattress. I can't see. "You are definitely the poster girl for the international sisterhood of blondes," he said. "Take the clothes off your head professor."

"I'm sorry, but I don't understand what-"

"Don't you dare say it!"

What have I done to make him so annoyed? As I pulled the clothes from my head, my lower lip trembled as I looked at him. Nothing I try seems to please him. "Look, I know things are rough for you now," he said. "It's just I really want to be elsewhere and can't. Tell you what; you haul your ass to the shower and that'll please me."

How wonderful; now I can make him happy. I moved both hands behind to grab my hips and started lifting. "Now what're you doing?" He asked.

"I'm trying to haul my ass but it isn't working."

He blinked several more times watching me struggle, and then shook his head while looking at the floor. "This has to be a set-up," he said. "Hank's evening the score. Place one foot in front of the other repeatedly until you reach the shower. Is that simple enough for you?"

Again he sounds angry. I don't know what I can do other than follow his instructions. While holding my hips, I placed my right foot directly in front of my left carefully making sure it was precisely positioned. Then I slowly lifted my left, putting it on the floor. Oops; it's not in front. Maybe if I slide it a little he won't notice.

"Would you pick up the pace?" He asked. "No wait, don't pick anything up. I mean start-; oh for GOD'S sake! Now you're getting ME confused! Move faster!"

His voice sounds upset. Maybe if I forget about placing my feet directly in front of each other and just walk quickly, he'll be pleased. As I began moving faster, his expression softened. But when I reached the doorway, I wasn't sure which way to go. When I turned around to ask, he already had his hand pointed to the left.

Shortly after I left the room, he brushed by me to stand in front of a big steel door. Before I reached him, he placed a key in the lock and opened it, stepping to the side. I moved past him, and he fell in so close behind I could feel his breath on my neck.

"A message from Earl," he said while slapping my fanny.

I abruptly halted totally perplexed. Fred bumped into me at full speed nearly knocking us over. We stumbled in different directions before regaining balance. "What the HELL did you stop for?" He asked.

This doesn't make any sense. As I stared at him, my head tilted slightly to the side. "I'm sorry, but Earl told me to tell you if you touched me for me to say he said for you to stop, and then tell him about it. But you said the touch you just did was a message from Earl and then touched me, yet he doesn't want you to touch me but you said it's from him and now I'm so confused!"

Fred stared blankly at me for a few moments, rapidly shook his head, and then stared a little more. Slowly a smile grew on his face.

"Congratulations seven forty-two," he said; "you've passed the first portion of our test. In order to pass it all, you must tell me what Earl said for you to do."

This is great. Not only have I passed a test, he's smiling. Now I must complete the test which will please him more. "He said if you touch me below the neck, to tell you he said stop and then tell him about it."

His eyes drifted to my lips briefly, before turning toward the far end of the hall. "That's absolutely correct," he said. "You remembered it flawlessly. You have pleased both Earl and me. I'll tell him all about this."

At long last he said I've pleased him, but there's something I need to better understand. "You will tell Earl?"

"Yes," he said, "you have fulfilled your instructions perfectly. Now the shower is the middle door on your left. It's okay to resume walking to it."

I feel wonderful. He's happy and so is Earl. The thought of it all put a little skip in my step as I walked to the door he mentioned. Then he placed a key in that lock, opened the door, and reached around to turn on the lights. "What you need is already in there," he said. "I want you to wash everything twice, but don't take too long. I'd love to stay and watch but another lady is in dire need of my services. I'll be back in twenty minutes. Be sure you're ready for me; capeesh?"

Before I stepped into the room, I faced him confused again. "I'm sorry, I don't understand. What does cap-eesh mean?"

A frown grew as he shook his head twice. "Do you understand?"

"No sir, I'm sorry."

He drew a deep breath still appearing annoyed. This is not good. "Listen you blank blonde; it means do you understand!"

While he exhaled, I stared at him. "Do I understand?" I asked.

"Yes," he said while turning.

"No sir, I'm sorry."

That slowly returned his face to me, making me cringe from the evil expression. "No sir what," he asked.

He's really mad. But how do I answer him? "No sir-; Fred?"

"Just get your ass cleaned! Oh SHIT; don't even think of asking about the rest of your body. Clean it all! DAMN it I have GOT to get away from you before I do something you'll seriously regret!"

Sadness crept into me as I stepped down. Before I could face him, he slammed the door. There's nothing I can do to make him happy other than being ready when he said he'd return. With that in mind, I hung the outfit on the wall hook, slipped the bikini off, walked to the nearest showerhead, and adjusted the water temperature.

It feels great having warm water cascading down my hair, across my shoulders and legs. The tub of soap and shampoo started flooding, so I moved it slightly out of the way. Suddenly the door yanked open. Mark stood in the hall glaring at me. As I started to scream, he held a squirming bug out for me to see. Breath froze in my throat.

"Hello lover," he said. "You don't remember me, but I remember you. It's a shame really. This would be so much more enjoyable if you recalled our last talk. Oh well, I did say I wanted my revenge to be memorable. How does this suit you?"

The insect flew from his hand on a direct course for me. Terror locked all joints as it landed in my hair. I could feel it crawling on my scalp, accelerating my heartbeat. Absolute dread seized me into a silent scream staring at Mark as he casually lifted a box.

"Goodbye, seven forty-two," he said and then slammed the box to the floor. It burst open, letting loose hideous bugs that crawled and flew. Then he quickly cut off the lights and shut the door.

Sounds of heavy buzzing reached my ears, slowly pushing me to the edge of madness. Dozens of tiny legs crossed my feet, unaffected by the flowing water. My hair became entangled with airborne horrors, quickly forcing a mental retreat. Sanity began fleeing, my mind seeking anything for salvation. Rising from a deep recess of my brain in answer, a comparison to an actual event from the past began playing as if I were there.

From the kitchen downstairs dad angrily shouted "WHERE IS SHE?"

Earlier today, mom wasn't around and the Thomas family needed a babysitter right away. Now that I'm twelve some of the neighbors have asked I watch their kids. It's easy money and up until now it wasn't a problem. When I called dad to ask if he minded, I interrupted a sales meeting and he said I was going to pay. Since then I've been quivering in my room.

"Calm down," mom said. "Here, have a drink."

A moment of silence ended with shattering glass. "DON'T tell me what to do woman! Do you KNOW what she did?"

Sounds of a chair dragging across linoleum followed.

"She just wanted permission", mom said.

"She interrupted a very important meeting wanting her permission! Get out of my way! The TV's off; she must be upstairs."

Angry footsteps pounding across the first level sounded like exploding bombs of an advancing army. Tears ran down my cheeks, my arms and legs trembling violently.

"GET DOWN HERE THIS INSTANT!" He said. "DON'T MAKE ME COME UPSTAIRS OR IT'LL BE MUCH WORSE!"

This is it; he's going to kill me. I knew he said for me to never call him at work no matter the circumstances, but I thought this different. As soon as he heard my voice, I realized the depth of my miscalculation. My prayers for a miracle have gone unanswered.

Slowly I left the mattress, saying goodbye to Robbie Rabbit, Sir Scratch-A-Lot dog, and all the other stuffed animal companions as I walked to my certain doom. Dad's arms were crossed over his chest watching me descend the steps, his face red, and a vein throbbing in the left temple of his head. That only happens when he's seething with rage.

"I'm sorry daddy," I said.

His hand lashed out so fast grabbing my wrist I had no time to react. Squeezing pain instantly ran up my left arm under his tight grip, my hand already tingling from lack of blood. Then he began yanking me toward the kitchen. "It's time you learn I mean what I say," he said. "You need a lesson in the room."

For years he'd used the room as a threat, a storage area dug out in the basement wall. It is three steps lower than the basement, with earthen walls and flooring, shelves, and upper-level support beams for the ceiling. Numerous bugs made a home there. All efforts of extermination failed as they managed to return. Only a tightly sealed door prevented an all-out invasion of the rest of the house. Terror filled my thoughts as I began imagining meat-eating insects waiting to pick my bones clean. While struggling against his iron grasp I pleaded "No daddy, please no."

Mom appeared in the doorway to the kitchen, her hands on her hips while blocking the entrance. "That's enough," she said. "This is abuse and I won't tolerate it! Let go of her this instant."

Fresh hope was quickly killed when dad faced her with an unbelievably ferocious glare. Her hands fell from her hips, she looked toward the floor. "You want to leave?" He asked. "Fine; don't let the door hit you in the ass. In the mean time, if you don't get out of my way I'll move you myself."

A heavy weight descended on my chest, almost feeling like I was being crushed as she moved aside. Then we were back in quick motion, dad turning the corner so fast I bumped my shoulder on the doorframe. Spasms immediately racked my upper body while I was yanked down the basement stairs. Twice I nearly fell trying to keep up.

In what felt like a nightmare environment, we stood before the sealed room. To my eyes the door heaved and shivered like a hungry beast anxious to be fed. My mind defensively shut down giving this a strange feeling of unreality.

"If you call me again," he said, "I'll put you in here forever."

The door creaked open with the sound of nails across a blackboard. Darkness as absolute as a bottomless pit yawned before me, temporarily chased away by dad throwing a switch on this side. Shadowy multi-legged shapes scurried for cover, fleeing under shelves and out of the light.

"Move," he said while releasing my arm.

Thoughts of running entered my mind, but he'd only catch me. My last hope was that if I stepped across the threshold, he'd change his plans. While silently asking for help from above, I entered the room. "Go down the stairs and take ten steps from the door," he said.

If I do as he says, maybe he'll let me go. By making me go in there under threat of being locked up, he's scared me so much I can hardly breathe. Please let that be all he wants to do. Once I'd climbed down and walked the distance, I turned to face him. Suddenly I was thrust into darkness, the door slamming shut. "Daddy please, I'm sorry please! Let me out of here!"

No response; oh God save me! "I promise I won't call you again. Please let me out!"

My only hope is to get near the door. Those horrible creatures can't reach me once I'm on the steps. "Let me out!"

Slowly I began moving in the direction I thought would lead me to safety. My hands bumped into a shelf, something falling into my hair that began crawling. Sheer terror filled my being, tears running down my cheeks. "THEY'RE ON ME PLEASE; LET ME OUT LET ME OUT LET ME OUT!"

A terrible six-legged monster began prickling my leg, freezing the words in my throat. Loud buzzing flew past my ear, moving my hair in the process. The creature that fell off the shelf now began to crawl down my forehead, and that was when a hate rose from the deepest pit of my mind. All I did was call him to ask a simple question. All he had to do was say yes or no. Instead he yelled at me over the phone and as punishment put me in this nasty place. What a real bastard. I refuse to let him break me.

Anger changed to determination. Mom isn't coming to my rescue, I must do it myself. These bugs are in my home. How dare they side with him to attack me? With a rage I've never before experienced, I plucked the bug from my eyelids and squeezed until I felt liquid between my fingers. Strength rose from the power I just discovered. "They can't hurt me, but I can kill them."

Just the sound of my voice in this near-total quiet soothed my nerves. The bug halfway up my leg was next; soon it was nothing more than a disgusting substance. As I worked my way toward the door using the shelves as guides, any insect I came across was extinguished. Finally my toe bumped into the bottom step, and I turned to sit down. It was like the insects knew I held absolute dominion over them and left me alone. "I've won. Dad can no longer frighten me with this room. If he thinks bugs will terrify me, he's in for a big surprise!"

A rattling doorknob partially brought me out of the fugue condition. In my semi-hallucinogenic state I saw Mark tossing insects on one side of me, my father yanking me to the room on the other. Both sides merged into swirling colors when one insect landed in my hair. Memories of false commandments crept forward.

From deep inside my mind, swarming bugs seemingly formed one large mass that shrunk into a point, and then slowly grew to a door. It opened to a sight of devastation. Snakes and insects on the other side were dead, scattered as far as I could see. A hand curled by arthritis dug through the ground, opening its grave. All vermin faded away as a very old woman climbed out. Fascination over the draw she had on me kept me immobile. Her eyes were gentle, a soft smile on her face.

Then she started moving toward the door, miraculously reversing years the closer she came.

A little girl pulled from me, rushing through the door to the woman. For a moment they looked at one another, and then gently moved into a hug. Each held the other tightly, slowly melting into one. That was when I knew it was the other Joyce smiling kindly at me.

I held no fear even when she crossed to my side, her age identical to mine. She stopped six inches in front, holding her arms out. Curiosity above all else moved me to her embrace, our arms tightly hugging one another. Then she let go, slowly turning around to back into me. Our bodies painlessly merged, a flood of memories both past and present rushing to my thoughts at a dizzying rate. When it settled my mind cleared. The other two were a part of me. I am Joyce Allison Jackson!

CHAPTER 13

Light expanded downward from the opening door, forming a triangle quickly changing to rectangle on the shiny tile floor. Two human shadows darkened the brightness. Here they come. My only hope is to act lost.

An arm reached around the frame, briefly searching for a switch I could now see. Brilliant illumination forced my eyes to squint momentarily before I forced them open staring at the wall just below their feet. Fred leaned to look at my eyes, his expression gravely worried. "Look at her God Damn it!" He said. "You've killed us both!"

Shuffling sounds came from the hall as Fred left the entrance and Mark took his place. He didn't bend down; just stood still. Faucet water spraying on the floor made the only noise for a few moments. I didn't move, not exactly sure how to react. Two footsteps angrily walking away preceded Mark's arm-reflection off the tiles reaching for something beyond the doorframe. "Would you relax?" Mark asked. "This isn't the first time one of them has lost it. You take her to the room; I'll clean up the mess. Then we'll both act surprised when Earl sees."

"Like hell you're pulling me in," Fred said. "I'm telling Earl this is your doing!"

Mark leaned to where I could see his face, an expression of indifferent curiosity studying me. "And how will you tell Earl I was able to get this close to her?" Mark asked. "I became invisible?"

When Mark pulled back, I chanced a quick glance at the floor just below the wall. Numerous unmoving insects littered the entire area. I think they're all dead, but how?

"You set me up, you son of a bitch," Fred said.

"No, I didn't," Mark said. "But if you keep insisting on telling Earl the truth, I will let him know how I waited until you went to play husband with six ninety-eight when you were supposed to be standing guard."

Good God he raped that girl. I've got to focus on calm. Any facial changes will betray me. More shuffling sounds came from the hall as Mark turned to face someone out of view.

"I'll kill you for this," Fred said.

"And I'll say it again; relax. Earl doesn't need to know. You take her back, I'll clean up, we both get Earl, and he terminates this model. We get off scot-free!"

Dear lord, he's talking about killing me. I have to do something now or I'm dead. Since they expect me to be horrified of bugs, I slowly raised my arm to point at the many dead ones on the floor.

"Look, she's moving," Fred said.

My face grew into a terrified expression, followed with closing my eyes tightly.

"She's responding," Mark said. "Do you understand me, seven forty-two?"

"B-bugs," I said, "please, take them away!"

Both jumped into the room, the sound causing me to open my eyes. Fred moved around me to shut off the water. Mark approached my face, carefully looking into my eyes. His expression softened while I maintained my shocked stare. "It's okay," he said. "They can't hurt you."

Before I could react, he scooped me from the floor, gently cradling me in his arms. A surprised noise slipped out, bringing a kind smile from him. This is becoming an interesting change of attitude, one I might be able to use. I formed a pitifully frightened expression while wrapping my arms around his neck, tightly pushing my face into his chest as he carried me toward the door. "I'm sorry," he said, "I thought you were someone else. The person I'm angry with no longer exists."

Loud crunching sounds caused both of us to glance at Fred stomping across dead bugs. "That ain't going to cut it," he said. "You think all you need to do is kiss and make up? The first time Earl asks if she adjusted to showering, it's over and so are we!"

When we reached the door, he carefully placed me so I was in the hall. For a brief moment, I thought about running to the other door even though I'm naked. Then I remembered this collar and their remotes. It's not yet time. Mark looked at Fred as he arrived by his side, and then returned his eyes to me. "It would please me very much if you'd forget this ever happened," Mark said. "Even if anyone asks, tell them all you did was shower. Can you do that for me?"

Much as I abhor the memory of my moronic state while under the influence, I forced the same idiotic smile I lived with back then. "Yes, I can do that for you."

Fred slammed my new outfit to the floor next to my feet. "I don't buy it," he said. "Back away from the door seven forty-two."

He didn't tell me to pick up the clothes. Though I have an overwhelming desire to cover myself, I complied without hesitation. Fred climbed out followed by Mark who scooped the clothing. Both approached me, Mark smiling as he held the clothes out to me and Fred frowning. "Here," Mark said.

The urge to grab, turn, and dress was pushed aside as I accepted the outfit and waited. Fred squeezed between Mark and me, staring at my eyes. "It would please me tremendously for you to tell me what happened while you were showering," he said.

This is dangerous ground I'm on. If I lean too far in either direction chances are one of them will kill me right now. It was Mark's confident face that hinted at the direction to pursue. "I'm sorry, I don't understand. Do you mean water running?"

Mentioning water reinforced the chill I felt standing in a hallway dripping wet. Mark's shirt and pants were soaked from where he'd carried me, but it didn't seem to bother him. Fred appeared livid as he pushed his nose against mine. "No you vocal vacuum! I mean what about the bugs?"

As I forced a horrified expression on my face, Mark's hand appeared on Fred's shoulder pulling him away while coming between us. "How in the hell do you think Earl, or even Hank for that matter, will come up with that question?" Mark asked. "Let it go and no one will ever find out. She just proved it to you."

Oh I'm going to prove a lot of things to you soon, but for now I must act the part they expect. My face remained locked in mortal fear, staying absolutely still even when Mark slowly turned to me. "It's okay," he said. "The bugs are gone. It would please me for you to forget about what just happened."

My head suddenly felt like it was splitting in half, cloudy remnants of another Joyce trying to pull free. It forced me to step back two paces holding my scalp, the clothes slipping from my hand. For a brief horrifying moment I forgot where I was. Then it all returned with what seemed an audible pop that slammed my ears. Nerves slowly settled, my wits returning. Mark and Fred watched anxiously, no one moving to intervene. I forced a smile at Mark even though I felt exhausted. "Yes, I can forget them for you," I said.

Fred jumped into the shower room, returning with the towel in moments. He climbed out, walking rapidly to me with the towel outstretched in his hand. "Dry yourself-; I mean it would please me for you to dry yourself quickly and get dressed."

He faced Mark. "Get moving. If this isn't a drug after-effect I want all evidence gone now!"

Those words chilled the marrow of my bones. What kind of after-effects are they expecting? Does that mean the drug is still working to take away my identity?

Covering those grave fears took more strength than I've used before. Even with my calm appearance, out of the corner of my eye I could see Fred watching me with as much concern shown as I had hidden. Mark jumped into the shower room while I was dressing, and soon Fred escorted me back to the cell. Once he closed the door and I was alone, fatigue hit me like I hadn't slept in two days. The bed looked like a welcome cloud of relief, my legs moving with numbness like they belonged to someone else when it happened again.

My head felt like it was splitting in two, my hands grabbing it. Vision blurred. The bed became three shimmering forms on the floor. Ghosts of dad and Mark materialized pulling against my elbows in opposing directions with a ferocity that caused real pain. "I am Joyce Allison Jackson," I said. "Their drugs cannot beat me."

Slowly the images dissipated, the bed returning to one but it wasn't over. My head hurt like I'd hit a brick wall, room lighting creating uncomfortable halos around everything. It felt like spikes were being driven between my eyes. Then I bumped into the mattress, just letting myself fall to a soft landing. "I'm so tired. Please God, I can't stay awake any longer. Protect me and make sure I'm Joyce when I wake up."

Exhaustion halted all movements, the lights started dimming.

Katie was dressed watching me with an impatience that rivals my father. She might think a double-date with gun nuts is an interesting change of college entertainment, I don't. How I'd let myself get talked into this still angers me. "You promised," she said.

Yes, I did. Had it been anyone else, I'd have politely declined. Katie and I have been rooming together for two years, becoming fast friends in the process. She wasn't Mary but came in a close second. When she said there was a guy she liked and wanted to know better, I thought it was great for her. Weeks passed with the two of them growing close. Then one day she said he had a shy friend with trouble meeting people. I and my stupid sympathetic nature showed sorrow. Well one thing led to another, and here I am preparing to go off into the wilds with one guy I only have fleeting knowledge about and another who's a mystery. As if that wasn't exciting enough, they're coming armed for World War Three. "If we get killed," I said, "I'm telling your parents."

As I pulled jeans and a matching blouse from the drawer, she came to me. "I know you don't think this is going to be fun, but who knows what Mike looks like? Besides you've been working too hard. It'll be good for you to blow off a little steam."

"I'm afraid someone's going to blow off a little toe," I said.

She snorted once while turning to walk toward the window. A quick peek between the closed blinds at the parking lot below brought a disappointed look to her face. "You'll be all right," she said. "Just do what Sam says. He's an expert marksman."

The struggle of tugging tight jeans over hips begins. "How come you never hear about any expert markswomen?" I asked. "You know why? I'll tell you."

Her hand slipped from the blind, facing me with an amused expression. Finally the jeans were up allowing me to slide the blouse over my arms. My eyes opened wildly as I faced her while buttoning. "It's because they go insane and start shooting everything. A tree, bushes, cats, dogs, butterflies; it's just targets for them. Sure they mingle with folks appearing normal as can be, but put a gun in their hands and they change. Oh how they change."

My blouse was buttoned, tucked into the jeans, and zipped. I started creeping up on her saying "So while we're out in the woods today, if I should start acting, you know, terrifying, it's because I, am an expert markswoman!"

While laughing evilly I threw my hands overhead. She feigned fear, raising the back of her hand to her mouth while opening her eyes wide. Then the phone rang.

Katie giggled a few times while walking to answer. My arms lowered; feelings of near doom rising. As she lifted the handset, I walked to the closet for my shoes.

Had it not been for my promise, I would've conveniently been in the library long before now. I've never touched a gun, though I watched a tremendous amount of television where I imagined aiming one and squeezing the trigger. That was during my torturous childhood. Now that I'm on the verge of freedom, handling a real weapon might bring back unpleasant memories.

Based on Katie's hushed tone, it was as I suspected our dates. Her expression did not reflect a cancellation of plans much to my disappointment. She returned the phone to the cradle, looking at my feet. "They're here," she said. "You're going in those shoes?"

That question caused me to glance at my sneakers for a brief moment before looking at her. "My army boots are at home. If we get invaded while we're out, I promise to run get them."

Her head shook a few times while walking toward the door. The choice for her foot attire was hard-soled pumps. In no way was I going to chance ruining a good pair of shoes like those. When she placed her hand on the knob, she faced me. "Are you ready?"

"Bang, bang."

Introductions were brief with Sam doing all the talking. Mike seemed fascinated by his own feet, looking at me for maybe two seconds before rechecking to make sure his laces were still tied. Oh this is going to be fun.

The metal clap-trap Sam calls a car scares me more than thoughts of going to some isolated place with armed men. It sounds more like a person suffering emphysema than an automobile as he kept twisting the key. Then with a bang like he shot the dashboard and a burp of fumigating smoke, it vibrated to life or something akin. We pulled out of the space leaving behind a slimy black puddle as a memento. Mike sat next to me in the back, watching buildings go by rather than glance at me.

He is kind of cute but I can tell he has the personality of a clock. You look at him every now and then just to make sure he's still ticking, and then drift back to your previous activity. I owe Katie big time for this.

At least the vehicle gave reason for the lack of small talk. The deafening roar made conversation difficult as high-speed vibrations rattling the floor began numbing my legs. Katie and Sam carried on like it was normal for a car to give massages. Mike was staring calmly out the window. Am I the only one who fears this car is breaking apart?

A reduction of teeth-rattling indicated our deceleration just when a dirt road became our new direction. There were no trees as far as I could see, only some kind of a mound off in the distance. After a mile of pock-marked driving that added bounces to shakes, Sam put the car into park and turned the key. Ten seconds later the car stopped. "We're here," Sam said.

"We're where?" I asked.

Sam and Mike opened their doors simultaneously, Katie looked at me. Mike took off running toward the rear, but Sam faced me. "This is a place we have permission to target practice," he said. "We don't have much money, so we shoot at cans. They're already set."

Katie had a pleading expression on her face to which I smiled. But when my door yanked open, it nearly scared me through the rusted roof. My hand flew to my chest as I quickly turned toward Mike. He held the door open, looking very sad. "I-I-I'm s-s-sorry," he said.

His gallant gesture coupled with that struggled apology touched my heart. Once I was outside and clear, he closed the door while staring at the ground. I stepped in front of him, placing two fingers under his chin and lifting until he was looking at me. "Thank you," I said.

Red instantly exploded across his face. Katie had climbed out, watching this exchange with a soft smile. Mike nodded and turned away. Sam walked around the rear, approaching us. That must've sent a signal of some sort since Mike accepted the keys from him and proceeded to open the trunk. "He's been working on overcoming that stutter for as long as I remember," Sam said. "It's hardly noticeable unless he's in the company of beautiful women. He really is a nice guy once you get to know him."

Now I understand the attraction Katie has for Sam. His explanation shows this concern for Mike isn't about sympathy felt for someone with a speech impediment, but a friendship that sees beyond physical differences to the real person. Sam and Mike are both kind people.

"Have you ever fired a weapon before, Joyce?" Sam asked.

How can I say shooting guns doesn't interest me in the least without insulting them? Oh well, just for the sake of peace I'll go along with this. "No."

A large smile grew on his face. Mike began placing pistols of various sizes on the top of the car. "That's okay," Sam said. "Stick with us and we'll turn you into a real markswoman!"

My eyebrows went up as I faced Katie. She struggled against the forming grin. "Lord I hope not," she said.

The absolutely confused face on Sam was all I could handle. Laughter broke out, bringing a smile to Mike's face. Sam appeared insulted, calming the chuckles quickly. "I'm sorry Sam," I said. "It's just a private joke that has nothing to do with you."

He still looked angry while facing Katie. "Maybe you'd like to share the joke?" He asked.

Katie took his arm in hers; putting on one of the most alluring expressions I've ever seen. It was almost like he melted under her gaze, the hardened features instantly vanishing. "I'll tell you later," she said. "Right now, why don't you show us how to shoot?"

This was astonishing watching how he became an automaton totally under her control. It was like he completely forgot about being upset. An expression of happiness grew on his face as he walked toward Mike. Katie moved with him, glancing briefly at me while winking.

Four handguns were placed in the sun on top of the car, glinting like deadly diamonds. Mike tossed a green duffel bag over his shoulder, slamming the trunk. It reopened, forcing him to slam it harder. Then he and Sam grabbed two guns each and began walking a downhill path leading toward the mound.

We fell in behind, dipping below the prairie grass surrounding the car until we reached a leveled-out section a hundred feet in front of the mound base. About a foot away from the base were long steel shelves four rows high, each lined with at least ten empty bean cans. Either these guys have a lot of fiber in their diet or they spent a great deal of time setting this up. "That's soft soil behind the cans," Sam said. "There's no danger of a ricochet. Who wants to go first?"

Mike placed the bag on the ground, opened it, and put his guns inside. Katie and I remained quiet, a strange fear building inside my gut. "Relax, everything will be fine," Sam said. "Tell you what; I'll go first."

As he started walking toward the bag, Mike searched the contents until locating a box of bullets. Sam placed one of the guns in the bag, took the box from Mike, removed a handful of bullets, and loaded his chosen weapon. "This is a forty-four magnum," he said. "It's so powerful; it can shoot through an engine block."

I came perilously close to asking if he'd tested that theory on his car, but decided not to anger the man with the cannon. Mike began loading the other guns as Sam took a stance facing the shelves. His legs spread slightly; held the gun straight out in front of his face, looked over the barrel, and squeezed the trigger.

Thunder exploded from the end of his pistol startling my feet off the ground. None of the shows I'd watched prepared me for that. A cloud of dust rose behind the cans, but it was a miss. His expression showed disgust as he took aim again.

The second shot was no better as I still jumped, but he did kill a can. It hit the mound with incredible speed, a mortal wound showing from its guts. He smiled at it like a sheriff watching a wounded outlaw tumble down the slope. Then he aimed at another one but that was all I could take. "You guys enjoy yourselves," I said. "I'm going to catch some sun by the car."

Mike anxiously looked at me. Katie appeared apologetic but made no move to try convincing me to remain. When I started moving off, Mike rushed to stand next to me. "P-P-Please d-don't go," he said. "I-I th-th-think you sh-should learn how t-to sh-shoot. You're very p-pretty and sh-sh-should be able to d-defend yourself."

In a bizarre way, I thought his concerns were kind of sweet, but those loud sounds were downright obnoxious. I wanted nothing more to do with them. "Thanks Mike, I'll be okay. You stay here and have fun."

It wasn't my intention for that to come across as a rejection, but based on his expression that's how he took it. Slowly he turned away with the most depressed face I've ever seen, walking back to the duffel bag. "Oh let her go Mike," Sam said. "I bet her joke was about not being able to hit the ground with a stone."

Normally I let rude remarks fade away, but something about this afternoon changed that. With a slight smile, I did an about-face and marched to Sam. When I looked him in the eye, I held out my hand for his gun. "Hold on a moment Annie Oakley," he said, "this gun has a kick that'll send you to the next county. Better try something smaller first."

My head shook without breaking eye contact, but my smile grew. "If you can do it, I can do it."

His shoulders shrugged as he handed the gun over. Then he quickly moved out of the way like he thought I was going to shoot wildly. I held the gun out just like I'd seen hundreds of times before, aimed a little above one of the top cans, and gently squeezed the trigger. Nothing happened, the trigger wouldn't pull back. Sam started laughing loudly as I looked at him. He settled down, briefly wiping tears from his eyes. "You need to release the safety," he said. "It's a lever on the right side beneath the hammer."

That mean-spirited laugh intensified my resolve. Just like he said, a lever was below the hammer that I moved into a new position. Chuckles came from Sam as I took aim again. Then I slowly squeezed the trigger. A deafening explosion rocked the ground as a can flew backwards, the gun-kick nearly catching me by surprise. No more laughter was heard as I lowered the gun and looked at Sam, a smug expression on my face. He appeared shocked for a moment, followed by a frown. "Beginners luck," he said. "You couldn't do that again at half the distance."

It must've been my upbringing that instilled such a strong dislike for any man to tell me I can't do something. As I aimed at a second one and squeezed, the can went airborne. Just for my own laughs I shot another one, tagging it with two more bullets on the way down the slope. All three were staring at me slack-jawed as I moved the barrel under my mouth to puff out some smoke. Sam began grinning while walking toward me.

"Folks, we've been conned," he said. "This isn't the first time Joyce has shot a gun. Man I've never seen things like that before. You are amazing!"

When he arrived, I handed the gun back and turned to leave. "I assure you; that was my first and last time to handle a gun. I hate loud noises. No offense but I'm not interested in any more shooting. You go ahead and-"

"You have company coming, seven forty-two."

CHAPTER 14

Memories of a strange date slowly dissipated as I carefully opened my eyes. The headache I had before sleeping was gone, hopefully for good. Thank God I remember who and where I am. Does this mean I've won?

Earl stood in the doorway for a few moments watching me. Once he entered and shut the door, I sat up smiling. Without saying a word he walked to the chair, sat down, and placed his remote on the table out of my reach. Dread immediately built, taking an inordinate amount of willpower to conceal. He continued his close study of me until drawing a deep breath while glancing to the ceiling, and then exhaling while looking back at me. "I'm at a quandary," he said. "People are becoming impatient, sending e-mails that could be considered downright threatening. They want you now, not in two weeks. As if it isn't burdening enough calming them, one of my clients from Las Vegas has flown in. She'll be here soon. I simply don't have time to constantly placate eager beaver-types, pardon the pun."

His attention drifted to the remote while placing his hand on it. "There're some things about you that worry me. For instance, the clothes you had. Someone with your stunning beauty normally packs items that flatter their bodies, but you didn't. It's like you're unaware of your own sex-appeal which makes you dangerous. You haven't relied on Nature's gifts to get by. No; you developed a sharp mind instead."

He lifted the remote, pointing it at me. Even though my insides were shivering from terror, I struggled to maintain a calm appearance. "Doc got me to thinking. Is all that money really worth the risk? He's right about your eyes. There's something different about them."

Time seemed to slow as the arm muscles to the hand holding the remote tensed. His wrist jerked suddenly, coming extremely close to making me jump. Lord I hope my expression hasn't changed. For a few more moments he pointed the remote at me, staring intensely at my face. Then his hand lowered almost causing me to exhale loudly. "Every time I look at you I see two things. One is an overflowing bank account, the other is total devastation. My instincts are telling me to terminate you immediately. What do you think I should do?"

Oh how I wish I could call forth the other Joyce to answer him. He watched with the scrutiny of a scientist looking into a microscope as I gathered my thoughts. "I'm sorry, I don't understand. Would it please you for me to think?"

The remote remained in his hand, his expression unchanged. A knock on the door didn't detract his eyes from me, nor mine his. Chest pressure so intense I grew fearful of my heart imploding built while he stared at my smiling face. Then he sighed while rising from the chair. "No one could fake that," he said. "Still I need a little time to think it over. I'll let you know my decision in three and a half days. To answer your question, it would greatly upset me if you started thinking. For now it would please me for you to get out of bed and come with me."

Though I really wanted to release a huge sigh of relief, I calmly moved my legs off the mattress to the floor. Dizziness hit the instant I stood up, forcing me to place one hand on the bed. Before it passed, Earl came to my side dropping down to gaze into my eyes, slowly shaking his head while rising. "That's another mark against you," he said. "Sporadic fatigue hit just about everyone else after the first treatment yet you seemed fine back then. I wonder what it means when it starts now."

A second knock sounded, this time drawing Earl's attention. For a moment I thought he was going to ignore it, but then he walked across the room. "Come on seven forty-two," he said; "company's waiting."

When he opened the door, I nearly made a break for it. My time is quickly running out and I'll have to take a risk soon. Then what he said about three and a half days calmed me momentarily. As long as I continue acting like a mindless zombie, I think he'll live up to that promise. I pray that one of them will grow careless soon. Yes, for two days I'll behave. Then if nothing presents itself I'll make my move no matter what. Better to die trying for freedom than live in slavery.

Earl had cleared the doorway by the time I arrived. He didn't look at me after his last words. Hank stood in front blocking my view, smiling so big I wanted to rip his lips off. I maintained that moronic smile as he walked away and permitted me entrance.

The redhead was close to the main door, her arms held over her head by two cables from the ceiling identical to the ones I'd seen before, only these were in a different location. A moan coming from the other side of the room pulled my eyes. Two more cables held the arms of a semi-conscious naked oriental brunette with a short haircut. Wait, is that; oh my God that's Fugi. Doc did an extremely professional job as Fugi looked like she'd always been a well-proportioned woman.

"Over here, seven forty-two," Hank said.

He stood on the back side of two loose cables dangling between the other captives. Earl had been watching me so closely I could almost feel his eyes. Something seemed wrong like I'm now on deadly ground. Since I don't know if they'd been talking about Earl's concerns, he might be testing to see if I was still under their control. I hope what I'm about to do is the right thing. "I'm sorry, I don't understand. What is over there?"

Fugi slowly looked at me, her eyes barely open. Earl turned to walk out of the room apparently satisfied. Hank's smile grew larger though I didn't think it possible. "It would please me for you to come over here," he said.

Out of the corner of my eye, I watched Fugi turn away, a look of utter defeat on her face. Hank held the manacles ready when I arrived. I lifted my arms into them while holding that stupid smile. Cold metal gripped my wrists with a painful tightness. It took a considerable amount of concentration to keep my expression.

"I'll let the three of you get acquainted," Hank said.

He laughed while walking to the main door. A few seconds later he was gone with the door closed. While I held that silly face in case we were being watched, my mind began working on a new plan.

There are three of us, although I don't know about Fugi. Chances are she'd leap at the opportunity to escape, but the possibility exists she could switch sides at the most inconvenient moment. She is wearing a collar just like mine. That means she has incentive to instruct me on proper usage when I get a remote. But the real question is does she remember how?

Sounds coming from the outer hall drew her attention my way.
Her face formed a quizzical expression when she saw me looking at
her, which she quickly lost as the door opened. My attention drifted
toward the door just in time to see Fred enter. He stared at me with
a hunger that nearly made me shiver. Hank came next, followed by
Mark. Then Earl walked in holding the arm of a middle-aged woman
who looked and dressed more like a man. The woman disengaged
herself, quickly crossing the room to Fugi. Her hands went to her hips
as she smiled at Fugi. "Oh how the mighty have fallen," she said.
"You've got to let me have her!"

Fugi looked from the floor, a frown forming on her face as she
stared at the woman. She yanked the cables, making the woman back
up. That brought a slight smile to Fugi's face.

"Yep, that's Fugi Mago all right," the woman said. "Is she like the
other transies?"

What in the world are transies? My lord, does she mean
transsexuals? How many forced operations have they done here?
That question can be answered later. Her attention was focused on
Fugi which also interested me. Fugi's reactions to that woman's
provocations could shed some light on her mental status.

Earl had been quietly approaching from my blind side. He was
directly behind me as he spoke, almost making me jump. "No; Doc
used his serum on her after the operation. Though it's too early to tell,
I think it's an incredible break-through. Fugi now has the body of a
twenty-three year-old woman. The treatment does have drawbacks
though. Her muscles are weakened like those of a baby, but we're
working on it. On another note, his anti-aging drug could be available
by the end of the year."

The allure of immortality didn't detract her attention from Fugi.
She casually circled her, staring in a most lewd manner until returning
to the front. Then she started laughing while cupping one of Fugi's
breasts. "This is astonishing," she said. "Everything looks and feels so
natural, like Fugi has always been a girl. When will she be ready?"

Earl moved to where I could see him, approaching the woman
with a confused expression on his face while pointing at me. "I thought
you were interested in this one. She'll be ready in about two weeks.
Fugi won't be for at least four, depending on muscle development."

An evil smile grew on the woman's face as she returned her gaze
to Fugi. "That one is out of my price range," she said, "but this one

I MUST have. Oh the things I'm going to make her do send shivers down my back. You have *no* idea how much I've longed for this day! Let's cut through the bullshit. I'll give you a million right now if you'll keep her off the market and let me know when I can expect delivery."

A million for Fugi and I'm out of her range? This is unbelievable. "I'm afraid it's too late," Earl said. "We've already notified two foreign interests about Fugi's successful operation. I'll let you know about the auction date in plenty of time for you to be here, but that's the best I can do. I'm sorry."

Disappointment grew on her as quickly as a wind-blown storm cloud covering the sun. She released Fugi's breast facing Earl. "What about his, I mean her Tae Kwon-Do skills?" She asked. "Will she be as dangerous as before?"

Earl shook his head. "Based on preliminary observations, she more or less remembers everything. That means if we were to give her the time to fully develop the muscles, yes she'd be a serious threat. But after I've finished with the mind modifications, she'll be whatever you want."

Another yank on Fugi's manacles drew both their attentions. "I'll find a way," Fugi said. "And when I do, I will destroy all of you. Though it may take ten years, your house will fall Pinkerton. Get your affairs in order now."

The woman's name must be the Pinkerton I'd heard before, as she appeared concerned looking at Fugi. Earl calmly walked behind Fugi, reaching down to pinch her butt. Even though his fingers left flaming red marks that caused Pinkerton to grin, Fugi remained glaring at her without moving. "Such strong words from such a soft powder-puff," Earl said. "In one month, the only thing falling will be you on beds."

Pinkerton smiled but Fugi remained undaunted. Her quiet defiance unnerved the smile off Pinkerton, turning her toward me. "So this is the one everybody's all excited over," she said.

Her eyes leisurely strolled down the front of my body, creating involuntary shivers that nearly became visible. Then she slowly circled me like a proud tiger taking inventory of its mortally wounded prey. Fugi watched my reaction out of the corner of her eye, eventually losing interest. "I can see the appeal" she said. "Maybe I will show up for the big day. If nothing else, I'll see Fugi with a different attitude."

"That you will," Earl said.

A nod from Pinkerton responded as she turned toward the main door. "I must fly, literally," she said. "As always, thanks for the hospitality Earl. This truly made my day!"

"The walking dead," Fugi said.

No one else in the room acknowledged her threat except me. The tone of her voice made me cringe inwardly. It was enough to give nightmares to anyone that threat was directed toward, and gave me pause to wonder if she could be trusted.

Earl and Pinkerton continued moving toward the door, obviously sending a signal to the rest. Fred and Mark went to Fugi, releasing her hands and then roughly hauling her to the cell. Hank freed me, walking to my front with that irksome smile splashed all over his face. "So what do you think about Mrs. Pinkerton?" He asked. "She's purchased a few of our lesser attractive packages in the past. How would you like to go with her?"

Alarms clanged loudly inside as he calmly waited for my response. Why are they continually testing me? Is my appearance faltering? "I'm sorry, I don't understand. Would it please you for me to go with her?"

Mark left Fugi's room, quickly walking behind Hank with a worried glance at me. He continued moving toward the redhead as Fred stepped into the main chamber closing Fugi's door. "What do you want to do?" Hank asked.

Fred nearly ran to us, drawing Hank's attention. "I only wish to please," I said.

Before Hank could look at me, Fred grabbed his shoulder. "Would you cut the shit? She just finished the first set yesterday. Stop mentally torturing her!"

Oh I get it. They aren't worried about me recovering. This is a sick game to them. Hank's eyebrows went up as he turned to fully face Fred. "Since when did you become the knight in shining armor riding in on a white horse?" He asked.

"Since Earl threatened to set Doc loose on me if anything went wrong. Now please, for the love of God, leave her the hell alone! Don't you have things to do?"

Hank smiled in an ingratiating manner as he looked at me, like he was being charitable. I must stay calm. In two days they're all going to be surprised. "It would please me for you to return to your room," he said.

With that simpleton grin on my face growing, I quickly complied. Fred walked behind me, closing the door once I was inside. Muffled chatter could be heard outside for a few more moments, followed by silence.

I wonder if my door is locked. Do I dare try it? No; not yet. If anyone is lurking out there they'll realize I've recovered. Even if all they hear is the rattling of a locked knob, it'll be enough. For now I'll patiently wait.

My stomach growled turning all thoughts toward the remaining fruit. I have to eat to maintain my strength. When the chance arrives I must be fully alert and ready.

That thought more than hunger guided me to the table. Then I looked at the spot Earl laid his remote. It was like a shadow as dark as death remained in its wake. Shivers coursed through me briefly before I sat down, carefully avoiding that area.

I was working on my second banana when the door yanked open. No sounds of keys were heard beforehand. That may have answered my question about the door lock. Fred quickly entered the room holding a plate of sandwiches. After he placed them in front of me, his face developed a sneer while casually looking at my breasts. It took all of my inner strength to hold my calm demeanor. "Eat up my pretty pinhead," he said. "Soon you'll be mine!"

What's that supposed to mean? I thought there was grave danger for him to touch me. It must be another of their twisted games. Well it's time to continue the act. He started walking to the open entrance as I spoke. "I'm sorry, I don't under-"

"You will," he said while leaving and shutting the door.

This is becoming scarier by the moment, even though I wouldn't have thought it possible. If he rapes me, I won't be able to contain myself. I'd rather die than surrender and will fight him to my last breath. Perhaps it's time to end my charade and see what happens. At least I'll be free one way or the other.

Dizziness immediately hit, nearly causing a tumble out of the chair. The mental Joyce was trying to rip away, making my head pound in agony. I gripped the table so tightly my hands ached. "I am Joyce Allison Jackson. Leave me alone!"

The floor started heaving, walls closing in on me. Moans floated through the air like the anguished cries of the doomed. One of the apples split open letting loose dozens of crawling insects. Snakes slithered from the bottom of the basket; their dripping fangs striking at my wrists. I shut my eyes tightly. "This is not real. It's all in my mind. Go away."

Slowly my balance was restored. When I opened my eyes, the room was as it had been before, no bugs or snakes. Silence returned; the terrible cries just stopped. Incredible fatigue fell over me like heavy chains, making my journey to the bed difficult. When I arrived, I dropped to the mattress with the lights dimming on the way down.

"Is that the last of it?" Mary asked.

I'd counted eight more boxes before we moved this one to its new location. "Not yet."

An exasperated sigh rose from her. For the past three hours, we'd been moving heavy boxes and furniture out of what I termed deep storage to the front of Hammonds' Department Store's lay-away floor. This wasn't the job we applied for.

In order to earn extra money for Christmas, we decided to hunt for jobs. Now that we're sixteen, many opportunities presented themselves. The ad we answered was for cashiers. Mr. Black was so impressed he offered the positions after the initial interview. But when we arrived earlier today, he told us the only openings he had left were what we're currently struggling to complete; stock clerks. "I don't know how much more of this I can take," she said.

It was obvious to me what went wrong. "Hang in there kid," I said. "We're almost finished. I'm so sorry."

Her face took on a perplexed expression while wiping sweat from her brow. "It's not your fault. I wanted this job as much as you."

"That's not why I'm apologizing."

With her looking at me more confused, I turned to walk for another box. Rushing footsteps stomped the wooden floor until she reached my side. "Would you care to enlighten me about your meaning?" She asked.

The next box loomed in front. I started sliding it across the floor, moving it to where I could get on the back side while Mary takes the front. "This has to be the work of dear old dad. He gets thrilled at squashing everything I try doing for myself. One phone call from him and here we are. I'm sorry you got involved."

Mary had years of secondhand reports regarding dad's animosity to me confirmed at my birthday party a few months back. Even with that eyewitness account, she still developed a skeptical eye while placing her hands beneath the box. "That's totally ridiculous," she said. "Your father isn't all-powerful. I think you're becoming paranoid in your old age."

Together we lifted the box. Good lord, there must be weights in here. A serious grunt flowed from her as she slowly began backing up. "You don't know him like I do. I'm sure he set this up to watch me fail."

Slowly we continued struggling with our burden until at last reaching the designated space. It went down with a thump, almost catching Mary's fingers in the process. "Are you okay?" I asked

A few gasps for air responded first. "Yes, wow that was close," she said.

Stomps on the metal stairs leading to the storage area eerily sounded like they were keeping time with our deep breathing. I didn't care who was coming, we both need a short break. Mr. Black arrived on the floor, looking at everything we'd moved with an astonished expression. When he noticed us watching, he instantly changed into something more intimidating. "Come with me girls," he said.

Based on what I saw, he wasn't going to offer us a promotion. Walking behind him down the stairs and through the store seeded a growing anger. I had to fight the urge to lash out. Let me hear what he says before jumping to conclusions. Once we were inside his office and seated, he casually leaned back in his chair. "First I want to say you've exceeded my expectations," he said. "Moving items that heavy are hard work, too hard for you I'm afraid."

Here it comes. Mary glanced at her lap saddened. As he looked toward the ceiling obviously gathering courage, I took the initiative. "With all due respect Mr. Black, we can handle it."

Mary's head nodded as she looked at Black. He formed a sympathetic smile while returning his attention to us. "I know you *think* you can," he said, "but I can't afford risking either one of you getting injured. I'm going to let you go. You will be paid for your time tonight."

Mary's eyes returned to her lap as she started to rise, but this unfair termination infuriated me. I had to respond. "You knew what you offered us three days ago wasn't the job you started us on, but did we complain? No; we jumped right to work. You also knew those heavy things we moved might be enough to send others packing, but we stuck with it until you called us here. If anyone knows what's too much for us, it's us and we can handle it. Yet here you are sitting behind your desk saying we can't. Why? Why would you put us to work on a job you obviously wanted us to quit, and when we didn't, fire us? Could you at least do us the courtesy of explaining why?"

His face became slightly irritated, causing Mary to head toward the door. I remained seated waiting for his answer. "Goodbye Miss Jackson," he said. "Your paycheck will be mailed at the end of the week."

I came dangerously close to telling him where he could shove my paycheck, but the calm voice of reason soothed my tongue. Instead I sympathetically looked at him while shaking my head and rising. "I thought you were a man," I said. "You're just like all the other spineless cowards afraid of my father. It sure is good not being you."

He appeared mad enough to jump his desk at me, so flustered he couldn't think of anything to say. Mary stared at me gape-jawed as I calmly walked to her, and together we left the office. On our way out of the store, she took my arm in hers and started giggling. Once we were outside, she released my arm. "I can't believe you said all that," she said. "You are the queen of courage. He didn't know what to say. I am humbled to be in your presence."

Anger still filled me, her praise sounding sarcastic. "We just got canned. How can you make jokes?"

Her hand on my shoulder pulled me to a stop. As I faced her, my impatient expression quickly fled. She looked at me with awe. "I'm not kidding," she said. "I didn't have the guts to face him the way you did. Chances are nearly everyone on the planet would have just gotten up and left, but not you. Oh no, you had to have the final word. That's the Joyce I know and love. You never surrender even when it's hopeless, but go down fighting. It's his loss not ours."

My mood slowly began improving as we resumed walking. When we reached the first stop light, I faced her while waiting for it to change. "He did lose a couple of hot chicks," I said.

She glanced at me with a confused expression. "Well, I'm gone that's true, but who else did he fire?"

As I tried appearing angry, her innocent expression forced laughter from me. She joined in. Then the light changed and we crossed the street giggling.

"It's time for you to shower with my special soap. Get up!"

Foggy remnants of sleep began evaporating as I looked toward the open door. Fred stood outside, a sneer on his face. His last talk with me reverberated in my mind, but he wouldn't dare. "I'm sorry, I don't-"

"Let me make this real simple for you," he said. "It would please me beyond your wildest imagination for you to come with me to the shower."

That sounded ominous. Even though I wanted to hide under the bed, I forced one of the biggest smiles my face could handle and climbed out. As he watched closely, I walked by him heading toward the main door. He ran in front, quickly unlocking it and holding out his arm in a horrible mimic of a gentleman waiting for a lady to enter. The rest of our journey was done in frightening silence until he started unlocking the shower room door. "It would please me for you to thoroughly wash your body," he said.

He remained in the doorway, watching me step down and then undress. Oh God I don't know how much longer I can conceal the utter contempt I feel at putting myself on exhibit. Once I set the outfit on the floor next to him, I moved to the showerhead.

By turning my back, I was able to garner a slight amount of self-respect. I adjusted the water to a comfortable temperature, and then lifted the shampoo from the plastic tub. Just in case I wanted to lather a second time, I left the lid off the bottle. Then I worked it in thoroughly, starting to rinse when a nearby footstep reached my ears. "Look at me, seven forty-two," he said.

It took tremendous strength not to spin, but to casually turn. He was naked, his clothes hanging on a wall hook close to the door. His excitement was disgustingly obvious. Something's strange. Why would he risk being seen this way? "I'm sorry, I don't understand. Why did you come into the shower?"

His smile grew. "I'm going to do much more than just come in the shower, my beautiful blank bimbo. For the next three days, I have you all to myself."

What does that mean? Is it what I think? "I'm sorry, I don't understand. What about Earl and Hank and Mark?"

A chuckle came from him as he leisurely looked my front over. "They're all gone," he said. "I'm the lone rooster in the hen house. You have no idea how happy you're about to make me. It would please me for you to come here."

On my first day out of Burksdale when I stopped at that bar, my instincts told me to leave. I didn't listen and here I am. Now my instincts are talking to me again only *this* time I'm paying attention. They're saying he's telling the truth, this isn't some sort of test or trick. He really is alone. They're also telling me one more thing; now.

CHAPTER 15

Shampoo oozed into my eyes while I plotted my next move. The sting forced them closed as I quickly rinsed my face and hair. Then as water cascaded down my back, I smiled seductively while slowly inching toward him.

"I only wish to please," I said.

What I was going to do, I didn't know. If I tried running past him, chances are he'd catch and kill me. I have to find a way to get his guard down, and then slip away.

His smile was unbelievable, his gaze staring at my upper thighs. As I drew close, he looked at my breasts, almost foaming at the mouth. *Oh* he's one sick bastard, but doesn't suspect a thing. With his vulnerable places exposed, a plan came to me. I pointed between his legs asking "Would it please you for me to touch you there?"

If I tried to hit or kick him, I'd have one chance. Should he block me I'm finished. If I grip his tender spots and squeeze as hard as I can, it might incapacitate him. His eyes drifted to my face, his nose flaring with desire.

"In a moment," he said. "For now it would please me for you to slowly turn around, with your hands on the back of your head."

Earl's warning about his touching me below the neck must be a legitimate threat. It's the only reason I can think why he hasn't pounced on me. Then I remembered the way he looked at my mouth, filling my entire body with revulsion. As I placed my hands the way he wanted and slowly turned, I searched for something to use as a weapon. Nothing other than soap, shampoo, and a plastic tub were here. "Oh baby that is SO sweet," he said. "It would please me for you to face me quickly, but keep your hands where they are."

Nausea threatened to overtake me thinking about what he was commenting on as I spun so fast it surprised him. "Whoa you really are anxious to please," he said. "Get on your knees."

In an effort at buying time, I lowered my hands to stare at him with a confused expression. "I'm sorry, I don't-"

"Damn it to hell! It would please me for you to return your hands to the back of your head and get on your knees now!"

His anger wasn't directed at me, but at his sexually motivated forgetfulness over the correct commands. There's no more time. The door is too far for me to escape, and I see no other recourse. May God forgive me for what I'm about to do.

With his irritated glare slowly dissolving watching me kneel, his enthusiastic expression returned once I was in his commanded position. "I hope you have gills," he said. "You're going to live here for the next three days. Now it would please me enormously for you to open your mouth."

While obeying him but closing my eyes, I began recalling his true nature. Even though the stench of his unwashed body assaulted my sinuses, I mentally returned to when I was locked in that pillory as he yanked my suit bottoms down, and began spanking me so hard splinters jammed in my wrists and neck. Anger grew at the same time he began fulfilling his fantasy. His excitement built, movements increased. I remembered the helpless man they brought before me, and how he tortured that poor soul before I fainted. Thoughts of the redhead repeatedly raped by him flooded me with unbridled fury as I allowed it to flare. Grotesque murmurs of pleasure gave me the final push. I took a deep breath, held it, and bit down as hard as I could. "Ah SHIT you bitch! Let me go!"

Hands painfully yanked the hair on the back of my head only for a moment. When he pulled me, I pulled him. Panic filled his rigid body. As he tried prying my jaws open, I scratched his hands and bit down harder. Then he moved one way and I the other. My teeth drew blood as I violently yanked my head to the side. Then I was free with something in my mouth. "Oh my God; oh shit! Look what you've done!"

Blood was spurting from between his legs as I quickly spat my mouth clean while backing away. Shocked terror changed to enragement as he frowned at me with clenched teeth. This is horribly wrong. My hopes for him to buckle in agony have failed.

"I'm going to kill you slowly," he said, and then headed toward his clothes.

If he gets there I will die. Adrenaline pumped through my veins, giving me incredible speed as I screamed madly while leaping on his back. He couldn't dodge me as I gripped his hair, wrapping my legs around his waist and biting deeply into his shoulder, my fingernails digging into his face and sides. His arms flailed trying to hit me. "God damn it, get off," he said.

Each swing he took, I quickly moved the intended target out of the way and caused new pain for him when I bit or dug my nails into a fresh area. When he tried prying my legs loose, I bit down so hard on his shoulder blade blood flowed freely. Then he began rushing backwards, moving us under the water spouts just before slamming me into the wall.

A thousand points of light filled my head, breathing became impossible. As I gasped for air, I fell to the floor. Water sprayed my lower belly for just a moment before a shadow stepped over me and sat on my belly. "I'm going to twist your filthy head off."

My breathing finally eased just as he grabbed my neck. I was only able to take in a partial breath before his angered grip cut off all supply. Water ran down his stomach to my chest and shoulders making my neck slippery. It wasn't enough to loosen his grip.

Pressure built inside my head, feeling like it was about to explode. His snarl intensified as his grasp tightened, my chokes now cut off. As I tried pulling his hands free, it was like a rusted-shut bear trap. Light started dimming, my head rolled to the left. There in the tub less than a foot away was the open bottle of shampoo. With the last amount of strength I had left, I grabbed it and squeezed it in his face. His hands immediately released me, allowing me to gulp air while coughing.

"Ah shit I'm going to make you suffer!"

Strength was slowly returning, making it possible for me to look at him. He'd ducked his face under the water spray, quickly removing the shampoo. In a few moments his eyes will be clear. There's only one chance left. As I formed a claw with my right hand, I scratched out with all strength toward his testicles. His attention was so focused on cleaning his face, he never saw it coming. Contact was made; a nail broke into him, three deep gashes formed after my hand cleared. He tumbled to the side moaning.

From somewhere deep inside, new energy revived me. I sprang to my feet, rushing toward the door. No sounds of water splashing proved he was still down. When I reached the hook holding his clothes, I removed them and tossed them into the hall. Before I could leave, hacking from Fred caused me to face him. As he kneeled with the water pummeling his shoulders, I stared at him smugly. "I'll send help once we're safe," I said, "even though you really don't deserve it."

His face became a mass of confusion as he slowly shook his head in disbelief. "H-How," he said, stopped to lower his head coughing, and then looked at me.

A smile grew on my face. This was the first legitimate one I've had since meeting Hank. "Would it please you to learn your treatments failed?" I asked.

My smile dropped. "You're pathetic; you all are. I'm going to send you to prison for so long my great grandchildren will be out of college before you're freed. Enjoy your watery cell. It's the last time you'll shower alone."

As he stared at me like he couldn't believe this happened, I casually turned away. My triumph gave me a feeling of invulnerability as I took a deep breath, and then stepped over the stoop. When I faced the room to close the door, danger was rapidly approaching. Fred had been sneaking up without making a sound. He was less than five feet away as I gripped the door edge and began pushing.

The air felt like syrup, slowing the movement of the door. He leapt into the air like a guided missile. An ugly sneer was on his face, his weakened appearance from before only a show. Both he and the door seemed to move impossibly slow, seconds feeling like minutes. I put all my weight behind the door, yet it still seemed to fight me. Just as he screamed, the door slammed shut with a click. Instantly a loud impact against it sent shock waves though my shoulder. As I slowly backed away, I prayed the door was locked. With my eyes widening, the knob rattled a few times, but the door remained closed. "Let me out of here you bitch!"

My heart was still racing as I backed completely across the hall, his pounding on the door kept me cringing. "If you let me out, I'll be merciful."

Maybe it was the life or death fight I just won, or possibly the giddiness of freedom just around the corner. It might even be something else that caused me to think his last statement was hilarious.

Laughter bordering on insanity filled the hall, apparently inspiring Fred to pound harder. "You'll never make it without me," he said. "Let me out and I swear I'll help."

He must think I'm still under the influence of those drugs. My head shook in disbelief as I moved closer. "Calm yourself," I shouted. "It'll be over soon."

"God damn it! Let me out!"

More pounding followed, and then a moment of silence before it loudly resumed. "Oh shit it won't stop bleeding," he said. "Let me out! I'm bleeding to death!"

In all of the excitement, I'd almost forgotten how I became free. Coppery tastes in my mouth made me gag, forcing me to quickly face the wall. As his beating continued, I threw up. More shouts came from the room, but I really didn't understand them. Sickness claimed all food I'd eaten, and then dry heaves took its place. His pounding slowed, his shouts stopped, and then all was silent. Slowly I regained composure, turning toward the door.

It remained quiet. I started walking toward it when I remembered the last time I thought he was finished and how he'd nearly gotten out. Rather than chance opening the room, I lifted my clothes from the floor and got dressed.

The hall remained eerily silent as I backed from the door, moving toward Fred's clothes. I felt like a grave robber searching through them considering Fred's last words, but he has what I need.

Looking through his pockets turned up some change, a wallet, his keys, and thank you God, his remote. He carried nothing else, so I walked to where I'd thrown up and dropped the clothes over the mess. My eyes wandered to the door at the far end and I started moving toward it, but Earls warning about hidden sensors coupled with my own experience involving the first cell reversed my direction.

We have three days before the others return. There's no immediate urgency to take risks. Though I want to put as much distance between me and this place as I can, there are other captives here. My first order of business is to set them free and hope Fugi will be appreciative.

Like a whisper in the wind, Fred's wallet seemed to call out. Curiosity over the contents momentarily rose to the front of my mind as I opened it. Pictures of a woman with two little boys were the first thing I saw. Good lord; does that mean he's married? How in the world could any woman fall in love with a monster like him? And what kind of parent would a pervert like Fred make? Even my father wasn't that bad. Then his driver's license grabbed my attention. His address shows a town in Ohio?

This is unreal. I was in North Carolina when they nabbed me. It can't be; it just can't be. I had to place my hand against the wall for a moment to let it sink in.

Either he had one heck of a commute or I've been transported across three states; unbelievable. Okay get over it. Even though it's almost finished, I can't afford the luxury of wasting time. The keys I placed in a pocket, and then looked at the remote.

It's a small black box without any letters on the four buttons. Just like I remember, some kind of strange language is on the back spelling words I don't know. Fugi's help is definitely needed. While holding the remote in my hand, I walked down the hall to the main chamber outside our cells, leaving the hall door open as I detoured to enter my room. Fred left Fugi's room so fast when he rushed to my aide during Hank's game I don't think he locked the door. If I'm wrong, I can always come back and get the keys. In case Fugi tries turning on me, I don't want her to have access to them as well as the remote. Eight steps into the room, the main chamber door shut with a bang.

So this was a test after all; one that horribly backfired on them. Or maybe they tired of Fred and decided to use me for their depraved purposes. Whichever the case I'm going to stand proud; I refuse to give them the pleasure of seeing me cower. At least this horrible nightmare will end soon.

Minutes ticked by without a sound. My attention remained focused on the back wall waiting for the jolt of intense pain. Nothing happened; these lowlifes are hoping to see me crumble. "What are you waiting for? Finish this you bastards!"

No footsteps, threats, or even laughs responded. It was absolutely quiet. They must want to see my expression as I die. I've had enough of their perversions. One way or the other, I want it over.

With a defiant smile on my face, I turned toward the open doorway. It was empty. Confusion built in my mind, causing me to carefully approach. When I looked out of the room, the main chamber was empty. What's going on? Surely they aren't afraid of me?

There's no place for them to hide, and I would've heard had they dashed into one of the rooms. For whatever reason, they must've run to the other hall. I have to know if they're waiting to spring a trap just when I think we've made it. As sick as these bastards are, that must be the plan.

Keeping as quiet as possible, I ran across the main chamber floor until arriving at the door. It was absolutely silent on the other side. I tried ten keys before finding the right one, and then yanked the door open. No one was waiting out there, grinning while holding his remote at me, and all the doors were closed. Even with the time I remained in my cell waiting for them to strike, they couldn't have gotten this far without my hearing. It doesn't make sense. Who slammed the door?

For now I have to maintain the real possibility someone else is toying with us, but I've got to keep moving. Once I pulled the door closed, I started walking toward the redhead's room. Then I stopped, remembering the hidden sensors in my old room and realized they might be in hers. This collar must go first.

Eerie silence permitted my steps to echo across the room as I walked to Fugi's door. This time I didn't worry about hiding the keys. If she turns on me and wins, she'd find them anyway. As I opened the door, she slowly looked at me.

She was naked and tied to the bed. One short glance at me formed an irritated expression followed by her closing eyes. "Who let you wander around?" She asked. "It would please me for you to go away."

"And it would please me for you to tell me how to get rid of this blasted collar."

Her eyes popped open staring at me in mass confusion. A smile grew on my face as I held the remote up for her to see. "Son, of, a, bitch," she said. "How'd you get that?"

As I lowered the remote, my smile dropped. "Suffice it to say I took advantage of a situation. Are there sensors around this door?"

Fugi just stared at me, her head shaking with an expression of disbelief. "SNAP OUT OF IT," I said. "Are there sensors around this door?"

The tone of my voice caused her to blink rapidly a few times before she faced the ceiling. "Very funny Hank," she said. "The game's over, come get your toy."

My patience was nearly spent. An angry exhale noisily exploded through my clinched teeth. "I'll give you one, more, chance," I said. "Fred is incapacitated and the others are gone. In three days they will return. I don't plan on being here when that happens. If you want to stay that's fine by me. I'll get the redhead and we'll be on our way. The choice is yours."

She faced me. "Assuming for the moment I believe you, why would you be willing to help me?"

I really don't want to, but is there a choice? "Because I need you as much as you need me. Now I want your solemn word. If I release you, will you help us all escape?"

A wicked smile grew on her face that sent shivers down my spine. "Yes; you were wise to remain in the doorway and not come in here."

That ominous compliment caused me to take an involuntary step backward. Her smile faltered until she realized I wasn't leaving. "Tell me how to take these collars off," I said.

Slowly she returned to watching the ceiling. "Now it's your turn," she said. "Give me your solemn word you'll release me if I help you."

Leaving her here for the authorities once my collar is off had entered my mind, but in case there are surprises around I quickly discounted it. As I held the remote up for her to see, she looked at me. "You have it," I said. "What do I do?"

For a few moments I didn't think she was going to tell me. Then she drew a deep breath and allowed the smile to fade. "This is *very* dangerous," she said. "If you don't do it exactly as I say, we'll both die. Can you tell the top from the bottom?"

To make sure I was holding it correctly, I flipped it over to check the lettering. "Yes," I said. "What language is this?"

"Russian; Earl has connections all over the world. Listen carefully to me. The top button places the collar to sleep, second from the top is stun, second from bottom is on, and bottom is kill. Are you sure you know which way is up?"

A look of impatience grew on my face. "I've handled it before," I said. "Earl tested me, which I'm sure you know how; satisfied?"

Her eyes developed wonder looking at me, and then changed back to seriousness. "Every time a collar is removed, two of us were needed just in case. If one slipped up, seconds counted. The other had to act immediately or death could not be averted. Push the top button, come in here, untie me, and I'll remove the collars."

Three chuckles escaped before I could prevent it. "I'm a quick study," I said. "Besides, at this point the only person I trust is me. Now how do I take these things off?"

She glared at me while slightly shaking her head. Her eyes closed, mouth moved saying something I couldn't hear, and then she looked at me. "Pray to whatever God you worship you get this right. Don't start anything until I've finished telling you the procedure. You'll need both hands. While keeping the top button down with the thumb of your hand holding the remote, use your other hand to press the bottom button for one second and release, wait a second; then hold the second from the top in for five seconds and release both buttons. This is critical; one second release; wait one second, and hold five release everything; otherwise a chain reaction begins that turns us into light bulbs. Have you got it?"

Why can't there be a simple unlock button? A deep sigh escaped as I scowled at her worried face. "Yeah, I got it; ready?"

My hands began trembling as I turned the device toward me. Fugi watched my movements with the intensity a cat guarding a mouse-hole. The pounding of my heart filled my ears with the sound of a drum like the start of a firing squad; then I began.

Fugi gritted her teeth watching my fingers move. First I held the top one down, pressed the bottom, released it, briefly waited and then pressed the next button. After counting to five, I let go of all buttons. Mechanical whirring sounds came from the back of my neck as an immediate rush of blood flowed under once restricted skin. A smile grew on her face as she nodded. I dug my fingers under the collar front and yanked it away leaving scrapes in its wake, letting it drop to the floor. My free hand began rubbing the area where the collar had been as I entered her room. She watched my progression with a gleam in her eyes. Once I was next to the bed, I looked at her without moving. "Before I untie you, I want to remind you of our agreement. As a show of good faith on my part, I'll take the collar off first."

Her eyes followed my every move, giving me a creepy feeling. The collar came off easier than mine; I wonder why? Still she remained silent and vigilant. Since I was next to her left hand, I untied it first. When it was free she immediately went to her right hand while I moved to her ankles. They were tied together, I only had one knot to deal with. She freed her hand before I was finished, lying in bed watching me. Finally I had it loose enough to remove the rope, but before I could get out of the way her right leg moved with incredible speed to clip my bottom jaw. Pain blossomed when my teeth clicked together, the room spinning as I started to fall.

"Sorry toots but I have other plans," Fugi said.

As I hit the floor hard, she jumped off the bed to sit on my stomach. Wooziness threatened for a few moments, giving her time to start patting my pockets. My head cleared when she found the one with the keys and began reaching inside.

My right hand formed a fist as I cold-cocked her on the side of her head. Obviously she wasn't expecting it; I caught her by surprise. When her balance was slightly thrown, I rolled to my side knocking her off. Then I jumped to my feet placing one foot on her throat. Her pitiful attempts at removing it failed. She was no match for me. That assault pushed me to the brink. Animal fury overtook my better judgment as I placed a great deal of weight on the leg, my teeth gritted together. "Tell me why I shouldn't finish you," I said.

All struggling stopped. Her expression changed to the calmness of someone completely at peace. It seemed she wasn't afraid to die. The serene expression softened my rage; I lifted my foot while back-stepping to a safe distance. She slowly rose, rubbing her neck while eyeing me suspiciously.

"I'll try this again," I said. "If I let you live, will you stop fighting me and help?"

A chuckle flowed from her as she took a step toward me. I answered it with a step toward her, my hands made into fists at my sides. We stared at each other for what felt hours until she broke eye contact looking to the floor. "Why should I?" She asked. "The moment we're free you'll turn me over to the police. I'd rather be dead."

That had been my plan all right. Then I started recalling how she went out of her way to avoid hurting both the redhead and me, and how her refusal to shoot the redhead resulted in Earl turning against her. It told me problems between them existed long before I arrived, possibly a testimony about her regrets over being here. "I'll make a deal with you," I said. "You help us escape; I won't tell the police who you really are. By the time they sort this all out you can be long gone."

She looked at me with a highly skeptical face. "How can I believe you?"

My fists opened. I looked at her with a softening expression. "I'm not the one who attacked. Besides, there's something different about you. You're not like the others. I give you my word; I won't try stopping you when we're out. Do we have a deal?"

As I lifted my right hand in truce, she stared at it briefly before accepting it.

"We'd better get moving," she said. "There isn't much time."

"We have three days."

Her head began shaking. "No, we don't."

CHAPTER 16

Staring at her suspiciously I asked "What do you mean?"

She walked toward the door without looking at me. "Based on what you said, Fred mentioned the three days. Am I right?"

Once she stepped into the main chamber heading to the exit door, I quickly followed her. "Yes, and I'm certain he wasn't lying. He was very, excited about it."

A chuckle acknowledged my answer as she continued walking. "Figures," she said. "That tells me they went hunting. The only way they'd do that is if they believed everything was under control. Six ninety-eight is lost, to be honest I thought the same about you, and I posed no real threat. By the way, were you faking the whole time?"

Chills coursed down my spine thinking about how those drugs enslaved me, and that they were out looking for innocent people to put through the same thing. She faced me with a curious expression. Her question gave me a combination of fear, sadness, and anger at the same time. "No," I said, "but I found a way to overcome it. Please continue. How much time do we have?"

Her face reflected wonder as she stared at me briefly before turning her back. "I'll tell you in the next hall," she said. "It's the orange key."

Obviously she wanted to leave the redhead behind. Rather than remove the keys from my pocket, I crossed my arms over my chest and stepped back.

"That girl, the one you called six ninety-eight, what's her name?"

Irritation was on Fugi's face as she turned to me. "I don't remember and it's irrelevant," she said. "She's gone. We have to keep moving or we will be as well!"

The lack of panic in her tone informed me the others weren't closing in on us. We still had time, though possibly not three days. "She's coming with us," I said.

Her face became frightening, like something out of a nightmare as she slowly walked within striking distance. "Let me explain the facts of life," she said. "Earl never hunts close by. He always drives for at least five hours. That way he remains above local police suspicion. Are you following me?"

When she paused, I turned away and walked to the girl's door. It was locked.

"If there are people in the midst of treatments, he always leaves someone behind to tend to them," she said. "Even though he never travels unless he feels safe in doing so, he still has a system. After they arrive wherever they're going, he calls. Then they sleep. He calls again when they wake up. And every so often he checks in. The times are set right down to the minute. Fred knew what time Earl was going to call. The real question remaining is did Fred come to see you before Earl's initial call or after it?"

It didn't take much thought to answer her question. "Afterwards; he woke me from sleep and was in no hurry for me to-; he wasn't in a hurry."

My face flushed as Fugi softened her expression. She approached me, placing her hand on my shoulder. "I don't know what you did to get free, but always remember you were justified," she said. "I had no love for Fred. He deserved whatever you did to him. And what you said about his waiting for the call makes sense, but it could still be debated that he ran down the moment Earl pulled off. Whatever the case, we have between five to ten hours to clear out and it's not going to be easy."

So far nothing she's said gives good reason why we all can't go. Does she have an ulterior motive? "That's plenty of time," I said. "Why don't you want her with us?"

Fugi picked up on my thinking she'd raped the girl and might be afraid of what was said. Her expression changed to near anger. "Drop the look," she said. "I never participated in their rampages. It's just you have no idea where we are. Would it surprise you to learn we're in the third underground level of a gigantic system of basements?"

Her head nodded as my eyes widened. "And that's not the best part," she said. "This level has four sections. We're in one of them, the shower is in another, various storage rooms are in the next, and then comes the real treasure; an electrified hallway ending with a magnetically sealed door. A code must be entered before the door can open, and the juice can only be turned off by a key in Earl's pocket. That means we go together. There is a great danger involved. In order to safely cross we must follow a narrow unmarked zigzag path. That path is hard enough to follow with a clear mind."

Everything she said caused me to start feeling lightheaded. It forced me to lean against the door looking at the ceiling. What kind of monsters built this formidable dungeon? Though her efforts were clearly designed to talk me out of freeing the girl, it only strengthened my resolve. When I looked at her with a determined expression, she appeared mad. "I don't care what the obstacles are," I said, "we're all leaving together. Got it?"

She gritted her teeth staring at me with seething rage. "If any one makes a wrong move in that electric hall, we all die! But let's just say for the sake of giggles we survive, and Earl comes waltzing down the trail before we're safe. We can't hide from him or even fight with six ninety-eight in tow. All he'd need to do is command her to rise or get in the way and we're finished! She is not coming with us."

Anger rose in me as I narrowed my eyes and snarled, making Fugi move back a step. Then I smiled patting the pocket with the keys. "You are *not* in a position to make demands," I said. "Either she comes with us or we stay with her."

My expression softened, changing into a more pleading one. "We're wasting time arguing. Which color key opens her door?"

A resigned sigh preceded her answer. "Blue; look for small dots near the top."

She started walking to the main door while I fished the keys out. Just like she said, small colored dots adorned the top of almost every key. It didn't take long to find the blue one, and then I had the door open. Oh my God; no wonder Fugi tried talking me out of opening this room. Those monsters have it set up like something out of the Spanish Inquisition.

The girl was naked in a bed that looked more like a rack, tied spread-eagled to wheels at both ends. Those bastards had her pulled so tightly her muscles were like taut strings. Two powerful spot lights on nearby poles were shining on her so close they created sweat. She must've been delirious from the heat. When I entered, she didn't even acknowledge my presence. "It's okay," I said, "I'm going to get you out of here."

Her eyes stared at the ceiling, not moving as I looked under the bed. Just like my first cell, an outlet was on the floor with two plugs. It took a little stretching, but I reached them to yank out the wires. Semi-darkness indicated my success.

"The wheel locks are on the other side of the bed," Fugi said. "I'll get her feet."

That sudden appearance startled me momentarily, but when I saw the absolute remorse on her face, it made me feel slightly better about my agreement not to turn her in. By working together we had the girl free from her bonds, but she just remained on her back.

"It would please me for you to sit up," Fugi said.

Instantly the girl obeyed and my anger flared. "Don't you ever say that to her again," I said.

Fugi appeared apologetic but didn't back down. "It's the only way to get her to respond," Fugi said. "She'll never be able to think for herself."

"Yeah? Well we'll see about that!"

As I dropped to my haunches close to her face, she looked at me. The absolute blankness in her stare made me shiver. "Do you understand me?" I asked.

Her head tilted slightly as a smile grew on her face. How she could appear happy so soon after being tortured astonished me. "Yes," she said. "Are you my new mistress?"

I felt sick. It took a few moments before I could respond. "No honey, I'm not." I briefly glanced at Fugi. "And neither is she, or anyone else for that matter. You are your own woman."

A look of total confusion crossed her face as Fugi shifted her feet. "Seven, I mean Joyce," Fugi said. "She doesn't understand. You're going to have to trust me on this. There's no more time. We've got to move now."

That little tongue-slip regarding me indicates Fugi can't be trusted, but I fear she may be right about this poor girl. We simply don't have time to help her recover. Calling her a number would be an insult, one that I refuse to do.

"Fugi go into my room next door and bring the water bottle and fruit basket here," I said. "We can't go anywhere until she's stronger."

For a moment it looked like Fugi was going to argue, but then sighed and left. I returned my attention to the girl when we were alone. "I want you to think about this," I said. "Go back to before you were brought here. Do you remember your name?"

She smiled so innocently I wanted to cry. "I'm R six ninety-eight, but everyone calls me six ninety-eight."

Tears formed in my eyes as I shook my head. Fugi returned, watching from the doorway holding the two items. "No, it isn't," I said. "I swear to you, I will see to it you receive the best possible help when we're out of here."

A single tear ran down my cheek as I rose. Then sadness turned to fury as I faced Fugi. "You did this to her," I said, "How can you live with yourself?"

Fugi's face reflected regret for a second before hardened determination returned. "It's a long story how I got involved here," she said. "Believe me when I say I wasn't happy. Why do you think I'm here with you and not out with them? And I really don't give a damn what you think about me, but if we don't start moving none of us will get away."

My head shook in disgust as I slowly looked at the girl. She was still smiling sweetly. As much as I hate doing this, I remembered what it was like being enthralled under those drugs and what needed to be said. "I refuse to call you a number," I said. "It would please me for you to accept-, Hope, as your name, and for you to remember everything."

"Yes ma'am," she said. "I am now Hope and will remember everything."

Oh how I want to hurt something. It took incredible energy for me to remain calm. "Very good Hope," I said. "My name is Joyce, and she's Fugi. Now I want you to eat some of the fruit and drink the water slowly while we're gone. Stay in this room until we return. We'll be back in a few minutes."

Fugi loosed a loud explosive breath as she entered the room. "Do you want them to catch us?" Fugi asked. "Or is it you really want to die?"

"Put the stuff on her bed and come with me outside," I said.

Without waiting for a response I brushed past her, nearly colliding in the process. She must've thrown the items on Hope's bed as quickly as she was standing before me in the chamber. Her face was red with rage, her eyes showing the intensity of a warrior. Mine reflected quiet resolve in spite of my true feelings.

"We do not have time to play nurse," she said. "Have you forgotten everything I told you?"

Even though I really want to finish the fight she began in her room, we need her. That's the only reason I'm not smashing her head into the floor. "First off, calm down," I said. "Now, we need clothes from the storage room. Are they in the hall you mentioned?"

It looked like I jabbed her in the chin, the way her head jerked back. "Well, yes; how did you know?"

A smile grew on my face. "It's simple," I said. "I didn't pack these clothes or that bathing suit I wore before. Plus Hope had a similar outfit meaning there's a supply kept nearby for convenience. We need them. I don't want to be seen with two naked women."

That last statement made me think for a moment. Hope I can understand, but how Fugi is able to act normal while nude made me wonder about her. It's like she doesn't care. Had it been me naked, my first order of business would be finding clothes. She glanced at me and then her chest, looking back at me with a lopsided grin that favored her right side. "To tell the truth," she said, "this isn't my body. I feel like I'm wearing a woman's costume and not really nude. But you're right. I don't want to be seen in public like this. It would be difficult to slip away. Let's hurry it up."

Though what she said about her lack of modesty might make sense, it still didn't quell my concerns over her sincerity. Thankfully it was like she could read my mistrust of her, stepping away as I removed the keys from my pocket. She made it comfortable for me to turn my back. The key slid easily in the lock and then we were on our way. After walking a few steps in silence, she glanced at me out of the corner of her eye.

"Had you tried stepping into the next hall before removing Earl's, *jewelry*," she said, "sensors around the doorway would've brought you down. Even if a collar is asleep, the signal sent will trigger the tamper guard. Before I forget, what did you do to Fred?"

Ironically enough, our progress had us next to the shower room when she asked. My head tilted in the direction of that door as we walked past it. "He's in there," I said.

Fugi noticed his clothes lying in a heap, looked closely at my neck, glanced at the shower room door, and then started grinning again. "That must've been some kind of war," she said. "I attributed the neck bruising to how roughly you yanked the collar off. Is he dead?"

We'd arrived at the end of the hall. Her question brought mental echoes of his pounding and pleas to the front of my mind. Shivers coursed through my body that I didn't worry about concealing.

"When you're ready to talk I'll listen," she said; "orange key."

The genuine compassion of her voice came though clearly. Her previous statement about not being happy here began making me think she might have become trapped and couldn't find a way out. As I opened the door, I looked at her closely, which in turn caused her to look at me. "He said he was dying, but I don't know," I said. "He tried to trick me before I got out and nearly caught me. That's why I didn't open the door to see if he was dead; for now that's all I'll say. But what about you; how did you become involved with those bastards?"

Fugi glanced at the shower door, looked at my arms, and then started grinning. "You don't have any real fighting skills or training, do you?" She asked.

Why would she ask that and not answer me? Deep concerns began forming in my mind. Even though I threw a round-house punch that stunned her, she's right. I have no formal training in self-defense. It also seemed like an evasion to my question. "I know enough" I said. "Why do you ask?"

Her grin didn't falter as she stepped into the next hall. Without looking at me she said "I'm not plotting against you. I'm only trying to picture how someone half Fred's size could put him down. No offense, but your arms give you away yet you bested a man who works out on a regular basis. To say I'm astonished would be an understatement."

Once she moved through the opening, I could see into the next hall. Ten wooden doors, five on each side, caught the breath in my throat. Another steel door identical to the other hall separators was at the far end. My God it's incredible. "This is all underground?" I asked. "Do you know who built it?"

My questions seemed to hit her back. Her step faltered briefly before continuing toward a specific door in the middle. "Though I'm not the one who dug it out, I guess you could say I'm responsible," she said. "It's part of my long story. Tell you what, you explain how you got past Fred, and I'll tell you my story on our long walk out of here."

Anger instantly flared causing me to form fists. Plans to tear her apart grew in my mind as I stepped through the doorway, quickly marching to where she was standing in front of a door. My breaths left in enraged puffs. She faced me when I arrived; wearing one of the most sorrowful expressions I've ever seen. It wasn't bragging. She was performing a confessional. My heated fury began calming just looking at her. Then she drew a deep breath while facing the door. "Purple key," she said.

When my head cooled, I processed all her words. Why did she say something about walking? I guess in order to get her to talk freely I have to do my own confessional. My attention fell to the floor as I said "Fred climbed in the shower naked. I bit him in a, vulnerable place. He may have bled to death."

Her legs indicated she'd turned to me; her hand touching my shoulder drew my attention. "You did what you had to do," she said. "On behalf of my part in your being abducted, I'd like to say I'm truly sorry."

A soft smile formed as she held out her right hand in friendship. With the exception of two times, Fugi always looked regretful at what was happening. There's more to her than being a criminal trying to escape. Even though I fooled my father with phony sorrow, my instincts told me she was legitimately apologizing. I decided to give her a chance and accepted her hand. Once we released she said "We need to get moving. There's about five miles we have to cover before we can call for help."

There she goes with the walking again. It makes no sense. "You said Earl checks in by phone," I said. "Why can't we call for help?"

"I wish we could," she said. "Earl assigned each of us a hiding place for our cell phones. None of us knew where the other's was located, and you can bet my spot is empty. It was to be used only when one remained behind while the others were out."

She glanced past me, staring at the wall to my rear like she was seeing something else. "Right after I teamed with Earl, a guy named Phil started talking about how ridiculous Earl's precautions were. No slave would ever manage to get above ground until the treatments were finished and they were being transferred. It was like he wanted me to agree with him when he told me precisely where he hid his phone. Hank was eavesdropping which also meant Earl found out. Judgment was swift. Phil is now one of Pinkerton's transsexual prostitute slaves in Las Vegas, or transies as she calls them."

This is becoming more unbelievable by the minute. How many men were forced to undergo Earl's decision of a sex change? At least now I know where some of them are. Once we're clear of this mess, I'm going to shut Pinkerton down for good.

Fugi stood next to me watching as I found the right color key. Her face developed a strange appearance of gritted-teeth concentration as I placed the key in the lock. A loud gasp came from her just as I started to turn. "STOP," she said.

She grabbed my arm tightly, yanking me ferociously. That move caught me by surprise. I stumbled away from the door, leaving the keys dangling. As I prepared to fight her, she moved away from the door still deep in thought. "Why'd you do that?" I asked.

Her eyes focused on me, a look of enragement on her face. "Damn it to hell," she said, "I nearly forgot. What is *wrong* with me? You came within one twist to killing us!"

As I looked from her to the door, doubts rose in my mind. What is she up to? Is there something inside that room she doesn't want me to see? "Explain why you pulled me off the door," I said.

Something was obviously shaking her up. She positioned herself between me and the door, but did not look at the keys. "The doors in this hall are all booby-trapped," she said. "There's enough plastic explosive inside each one to splinter the wood, sending out large shards like bullets. What the concussion doesn't kill, the flying wood finishes off. Turning the knob either direction acts as an electrical detonator. Shit how could I have forgotten that?"

Even though she's the one in need of clothing which lends credence to her warning, I still had a hard time believing what she said. "Why," I asked, "why would anyone do this?"

Concern changed to sadness on her face. Her shoulders shrugged while glancing to the floor. "It is part of my long story," she said. "Earl put these in after an ambush that began in several of these rooms nearly took his life. We can only get inside by keeping the knob still with one hand and turn the key with the other. If the door closes while you're inside, there's no safe way for you to open it which is why they're here. To this day Earl hasn't figured out how they got in, thus he insured no more surprises could leap from this hall."

Everything here seems to be part of her so-called long story. Who is she? "Okay I think it's time you tell me your long story," I said. "How do you know Earl so well?"

She turned to the door so quickly I had no time to react. When I grabbed her shoulder, the door was open and keys in her hand. As my grip intensified, she simply held the keys over her shoulder for me to take. Then she reached inside the room and threw a switch. Dozens of rows of clothes-racks took my breath away.

Good lord this looked more like a clothing store than a storage room. Some appeared to be men's clothes, but most were female. Underwear, bathing suits, jeans, and see-through blouses hung from hundreds of hangers. Fugi watched my reaction, an indeterminate expression on her face.

"This whole thing keeps getting more confounding by the moment," I said. "I expected some but not this many. My lord there's enough here to clothe a small army. What is the purpose for all these outfits?"

"People come in different sizes. If you look closely, you'll notice how most of them are identical to what you're wearing. Every now and then Earl uses transportation methods requiring attire that won't draw the attention of an institution jumpsuit. That's why there're also jeans and tee shirts."

My mind was spinning to the point I had to lean against the frame. Fugi placed her hand on my shoulder, looking at me with concern. "Are you all right?" She asked.

I shook my head as I drew a deep breath. "No; but I will be as soon as we get out. Is the door to the last hall armed?"

Her expression changed to confusion. "No; that would be too dangerous. If the electricity started arcing, it would hit the knob and blow out this hall. That could cause a chain reaction that-"

I started walking toward the door asking "What color key?"

In spite of my head-start, she still caught up to me quickly placing her hand on my shoulder. "You can't go in there," she said.

As I continued walking, I looked at her. "I have no intention of going in there yet. What color key?"

For a moment it looked like she wasn't going to say. Then she sighed. "Black; but don't even step in the doorway."

How fitting a black colored key would open a hallway of death. The key was easy to find; slightly larger than the others. Once the door opened, lights instantly flickered on. My mouth dropped open at what I saw.

Crisscrossing the walls and ceiling were thick single-strand silver wires intersecting to form small rectangles. This entire hall looked like a gigantic crossword puzzle without any blackened squares. Hundreds of wires were evenly spaced apart and ran perpendicular to the floor, over the wall and ceiling to the next side, while hundreds more ran parallel to the floor from one end to the other. The floor had thick metal grating that looked like large square drain covers running from wall to wall the entire length. We need shoes. Before I turned away, a door in the middle of the hall caught my attention.

"What's in that room?" I asked.

"Earl's museum of his past; every time he shot someone, he used a different gun. He made plaques with the names of all his famous kills and keeps the gun stored underneath. Before you ask, yes there's ammunition for each gun but no, we can't get to them. He has the only key to the room."

That explains the question I had about the gun Fugi brought to Earl when they planned on shooting Hope. I just know the police are going to love learning about Earl's egomania room. It may solve many mysteries.

"Okay let's go," I said. "We have a lot of work to do. I didn't see any shoes in that room. Are they somewhere else?"

Fugi shook her head. "No; Earl didn't see the need for storing shoes down here."

That's going to make things difficult, but not impossible. "Please tell me there are some tools in one of these rooms," I said.

She looked at me like I was going insane. "Yes, small tools; nothing that can be used as a weapon. Why?"

Relief flooded over me, bringing a smile to my face. "Okay this is what we have to do," I said. "Find suitable clothing for you and Hope, plus make covers for our feet using jeans. We can't risk walking around outside in our bare feet. Now I have one more question which I really hope you say yes. Did Earl keep wooden doors or building supplies in any of these rooms?"

Anger replaced confusion as she stared at me.

"Tools, doors; are you planning on building an addition down here? We're wasting precious time!"

"Please answer me," I said while starting to walk to the clothes room.

A disgruntled sigh filled the air as she fell in behind me. "No," she said. "There's absolutely no doors, plaster, carpeting, nails, curtains, or paint in any of these rooms. Are you sure those drugs aren't affecting you?"

Her question made me chuckle as I stepped into the room. "I'm fine but I'm not so sure about you no offense," I said. "You almost forgot about a bomb that would have killed us. I'd hate to get halfway down that electric hall only to find out you made a zig instead of a zag. What causes the electricity to start arcing?"

She ran in front of me, and placed her hands on her hips. The look on her face was one of fury. "If you so much as push one of the grate-edges to a ground, all hell breaks loose! The only way to get across that hall is by following the path."

That attempt at blocking me failed as I stepped around saying "It is pressure sensitive only in specific areas then."

Her hand on my shoulder stopped me. "Yes it is," she said. "Where are you going with all this?"

The tone of her voice was like that of a schoolteacher reprimanding a problem student. It brought a smile to my face, which made her look more concerned. "If I understand how electricity works, the only way an arc forms is if it can jump from one conductive surface to another," I said. "What would happen if that arc was buried beneath a non-conductive element like a solid wooden door?"

A smile formed on her face, followed by a frown. "In theory, it wouldn't go anywhere," she said. "Rubber between the grating and walls prevents accidental discharges while walking the path. Whatever is on top of the door would be safe. If you're talking about what I think, we don't have time to remove any doors!"

"You'd better wear a bra," I said. "If things get heated and you have to move quickly, I think you'd find the support to be worthwhile."

Before I could move past her, she stepped in front again looking prepared to kill. "You can kid around all you like," she said, "but you'd better damn well listen to me. It's your only chance to live! Earl *will* come after us; count on it. He's the very best at hunting people down and his aim is unreal. Once he gets you in his sights it's over. If we're anywhere other than the safety of far from here when he returns, we'd be better off hopping on those electrical wires. Now we have at best nine hours before he walks down this hall, possibly as little as five. I want to be out of here in fifteen minutes while you want to remodel! This isn't fiction where everyone lives happily ever after girlie; it's real life with deadly consequences!"

My humor fled the instant she started talking down to me like my father. The look on my face caused her to step back. "Don't you EVER speak to me like that again," I said. "You think I don't know what's going on here? I have been kidnapped, humiliated, threatened, drugged, and told by Earl he thinks I need to be terminated when he returns." A chuckle escaped. "I was already ON his death list *BEFORE* I fought Fred! Plus those drugs work with frightening efficiency. It's only by the grace of God I was able to regain my identity and I do NOT want to go through that again. No one, not even you, wants to get out of here more than me. But I want to get out alive. The three of us can have the two wooden doors from the other hall down and the knobs and hinges removed within an hour. Then we can stand on one while sliding the other across the floor and be gone thirty minutes later. Without them, one wrong step in that hall will kill us."

Her eyebrows were up, her taut muscles appearing ready to run. I took a deep breath and allowed a small smile to form while exhaling. "We'll still have three and a half hours to walk five miles, worst case scenario," I said. "Even with make-shift slippers on our feet, there'd be plenty of time for us to be safely sipping wine in a nice cozy restaurant watching the news about Earl's arrest. Together we can do it but alone we will fail. I need your help, so does Hope. Otherwise like you said, we might as well hop on those wires. What do you say?"

Silence sounded deafening as we looked at each other. Tension mounted to the point it felt like a wall was going to blow out. Then she started grinning. "I knew there was a reason for me to make my move," she said. "For over eighteen years I've been trapped doing things I deplored. Much as I hate to admit it, I was afraid to do anything about it. Then I saw how you bravely faced situations others before you have cowered, and it gave me the strength to change. For that I thank you."

My face reddened as I started to turn away, but her hand on my shoulder returned my attention. A gentle smile grew as she said "I'm not done. It isn't my intention to embarrass you, but I want to finish.

The fact we're standing here having this discussion is testimony to your determination. Your wisdom is beyond your years, your calm courage inspirational. Who am I to question such intelligent logic like you've presented? As you said let's go. We have a lot of work to do."

CHAPTER 17

Even though her compliments could be a ploy of some sort, I can't let that worry me. Every minute counted. We must assume our time is limited to five hours. A sense of urgency filled the clothes room as Fugi went one way and I the other. My target was six pairs of jeans, while she went off in search of two jumpsuits and underwear. She pointed me in the right direction and was already standing in the hall dressed before I'd finished.

"The wooden doors appear smooth enough for us to walk across barefoot," I said. "That'll give us better traction while we slide them. We should wear the jeans around our necks until we're outside and then wrap our feet."

Her nod preceded our walk to another room containing tools. "Purple again," she said. "Do you remember how to open the doors?"

It's time to see if she can be trusted. I need to know what side she'll be on if Fred comes dancing out the shower room when we open it. The jeans dropped to the floor as I held out the keys. "You'd better do it," I said.

She accepted them without as much as a blink. In a moment the door was open with the light on. Then she turned, holding the keys out for me.

"I know keeping these will make you feel better," she said, "so I want you to. And I want to thank you again."

Why is she thanking me for feeling unsure about her? "For what?"

A smile crossed her lips as she handed me the clothes she held and turned to enter the room. "For helping me find what I thought was gone," she said. "I will tell you my story once we're out of here, but don't forget to keep an eye open for all traffic. If you see a black van off in the distance, start running."

That made me think of something I should have asked by now. Is my forgetting it really a sign of those drugs working against me? "Does Fred have a car?" I asked.

Some of the keys had no color markings, appearing like vehicle and house keys. Fugi's shaking head crushed that hope. "He has a car," she said, "but we can't get to it. Just before Earl goes off, the person selected to guard the captives drives his car to a parking lot with Hank following. The car is left in the lot until they return. That guarantees the guardian won't slip away at a critical moment. And this is why I said we can't get to it. For as long as I've been here, Earl always uses the same place. It's further than the gas station we're going to visit."

Fugi entered the room, leaving me to my thoughts. I'm beginning to understand how Earl has been so successful all these years. He planned for nearly every contingency.

Loud sounds of items being shifted and heavy boxes smacking the floor returned my attention to the room. It resembled a true storage compartment with shelves lining every wall and a few cabinets on wheels. Fugi came out grinning, holding three screwdrivers, a wrench, and a claw hammer which she swung a few times. "I feel a little better," she said. "In three months I'll be back, but now my muscles are too weak to be of any good. All my Tae Kwon-Do training is useless. This hammer equalizes things at close range. Now if you're ready, let's get Hope."

This was a remarkable change. She had a weapon that could easily kill me, yet it looked like the thought never entered her mind. Plus she just called the redhead the name I chose instead of those numbers. Without saying another word, we turned together walking down the hall. A question rose that began nagging me until I drew a breath, glanced at her from the side of my eye, and asked. "You thanked me for helping you find something you thought was gone. What did you mean?"

A sparkle was in her eye as she glanced at me. After we entered the next hall, a smile grew on her face. "My humanity; for that I'm in your debt. But let's not get all mushy, okay? We have to keep focused."

I don't know if mushy would be the word I'd use, more like relieved. Granted I've only known her a short time, but there seems to be a spring to her step in spite of the dangerous task ahead. She appears happier than when I first saw her. That leads me to believe she is sincere in her gratitude. Since she really did me no harm other than be at the wrong place at the wrong time, I decided to take a chance. The steel door between us and the chamber loomed in front. It was closed. Rather than go for the keys, I placed my hand on her shoulder. "I accept your apology," I said.

My hand came off her shoulder, held out in a gesture of friendship. She looked at it, and then me. Tears lined her eyes as she shook it. Her mouth opened, closed, and then she drew a deep breath while releasing me. "If we make it out of here," she said, "I'd like to consider you a friend. Do you think that's possible?"

That is something I hadn't considered, thinking we'd go our separate ways after this. Could I ever really think of someone with a criminal background as friend?

People make mistakes. She did talk about unhappiness and being trapped into something she didn't like. Though my chin is still sore from where she tried overpowering me, I think that was an act of desperation. Had the roles been reversed I might've done the same. Anyone can unwittingly get involved with the wrong crowd and then find it difficult to change. They can change, but only by finding the courage to do so. A smile growing on my face caused one to form on hers. "I would be honored to call you friend," I said. "But only if you stop talking like you think we won't make it. I will never stop until I see Earl behind bars."

Her smile changed to that lopsided grin as she faced the door. "Your terms are acceptable," she said.

When I moved the clothes to one arm so I could reach in my pocket for the keys, I remembered the door mysteriously slamming before. "Didn't we leave this open?" I asked.

She appeared unconcerned, her shoulders shrugging, but I turned to look the other way. All doors were open leading to the one outside the electric hall. "I guess not," she said.

Simple hinges adorned the edge. No indication of a closing mechanism was seen. Maybe it's out of alignment or something, or Hope may have closed it. If Fugi isn't concerned, it must be okay. Suddenly a foreboding sensation befell me, almost like a sixth sense. What if Fred somehow managed to get out of the shower room and was waiting for us on the other side? "Just in case," I said, "keep that hammer ready."

Her expression was one of confusion as she glanced at me with raised eyebrows, but then moved the handle up like she was prepared to drive in nails. When I fit the key in the lock, she raised the hammer over her head. The door pulled open without a struggle, no one was there. She lowered the hammer, looking at me with growing concern. "I was sure we left this door open," I said. "Until we're out of here, I'm not going to assume the only danger we face is what we see."

A grin crossed her face as she stepped over the threshold, looking the entire room over. Then she moved aside, allowing me entry. "Now I know we're going to make it," she said. "What I don't think of, you will."

It relieved me for her to take that attitude instead of thinking I was delusional. We have to keep alert at all times. She jogged to her old room, looking in as I walked toward Hope's. Fugi rushed to my room just before I reached my destination. Then we arrived at the same time in front of the room only to see Hope cowering in the corner. The clothes fell from my hand as I ran to her. "What's wrong?" I asked.

Tears streaked her face as she looked at me. "Please don't hurt me," she said. "I'm sorry. I didn't mean to."

Why is she acting this way? It's no big deal she closed the door. Fugi sighed deeply, looking sorrowful again. "It's okay Hope," I said. "Nobody is ever going to hurt you again."

Her body was visibly shaking as she raised her arm to point at the bed. A small piece of banana was sitting on top of the mattress. "I didn't know where to put it," she said. "I'm sorry. I promise not to do it again."

Fugi placed her hand on my shoulder, pulling me away. When we were by the door, she started speaking softly. "That's why she's here. Apparently she spilled something on her master and he became enraged. When he went to punish her, she cowered away. Earl's successful transfers are supposed to be willing to commit suicide at a command. Her desire for self-survival indicated something went wrong."

Seething rage formed as I wanted to tear this building apart, but then the calming influence of logic slowly replaced my frown with a smile. "Don't you see?" I asked. "Nothing went wrong, it went right. She's starting to remember. If only I knew what would push her over the edge."

A light started shining behind Fugi's eyes as a smile grew. "You may just be right," she said. "Damn I wish I could remember her name!"

"Think hard on it," I said. "For now we have to convince her we're not going to hurt her."

She remained balled-up in the corner, violently shaking when we approached. I can't even begin to imagine what her life was like, but I can change it starting now. "It's okay sweetie," I said. "Nobody is going to punish you. Did you have enough food?"

Fugi withdrew deep in thought, quietly mumbling names and shaking her head. That self-whispering brought Hope's attention away from the floor looking at her and then me. A gentle smile rose on my face as I held my hand to her. At first she cringed, but when she saw I was waiting patiently, she gradually accepted it. Her trembling diminished; she stood. Uncertainty about what we were going to do next was obviously in her thoughts, but a bigger smile from me seemed to quell the last of her anxiety.

"Y-Yes ma'am," she said. "I had enough food. What would you like me to do now?"

"I'VE GOT IT!" Fugi said.

That loud exclamation nearly sent Hope back to a terrified ball pulling me with her. "Your name is Penelope Ashton Carver but you go by Penny" Fugi said. "You're originally from Virginia Beach, Virginia. Oh man I can't remember the name of your parents, but you were kidnapped outside a bar near the oceanfront a little over three years ago. Do you remember any of this?"

For a brief moment, it looked like a spark ignited behind her eyes but it quickly went out. "I only wish to please," she said. "I'm sorry, but I don't remember."

Even though I maintained my smile, inside I was crying for her. Fugi began mumbling again, and it took a few minutes for me to build strength so I could speak without breaking up. "Honey," I said, "it would please me very much if you now accept Penny as your name, and concentrate on everything Fugi told you."

Oh how I remember that false feeling of joy you get when you're under those drugs and someone says something will please them. Her entire appearance changed, like she was ecstatic. "Yes ma'am," she said. "My name is now Penny and I will concentrate on everything Fugi told me."

My lower lip quivered, I had to turn away.

"It would please me for you to get dressed and then meet us in the next room," Fugi said.

"Yes ma'am."

As Fugi walked by, her hand tugging on my arm sent a signal she wanted to talk. My God that poor girl, her mind is gone. All I want to do is cry. Everything began feeling like a nightmare, my legs rubbery as I followed Fugi out. When we were away from Penny's door, Fugi spun and slapped my face hard. Instantly my fists formed and teeth gritted; a snarl unlike any I've felt before rumbled in my throat. "You'd better have one MIGHTILY good reason for doing that," I said.

The hammer and screwdrivers fell from her hands; she kicked them out of reach. Then she took on a martial arts stance I've only seen in the movies. "You can probably kill me right now," she said, "but if it takes a fight to snap you out of that damnable pity, then let's have at it."

My breathing accelerated as rage nearly overtook. She remained perfectly still, closely watching me. Her words finally sank in, my fists opening. While holding her stance she said "Good. Do not lose sight of our objective. We can cry later. Now we must remain focused. It's the only chance Penny will ever have of finding a better way. I owe her that much and refuse to allow self-wallowing to jeopardize it. Have I made myself clear?"

Astonishment replaced slowly dissipating anger. This was about as far a reverse in attitude as I've ever seen. Less than twenty minutes ago she wanted to leave Penny behind and now she's willing to fight for her. Stinging on my cheek made my hand involuntarily massage it as a smile formed. "You are amazing," I said. "But you didn't need to slap me so hard!"

Her position relaxed. "Yes, I did. Pain directs attention to its source. You looked like you were falling apart and we don't have that luxury."

As I continued rubbing my jaw, sounds of walking from Penny's room brought both our attentions. "I was," I said, "but if it happens again, try talking first okay?"

A half-grin formed on her face as she glanced at me, and then Penny stepped into the room. The innocent smile on her face showed little, if any, improvement. Fugi's right; first we get out and then work with her. "Penny," I said, "we're leaving this place. It would please me for you to come with us."

Fugi moved to gather the tools as Penny came to me, smiling like a child opening presents. Once Fugi was back, we entered the next hall. Before we started walking Fugi nodded her head toward the large overhead door. "We need something from there," she said; "yellow key."

This was becoming monotonous. Fugi has proven she can be trusted. Rather than waste any more time, I held the keys out for her. "You keep them," I said. "It'll save time."

A grin grew as she accepted them. "Maybe I should slap people more often," she said.

I chuckled while Penny just stared with the smile. When Fugi faced the door, her mood seemed to darken. As she placed the key in the handle, she looked at me. "I hope you have a strong stomach," she said.

Oh dear God what's in there? Before I could ask, Fugi yanked the door up and stepped inside. Shortly afterward numerous ceiling lights illuminated a cavernous room, reflecting off gigantic machines that looked like industrial baking ovens. Exhaust pipes ran to the ceiling. I started feeling queasy as I realized this was where Earl cooked his human dog food.

"There's something you should know," Fugi said. "I'd hate for it to be used against you later. As you've probably guessed, this is where Earl cooks all his victims once they've been ground to bits with this." She pointed toward another large machine on wheels. "Not all were cooked to a dry food. Pieces were used to feed his captives."

Memories of those plates with strange meat flooded my mind with sickening clarity. Bile rose in my throat, forcing me to gag. I quickly turned away heaving against the wall. Fugi placed her hand on my shoulder, patiently waiting for me to look at her. "I'm so sorry," she said, "but when this becomes public knowledge, I wanted you to be prepared."

My sides ached. After I gasped a few more times, I glared at her with the same rage I'd felt when she slapped me. "Is this why you brought us in here?" I asked.

"No; there's a cart in here we can use to move the doors down the halls. I really didn't want to tell you, but I knew sooner or later you'd find out. Then you might think I hid this from you for a reason and never forgive me."

She appeared extremely depressed as she turned to walk into the room. Lingering pains made my body quiver just watching her move. Squeaking wheels filled the air, and soon she was pushing an open four-wheeled cart with a rear handle toward me.

"Is there anything I can do to make you feel better?" Penny asked.

Fugi stopped the cart, looking at Penny with amazement. That expression coupled with Penny's concern helped me start recovering. "I'll be okay in a few minutes, thanks."

Penny worriedly watched me rise. Fugi resumed pushing the cart, but stopped just before the doorway. "Penny, would you wait for us by the shower door?" Fugi asked.

Her smile returned as she nodded and walked out of the room. Fugi watched her departure with her own growing smile. When Penny was across the hall, Fugi leaned close to me. "I'll be damned, independent thinking" she said. "She's almost there. You were right. She is remembering!" Then Fugi's face changed to a more serious expression. "I know I told you the monster of all shock, but you have to get over it. Never forget you had no idea and that they forced you. Focus on making them pay for it."

As I glanced at her with my wits returning, a smile grew. "Thanks," I said; "I'd rather hear this news from a friend than anyone else."

The look of relief that washed over her was so profound it moved me. One thing I learned long ago was if you want to maintain a flow of information never shoot the messenger. Plus I realized she'd never brought any food to me and in all likelihood was abhorred by the practice. Her reluctance at telling me followed by concern for my well-being afterwards proves it. "Let's move," I said.

Penny's attention was toward the door, not our squeaking approach. Water was flowing from beneath the bottom jamb trickling to the drain out here. This flow wasn't present the last time we went by. Sure I'd left the shower running, but I thought the drain in that room would've kept it under control. Obviously something is plugging it up. Then erratic thumping against the door was heard when Fugi stopped pushing the cart. There was no pattern, more like a heavy object bouncing against it. "That's creepy," Fugi said.

Water spilling into the hall drew my attention away from the sounds. It seemed to rise momentarily higher along the sides, spilling down slightly and rising again. Based on what I saw, it looks like the room is flooded about three inches above the jamb.

"Penny, would you wait for us in the next hall?" I asked.

"NO!" Fugi said. "Wait for us in the room we just left."

The poor girl looked as confused as I felt. Fugi remained stern-faced watching Penny, not even glancing at me. There must be a reason for that command, as it really makes no difference to me.

"Okay, please wait in the room," I said.

Her smile grew as she turned and walked across the hall. When I looked at Fugi with a questioning stare, she shrugged her shoulders. "I'll tell you later," she said. "Right now we'd better prepare for the real possibility Fred is alive. You take the hammer and I'll use a screwdriver."

My head started shaking as I stepped to the side of the frame. "He's either dead or too weak to be of any bother. Something's plugged the drain and I left the shower running. Look at the water around the door. It's rising and falling making something hit against the door. If Fred were in there, it would be up to his knees by now. Don't you think if he were alive, he'd want to move quickly once the door opened? High water like that would impede his ability to escape. He would've turned the spigot off. Relax, but stand clear of the doorway. When that door opens, water is going to flood out."

She ignored my logic, reaching to the cart where she'd placed the tools and lifted both items she'd mentioned. Then while she held the hammer toward me, a chilling expression on her face was so intense it caused me to shiver. "Listen to me," she said. "You could be right and I sincerely hope so, but all of us knew how to trick our adversaries into believing we were no longer a threat. You of all people should understand what I mean. Now if he's gone, we'll put the tools back. But if he's hanging on to the knob just waiting for the water to carry him past us, be ready to move quickly."

Memories of how he'd acted so pitiful while on his knees, and then charging me full-speed once my back was turned, served as a terrifying validation to Fugi's warning. Tension built as I accepted the hammer, another thump added to the suspense. Fugi lifted the screwdriver over her head like a knife, placed the key in the lock with her other hand, and looked at me; "Ready?"

There were no other unarmed wooden doors except the two in this hall. We have no choice but to proceed. "Yes; please don't be heroic."

A grin crossed her face for a second before the expression returned to grim determination. As she started reaching for the knob, a danger rose to mind. "Wait a moment," I said.

The cart was within reaching distance of the door. If Fred was just on the other side, he might be able to grab a screwdriver before we could move through the rushing water. I lowered the hammer and pulled it closer to me, away from where I think the water will flow. Fugi glanced at the cart, and then looked at me nodding her head. She faced the door as I raised my hammer, placed her hand on the key while stepping slightly to the side, and turned the knob.

Movement seemed sluggish. Although the door burst open in my direction, the knob appeared to creep toward my stomach while shoving the cart against my ankles. It pinned me to the wall. Wood blocked my view. Gurgling sounds intensified in the hall drain. I couldn't push the door away forcing me to try sliding the cart from my legs. Bumping sounds came from the other side before I could move.

"Are you all right?" I asked.

My question seemed to come out in slow speech. Splashing noises responded, and then the gurgling diminished. "Yeah," she said. "He's gone; really gone."

Sounds of rain falling into a lake filled the silence as the shower continued spraying the collected water. Pressure against the door dropped to the point I could push it away, and then step over the cart. Ghastly grey-colored legs hanging into the hall was the first thing I noticed.

Fred was face down in the water, perfectly still except when the level slightly lapped over the jamb. Then it looked like he was trying to float away. A slight rusty-colored tinge clouded the moving liquid. My eyes closed as I tried pushing the reason for that discoloration out of my mind.

Fugi was already in the room, carefully moving across the floor toward the showerhead. She turned it off and walked to the drain. Her feet scooted the bottom, and then nearly lost her balance as the water started to quickly drain away. As the level dropped, it pulled Fred into the room. The movement of his lifeless body held me enthralled. "Stop looking at him," Fugi said. "Go get Penny and the two of you start removing the hinges from behind the door."

Water had drained low enough for Fugi to move without risk of falling. Her eyes were gazing behind me as she drew near. "Don't look in here Penny."

That snapped me out of the hypnotic state. She'd quietly come up, staring at Fred as intently as me. Though I believed he was dead before the door was open, I'd never seen a body before and didn't know what to expect. Fugi grabbed the hair on the back of his head to pull out of sight and then returned.

"Was that Fred?" Penny asked.

"Yes," I said. "I killed him."

Nausea threatened to return as my own words echoed in my ears. I am now a murderer. A life ended because of me. Ghostly images of our struggle played out in my mind, with me killing Fred and then his rising from the dead to accuse me. God I hate this place and what it turned me into.

"Good," Penny said. "He deserved to die. Can we go now?"

The images popped out of my head as I stared at Penny gape-jawed. Fugi smiled, climbing to the hall dripping wet. Somehow a towel had clogged the drain which became visibly obvious after she cleared the entrance.

"We have to take down two doors first," Fugi said. "Do you remember the name of your parents?"

Her eyes gave the appearance of concentration for a few moments, and then relaxed. The smile returned. She stood to the side apparently waiting for instructions. I can feel her recovery nearing, but in dire need of something huge to complete the task.

"We'd better get going," Fugi said. "The clock is ticking. Are you going to be all right Joyce?"

Time for seeking forgiveness will have to wait. We need to move. "Yeah I'll survive. Listen, these doors are going to be heavy. Fred's wallet is near his clothes. If we wedge it under the front edge, it'll make taking the hinges out easier."

Fugi smiled nodding her head, but Penny took the initiative. She walked quickly to the heap, located the wallet, and returned to jam it in place.

"Nice job Penny," I said. "Now if you and Fugi will hold the door steady, I'll work the hinges out."

With the hammer and screwdriver put to use, the door was free in a few minutes hitting the floor with a solid bang. The highly polished surface was rapidly losing beads of water while I moved toward the back edge. Penny watched as I began unscrewing the hinge, moved down a few feet, and started working on another. Fugi took the last screwdriver and soon had the knob off. I removed the last hinge, and then a monumental struggle began as we lifted the door to the cart. Final remnants of water ran off once we had the door settled. It now looked dry but we can't stop. Even though my muscles ached we couldn't afford the luxury of rest. Moving these heavy doors across electrified grating worried me about how much time it would take until I came up with an idea. Fugi started pushing the cart toward the next door. Before I could talk, Fugi spoke with a tone bordering on threat. "Do you still have the remote?"

Squeaking wheels echoed down the empty halls as I stared at her. Why is that needed now? A quick check of my pocket proved it was inside. "Yes; why?"

The cart stopped far enough away from the next wooden door to avoid damage when it toppled. Silently Fugi backed to the doorway between halls, guarding it like Mark had done before. When Penny started approaching, Fugi's hand rose. "Stop right there," she said.

Then she drew a breath, glanced behind her, and faced us. "I can't put this off any longer. God I wish this wasn't true."

Tension mounted while I waited for Fugi to continue. Penny simply looked at her with a calm expression, but remained where she was. Finally Fugi glanced briefly at me and then turned her attention to Penny. "Before Earl ships anyone, he gets Doc to surgically implant a little sleeper device deep in their thighs. It's a tiny bomb set to detonate if it crosses this one doorway."

She paused to look overhead briefly before returning her eyes to us. "Since the hidden sensors around the entrance are designed to beam in all directions, there's no way to prevent the signal from reaching the bomb's receiver. The explosion will rip the leg off, killing the person in a matter of minutes. He was always concerned over the possibility someone would send their slave after him. That little demon eliminates all risk quite efficiently. Penny has one. Rest assured it is active. Only Earl and Hank know which remote button will disarm it. I have an idea but it's just an educated guess. There's only one chance. If the remote control detonate signal reaches an active bomb, it will get ugly. And if I only push the sleep button, there's no stopping the chain reaction that'll occur once she crosses this threshold. Assuming I don't push the explode button, when Penny steps into this hall, either she keeps going or doesn't. Now is the time to pray my idea is right."

CHAPTER 18

Those monstrous bastards! Isn't it bad enough they destroy people's minds without setting them up as human bombs? Oh how I'm going to make them pay. There has to be a way to eliminate the risk. "Can we turn off the sensors?"

A sigh rose from Fugi. She looked depressed. "There's a master panel upstairs in a steel vault, but again Earl has the only key to fit the lock and switch," she said. "The sensors are always on. An alarm sounds if they're turned off."

"What if I take the hammer and smash the area as hard as I can?"

Fugi's head was shaking. "This is steel reinforced concrete fortified to withstand multiple door blasts," she said. "In order to make certain all sensors are destroyed, you'd have to reduce about three feet worth of floor, walls, and ceiling to dust. A claw hammer won't do the job. All it takes is one to set the bomb off."

My mind started racing, another idea came up. "Is there something we can cover the area with, like aluminum foil, that'll prevent the signal from getting through?"

For a moment Fugi thought over the idea, and then shook her head again. "Foil would prevent the signal from passing through, but there's nothing down here we can use to hold it against the ceiling. It wouldn't work wrapping her thigh either. The signal could still reach the antenna either through her heel or shoulder."

This is unbelievable. I refuse to give up. "Then let's push every button on the cursed thing just to make sure."

"Joyce, if we do that the bomb will go off. There's no other way."

Thoughts of wrapping Penny up like a gift crossed my mind, but one tiny tear would most likely spell disaster. Oh God this isn't fair. Why did you let me help her this much only to watch her die horribly? Tears clouded my vision as I pulled the remote out and handed it to Fugi. Penny's expression changed to terror watching Fugi point it at her.

"Relax," Fugi said. "You won't feel a thing."

First Fugi checked the back to make certain which way she held it, and then put her finger over the kill button. "What are you *doing*?" I asked.

"This would be the kind of irony Earl likes," she said. "I hope I'm right."

Panic accelerated like a runaway train. "Wait a minute," I said. "Let's think about this. The kill button sends out a signal that activates electricity in the collars. Is it even possible a signal of that type could be used to disarm a bomb?"

Her head started nodding as she sadly looked at me. "Yes since the signal only activates a switch. That switch could either be to kill or release."

She lowered the remote, a compassionate expression now on her face. "The remote range is about fifty feet plus the cells are shielded which is why you were able to push buttons without affecting Penny," she said. "Getting back to the matter at hand, Earl has always been super paranoid. Take a look at the exploding doors and you'll know what I mean. A moment ago I crawled inside his mind to think about this. If someone with my knowledge got hold of a remote and tried sneaking a slave in here, my logical choice for disarming would be the sleep button. He'd know that and probably have it set to detonate the damn thing. Out of all the buttons, which one would someone like me be least likely to push? That's why I think I'm right. Does that make sense?"

My eyes closed as I nodded my head. Fugi knows Earl better than me.

"W-Will it be a big explosion?" Penny asked.

Tears flowed down my cheeks, forcing me to turn away.

"If I'm right there won't be an explosion," Fugi said.

"And if you're wrong?" She asked.

God I can't stand this. Now I want to tear Earl apart with my bare hands. Silence responded, no vocal answer given. Suddenly a hand was on my shoulder, drawing my attention. "You'd better move away from me," Penny said. "Before anything happens, I want to thank you for being so kind to me. If I don't make it, don't be hard on yourself. You and Fugi have made me feel good and I know this isn't your fault; thank you again; good bye."

I had to close my eyes again as the tears became quiet sobs. All I could do was blindly hold my arms out, which she gently came to me in a hug. Then she pushed away which opened my eyes. "O-Okay," she said, "I'm ready."

Fugi raised the remote halfway up, and then looked at me saying "You'd better take five steps back, just in case."

Please dear God guide Fugi's hand. As I stepped away, Fugi pointed the remote toward Penny, held her finger over the button for a moment, closed her eyes briefly while muttering silent words, and then pressed down.

Penny watched her closely, standing still and proud. Fugi lowered the remote looking at Penny's legs. Nothing happened. Though I felt great relief and it showed in my smile, Fugi remained grim.

"Is it over?' I asked.

"Maybe," Fugi said, "but I don't know if all I did was push a useless button. We won't know until she steps in the hall."

While Penny remained absolutely still, I ran the few steps and grabbed Fugi's shoulder. "What do you mean by useless button?' I asked. "Why don't you push more of them?"

A soft smile grew on Fugi's face. "If I do that, I chance reactivating the thing assuming I turned it off, or worse causing it to blow. I hate having this pressure, which I find astonishing as weird as that sounds. But I honestly believe Penny's best chance is right now. It's up to her. What do you say Penny?"

"My mother's name is Frieda and my father is Bernard. I have a boyfriend named Benjamin which my parents always said would make a funny if we married; Pen and Ben. Oh my God, when you pointed that thing at me it was like a door opened in my mind. I remember everything!"

She rushed to me yanking me into a tight hug. Then she held out her arm for Fugi, who apprehensively approached. When Fugi was close, she was pulled in. "Thank you so very much for everything," Penny said.

With no warning she shoved both of us away so violently we stepped back several feet to avoid falling. Before we could recover, she dashed into the doorway and halfway down the next hall. A smile grew on her face as she jumped in the air and kicked her heals together. "I am back," she said, "I'm back, I'm back, I'm back!"

Fugi and I exchanged smiling glances. "I'd call that a successful disarming," Fugi said.

Snickers broke to laughter as I pulled Fugi into a hug. Penny literally came skipping back to us, a genuine smile on her face as she focused on Fugi. "I recognize you," she said. "You were the only one who wasn't mean to me."

Then she looked Fugi over, her expression changing to confusion. "It must've been what I went through," she said, "but I swear you were a man before."

Her honest confusion nearly made me laugh, but Fugi tensed and appeared upset. "I didn't mean to make you mad," Penny said. "Your secret is safe with me. I owe both of you more than you know."

She ran to the shower room, leaning over the frame to look in the direction Fugi pulled Fred. Her head nodded, she spit in the room, turned to pick up the wallet, and ran back to us. This girl's recovery is like a rocket ship liftoff. "It's like there were two of me," she said. "Until we get out of here, I'm going to think the terrible things that bastard did was to another person. It helps. Now shall we take down this door and go home?"

Her question brought up a point I hadn't considered. With everything I own gone, where could I go? Crawling back to dear old dad is just what he wants, and something I can't stand thinking about. "If I had a home I'd say yes," I said.

It wasn't my intention for that to be heard, but it was. Both of them looked at me in astonishment. Rather than discuss embarrassing family problems, I faced the closed door. "Let's get moving," I said. "We're behind schedule by at least ten minutes."

Two shadows covered mine on the door, one hand touched my shoulder. "If you want to talk about it I'll listen," Fugi said. "In the mean time know this. I have a whole lot of money tucked away that even Fred couldn't find. Whatever you need it's yours."

"And it would make me very happy if you came to Virginia Beach with me," Penny said.

I was so moved by their offers, tears threatened to fall again. They stood patiently by as I turned to them. "Thank you both so much," I said, "but I'll be okay."

A frown formed on Fugi's face as she looked at Penny. "There's that damn stubbornness that made it possible for us to be here now," she said.

Her attention changed to me. "This isn't charity Joyce. It's genuine care. Accept it or I'll be gravely offended."

She backed up three steps, placed her arms at her sides, and bowed. "According to ancient traditions, if one party offends another it can only mean war. Now either accept this or prepare to do battle."

Penny giggled, making me smile. It felt like a weight had been lifted. "Thank you Fugi, and Penny. It truly is a relief. I gratefully accept your help. Now shall we get out of here?"

As I turned to the door, curiosity got the best of me. "What's in here?" I asked.

"That's a small meeting room that looks more like a living room," Fugi said. "Sometimes Earl entertained his extremely affluent customers in there. The wooden door gives it a more comfortable appearance."

"I got it," I said. "The door over the shower is wood so it won't rust, and this one is just for show." A smile grew. "Let's show Earl the error of his ways using them!"

No one moved; all was quiet. When I faced them, they both looked concerned. "Okay so I'm not the best comedienne," I said. "Can we get to work now?"

Fugi grinned, glancing briefly at Penny while fishing the keys out. Soon after that, the door opened to a place so alien from the rest it appeared like a different world.

Two ultra-expensive sofas adorned a wall corner perpendicular to each other, with an antique coffee table set at an angle in front. Three cushioned Queen Anne arm chairs dotted the far wall, and two small tables at each end of the farthest sofa edges held lamps, providing soft light as compared to the harsh hall illumination. Landscape paintings hung in numerous places. Plush beige carpeting gave the final touch in creating an illusion of warmth amid horrors. "This is better than what my parents have," Penny said.

When I looked at the luxurious furnishings, I saw people suffering to make it possible. Anger built, forcing me to grit my teeth. Penny gasped noticing my rage as I looked at them. "We're about to close this show room down," I said. "Let's go; we still have a long walk in front of us."

By following the same procedure we did with the shower room door, this one was quickly off the hinges and free of all metal parts. Moving it to the cart was more difficult because of the first door constantly trying to slide off, but we managed to set it on top and were rolling into the next hall. When we arrived in front of the clothes room, I held up my hand indicating for Fugi to stop. "We need two more pairs of jeans," I said. "That way we can loop them through the knob openings of the doors and have handles."

Both smiled while Fugi started heading to get the clothes. "Wait here," she said. "I'll be right back."

It must be the tension that nearly made me laugh wondering where she thought we could go. As she ducked out of sight, Penny moved close enough to whisper. "Don't get me wrong, but are you sure Fugi can be trusted once we're outside? I mean my father works in an assembly plant and they've gone on strike from time to time. People who crossed the picket lines were called scabs and switchers and threatened to undermine what they were trying to do. For now Fugi needs us, but when this danger is gone she might turn on us to save herself. My dad had a saying; watch out for switchers. I think we need to listen to it."

"Listen to what?" Fugi asked.

She'd stepped into the hall so quietly we hadn't heard. Penny turned from me, walking toward the cart. Fugi watched her with growing confusion. When she faced me, I really didn't know what to say.

Though her concerns might be considered justified, I can't see Fugi attacking us. Something inside told me she's sincere with everything she's said, but at the same time it proved Penny was unsure about who to trust. I have to keep what she confided to me secret. I smiled while looking at Fugi. "She's just worried about listening to approaching traffic," I said. "While we're walking down the road, we can't assume Earl will come at us from the front."

Fugi's right eyebrow shot up as her left lowered. "This had to be *whispered*?" She asked.

My shoulders shrugged. Fugi dropped the jeans, walking to where Penny was watching us. "I know you have every reason to doubt me,"

Fugi said, "and when this is over if you want nothing more to do with me I'll honor it. But I am not your enemy."

As Fugi paused, a deep breath was drawn while glancing at me and then exhaling it while returning her attention toward Penny. "About eighteen years ago, I accidentally set my house on fire," she said. "My entire family died that night. Since then I've been trapped doing things that repulsed me. Joyce gave me the strength to start fresh, and I will not jeopardize that opportunity. Believe me when I say I want out just as badly as the two of you."

A chuckle rose from her. "You both kind of remind me of what my sisters would be like had they survived, and to be honest that's how I think of you. I know it's corny and all that, but I can't help it. Now if it would make you feel better, I'll stay on one side of the road and you stay on the other. For now let's just get to the road; okay?"

Eighteen years ago would put Fugi in her early teens. Visions of a house completely engulfed in flames with a young boy screaming outside sent shivers down my back. I never would have guessed that began her life as it is today. My own harsh upbringing pales compared to that, and a new sense of admiration for her courage grew. Penny remained silent looking at Fugi, but I gathered the jeans and walked to them. "I can't even begin to imagine what you felt back then," I said, "but what you've done today atones for everything. Your sisters would be proud. As crazy as it sounds, I've started thinking about the two of you like extended family."

Penny looked at her feet apparently feeling shame. I moved closer to her, placing my hand under her chin to gently lift it. "Everything will be okay," I said. "Let's get out of here and then decide what to do next. We need each other or we'll all fail. What do you say?"

Her eyes sparkled as she gently smiled. "I say let's go home," she said.

Fugi cleared her throat unnaturally loud, drawing our attention. "I'll tie the jeans off," she said. "I'm really quite good at knots. The code to release the magnetic door is one, six, five, eight, two, and one. Keep quietly repeating that sequence until you're out. If I don't make it, be sure to enter those numbers on the keypad next to the door exactly as I said. You only get one chance at it."

Both of us looked at her like she'd lost her mind. What in the world is that supposed to mean? "I'm confused," I said. "Is there something you haven't told us yet?"

Her lopsided grin returned. "Lots; and I will tell you on our walk if all goes well. What we're about to do has never been done before. In theory it should work. Just in case we topple the doors and it starts a chain reaction of electrical arcs, I want you two safely under the cover of any open room when I check the hall."

As I opened my mouth, Fugi shook her head and spoke quickly. "My muscles are too weak to be of any good if it comes to a fight," she said. "Besides I'm partly responsible for the both of you being here. This is my way of getting you out. No arguments; together you can make it. And this should work. It's just I like being dramatic."

Penny looked at Fugi with a strange expression. It looked to be a combination of mistrust and worry. "I'll stay with you," she said.

Fugi's head shook a few times. "You have to make it out. If this doesn't work and one of you should die with me; no one will escape and Earl cleans up the mess. He must be stopped. I'm too weak to tug a door which makes me the logical choice to be the guinea pig. The safest way to do this is for both of you to move the doors to the entrance, and give them a push while I shut the hall door. Then get as deep as you can in the clothes room and duck for cover. If an electrical discharge reaches the knob, you won't believe the explosion that'll follow. Use clothes as protection. I'll wait until you say you're ready before reopening the door. If all goes well, I'll give a shout."

What she said made sense, but I hate it. "Isn't there another way to see if it's safe?" I asked.

Her lopsided grin returned. "Why Miss Jackson; if I didn't know any better I'd think you were worried for me. I'll stand behind the door as I open it. In case there's a problem, I might be able to close it before a nasty happens. You'll know one way or the other, believe me. There's no more time for debates. We have a lot of ground to cover and must get going. This matter is closed, excuse the bad joke."

The silence of a funeral procession followed as I just stared at her. Nothing I could think of would make this task any safer, and though I really thought we should draw straws or something she's right. Penny and I have been doing the heavy work with Fugi struggling to keep up. I wouldn't be able to lug heavy doors across grating with only her, and I doubt Penny would either. For just a moment I considered suggesting we try walking the unmarked path, but decided that would be riskier.

A smile was on Fugi's face as she tied knots in the pants, but Penny's expression reflected how I felt; depressed. When Fugi was finished, we carefully moved the doors from the cart and slid them toward the doorway. Fugi helped us lift the doors on their bottom edges, with Penny holding one and me the other. Then she unlocked the electric hall and pulled the door wide open. "Slide them at a forty-five degree angle to the entrance and let me know the moment you release them," Fugi said. "Once you shout, get the hell out of the way!"

It was a real struggle keeping the doors steady. I grabbed the jeans with my hand, giving Penny the same idea. That made handling them a little easier until we were in position. First we caught our breath and then I glanced at Fugi. "Ready?" I asked.

She nodded; a look of dead seriousness on her face. "Okay Penny," I said; "and-, NOW!"

We pushed the doors simultaneously, and then jumped clear. Fugi began slamming the door, catching the bottom edge of the door I'd handled and sliding it into the hall. The doors fell like trees, drawing closer to the grids as Fugi grunted. My eyes widened when it appeared Fugi wouldn't make it in time. Then a loud bang sounded as the hall door slammed an instant before two pinging noises filled the air.

"Is everyone all right?" Fugi asked.

"Other than my heart being in my throat, yes," Penny said.

I nodded on my way to the hall door where I leaned my ear against the wood panel. It sounded like tightly wound springs were being plucked for a few more moments, and then all was quiet. "If the electricity was being, I don't know, zapped around, would it make noises?" I asked.

Fugi's shoulders shrugged. "I've only seen the aftermath. I don't know."

My head pulled away from the door as I looked at her. I don't ever want to know what she meant by aftermath. "It's real quiet," I said. "I think it's safe."

Her face hardened, a deep frown forming. "It could very well be," she said, "but that doesn't change a thing. If the electricity is silently arcing around, it'll get spent on the first ground it contacts. We're wasting time. Move to the room quickly and let me know when you're safe."

We exchanged looks, my mouth opened and then closed. I pulled her into a hug. Then we separated; that goofy grin on her face. Penny approached, giving her a hug as well. "Be careful," Penny said.

As they pulled apart, Fugi glanced at her chest before looking at Penny. "Most of the time that's what I do best," she said. "No tearful goodbyes; just get to the room and wait for my shout."

That almost had the ring of the condemned's last words to me. As I turned to walk to the room, Penny silently followed. Once we were in the far corner and had clothes on the floor like a make-shift fort, I sighed.

"Why is this necessary?" Penny asked.

"The knobs in this hall have some sort of explosive. If the electricity hits them, the doors will explode."

Her eyes widened as she grabbed some from the floor and hugged them.

"WE'RE SET," I said.

No answer from Fugi; the quiet was maddening. I know she heard but did not acknowledge. The thumping heart inside my chest was the only response, until I could stand it no more. As I started moving away, Penny grabbed my shoulder. "Don't go out there," she said. "Fugi might be working up the nerve."

She's right, but I still couldn't stand waiting any longer. "Then I'll go hurry her."

"All clear," Fugi said. "Oh DAMN it!"

Squeaking from the cart wheels now came from the hall. We exchanged horrified expressions, and then rushed through the door running down the hall. The cart held the hall door open, but Fugi was nowhere to be seen. "WHAT'S WRONG?" I said.

More of those pinging springs filled the air before we'd gotten close enough to see. It felt like soft tar was on the floor, slowing my run toward the cart. Relief washed over me when I reached the entrance. Fugi was standing on one of the fallen doors looking at us, her smile the biggest I've seen as she pointed at the door edges. "We're in luck," she said.

When the doors toppled, they landed so the tied jeans in both knob openings were literally touching. It's going to be easy standing on one while pulling the other.

"Then why'd you cuss?" Penny asked. "That scared me half to death!"

Fugi grinned, glancing to the rear, and then looked at her. "Well, the doors didn't exactly fall like this, but they landed to where I could push them apart."

My head lowered as I silently chuckled. When I looked up, Fugi was grinning at me. "Hang on one more second," I said. "Let me get the jeans we'll need for our feet."

I looked at Penny. "For now tie two pairs around your neck. When we're out of this hall, we'll stop long enough to wrap our feet with them, and then be on our way."

The sound of my own words rang sweetly in my ears. We're moments from ending this nightmare. Penny's lower lip trembled; I guess truly believing we're almost free for the first time. Excitement lifted my step as I quickly dashed to where I dropped the jeans, picked them up, and ran back to the others. In very little time we had our pairs secure on our necks and standing in the hall. Fugi pointed to the right far corner. "We need to angle the doors in that direction," she said. "The locked door at the end will automatically swing inward to the left, so we can't block the bottom. And remember; don't touch the walls or floor. Let's go!"

All our hard work was paying off. We were on the way. As an added bonus, the doors slid across the grids like they were on wheels making our door to door hopping and pulling that much easier. Enthusiasm grew with each passing moment until at last we were close enough for Fugi to reach the keypad. A tremendous smile was on her face as she looked at me. "Thank you again for helping me get here," Fugi said. "We are now six buttons away from freedom. Once we're through this door, there are no more traps or surprises. What do you say we blow this joint and go for pizza?"

"No anchovies for me," Penny said.

Fugi laughed as she faced the wall. My enthusiasm was so overpowering I almost felt like I could tear the door down. Tears clouded my vision watching Fugi's hand reach out and start pushing buttons. All the horrors I'd faced were almost over. In just a few hours Earl's torture of innocents would decisively end. In a way I wished I could be here to see his expression, but that's best left for the police. A beep followed each keypad tap, and then after five she spun her hand in the air a few times before pressing the sixth.

One powerful jolt instantly hit the door beneath our feet just as a horn started blaring in one second bursts. Rumbling shook the hall, a wall of thick metal bars rolled down in front of the magnetic door barely missing the one we were on. It now felt like angry bees were trapped underneath the door, rapid vibrations tickling my feet. Then the keypad lights died. "WHAT IS IT; WHAT'S HAPPENING?" I asked.

Slowly Fugi looked at me, for the first time with absolute fear in her eyes. "They changed the code," she said. "This keypad is designed for one entry only and then it shuts down. There's no other way to open the door, but bars drop just in case. They're locked in place and can only be raised from the other side."

She drew a deep breath and walked to our door's edge. "The floor is now fully armed. Had we not been on these doors, we would be dead which might not be such a bad thing. Earl's cell phone receives an alert when the alarm sounds. It keeps beeping until he responds. If he didn't know about us before, he does now. We're hopelessly trapped and he's coming for us just as fast as he can."

CHAPTER 19

Monotonous tones blasting from the hidden siren made it hard to think, but I have to do something. Penny's cheerful demeanor was gone. She stared at Fugi with horror on her face. Fugi just looked at the metal grids in front of her. I refuse to give up. "Okay let's go back," I said. "We need to do some serious brainstorming."

Fugi slowly looked at me, her expression identical to when I was pressing my foot to her neck. "What's the use?" She asked.

I stomped across the door to grab Fugi by the shoulders, yanking her away from the edge and then shaking her. "PULL IT TOGETHER," I said. "We have to get out from under this noise. Now move it!"

Her head slowly shook, looking at Penny over my shoulder. "I think we should vote," Fugi said. "Penny, do you-"
"Like hell we are," I said. "I have an idea or two, but I need to be in a less noisy area to discuss them. Let's get out of this hall and go someplace quiet."

In all honesty my mind was a blank, but I had to say something encouraging. Both looked on the verge of suicide. Once I felt comfortable in turning my back to Fugi, I moved to the jean handle of the free door and tried pulling it toward the other hall. Thankfully they joined in, but with far less enthusiasm. Our efforts at reversing direction went much slower than before, which gave me a chance to examine the door closing off Earl's museum.

It looked strange, almost like it was rubber with a rubber knob and frame. Then it came to me. The dangers Fugi mentioned about electricity entering the other hallway gave me that idea we so desperately needed. A smile grew as I increased my pull. Five minutes later we were sitting in the so-called living room where the noise was muffled, and then pulled the jeans from our necks.

"Let's think about this for a few minutes," I said. "Fugi, after the alarm sounded, you said the floor activated. Did you mean the path as well?"

She was slumped in her seat looking at me with an almost bored face; "yeah; so what?"

My growing smile was not contagious. They both appeared gloomy. "So Earl believes we're dead," I said. "Think about it; had he considered the risk involving two wooden doors being used to safely navigate his horror hallway, he would've replaced them with steel; right?"

Her shoulders shrugged and head nodded once.

"Okay, we agree. He believes the only way we could get to the keypad is by walking across the grids. Now the only reason he would have changed the code is if he thought there was a slight chance you'd get free. You see where I'm going? He thinks whoever set off the alarm is no longer a risk. He is coming back now, that much is certain. But he believes the threat has already been eliminated. We still have time."

"To do what?" Penny asked.

As I looked at Penny, my smile broadened. "To get weapons," I said and then faced Fugi. "Tell me, what would happen if we took down one of the exploding doors and positioned it in front of Earl's museum?"

A light shined behind Fugi's eyes for the first time since the alarm sounded. "If we can set the explosive knob close enough to any side of the frame, the concussion should demolish it. That's all we need to do. The door has a steel core surrounded by rubber, but the frame is all rubber. It might work."

"Can the knobs be removed from the door?" I asked.

Her head shook as she said "No. The explosives would detonate immediately."

Penny shifted in her seat, drawing our attention. "Would someone care to clue me in on what you're talking about?" She asked.

Fugi's grin returned. "Earl has what he calls a museum behind the door halfway down the electrified hall," she said. "It's there to serve as a warning for all who visit what he was and still is; the deadliest assassin to ever live. Each time he killed someone famous; he'd take that gun and put it in the room. There're over a hundred weapons and ammunition sitting around collecting dust."

Just the thought of touching one of those guns repulsed me, but in a way it could be considered poetic justice using them to end his reign of terror. Penny started smiling, and then began laughing hysterically. This did not look good. "Are you alright?" I asked.

She continued laughing a few more moments, making both Fugi and me grow concerned. Then her laughter subsided, she wiped tears from her eyes. "Earl may be a good shot," she said, "but so am I. My father is a member of the Rotary Club. Every year I take first place in the turkey shoot, pistol competition, and skeet shoot. Plus I was on the archery team in high school where I led the district. I do believe you've given us a fair chance Joyce."

Though I felt elated by this news, Fugi looked grim. She rose from her seat, walking to the door. Her actions killed the rising hope. While staring off into the hall she said "Do not underestimate Earl. What you said relieves me, Penny; but never let your guard down or it will get you killed. Just before you arrived, Earl was ambushed in the next hall. They came out of the rooms where they'd been hiding, which is why Earl booby-trapped the doors later. Anyway it didn't look good for him. He was surrounded with guns drawn ready to fire."

Fugi faced us, but her expression seemed focused on something long ago. "Five men approached, demanding he get rid of both his guns. That was their biggest error. They should've fired immediately. Earl slowly removed the pistols, holding them butt-side out. When they ordered him to drop them, he slowly released his grip, but not enough for them to fall. His relaxing arms sent a false message to the men; they also relaxed slightly. Then he dropped to his belly, rolling on the floor while flipping the guns to a firing position. Five shots rang out in about two seconds, five men fell mortally wounded. Not a single one of them got off a shot. If you get him in your sights, do not hesitate on pulling your trigger. You're only going to get one chance."

Suddenly the siren stopped, lending eerie emphasis to Fugi's conclusion. "Earl just acknowledged the alarm," Fugi said. "As long as it took him; that tells me he was asleep when it went off. We now have about five hours or so."

Before she could walk into the hall, I spoke. "We need an edge. Earl is experienced at this sort of thing. You may be as well Fugi, but I'm not and I bet good money Penny has never shot another person. He can patiently choose his timing, picking us off one at a time. There's got to be something we can do to shift the odds in our favor."

Penny was nodding her head in what I think to be total agreement but kept quiet. Fugi simply stared at me like it was a hopeless wish. Then an idea rose in my mind. I looked at Fugi; "Would the shock collars set off the exploding doors if they're hanging on the inside knobs?"

Her eyes sparkled as that grin returned. "Yes my dear. Even with the door closed, the signal can get through."

Okay that's part of the plan. Now we need to know the rest. "Is there any way to increase the range of the remote?" I asked.

Fugi's grin dropped but the sparkle remained. "I'm afraid not. As a matter of fact, since the ultra-sound will be going through wood, we'd have to be closer than the fifty foot range."

That pretty much eliminates my idea about arming two doors in the other hall. We have to make our stand here since we can't allow them to get behind us. There's too much risk involved with being in any other hall. I rose, walking to stand beside Fugi at the doorway. Penny also got up, approaching us with a concerned expression. She moved in front, hands on hips and a frown on her face. "If you're planning on doing what I think," she said, "wouldn't that endanger me?"

My head started shaking as I looked toward the shower room. "Not if we send the kill signal," I said. "That'll definitely provide enough charge to set the bomb off without harming you."

"Besides," Fugi said, "we can protect you from the single beam of a remote using aluminum foil that's stored in the next hall. It won't be comfortable, but it will be safe."

Foil; of course. That just might do the trick. "Okay," I said, "what if we formed a foil bowl surrounding the collar so it would trap the signal? Could that help insure a weak signal is received?"

That grin returned. "I believe it might," she said. "Just like foil will make the signal traveling to Penny bounce away, it could capture a weak signal and send it back toward the antenna. That should significantly increase the range."

My attention turned toward the shower doorway, the closed main chamber door, and then back to Fugi. "Here's the most important question," I said. "How far do we have to be in order to avoid injury?"

Granted this was an assumption, but I doubted Earl would put exploding devices down here that would topple the structure. That doesn't mean the halls wouldn't act like a funnel for the shockwave, killing everything within a certain range. She thought about it a few moments, and then shrugged her shoulders. "Upstairs was the first place I thought of. The plastic explosives in each door have a yield of a little over one and a half sticks of dynamite. Though it won't blow up the steel-reinforced walls or ceiling, it will take chunks out. Plus it'll probably blow out all the electrical wiring in the process. I'd say as long as you're under cover in a different hall, all you'll suffer is a headache from the noise. Don't forget about wood shards that'll fly around like bullets. They'll bounce around the hall so fast you won't see them, going in all directions with deadly velocity."

I think we might have gained an advantage. All we'll need to do is bait them, and then stand clear. "Tell me what you think about this," I said. "First we get guns. Those will keep them honest. I doubt Earl will come running when he realizes we're armed. He'll try sneaking up. We have to keep alert and not assume a closed door is safe. What I'd like to do is arm one of the doors in the other hall, and move one of the exploding doors to the shower room. Then we'll hold up in two places; one of us stays here with the other two in the main chamber. Whoever is in here will keep hidden, while the others fight but only as a decoy. We'll purposely miss and then act like we're out of bullets. One will stay near the door while the other screams and runs deep into the chamber. That'll lure them to come after us. When they get near the shower room we'll blow them straight to hell! In case that doesn't get them all, whoever is in here can finish the job as they creep by. The couches can be used for cover during the blast, but we'll have to think of something to put in front of the chamber door."

Fugi chuckled quietly, almost sounding evil. "The grinder is on wheels with a very low bottom," she said. "We can easily move it into position. It'll work quite effectively at stopping bullets and wooden shards."

A smile grew as I nodded my head. "What do you think about all this, Penny?" I asked.

She glanced at me, Fugi, and then faced me again. "I think we'd better get to work."

"One moment *please*," Fugi said. "Before we go off on this great crusade, there is a serious danger we have to address. Those exploding doors are almost as heavy as the ones we used before, meaning they're liable to fall once we have them off the hinges. If that happens, the knobs will jolt and Earl comes back to pre-ground dog food. We're going to need the cushions from these couches and one hell of a lot of those clothes tied around both knobs."

That tone almost sounded mocking, but she did have an excellent point. "Tell you what," I said. "Why don't you grab whatever clothes you think will protect the knobs; and Penny and I will gather the cushions?"

Her head nodded as she disappeared through the door. Penny and I returned to the room, where we started pulling cushions free. "Do you really think we have a chance?" Penny asked.

My efforts didn't slow, but I briefly glanced at her. She now appeared on the verge of total surrender. "Not only do I think we have a chance, I know we're going to make it." A chuckle escaped. "Earl won't see it coming. Right now he's arrogantly returning to fix whatever damage was done, probably thinking it's minor. He doesn't have a clue what we're up to. They might even be laughing over their ingenuity at changing the door's code while plotting their next caper. As long as we keep him so busy he can't really look around, he'll strut right to his death."

All cushions had been removed by the time I stopped talking. Though it took a lot of balancing, we managed to get them under our arms and walk into the hall. "I promise you Penny; you will see your family again. Believe me when I say I never break my promises."

She smiled slightly, but it looked like an expression meant to placate another. Fugi was stooped down already tying off jeans around the outer knob when we arrived, briefly glancing at us before returning her attention to the task at hand. "Nice of you to join me," she said.

We dropped the pillows, ignoring her sarcastic remark. I scanned the hall in the direction we'd come, selecting the door I thought best for a trap. "I think maybe the exploding door closest to the living room should be our backup ambush. Is there any rope stored near here or do I need to go back to the cells?"

Fugi stopped before she finished, keeping on her haunches while looking at me like she thought I was crazy. "You plan on taking up a new hobby?" She asked.

A chuckle escaped as I grinned. "It's to tie this door to the one in the electric hall," I said. "We can secure one knob to the other. I'd hate to be in there if the door slides to the grids."

She returned her attention to the knob, a grin slowly forming. "Yeah, there's an entire spool of it in the tool room. Give me a minute and I'll get it."

It didn't take long for her to finish, and then she quickly walked to the storage room. Penny approached me with that worried look I'm starting to expect from her. "Let's say we get the doors all tied nice and tight," she said. "How are we going to get out and set it off?"

Crashing sounds followed by an extremely rude comment came from the room Fugi entered, momentarily drawing our attention. "Anything metallic tossed in there will result in electricity flying around," I said which pulled her eyes back to me. "We can even use the hinges we take off this door."

Her head nodded at almost the same time Fugi left the room holding a large wooden spool of thick rope. "Then why don't we tie this door to the bars blocking the exit and blow that up?" She asked.

Fugi reached us, obviously being close enough to hear her question. Before I could speak, she dropped the spool with a thud and placed a hand on Penny's shoulder. "It wouldn't work," Fugi said. "That's a six-inch thick solid steel frame around the exit, the door is solid steel three inches thick, and the two-inch bars are also solid steel. The best we'd accomplish is damaging the bars to where someone would have to cut through with a blowtorch. Earl has them."

Penny looked toward the floor, appearing more frightened by the minute. Fugi gently lifted her chin; one of the most compassionate smiles was on her face as she said "Less than fifteen minutes ago I wanted to kill myself and came damn close to doing it. Joyce convinced me otherwise. We really do have a chance at beating them. Don't forget; it's three against three now. And we have something they don't."

She looked at me. "I've never seen such clever thinking on the fly as I have in her. We're still alive after the wrong code was entered because she figured something out in a few minutes Earl never thought about in years. The three of them combined wouldn't be able to match wits with her. Look at her Penny."

My face was flushing madly. Why was she saying all these things about me? I had to turn away or I might die.

"You see?" Fugi asked. "She isn't arrogant in the least but is without a doubt the smartest person I've ever known. I'm damn proud to stand with her. We will be the ones walking out of here. That I believe beyond a shadow of a doubt."

She's putting me on a pedestal. This is not good. It could tear us apart if something goes wrong. As I faced her, my expression changed to anger. "We're all contributing," I said. "The only reason we're here right now is because we've worked together. This isn't about me or you or even Penny. It's about us. We three can easily outwit those thugs, but I'm no more special than you."

Regardless of how I felt, Fugi's talk seemed to help. Penny looked slightly relaxed, smiling while ignoring what I said and turning away. Fugi approached me, coming so close she could whisper. "I'm sorry I embarrassed you, but it seems I did a more effective a job at describing the danger Earl poses than intended. Penny needs someone to believe in and it can't be me. Like it or not, everything I said is true making you that someone. We are preparing to destroy one of the worst villains the Earth has ever seen, and it's only possible because of your brilliance. That's all I'll say on the matter for now. We'd better get going."

What did she mean for now? Before I could ask, she stepped out of reach while turning her back. "If we do what we did before," Fugi said, "we can carefully pull the door toward the hall. The cushions need to be arranged to provide a soft landing."

Renewed enthusiasm guided Penny's steps. A nod of her smiling face preceded her rapid departure to the other hall for Fred's wallet. There was almost a skip to her pace as she returned, her lost confidence restored. I don't know whether to leave it alone or set the record straight. Fugi glanced at me with an uncanny awareness in her expression, like she was reading my mind. "We'll discuss things later," she said. "Right now we need you to remain focused on the matters at hand Joyce. You look like you're a hundred miles from here. Come back to us."

She's right. We're in grave danger and I'm allowing petty concerns to cloud my judgment. Later I'll tend to it, but for now we must concentrate. I smiled at Penny, and then focused on Fugi. "Once we get this door down, I'd like to remove the second one before going into the hall," I said. "That way after we're armed, all we need to do is put it in place and then prepare our defenses. How does that sound?"

Fugi smiled while nodding her head, and then looked toward Penny. She seemed anxious to get started, quickly moving the cushions with her feet so they were positioned close to the door.

In an almost rerun of what we did before, I used the hammer and screwdriver to remove the hinge pins while Penny and Fugi held the door against the frame. Once the last pin was out, we gently pulled it free and guided it to the pillows. All hinges were removed in moments, and the door was gently lifted on its back edge and slid close to the electric hall. "One down, one to go," Penny said.

Her enthusiasm was catching. Fugi and I both felt exhilarated just watching her. We gathered the pillows, moving to the open door in front of the tool room. Once the cushions were dropped, Fugi ran to the clothes room disappearing inside.

"So, Joyce," Penny said. "How good a shot are you?"

Somehow I knew that question would be asked. Even though I hit the mark on every shot I fired, I've only handled guns once. It's time to start restoring her self-confidence. "I guess I'm all right," I said, "but nowhere near as good as you."

The expression on her face showed confusion. She looked toward the clothes room just as Fugi left holding two more pairs of jeans, and then faced me saying "you're just being modest. Do you belong to any gun clubs or teams?"

"No," I said looking at Fugi when she arrived.

Fugi dropped one of the pairs to the floor, walking by me to go inside of the room. On her way past, she looked at me out of the side of her eyes. It was like she wanted me to lie.

That I refuse to do; it would make me as bad as those monsters we're preparing to fight. Penny started looking worried as I walked close enough to place my hand on her shoulder. "I'm going to be perfectly honest with you," I said. "I've only handled a gun once my entire life. You and Fugi are the gun experts. The relief I felt when you talked about your shooting skills cannot be described, but it's exactly what I meant when I said the three of us will make it out of here. Please don't look up to me. When I consider what you've been through and how fast you recovered, it makes me look up to you. We are all special. I feel honored to know both of you."

Fugi stooped to her haunches. "That's so typical," she said. "The brains always give a little pep talk so the muscle will get the job done. Yet do we ever share the limelight? No; we do the work while they get the glory. Not only that, they get paid big bucks while we draw minimum wage. I tell you it is just *wrong*, but what can we do? Such is our lot in life, right Penny?"

She looked at Fugi, almost appearing offended. I have to admit it slightly irked me the way she talked. "I have a brain," she said; "speak for you."

My lips pursed in an effort at concealing the grin. It failed. Fugi looked at me and started laughing. It caught on. We all laughed while watching Fugi work. The better I get to know Fugi, the more I like her.

Soon both knobs were covered, with Fugi looking on in pride. Penny forced Fred's wallet under the front corner, the pillows were set in the outside hall just like before, and I began removing the pins. But when the last one came out, the door shifted toward me with the sound of tearing material filling the air.

"SHIT THE WALLET RIPPED," Fugi said. "Grab that Penny. No NO stop the bottom! Oh dear God! Get out of the way Joyce! The door's going to blow!"

The hammer and screwdriver dropped to the floor, my mind racing for a solution. A two-hundred pound bomb is falling out of control, heading directly at me. Penny and Fugi struggled to prevent disaster but it was too much for them. When the wallet tore, the bottom shifted unevenly causing this tumble. I could not prevent it from hitting the bare concrete floor in front of me.

As I quickly backed up watching the door fall in what appeared eerie slow motion, my foot accidentally stepped on a loose hinge pin. It rolled underneath, forcing me to lose balance. Helplessly I fell toward one of the cabinets. So this is how I die, by my own idea killing two others as well.

Penny released her hold, quickly lifting one of the pillows. She threw it at my chest like a Frisbee, hitting me and bouncing off as I fell backwards. It flew at the descending door, stopping on the floor just as I slammed the cabinet. Pain blossomed my side where I'd hit, sounds of wood splintering from my impact filled the air. Then the door hit the floor at the same time the cabinet broke apart, the knob landing on the pillow. It bounced once before coming to a gentle rest while I slammed concrete hard. No explosion followed.

"Unbelievable shot Penny!" Fugi said. "That was one in a million!"

Dizziness threatened to overtake me. I saw two doors lying askew in the opening, splitting to three and back to two until merging into one.

"Are you okay Joyce?" Penny asked.

Before answering I shut my eyes, shaking my head a few times prior to looking at their worried faces. "I ache all over but I'll live," I said. "Give me a moment to catch my breath."

Slowly my senses returned, permitting me the opportunity to stare in wonder at how precisely Penny had thrown that pillow. None of the others moved or said a word. They simply stared at me with continued concern. While gently rising I said "that's an amazing feat Penny. Where'd you learn to throw like that?"

Her shoulders shrugged. "I grew up close to a Frisbee park. It's no big deal."

"We're alive because of it," I said. "To me it is a big deal. Thank you."

Light glinting off metal caught the corner of my eye before I walked away. The wooden cabinet was destroyed, lying in many pieces. It looked like several blades were poking from under the rubble, causing me to carefully sift through. Six steak knives waited for me, sitting there like a reward for all my suffering. Fugi started smiling when I raised them for all to see.

"Uh oh," Fugi said. "Mark's going to catch hell for that. He was supposed to remove all silverware after Earl entertained. I guess he forgot about those."

I laid them on the floor away from the wooden bits. "We'll come back," I said. "Right now we need guns. What do you say we go shopping?"

"Typical woman," Fugi said; "always wanting to go shopping."

Penny's mouth dropped open as she faced Fugi, acting like she was going to smack her. Fugi quickly stepped out of the way, and then pointed at the door still blocking me in. A grin crossed my face as I grabbed the end on my side and they the other. Together we carefully lifted it on the back edge, sliding it across the hall to gently lean against the wall. When the danger of it falling was eliminated by shoving a pillow between the floor and door edge, we returned to the one next to the electric hall door.

"Okay here's the popper," Fugi said. "Have you figured out how we can move this door with a stick of electronically-detonated dynamite across an electrified floor?"

A smile grew on my face, making them both smile in return. "The doors move across the grates like they're on wheels," I said. "We

196

can slide this door on its back edge between the two we used before. As long as we don't block the jean handles, we'll be able to keep moving. Fugi, you keep the exploding door balanced when Penny and I move the free door. We'll angle our approach to Earl's museum so the door on our right will go past it and the one to our left stops near the entrance. Then we slide the exploding door to the front and gently move it into position, tying the knobs together. It's not going to be easy and will be time consuming, but I know we can do it. Can anyone think of a better way?"

"Hiring out comes to mind but I don't think they'd do it," Fugi said. "That's extremely dangerous girl. Can't you think of a better way?"

My head shook, Fugi looked worried, but Penny seemed anxious to get started which surprised me. Fugi is right. One slip and we probably won't hear the blast. "If we had some kind of grounded crane to lift it over the grids, I'd recommend that," I said. "Is there something you can think of we might be able to use?"

Fugi started concentrating, first glancing at the cart still in the hall doorway and shook her head. Then she looked at the tool room rubbing her chin. After a few moments her head started shaking again. Her eyes dropped to the floor as she turned toward me. She slowly raised her face; a gigantic smile greeted my stare. "I love this plan," she said. "Who wants to live forever? Let's go!"

"Hold up one moment," I said. "How much rope should we bring?"

Both stared at the spool, but Penny quickly looked at me again. Fugi began walking toward the tool room. "It depends on whether you want to hang the door or us," she said just before disappearing through the doorway.

Penny started grinning, yet I can't shake the sense of doom hanging over our heads. Though I smiled in return, my insides were shaking. I really wish there was another way but I just can't see it, and we have to get in that museum. Without guns we're as good as dead.

Fugi left the room a few seconds after entering; walking to where she'd dropped the spool. She lifted the free end of rope, pulled out about five feet, and cut it with one of the steak knives. Then she glanced at the knife, and cut off a smaller section of rope. The knife and rope were placed on the floor and she raised her left pants' leg.

"What are you doing?" Penny asked.

"I hate being unarmed," she said, and then lifted the small piece of rope to tie just above her calf.

Once that was done she slipped the blade under the rope on the inside of her leg and lowered the pants. Next she kicked her leg twice and then picked up the remaining piece. "Just in case we've misjudged the time," she said while walking to us.

That looks like a real good idea. "Does it hurt?" I asked while pointing at her leg.

"Not really," she said, "but those assholes shaved my legs. If I had some hair, the rope wouldn't need to be as tight." A sparkle lit her eyes. "I'll fix you and Penny up when we finish here," she said.

My head was nodding, but Penny visible shivered. "Just give me a gun," she said. "I'll take my chances without cutting off blood to my feet."

Her shoulders shrugged. "Suit yourself. Shall we begin?"

She leisurely stepped past us, heading toward the electric hall. Her calm assurance we would survive not only helped Penny, but me as well. Even if it was my idea, I'm still worried over the dozen ways it could go wrong.

Fugi was the first to arrive, moving the cart into a position so that it opened the door wider. Penny and I carefully pulled the exploding door away from the wall, sliding it across the floor until it was pointed to the middle of the entrance. While Fugi stepped between us to hold the exploding door steady, Penny and I entered the hall on the door to the left while moving the other one so it slightly angled to the left.

"We're set," I said.

A grunt responded as the exploding door slowly moved onto the grid. I was closest. When it started crossing the threshold, I grabbed the front edge and began pulling it. Penny soon had hold, allowing Fugi to step into the hall. Once the exploding door was more than halfway in, it started moving easier.

"Okay stop," I said. "Penny, get on the other door and come back to this end. Hold our boom-boom key steady while Fugi and I jump doors."

Both looked at me in astonishment. "Don't give up your day job for the comedy clubs," Fugi said.

Penny snickered as she hopped to the next door and did as I suggested. I grinned at Fugi, who looked at me with an innocent expression. Once we stepped onto the other door and moved the one we left further into the hall, we slid our explosive one a few more feet and returned to the first. Though this slow progress of door-hopping and balancing took time, we angled our way through the hall and eventually had the door we were on halfway in front of the museum entrance and the other four feet past it. The museum was within our reach, the exploding door ready to be positioned. Now comes the dangerous part. "Fugi, would you tie the rope to the museum knob?" I asked. "And Penny, would you move to the other door so we can carefully slide this into position?"

"Just don't knock me off," Fugi said.

While she leaned over the grids to tie the rope, Penny climbed to the other door and we began inching the exploding door forward, stopping a few inches from where Fugi was working. Fugi watched our progress, exchanging her attention between us and the rope. It amazed me how fast she had a tight knot tied, and then a chill coursed through me as I realized she'd had a lot of experience at that sort of thing. Her head nodded once as she straightened up while holding onto the rope.

"Okay move it toward me," Fugi said. "Do it nice and easy. Push it all the way to the wall."

As the door reached her, she lifted the rope over the front edge with one hand while guiding the door away from the wall using her other. She changed the angle slightly, moving the end a little farther down the hall. Contact was made, Fugi smiled.

"That's close enough," she said. "The knobs are within three feet of each other." She allowed the rope to dangle freely on this side while crossing to my door. Her attention shifted to removing the jeans covering the outer knob. "Penny, I need you to come here and hold the knob absolutely still."

Her head nodded as she hopped to this door and moved next to Fugi. When the jeans were off and carefully placed away from the door edge, she grabbed the exploding knob while Fugi tied another quick knot. Then they backed off smiling.

"Would it be safe to jam the jeans between the grids at this end of the door?" I asked. "I'd like to try holding it in place until we get out."

Fugi's head shook. "Any moisture or metal from those jeans contacting the grid will give us a killer suntan. We'll just ease our way out."

The exploding door was leaning about thirty degrees from the wall, angled precariously into the hall. Fugi did a thorough job at securing the knobs, but it looked like there was still a chance for it to slip if we accidentally hit it while moving away. I really wish we could put it directly against the museum door, but that can't be done.

Slowly we reversed course, moving our foot-doors while carefully avoiding contact with the exploding one. Relief flooded over me once we cleared the exploding door, directing my attention toward the exit. When we were ten feet away; sounds of springs pinging followed by a groan echoed in the hall.

"Oh no," Fugi said.

She was looking toward the rear. Her eyes' direction pulled ours. The exploding door's back edge was slipping away from the museum with the taut rope slowly guiding the jean-covered knob to the floor. Our movements sent vibrations through the floor grate which caused the exploding door to start sliding. Another groan echoed in the hall from rope pressure straining two well-bolted knobs.

CHAPTER 20

Fugi's eyes grew wild with panic as she shouted "MOVE!" Another groan rang out like an executioner lifting a heavy axe. The covered doorknob was slipping closer to the grid as we yanked on the jean handle harder than before. Light glinted off a large metal braid sewn to the jeans pocket on the bottom of the knob, collision with the grid imminent. It was now a death-race.

There wasn't time for safety. We pulled the free door as far as we dare, quickly hopped on and yanked the other one closer to the entrance. I chanced a fast look behind us. The knob was now less than four inches from contact, drifting down like a falling leaf. Please God give us a few more seconds. One monumental tug pulled the free door close enough for us to double-hop out.

Penny left first, quickly moving to the side. Fugi ran and cleared the entrance by about four feet. Rumbling from behind me caught my attention briefly. I could no longer see any distance between the grate and knob.

"GET OUT OF THERE JOYCE," Fugi said.

Her panicked tone hastened my speed. Just as I leapt, super-heated air pushed me tumbling forward. Lights started dimming; I felt like I was falling into a pit.

Such pretty colors; wait, was that a note of some kind?

"You will not remember any dreams you have while sleeping. Do you understand?"

"Yes."

"Joyce, for the love of God; wake up!"

Slowly Penny came into blurred sight, faded out, and then returned. She was stooped close to me, looking on with a terrified tear-streaked face. Fugi lifted my right hand, drawing my attention. A slight smile was on her face.

"Got any more bright ideas?" Fugi asked.

I ache all over. It feels like I've been tossed around inside a clothes-dryer. "W-, -What happened?"

As I tried to rise, Fugi released my hand to push my shoulder back down. "Take it easy," she said. "You just went for a fifteen foot flight. The door blew up while you were in the entrance. It's a miracle you're alive."

Penny watched me slowly move, her lips quivering. Fugi stared at me with compassionate patience. Gradually all of our efforts came back to my memory; "the hallway?" I asked.

Fugi smiled, glancing briefly at Penny before looking at me. "The grate was destroyed," she said, "and it looks like the museum door is hanging on by a prayer. When you feel up to it, we can walk to the guns. Your plan worked like a champ."

My eyes closed for a moment, a smile grew on my face. When I reopened them, Penny had her back turned to me quietly sobbing. Why is she so upset? "How long have I been out?" I asked.

This time when I started to rise, Fugi helped me to a sitting position. "Maybe twenty minutes," she said. "You gave us a damn good scare Miss Jackson. The good news is I don't see any bleeding. That means whatever debris went flying missed you completely. Of course the two doors we used as snowshoes slamming the entrance helped shield us all; take a look."

Dizziness threatened to return just from the effort of moving my head. One of the doors was sitting on its back edge blocking the bottom four feet of the doorway, while the other one was leaning over it jutting upward in this hall. It looked like a sadistic seesaw with bits of metal and wood pocking the surface. While carefully facing the others I said "We'd better get moving. Penny, are you going to be okay?"

She faced me wearing a smile, nodding her head. Though her eyes were red, the tears had stopped.

Fugi helped me up, and then steadied me when I nearly fell. "Would someone please stop trying to pull the floor out from under my feet?" I asked.

Silent chuckles moved Fugi's chest as her grin formed. Penny rushed to assist, helping me literally walk it off. My balance gradually returned. Then I noticed how bright everything was. "I thought you said the exploding door would take out the electrical wiring." I said. "The lights are obviously working in both halls. Does that mean the grate might still be charged?"

Her head shook as we continued moving slowly toward the electric hall. "Check it out," she said. "Not only did it work, if you'll notice the slight cracks in four locations of this hall, you'll see where the only cameras down here were damaged."

That caused me to stop, looking at Fugi with grave concern. "Earl has cameras?" I asked. "If he recorded what we're up to it'll be over before it begins!"

"Yes Earl *had* cameras," Fugi said. "They were put in before the exploding doors and only in this hall. Obviously they did not survive the shockwave funneled to the ceiling. As for Earl recording anything while out hunting, he never did before. He used them to watch people attending auctions, looking for suspicious behavior. But let's say he felt differently this time. If that were the case, it would be to watch Fred and not us. Let me ask you, would that pervert have acted the way he did while being taped?"

She had a good point. Earl gave him stern instructions regarding me. Any lapse in filming would've been dealt with harshly. That tells me the cameras were off the whole time, thank goodness. Why Fugi waited until now to say something about them must indicate the drugs are still affecting her. A smile grew as I looked at her. "You're right, they were definitely off," I said.

We resumed walking. When we arrived at the entrance, a scene of total devastation caused my mouth to drop open. Just as Fugi said, the museum door was hanging precariously by one almost severed hinge. If need be we could walk around the door. The floor in front of the museum was completely clear of the metal grate, but the further away I looked in either direction a nightmare existed. Thousands of rods were twisted and bent to form sharp pointed daggers jutting from heaps of violently ripped metal. Directly in front of the magnetic door, the grate had buckled into what looked like a maze of winding bush hedges creating a path that's going to be treacherous navigating. That'll slow them down. At least in front of us the doors we walked on apparently acted like plows to clear a four-foot wide path for the first eighteen feet. Small bits of wood and metal covered the floor like a carpet of thumb tacks which will make the walk more dangerous. "We need our home-made shoes," I said.

"I'm way ahead of you," Fugi said.

Penny released my arm, quickly walking to the clothes room where she ducked inside. A few moments later, she left holding the jeans we'd removed from our necks while in the living room. Why were they moved?

"While you were goofing off recovering from a near fatal blast," Fugi said, "I did some experimenting. Watch what I do and let me know if you can think of a better way."

I smiled slowly shaking my head at Fugi's comment. Penny arrived beside us, dropping the jeans. Then she picked out two and Fugi selected two. Both sat on the floor, prompting me to do the same. Once I was situated, Fugi nodded her head and held one pair in front of her left foot.

"Okay first you open the jeans and slip your foot inside so the seat is under the sole," Fugi said. "Next, take one leg, say the left, and wrap it under your foot going to the right and bringing up to the back of your ankle. Wrap the other leg in the opposite direction and then tie the legs together in front; like this."

With Penny and me watching, she opened the pair. Then she slid her foot in just as she'd said, zipping up the fly and buttoning the front in the process. Once her toes were almost against the crotch, she wrapped the legs beneath her sole in opposing directions crisscrossing them under her heel. The waist was lifted from the floor using the legs to hold it up. One more wrap around her ankles preceded a simple knot in the front, and she tucked the excess pants' legs under the tied portions.

"I doubt the style will catch on, but what the hell?" Fugi asked.

Her foot was completely enclosed in denim, looking as safe as can be all things considered. Penny began wrapping her feet just when I grabbed my two pairs.

"Brilliant idea," I said.

"Coming from you, that's high praise," she said.

No sarcastic tone was used when she said it. Her words caused me to blush, bringing a gentle smile to her face. By following her suggestion all of us quickly had our feet semi-protected and were standing at the entrance to the once deadly hallway.

"I suggest we don't lift our feet out there," I said. "Slide them across the floor to sweep the metal bits away."

Of course what I just said was obvious, but I didn't want to chance anyone thinking the tough denim material could withstand our weight pressing against a sharp metal splinter.

The top door leaning into this hall could only be slid backwards as the grate formed a lethal hedge on both sides. It took a tremendous amount of effort pushing it off, and once it dropped with a loud thud, debris-riddled side up, we couldn't budge the second door. Grating had arched behind it, acting like iron mounds pressing it solidly in place. Heavy grunts ceased as they looked on in frustration. "Not a problem," I said.

Then I pointed at the door we'd just shoved off. "Would you grab some clothes to toss over that door Fugi?" I asked. "Penny, would you come with me to borrow two arm chairs from the other room?"

Fugi began chuckling softly while shaking her head. "So you want to use the chairs as footstools over the door, huh?" She asked. "Man that was one fast solution. Not bad Miss Jackson, not bad at all."

Penny smiled as she looked at me. Fugi had deduced my idea perfectly. I nodded in agreement, and then we started walking to gather what we needed. As she neared the clothes room entrance she said "The chairs are pretty light, but if you need any help, give me a holler."

She passed through the doorway, leaving Penny and me alone. Our journey to the door between halls was in silence, but after we entered the next hall she spoke. "At first I honestly thought we were wasting time and tried to be enthusiastic. But now I really believe you and Fugi. We are going to get out of here."

As we stepped into the living room I said "You bet we are. In less than a day, you're going to be reunited with your family."

A gasp escaped her, she stopped walking. I guess she hadn't really thought about it or considered the finer details involved with her experience.

She was forcibly snatched away from her loved ones three years ago, and then subjected to horrors beyond imagination. The only reason she's here is because someone sent her back to be killed. To her our goal must've seemed like a fantasy that only now became reality. After all this time, it's about to end. When I put a time frame to it, I guess it finally registered.

"Hey, are you all right?" I asked.

Her head nodded as she looked at me. "Yeah; let's get some guns."

There was something different about her, but I can't put my finger on it. She'd had a skip to her step before, yet now it's like a determination has risen to add to eagerness. We grabbed two of the three chairs and a few moments later were at our destination. Fugi was already there, looking at us while shaking her head.

"I'm going to stop sending you two on a mission together," Fugi said. "Every time I do, you end up making me wait!"

That sarcastic jab went ignored as we peered into the hall. Dozens of jumpsuits covered the door, completely cushioning all shards jutting up. It looks to be at least five layers of clothing from one end to the other. I must admit; when Fugi starts a task she finishes quickly. Penny and I lifted one of the chairs over the blocking door, bringing the seat down so one armrest touched the standing debris-riddled door face. Then another idea came to me. While looking at the museum door I asked "How heavy is that door?"

Fugi shrugged her shoulders. "I don't know; maybe eighty or ninety pounds. It was made mostly of rubber, but this side's blasted clean. It won't give us any trouble sliding out of the way."

Both watched me look beyond the door to the other end. A clear path just wide enough to slide the door on its back edge led all the way to the iron bars. "We need some more rope and a screwdriver, just in case," I said.

Penny's mouth dropped open. Fugi appeared skeptical. "What have you got in mind this time, and is it going to blow up?" Fugi asked.

A chuckle slipped out as I smiled at Fugi. She was staring at me with serious eyes that killed my humor. "I don't want them to be able to sneak up on us," I said.

I tapped the door in front of us. "This will act like a blockade once they're down here, but that's only going to slow them down. What would happen if we secured one of the knobs of that door," I pointed at the museum, "to the bars in front of the exit?"

A smile grew on Fugi's face. "They'd have to make a whole lot of racket coming in," she said. "The bars will jam when Earl tries lifting them. He'll either have to cut through with a torch or use an explosive. Chances are he'll blow the door."

That's something else I hadn't considered, first the prospect of being filmed and now high explosives. "Earl has bombs?" I asked.

Fugi chuckled, turning to walk down the hall. I'd not noticed it before, but everything we'd left in the hall was gone. They cleaned it all up while I was unconscious. "Yes he does," she said. "Keep in mind whatever he uses will affect him as well. Call it a balance of terror. If he tosses any of his big stuff, the building will come down on him just as quickly as it would us. Besides, he's greedy." She'd reached the tool room, stopping without facing us. "He wants to keep repair costs at a minimum. And I'd lay odds he'll want to take us alive."

Chills ran down my spine considering our fate if he should succeed. When Fugi disappeared inside, I faced Penny. She appeared as determined as before. "You don't have to worry Joyce. That will never happen."

I'm not sure how to take her comment. She turned from me before I could ask, stepping onto the chair. Fugi left the room holding two pieces of rope and a knife. When she saw Penny, Fugi's speed picked up. "Hold on a moment," Fugi said.

Penny stopped with her legs on both chair seats straddling the door waiting for Fugi to arrive. "Most of the pieces jammed into the door are small," Fugi said. "But some are long as nails. I did the best I could. You'd better let me go first."

Penny nodded, returning to this side. Fugi placed both pieces of rope on the floor. One was much longer than the other. "We'll get to the guns in a moment," Fugi said. "I wish I'd thought of this before you put on your boots, Joyce. If you're still interested, have a seat and I'll set you up with a knife like mine."

My head nodded as I smiled. "Thank you," I said.

Before I was settled in the chair, Fugi was already on her haunches untying my left jeans shoe. In very little time, she'd secured the knife to my leg exactly like hers and had my shoe tied. Though I could feel the twine's tightness, it wasn't restrictive at all. While rising I said "That's great, thanks. I hope I won't need it."

Both looked at me in agreement, and then Fugi started grinning. "It's really not bad in that hallway," she said, "so as Joyce put it, let's go shopping!"

She lifted the second piece of rope and began climbing on the seat. The screwdriver in her back pocket caught my eye for a moment. Soon she was standing in the other hall looking at us. Penny went next, followed by me. We carefully walked across the fallen door until we were standing on concrete. My eyes looked to the ceiling at the light fixtures covered with Plexiglas. "I realize those covers withstood the blast," I said, "but do you think it would be safe to shoot out the lights?"

Fugi's head started shaking as she started sweeping her feet across the floor. "The answer is no," she said. "It'd be nice to soften them up by making them blindly stumble through those razor bushes, but I'm afraid all we'd accomplish is sending slugs bouncing all over."

That's another point that needs to be addressed. We have to protect ourselves against ricochets in the main chamber.

Our journey continued without conversation, the only sounds our feet brushing debris out of the way. This hall looked like the aftermath of a bombing run. Fugi arrived at the door, placed her right hand on the front edge and gave it a pull. The door fell off, hitting the floor with a muffled thud a few inches from her feet. She faced us grinning. "Imagine what I'll be able to do after I've regained *all* my strength," she said.

Penny chuckled, bringing one from me in the process. Darkness from the inside seemed to swallow the hall lighting. Fugi reached around the frame, throwing a switch. Rows of glass-covered guns reflected the lighting, each one with a placard just in front. It looked like a hundred guns were stored in this gruesome exhibit.

"We'll come back," I said. "Right now we need to move the door into position."

Penny appeared hesitant like she hated being unarmed, but eventually relented. Fugi walked across the door to enter the museum and placed her hands under the door's front edge. I worked my way to the top edge while Penny remained where she was.

"I thought if you could raise the door, I'll start turning it," Penny said.

With a weight of only ninety pounds, that shouldn't present a problem. I nodded in agreement, and then took a closer look at the door.

Burnt steel on the outside gave testimony to the power inside each exploding door. The rubber had been blasted completely off the front, but it was still on all four edges. Through some miracle, the knob remained firmly attached.

"We can't slide this one," I said. "The rubber will make it impossible. It's not that heavy Penny. You and I should be able to carry it."

I was right. It took modest effort lifting the door, and then Penny and I had it hoisted by the bottom edge. The difficult part came when we started walking. Each time we turned to follow the twisted path through the bent grate the door shifted nearly dragging us into a painful mess. We had to continually stop and reposition it in our hands. Fugi was waiting for us in front of the bars, which had somehow been cleared of the grating by two feet. Her attention was on the bare floor as she said "I guess the blast slammed this wall and ripped the floor away in the rebound concussion."

No matter the cause, that space gave us what we needed to turn the door upright and lean it against the bars. Fugi tied the knob to one of the bars about three feet from the floor, and then stood back to admire it. "That's not going anywhere," she said. "Oh the bars will lift all right, but the door will jam near the ceiling and hold. They won't be able to open the magnetic door." She chuckled once. "Earl is going to be so pissed he's liable to turn on Hank."

Her last statement made me wonder why Earl would single out his second in command for this, and then I understood. Hank brought me here and now their world is over. A smile grew. "What an intriguing assumption," I said.

Fugi began making her way through the path, glancing at me with a sparkle in her eyes. "It'll take him about one second to realize who orchestrated the welcome home party," she said. "I really wish I could be a fly on the wall when that happens."

For some strange reason, I found the prospect of Hank squaring off with Earl oddly satisfying. It put a little skip in my step as we worked our way through the treacherous path. My mood was promptly ruined when we were standing inside the museum.

Dozens of small glass enclosures housed various styles of handguns. All of the exhibits were intact; surviving the explosion without as much as a crack. The guns appeared as if they hadn't even been jostled. Fugi causally reached into her pocket for the keys, separated one, and began opening all cases, including smaller cabinets underneath that held boxes of what looked like ammunition.

"Forgive me Penny but I have to ask," I said, "Fugi, when you were ordered to shoot her and refused, Earl mentioned something about the gun rigged to hurt you. Isn't it feasible more could be like that?"

Her head shook as she continued unlocking displays. "No; Earl takes great pride in this room. The fact he ruined one of his more famous kills astonishes me. In a way I feel honored, as bizarre as that sounds."

Penny listened intently to her answer, walking close when she was finished. Her hand on Fugi's shoulder stopped the progress. "I remember what took place," she said, "and I never did thank you for risking everything on my behalf. Whatever happened to draw you here was obviously beyond your control. I thought you should know that I consider you a good trustworthy person. I forgive your involvement in my abduction. As far as I'm concerned, you've always been a prisoner here and I'll tell that to the world."

All efforts momentarily stopped, Fugi slowly facing Penny. Tears lined my eyes watching this exchange. Then Fugi started grinning. "If anyone sings Cumbaya," she said, "I'm taking one of those guns to shoot myself. I hate that song!"

Penny snorted, and then started giggling. Fugi pulled her into a hug, eventually separating to open more cases. Just for spite, I started humming the song as I stepped out of the room. More of Penny's giggling responded, while Fugi said something below her breath. It's probably a good thing I didn't hear. I hadn't gotten three steps away when I noticed Penny leaning out the door.

"Where are you going?" She asked.

"We need something to carry all that. I don't want guns or bullets left for the others. Some of those jumpsuits look like they could double quite nicely as bags."

She started to follow me until I held up my hand. "Why don't you stay here and help Fugi?" I asked. "I'll be right back."

According to my estimate, we've used about an hour and a half. Fugi assumed they were far from here when the alarm sounded, but something in the way Earl talked to me just before leaving makes me wonder if that's true. We have to keep moving or we might get caught by surprise. She nodded and returned inside the room. Walking the straight path back toward the other hallway entrance was easy compared to that twisted chaos beyond the museum. After picking the first three suits, I returned.

Fugi and Penny had already loaded four guns with the rest waiting in open cases. I placed the clothes on the floor. Their attention shifted between me and what they were doing as I partially unbuttoned one. Next I tied knots in the arms and legs, and then carried it to the closest wall. There I started scooping up weapons and letting them fall freely into the suit. It became painfully obvious there were too many here for us to conceivably make it in one trip. "I really hate leaving any guns behind," I said, "but we have to move on."

"That's not a problem," Fugi said. "We'll toss what we can't carry into the bushes."

What a brilliant idea. Those bunched-up grates form a dangerous hedge along both walls. If they cut through the magnetic door, it'll take too much time to dig them out. And if they use an explosive, chances are the guns will be damaged beyond repair.

"Sounds great," I said.

A gun's bullet chamber snapping closed responded. Fugi reached under the case to bring out two shoulder holsters. Then she started walking toward me. "I know you said you're not experienced handling guns," she said, "but I'd feel one hell of a lot better if you'd take this six-shooter for now and a gun with a large magazine in a few."

Penny was in the process of putting two shoulder holsters on when Fugi arrived. I nodded and allowed her to latch one to each shoulder. It felt strange once the gun was inserted, like something was pulling a strap into my back. Instinctive shoulder movements tried alleviating the discomfort to no avail. "You'll get used to it," Fugi said.

When she turned to walk away, Penny approached with another pistol. "This one holds sixteen bullets," she said. "I'll show you the safety when we're finished with everything."

About fifteen minutes later, we'd cleaned out the room carrying a large cache of weapons and bullets while throwing the rest into the tangled mess toward the magnetic door. When we'd climbed over the chairs to the next hall, I removed the chair from inside the once electrified hall and slid both chairs out of reach. Then I smiled. "Let's go set some traps," I said.

On the way down the hall our sacks of guns were placed in the clothes room, and then we gently slid the waiting exploding door close to the shower room. Fugi jumped into the room, walking to the drain where she retrieved Fred's ruined shoes.

"You're not the only one to think of problem solutions," Fugi said to me. "The wallet is gone. We can use these to lift the door into the hinges."

A chuckle escaped from me as I shook my head and smiled. Fugi stepped out of the room, carefully lining the shoes upside down near the frame. Next we slid the top toward the middle of the hall angling it so the bottom would tilt on the shoes, and then raised the back edge carefully.

Squishing noises sounded when the door was full weight on the shoes. Water splattered out from under them in all directions, small streams flowing toward the hall drain. Then we carefully positioned the door so the back edge could slip into the hinge clasps. To my relief it slid in with ease. Liquid squeezed from the shoes acted like a lubricant. Fugi's idea worked flawlessly. With the two of them holding it steady, it took little effort for me to push the pin through the middle hinge. Once that was done, Fugi returned to the storage room for a steak knife and sawed the shoes loose. She tossed the remains into the shower room and faced me. "Should we put in the rest of the hinge pins?" She asked.

"I don't think it'll be necessary," I said. "When the door is closed no one will notice it from the hall. Let's move on to the next phase."

It was like a cloud suddenly built over Fugi. Her entire demeanor darkened. "You two rest," she ominously said. "I'll get the collars."

She turned so quickly we had no time to respond. Her hand fished out the keys, and she unlocked the main chamber door, leaving it open after stepping through. The collars were on the floor of her cell, requiring her to enter it briefly.

"What was that all about?" Penny asked.

At first I thought I was imagining things. "Beats me," I said.

Fugi slowly left the room cradling a collar in each hand. When she reached us, she gently placed one on the floor and carefully rose while digging the remote from her pocket. She slowly handed the remote to me saying "these puppies are now activated. Penny, please return to your old room for now. In the event I accidentally set this damn thing off, I'll need Joyce to push some buttons that might kill you."

Penny's face showed growing terror as she slowly backed in that direction, and then took off running. Once she was inside the room,

Fugi faced me. "I want to do the door in the other hall first," she said. "That way if anything goes wrong, you can figure something else out for here."

Now I'm confused. "What do you mean?"

Grim determination filled her features as she gently began walking toward the other hall. Her expression pulled me along like iron filings after a magnet, subtle fears now rising in my mind. "Remember the tamper guard?" She asked. "If anything tugs on the collar, it's set to punish at first, but slowly rise until it reaches enough electricity to kill."

We'd reached the next hall door, which forced her to concentrate on moving through without chancing a bump or stumble into the frame. Once safely through she continued. "I don't know what's going to happen when I let this thing go on a metallic knob."

"Then let's disarm it and put it on the knob."

A smile grew on her face as she shook her head while putting the collar in her other hand so she could reach the keys. "That won't work," she said. "Though you probably didn't pay it any attention, when the collar was released a small amount of electricity zapped your neck. It feels like a slight tingle or itch, but it is electricity. The same is true when the collar is armed, and it might be enough to set off the explosives. In case arming it won't cause the door to blow we can't risk setting the traps any other way. We're only going to get one chance at this. When Earl sees the remote pointed at him he will take cover. He may be many things but he isn't stupid; here."

She handed the keys to me. I accepted them, slowly looking into Fugi's eyes. Warmth and compassion were clearly visible in them. "Pick your door, but remember to keep the handle still when turning the key," she said.

As I walked toward the door closest to this entrance, great anger started building. When it first began I'm unsure, but it made me grip the knob so hard Fugi gasped. "I hate this," I said. "I hate this pressure and I hate having to jeopardize people I've grown to care about because of Earl; that son of a bitch! If anything happens to you I'd never be able to live with myself. It's my idea. Give me the collar. Let me put it on the door."

When I opened the room, chains hanging from the back wall reflected hall lighting. My mouth dropped open as I faced Fugi. "This is one of the rooms Earl uses for his less than perfect acquisitions," she said. "Those who end up here usually become targets for hunt clubs, slaves working dangerous tasks no one in their right mind would touch, or given to Doc for his fiendish experiments. Since I've been around, anyone put here, well, I did my best to liberate them the only way I knew how."

Chills coursed down my spine as I understood her meaning. She'd killed anyone she could get to who was assigned here. Fugi was looking at the floor, obviously worried about my reaction.

I am a woman of my word and won't turn her in no matter what else I might discover. In a strange way, she thought that was the right thing to do. When she slowly looked at me, I forced a slight smile. "What was in the past remains there," I said. "Now let me put the collar on the knob and let's move on."

Her head shook again. "No; I want to do this for two reasons" she said. "First it's because of the things I did. I hope this will tip the scales a little more in my favor. But the most important reason is you. You didn't ask to be here while I willingly joined. I did nothing the night Fred placed a cloth with chloroform over your face, and idly watched as they prepared you for the treatments. That makes this my sole responsibility to right one of those wrongs. No more arguments. Our time is running out. Go back to the other hall, close the door and wait until I knock. Either way you'll know I'm finished."

Something in that choice of words made me realize her recent murder admission matters little to me. All of her actions proved her heart is good. If she doesn't make it, I'd miss her tremendously. But what she said about my presence and Penny's as well is true. Out of the three of us, she's the only one who wasn't dragged here. A nod of my head followed. She smiled back, and then pointed with her hand for me to leave. "Get out of here before I lose my nerve," she said. "No tears now; one way or the other we will meet again. Remember; wait until you hear me knock before opening the door."

My legs felt rubbery walking away. After stepping through, I faced her. She was looking at the inside knob, her attention set completely on the task waiting for completion. A glance from her displayed impatience at my tardy movements. Slowly I closed the door wondering if I'd just sealed her doom.

CHAPTER 21

What is taking so long? It's been at least five minutes and this silence is maddening. Oh my God what if she's hurt and can't cry out? I can't stand this waiting.

Walking back and forth didn't alleviate my mounting anxiety. Each time I stopped to press my ear against the door, absolute quiet built the tension a little more. At least if she's in pain, I think I'd hear something. Approaching footsteps from behind drew my attention toward the main chamber door. Penny moved to the threshold, leaning against the frame asking "What's going on? Where's Fugi?"

"There's a danger placing the collars on those doors," I said. "If it should get jostled, the door will explode. She's putting the collar on one in there."

I pointed toward the closed-off hallway. Penny's eyes opened wide, her expression showing grave concern. When she stepped into this hall I held up my hand. "Just in case I need to help Fugi," I said, "it would be best if you stay at a safe distance."

She backed a few steps but remained close enough to watch. "How long has she been in there?"

"I guess about ten minutes now."

Penny's mouth fell open. She looked at the closed door, and then at me again. "Do you think we should check on her?"

My head started shaking. "No; she was very specific in telling me to wait until she knocks. Plus I don't want to risk startling her in any way. I tell you, this waiting is driving me insane!"

Her face changed to one of sadness, apparently thinking things I wouldn't permit myself to consider. If anything goes wrong, it'll rest squarely on my shoulders.

Sudden dizziness hit, making me lean against the wall. It felt like the floor started shifting underfoot, threatening my balance. Penny rushed forward to steady me. "What's wrong?" She asked.

Gradually it diminished; a slight smile grew on my face as I looked at her. "I'll be okay," I said.

A series of knocks pounded the door. Penny and I looked at each other smiling. I'd already placed the key in the lock, allowing me to quickly yank the door open. Fugi looked at us with a grin, entering the hall holding a large roll of aluminum foil and two strips of rope. "Piece of cake," she said while glancing at me.

I looked at the foil and rope, and then thought about how I'd been worried for her safety while she was simply gathering supplies. "You didn't think to let us know you were okay before going on a scavenger hunt?" I asked.

She shrugged her shoulders while walking toward the shower room. "I'm sorry about that," she said, "but I was right there. It only took a second for me to get-"

Dizziness hit again. Fugi dropped all items rushing to assist me. Penny was already by my side, helping me remain standing. "You need a nap," Fugi said. "Let's go to the living room where you can stretch out on a couch."

When my equilibrium returned, I slowly shook my head. "There's no time," I said. "I don't think we have the five hours you've deduced. The way Earl talked to me just before leaving makes me think he didn't go that far. We have to set-up the shower room, hang mattresses from the main chamber ceiling cables near the door to protect against ricochets, that dreadful grinding machine has to be moved into position, the living room has to be prepared; no. We have to keep moving. I have to keep moving."

Fugi looked at Penny, nodded her head, and they began pulling me toward the room. I tried fighting them, but it was like all strength had faded. They were able to move me without much struggle.

"Are your muscles feeling a tad weak now Joyce?" Fugi asked. "Listen to me very carefully. Your entire central nervous system has recently undergone a seriously traumatic event. Though it will soon fade, you're still susceptible to attack. The drugs Earl uses are so potent he can only administer three watered-down doses and then has to wait a week before continuing. You know why? Because any more would literally burn up the brain as has happened in the past.

216

Tremendous sporadic fatigue always follows the treatments. If you don't rest now, and let's say you're right about Earl getting here sooner than expected, you won't get another chance until this is over. Imagine that dizziness hitting just when you start exchanging gunfire with Hank."

"She's right Joyce," Penny said. "I remember that exhaustion vividly. It's not your fault nor is it a sign of weakness. It's your body's natural reaction to the terror they perpetrate. Besides you've done enough. Rest and let us finish."

As much as I hate to admit it, all they said makes sense. I do feel tired, and if that dizziness hits at a bad time I may never recover.

"Okay you win," I said. "I'm really sorry guys."

Both looked at me like they thought I was crazy, but I couldn't help feeling guilty. There's still a lot of work left and I'm forced to rest at a critical time.

As if to make certain I did as suggested, we entered the living room together. Penny released her grip while Fugi guided me to the couch adjacent to the door. While sitting on the couch, I looked at Fugi. "Tell me what it's like."

Fugi glanced at me with a puzzled expression. "What what's like?" She asked.

"I killed Fred because I had no other choice," I said, "but this is different. Tell me what it's like to kill someone from a distance."

Her face changed to one of understanding. She looked at Penny, motioning with her head for Penny to come close. Once she was nearby, Fugi looked at me with a gentle smile. "We've been so busy running in every direction, it's only now hit you," she said. "Before I answer, let me ask you a question. How did you manage to kill Fred with such a strong conscience that obviously abhors the thought of killing another person?"

My eyes closed as memories of our battle returned, like I was fighting for my life again. Shivers ran though my body, prompting Fugi to place a hand on my shoulder. That caused me to open my eyes. "I concentrated on all the things he did to me, and then started imagining the horrors he did to Penny. When I got mad enough, I acted."

Fugi's head was nodding, her expression changed to grim determination. "That's how you do it. Concentrate on how you got here and all the horrors they committed. Then you have to get vicious;

I mean mad-dog crazy and just act on instinct. Shoot your gun until you start the plan, and when the time comes don't even consider what will happen. Just push the button. Keep in mind there will be no truce. They cannot be bargained with, kept at bay without pulling the trigger, nor will they surrender. It's them or us. You have got to stay focused. They will be, believe it. And if our plan fails, you might not need to kill. I'm a pretty good shot if I say so myself. In any event, give them no quarter, and always keep safe. Earl can pick us off with what we might think an impossible shot. One final thing; never lose sight of why this is necessary. You didn't ask for it, but by God can finish it. Everything we do is completely justified."

She started to leave when I asked one more question. "I keep visualizing Fred's floating body, will that ever stop?"

Her eyes closed as she drew a deep breath. When they reopened, she glanced at Penny and then me. "No," she said and turned away.

They quietly stepped out of sight, leaving me to think about a future of horrible memories. I suppose that's better than no future at all. Then I thought about Fugi saying we were justified and knew she was right. Though it won't remove the sight of Fred spurting blood, it might help me live with the visions. I raised my legs on the couch to lie down. My eyes closed and I could feel myself drifting asleep almost immediately.

I'm floating through the air toward a bar with a bright neon sign outside. It looks vaguely familiar. Now I'm inside handing money to the cashier.

After I paid the bill and stepped through the door, I noticed both cars present when I pulled up were still here. My rational mind said John was simply walking home, while my creative side screamed run. Another quick scope of the area showed nothing out of the ordinary, but I still hurried my pace. Just when I reached my car door, tires screeching from the road rushed into the lot. A black van pulled between me and the bar, slowing when it was two feet away. The sliding door yanked open before it had stopped. Panic filled me as I desperately opened my purse in search of keys. Footsteps hitting the pavement started to draw my attention, but a cloth with an oily smell was placed over my face blocking the view. Everything started becoming fuzzy; almost surrealistic like a dream. All fear melted away as I relaxed into oblivion.

Beautiful swirling colors filled my sight, replacing the dread I felt a moment ago. Was that some sort of note in the rainbow?

The colors faded away, leaving me tied to a bed in a small room. I know that person standing near the door. His name is Hank and he has an evil smile on his face. An empty plate with crusted gravy is in his hands, which he shifted as he started talking.

"Everyone, and I do mean everyone, thinks Earl is insane with all the preposterous claims he makes. How in the world could he possibly sell over two thousand people without getting caught; they think. Then they start scheming, convincing themselves how they're going to be the ones to blow the whistle. Oh, and let's not forget his cavalier attitude about introducing us; some of our more strong-willed cut through the humiliation to really pay attention. Did you think it was out of arrogance that he talked like it didn't matter?"

A churning rainbow sprang from his belly, filling the air with beautiful colors. Why did they flicker a second ago? Now Earl is coming into focus, seated at a table close to me. I'm resting on a bed, nervously listening to his bragging while struggling to conceal my high anxiety.

"It all begins with homework," he said. "People who needed my services first contacted my associate. That way if it turned out to be a trap, when I struck they'd never see it coming. Only once did a set-up almost succeed, but that's not important for tonight's campfire tale. By understanding the habits and patterns of not only my marks but also my clients, I was able to precisely choose when to literally take-out one or the other. Hollywood glamorizes what I did, making it look like a guy in a suit hiding in bushes. Though I found it mildly amusing, it was as far from me as you can get. They always died. I'm still here."

His face started changing colors, patterns leaving the confines of his head to start engulfing everything in sight. Fears faded away watching the beautiful pastels flowing in circles so gently. It changed for an instant, becoming white and then returning. Slowly the colors began fading into Mark standing in the doorway pointing a small device at me. He'd just discovered how I was planning to seduce him in order to escape and was mad.

"I'm not going to say this again," he said. "Get that lying, conniving ass out of bed or I'll kill you on your back!"

My mind rapidly searched for something to disarm this situation, but nothing came forward. Then it dawned on me he was alone. These actions might not be sanctioned by Earl. Either this was a frightful test or he was acting impulsively. If it's the latter, he'd face an almost certain death sentence should he proceed, yet he doesn't seem worried. As I climbed off the mattress to face him, I silently prayed for the first choice.

A wicked smile grew as he said "I want to watch you squirm like the maggot you are. We'll start off slowly just so you enjoy the full spectrum of that collar. Do you have any last words before we begin?"

He wants me to beg for mercy. I will not give him the satisfaction. "No."

At this point my escape plans were back to the beginning, and since they have drugs capable of forcing me to tell them anything they want to know, perhaps death would be a welcome release. His eyes grew wild, jaw tightened, and he lifted the remote a little higher so it was pointed at the collar. My eyes looked at his in defiance. Then his hand lowered. "This would be too easy," he said. "You deserve something much more lingering for playing with a man's heart. See you soon, lover."

White light shot from his eyes, breaking into many colors as it spread out. Everything vanished under the intensity of the swirling rainbow. It flickered briefly before changing into the main chamber. I was tied to a chair looking at the male Fugi lying motionless on the floor, a dart stuck in his calf. Earl was talking to me, instilling great terror at what he was saying. Hank entered the room holding a hypodermic needle with a yellow serum inside. He smiled while holding the needle up for me to see, and walked to stand in front of me.

"A scant few have bad reactions to the character assassination, requiring us to administer tests that weed out those who can't adjust. I mean we hardly ever fail, but if you look at six ninety-eight, you'll see how once in awhile we turn out a dud. The first test always involves snakes. We plant an unshakeable terror that freezes movement at the mere mention of one. Then if behavior remains unchanged except for that glaring difference, we know the candidate could probably handle our modifications and move on to the second treatment. You passed it with flying colors by the way. Just in case that fear already existed, we find something for the second test the inductee isn't afraid of like frogs, birds, mice, or in your case, insects. Then we put out irresistible bait. If we succeed, you live. Had you overcome the terror to grab the phone, any button pushed would've activated the kill setting of your collar. Thank you so much for being alive!"

My head started shaking denial as Hank held the needle in the air, tapping the glass container and then squirting a tiny amount into the air.

"Goodbye Joyce Allison Jackson, hello BL seven forty-two," Earl said.

"Don't-; don't-; don't-; don't-"

Yellow serum inside the syringe began changing to many colors, streaming out of the needle to fill the air in a kaleidoscope of patterns. Constant flickering in the colors began hurting my eyes, forcing me to squint. Some kind of message kept flashing in front of me, disappearing too fast to read.

"You will not remember any dreams you have while sleeping," a voice boomed. "Do you understand?"

"Yes."

Snakes and insects began crawling on my feet, coming up my legs to my stomach. I was helpless against their assault which they seemed to know. Their casual exploration of my body froze the breath in my throat. One of the snakes opened its mouth, two fangs dripping venom as it reared up to strike my face.

"NO!" I shouted, startling myself awake.

As I bolted upright with my heart racing, Penny and Fugi seated in armchairs near me looked on with concern. A table set between them was covered with pistols apparently loaded and ready. Fugi was the first to speak. "Relax; it was just a dream. Do you remember it?"

Penny watched me closely, a very worried expression on her face. Fugi calmly waited for me to think about it. I have no idea why I woke up so frightened. There were no dreams. "I wasn't dreaming," I said. "It must've been a noise or something that startled me."

They looked at each other with puzzled expressions before facing me again. "We've been as quiet as possible," Penny said. "I'm sorry if we awakened you."

221

"It's okay," I said with a smile growing.

The foggy remnants of sleep finally dissipated enough for their seated presence in this room to register. A yawn escaped, I stretched my arms, and rose from the couch to walk next to them. "Do you need help with anything?" I asked.

Both grinned while continuing their task of loading guns. "Everything is set," Fugi said. "All that's left is to slide that couch into position. Save your strength. You're going to need it soon."

"How long have I been asleep?"

Fugi shrugged her shoulders as Penny snapped a bullet chamber into position. "Maybe an hour and a half," Fugi said, "maybe two. Do you feel better?"

My mouth dropped open. They remained seated and grinning as I quickly walked to the doorway.

Fred's bundle of clothes was gone. Nothing in any of the hallways indicated we'd prepared anything. They'd done a remarkable job at cleaning up the evidence of our door swapping. The door in front of the shower room was closed, and the grinder was positioned in front of the main steel door to the chamber holding it open. A small space between the wall opposite the closed overhead door and the end of the grinder permitted limited access to the room. Footsteps approaching from behind indicated they'd arrived.

"I'll take you on the ten-cent tour which for today is only nine and a half cents," Fugi said. "All major credit cards accepted."

Two surprised chuckles left me as I slowly faced her in wonder. Penny was standing to the rear, a large smile on her face. Fugi's eyebrows rose as she said "Your idea about mattresses hanging from the bind-cables was sheer genius. Check it out."

Her terminology about the hanging cables chilled me slightly, but not enough to supersede the astonishment I felt. They'd been working feverishly while I slept. It amazed me how none of the sounds they must have made bothered me until now.

I stepped into the hall, followed by Fugi and a limping Penny. That hobble of hers made me grow concerned. It played across my face. Before I could ask she waved her hand like it was nothing. "Fugi wrapped foil around my thigh," she said. "I'll be so thankful to take it off!"

Grins grew on Fugi's and my faces as we walked past the shower room to peer inside the main chamber. Two mattresses were hanging length-wise on each side of the entrance, providing a cushion from the rear eight feet wide. They were three feet away from the front wall, permitting freedom of movement while acting as a close shield. Two holes had been cut out at each upper corner where the cable clasps held them tightly. Fugi watched my expression with pride on her face. "Look a little closer," Penny said.

When I peered over the top of the four foot high grinder, stacks of what are obviously loaded guns were neatly placed close to both sides. We are ready.

"Excellent job guys," I said. "But why didn't you wake me up before now?"

Fugi's shoulders shrugged. "By my estimate, we have an hour or so left before the fun begins," she said. "I'm sorry we awakened you when we did."

"I'M NOT," Earl said, "IT WOULDN'T BE AS MUCH FUN. LOOK OUT KIDDIES, DADDY'S HOME AND HE'S PISSED!"

His voice boomed from inside the main chamber. Panic hit Penny's face as she started to run down the hall. I grabbed her shoulder, which took a lot more effort than I'd anticipated. "He's not in there," I said.

"AH JOYCE, MY BEAUTIFUL TREACHEROUS SIREN," Earl said. "DON'T YOU KNOW BY NOW I'M EVERYWHERE?"

I started scanning the hall looking for anything that could conceal a microphone. Fugi snapped her fingers several times, pointing toward the wall high above the chamber floor. Slight discolorations of the paint matched the size of small sunken speakers.

"WHAT; NO COMEBACK?" Earl asked. "I THOUGHT SOMEONE WITH YOUR LEVEL OF EDUCATION WOULD BE QUICK OFF THE HORSE WITH ONE."

Penny removed one of her guns, as did Fugi and I.

"I DON'T KNOW HOW YOU OVERCAME THE DRUGS SEVEN FORTY-TWO, BUT I WILL FIND OUT. YOU'LL BE JOINING SIX NINETY-EIGHT ON HER VISIT TO DOC'S LAB WHERE HE'LL DO A CRANIAL DISSECTION. OF COURSE YOUR HANDS AND FEET WILL BE NAILED DOWN, AND TUBES AND ELECTRODES WILL BE SLID INTO EVERY BODY CAVITY. OH; AND HE'LL KEEP YOU ALIVE AS LONG AS POSSIBLE. YOU WILL FEEL HIS CUTTING, DIGGING, AND POKING. DOESN'T THAT SOUND EXCITING?"

Six hidden speakers on the three visible walls were soon discernible thanks to Fugi's pointing. As we nodded at each other, I slowly started squeezing my trigger.

"Let's end this," I said.

My gun-barrel erupted into a thunderous blast, intensified by the close-quarters we were in. Ringing in my ears sprang as quickly as the splintered remnants of a speaker across the room began falling to the floor. Penny and Fugi stared at me in awe, grinning as they each took aim at another speaker.

"FRED HAS TO BE DEAD," Earl said. "HE LOVED IT HERE." Fugi squeezed off a round, killing another speaker. "FUGI," Earl said. "FORGET ABOUT STARDOM. I'M GOING TO SLOW-ROAST YOU ALIVE!" Penny squeezed off a shot, hitting a speaker on the side wall. "SIX NINETY-EIGHT, I'M GOING TO STRING YOU UP BY YOUR LIMBS IN A VERY SPECIAL ROOM AND LET YOU HANG NAKED AS BUG FOOD. BY THE TIME I TURN YOU OVER TO DOC, YOU'LL BE NOTHING MORE THAN ONE HUGE FESTERING SORE! BUT I HAVE THE BEST IN STORE FOR YOU, MY PRECIOUS JOYCE."

Fugi lowered her gun, slapping her forehead with her free hand. That grabbed our attention as she dashed to the hinge side of the main door and pointed at a wire running six inches below the top of the door to the frame. The cable went into the door and looked thick enough to pull it shut. She briefly held her finger to her lips before hopping on the grinder to grab the wire. "MAKE EVERY BULLET COUNT," Fugi shouted. "WE'VE ONLY GOT ABOUT EIGHT ROUNDS LEFT DAMN THAT FIRE!"

She raised her gun toward the back wall of the chamber and fired two shots in rapid succession. "NO JOYCE, STOP," she said. "LET ME TAKE OUT THE SPEAKERS!"

Another shot was squeezed as she yanked the wire out of the door at almost the same instant. Laughter sounded from the remaining speakers eerily timed with Fugi's jumping to the floor.

"ARE YOU HAVING TROUBLES MY CUTE ORIENTAL LAP-DANCER?" Earl asked. "TRY NOT TO BOTHER THAT PRETTY LITTLE BROW OVER ME. I'M ABOUT TO DO SOMETHING THAT'LL MAKE ALL OTHER WORRIES PALE BY COMPARISON."

224

Each of us took a stance to aim at three different speakers once Fugi gave a thumbs-up.

"HEY JOYCE, ARE YOU LISTENING?" Earl asked. "I KNOW YOU ARE SO HERE GOES; SWITCHER SEVEN FORTY-TWO!"

My body froze watching streams of colors beam out of the barrel to my gun, filling the air with rapidly swirling patterns engulfing everything else. A door appeared in the middle, opening to a barren wasteland on the other side. Soil flew upward from that side, slowly turning into an open grave. Snakes and insects started slithering across the ground moving to the door.

Two ghostly images painlessly separated from me, one an exact duplicate and the other a young girl. Golden light appearing to be shimmering twine connected all of us at the head. The transparent replica walked through the door, falling in the grave. Earth began covering her; a great sword appeared in the sky with the words "Switcher seven forty-two" written on the blade. It moved toward the gold cord coming out of the grave, swinging down to sever it. My thoughts became confused until the little girl backed into me. Everything began calming as the door closed and winked out of existence. All colors faded; the little girl telling me what to do. Slowly I pointed my pistol at Fugi's back.

CHAPTER 22

"WHAT ARE YOU DOING?" Penny said. "FUGI WATCH OUT!"

Fugi's head jerked toward me, immediately dropping on her belly rolling in my direction. The little girl in my mind told me to ignore Fugi and kill Penny. As I started to turn, a leg kicked my feet out from under me.

"ARE WE HAVING FUN LADIES?" Earl asked.

I tumbled backwards, the pistol flying from my hand. My head hit the floor hard. A hundred points of light filled my vision. Penny rushed forward to remove the remaining gun from my harness before I could recover.

"Shit, God damn him to hell I didn't believe it," Fugi said. "Quick Penny, shoot the speakers!"

When I tried to rise, Fugi stepped on my chest restricting my ability to breathe. Penny moved between the wall and the grinder, entering the room where she rapidly took aim. The girl said I must stop Penny, intensifying my strength. Fugi looked at me as I struggled, putting more weight on her leg. Then the girl said wait for the opportunity.

"You stay down or I'll put you down permanently," Fugi said.

An explosion sounded, followed by two more incredibly loud pops from her gun. Earl's voice sounded tinny coming from the last speaker. "You girls enjoy play time for now. If you survive you won't"; another blast from her pistol ended his talk.

Penny lowered her gun, slowly walking toward the grinder. As she looked at me, tears lined her eyes. "What's wrong with her?" She asked.

"I must kill you both," I said. "Let me up."

Fugi put more weight on me, causing my chest to feel like bones were about to break as she said "Yeah like that's going to happen." Penny's mouth fell open staring at me.

"God damn it!" Fugi said. "That son of a bitch really did it!" She looked at Penny, anger on her face. "Mark told me about a subliminal message imbedded in the hypnosis screen that's activated with a phrase. The command is to kill with whatever tools are available. Once everyone else is dead she's to kill herself. Shit he never saw it used and I didn't really believe him." Her eyes slowly set on me, narrowing to slits as her gun began moving. "We've lost her Penny. There's no other way."

Penny recovered from her shock. Her speed picked up working around the grinder. "Don't even think it," she said. "She didn't give up on you or me. I'll be damned if I'm giving up on her. We'll lock her in a room where she can't hurt anyone and get help when this is over."

A heavy sigh escaped Fugi as she brought her gun to aim at my forehead. "She's nothing more than a killing machine watching for the moment to strike," Fugi said. "The command is controlling her every thought. This is more merciful."

Sounds of a gun hammer being cocked came from behind Fugi, causing her to look concerned. "Lower your gun," Penny said. "We're doing this my way."

Another sigh preceded Fugi moving the gun away from me, but she kept her leg on my chest while facing Penny, whose gun was still pointed at her.

"I can't move off or she'll try something stupid," Fugi said. "Don't shoot; I'll turn her over to your custody. She's your responsibility though. Don't lower your guard."

Slowly Penny's gun went down, but she held it in front of her like she was prepared to shoot. Her expression changed to one of concern as she looked at me, and then back at Fugi. "Do I have a subliminal message?" she asked.

Fugi's head nodded as she answered, not paying much attention to me; soon. "Count on it. Obviously it isn't the same as with Joyce or I'd be squaring off against Earl alone." Penny's face showed fright, returning her stare at me.

"I wouldn't worry about it," Fugi said. "Earl forgot or he would've used it when he spoke Joyce's. Put it out of your mind and stay focused. Get prepared for all-out war. They'll give Joyce a little time to, finish, and then come rushing in to clean up what's left. You have to move her out of the way now."

Fugi relaxed her pressure just enough. I jerked upward, catching her by surprise. Penny rushed toward my back, flipping her pistol butt-side out just as Fugi landed on her back. A grunt exploded from Fugi as I started to rise.

"I'm so sorry for this Joyce," Penny said as she quickly raised her gun in the air. It came down too fast for me to block. My hands flailed outward just as it reached the top of my skull.

I'm a big girl now. My first real report card proves it. There's mommy standing in the door smiling at me. This is going to be great. "How was school?" Mommy asked.

She knows the report cards went out. I think I'll play with her a little. "It was gross. Stevie who sits next to me ate a worm at recess; yuck."

My face formed a sick expression as I acted like I was gagging. When I started to go past her, she scooped me from the porch and lifted me into a hug. "That's what we're having for dinner," she said kissing my cheek.

Her lips tickled my face making me giggle. Then she held me out forming a stern face, but I could see the grin behind it. "Where is it young lady?" She asked. "I want to see your report card."

As she turned to place me inside the house, I felt terrific. With one exception I'd gotten all excellent grades. Mrs. Branch said my writing could improve but I still scored a satisfactory mark. Once I pulled it out of my backpack to hand her, a smile formed as she looked it over. Her smile broadened as she lowered it. "I'm very proud of you," she said. "Wait till your dad sees this."

Her praise made me feel even better. Daddy never smiles when he sees me, and I don't know what I did to make him angry all the time. At last he'll be happy with me.

"Mommy, can Mary come over?"

"Of course she can sweetheart."

Though she had more toys than me, I had the complete Bunny and Sam doll set including her best friends, Kevin and Margaret. We liked to play house with them. Mommy phoned Mary while I went to watch my favorite western television show, *Rifleshot!* The show had been on fifteen minutes when mommy came downstairs.

"Your father just called," she said. "He told me to turn off the TV if you were watching anything with guns or fighting. He doesn't think it right for girls to see so much violence. I'll make a deal with you. If you don't tell him I'm letting you watch this show, I won't either. What do you say pumpkin?"

A smile grew on my face. "I won't; thanks mommy. Did he ask about my grades?"

The doorbell rang at that moment, briefly drawing her attention. Then she looked at me, her smile fading. "That must be Mary. No honey he didn't. Someone walked into his office and he had to go before I could bring it up. Don't worry precious; he'll see them very soon."

"Okay mommy."

She smiled, and then turned to walk upstairs. On the TV Marshall Fulton was surrounded by bank robbers shooting at him. It looked like he needed help. I rose from my seat watching how he aimed carefully. When he held out his pistol, I held out my arm pretending I was beside him. Bang; there goes a bad guy.

"Oh gross," Mary said. "Why are you watching this?"

Surprise grew on my face as I looked at her. "This is the best show," I said. "It's almost over anyway. Do you want to play with my dolls?"

Her expression changed from disgust to happiness. "Can I be Bunny this time?" She asked.

Bunny was the best, a fashion model, beauty queen, princess, and athlete. Her friends were no match for her. Since I've always been Bunny, and Mary has let me do things I wanted to do at her house, I decided to agree. "Oh, okay; let's go."

Marshall Fulton had gotten most of the robbers by now. It was down to just one more. He always wins. Even though I really like watching how he saves the day, this is more important. I turned off the TV and we rushed upstairs to my room.

For two hours we played house, eating a dinner Margaret made for Bunny's birthday, and going out to the movies on a double date. The sun was starting to go down when the phone rang. Mommy's muffled voice came through my closed door, but we both knew what it meant.

Mary helped me start cleaning up.

"Mary, that was your mother," mommy said. "It's time for you to go home."

"Okay Mrs. Jackson," Mary said. "I'll be right down."

Once Bunny and the rest were put back in her home, I walked Mary downstairs and to the door. She ran down the porch steps, stopping long enough to wave at me before running next door. Then I went to the basement to watch more television.

Sir Scratch-A-Lot, Secret Agent Pooch was on. That silly dog and his French side-kick Cat-Mandu were always getting into trouble, yet they managed to scratch their way out at the last minute. It made me laugh watching their clumsy antics.

Our kitchen door opened as Sir Scratch-A-Lot was digging a hole to escape the evil clutches of arch-enemy Hare Hoodlum, the meanest rabbit to ever live. Daddy started speaking softly at first but his voice rose in anger. Mommy tried talking softly yet he kept interrupting. Then I heard him stomping upstairs toward the bedrooms, silence for a few seconds followed by his thundering clomp downstairs to the kitchen.

"Up here NOW Joyce," he angrily shouted. "I want to discuss your grades."

My heart raced as I turned off the TV. He stood at the top of the steps watching me climb. When I was in front of him, he stood aside letting me see the table.

Bunny, Sam, Kevin, and Margaret were lying on their backs like they were going to be part of dinner. Daddy just glared at me a few moments before walking toward the living room entrance. He stopped and faced me.

"I'm very disappointed with your grades," he said, and then held up his hand as I started to say something. "You can speak when I say so. Even if you are just a girl, I still expect your grades to be better. There must be too many distractions around here. Part of it is television. You're still watching those war and western shows; aren't you?"

Tears started lining my eyes. I'd promised mommy I wouldn't tell him, but my best toys are at stake. "Yes, but not as-"

"That's-, what I thought," he said while glaring at mommy before looking at me. "Those shows are for boys not girls. They have fighting and bad guys and heroes, not magic castles or flying ponies. It's a waste for you to watch them since you couldn't possibly comprehend what they're truly about. Learn to cook and clean not fight."

"Now just a minute," mommy said, but another heated stare from daddy silenced her.

Why is he saying these mean things to me? What did I do to make him act like this? Tears started flowing down my cheeks, which only made him madder.

"You see," he said, "that's what makes girls weaker than boys. We don't cave-in to emotions like that. Stop crying and take your punishment. Until your grades are better, there'll be no more television or friends for you."

My eyes opened wide as his meaning registered. Those dolls are my friends just as much as Mary. "No daddy please; I'll do better in school I promise!"

His eyes narrowed and mouth frowned as he walked across the kitchen to a cupboard and removed a large bowl. Mommy stepped out of his way as he went to the sink and began filling the bowl with water. "Did I give you permission to speak?" He asked. "No I didn't. Now you're going to learn the consequences of disobeying me."

"What are you doing Brent?' Mommy asked.

He turned the spigot off without looking at her. But when he started moving the bowl toward the table, she stepped in front. "She's just a baby," she said. "Would you please calm down?"

Faint hope started rising watching mommy with a defiant expression standing in the way. Daddy didn't back down or look afraid. "Get out of my way," he said.

Her head started shaking in denial. "No; whatever you have in mind, I forbid it!"

An evil smile grew on his face, making me cringe. Mommy remained still, but her face seemed to be changing. "If you want to leave feel free," he said. "Keep in mind I know the judge personally and you'll be living in poverty before I'm finished. Now either step aside or start packing."

As her eyes lowered and she moved away, my breathing became difficult. He placed the bowl on the table, putting all my dolls under water head first. Bubbles rose for a few moments, which he made certain I could watch. When the water calmed, he casually lifted them one at a time to carry to the microwave oven. My mouth was open, frozen in shock. Dribbles of water traced four paths across the linoleum floor once he was done. Then he slammed the door shut and looked at me.

"From this time forward," he said, "any grades below perfect will be dealt with swiftly and decisively. You will also do exactly as I say when I say it without hesitation or argument. If you do not comply, more of your girlie things will end up like this!"

He slowly faced the oven, moving in what seemed sluggish motion. His hand appeared to leave traces of light as it moved to program ten minutes on the timer. When he pressed the enter button, my heart sank and tears streamed down my cheeks.

Nothing happened for the first few seconds, but then the dolls started moving almost like they were suffering. Margaret's head bulged, forming a misshapen horror until it popped with an audible sound. Her headless body writhed and twisted in what looked great agony.

Sam's arm began bending down in an impossible position like it was broken in a dozen places. His head began shrinking on one side while ballooning out on the other. Kevin's belly shrunk to a flattened mess. And my absolute favorite doll in the entire world, Bunny, began melting on one side. Her head started growing, building into a huge ball twice its normal size with smaller bubbles forming along her scalp. It continued expanding, growing larger and larger until it-

----

A tremendous explosion rocked me into a semi-conscious state. Bunny's head popped at the same time something happened here. My mind saw colors swirling, with a door opening in the center. Snakes and huge insects began rushing through the opening at me. The little girl was demanding I close the door, but I moved backwards two steps leaving her to face them alone.

For many months after watching the terrible destruction of my best toys, I endured nightmares. Over time I realized nothing I dreamt of would ever hurt me. It gave me strength to survive the worst punishments imaginable. This scene no longer frightened me, a determination rose to end it. As the little girl screamed in her efforts at ridding the vermin, I calmly walked through them to the other side.

All creatures moved out of the way like they knew I could kill them. Soil began heaving underfoot; a hand broke through reaching

up. I grabbed it, helping a transparent replica of myself rise to the surface. The sword with Switcher seven forty-two etched on both sides appeared at my feet, which for the time being I left alone.

Agonized screams from the little girl tried to interfere, calling for help. It was ignored as the other Joyce and I smiled at each other, and then she turned to back into me. A painless merger took place; two became one. Memories both past and present returned seamlessly. The little girl remained separate demanding I look at her. Those loud commands drew my attention.

At first she was alone, but then a strange mist formed near her. Dad standing next to the microwave as my dolls exploded appeared when the fog withdrew, alternating his attention between the girl and me. His expression was one of boredom waiting for me to do something.

Vibrations gently shaking the ground rose from the sword, prompting me to look at it. The girl cried out for me to ignore it, dad remained quiet. I lifted the sword, walking toward both of them. Neither moved when I arrived in front raising the sword in the air.

Without hesitation I brought the sword down on the head of the girl. She vanished when the blade touched her scalp. Dad watched me closely. As I looked at him, I dropped the sword and turned away. He called to me. When I looked, he pointed to the microwave and vanished with a pop that startled me out of the semi-consciousness.

My eyes opened to a disorienting scene. I was in a small room with the door closed. A terrible pain throbbed on top of my head. Gentle examination with my hand indicated a huge bump had risen. Where did it come from?

Remnants of dad pointing at the microwave stayed with my consciousness, reminding me of my childhood. Time quickly advanced to where I was forced to look at a screen with swirling colors. Abruptly everything came rushing back including how Penny knocked me out and why.

Oh dear God I was an automaton programmed to kill! It was like someone else had taken over my body and I couldn't resist. That's why she knocked me out. Then some loud noise happened to wake me up. What's going on outside this room? I've got to get out of here. There has to be a way for me to prove I'm on their side again.

This looks like my first cell and I'd bet money they've locked the door. Okay I'll have to bring them to me. Before I start making a racket, I'd better make sure Earl isn't standing on the other side waiting for me to awaken. Quietly I rose from the bed and crept to the door.

Everything outside is silent; perhaps too quiet. One check of my ankle showed the knife still there. Either they forgot about it or something happened to draw them away before removing it. Regardless of the reason at least I have a weapon. While pounding on the door I shouted "HEY, IT'S ME JOYCE. I'M ALL RIGHT. CAN YOU HEAR ME? HEY!"

The door was locked. My fist pounded again, but for all I could tell no one was alive out there. Absolute silence gave me an eerie feeling of being the only one left. "COME ON GUYS, IT'S ME. OPEN THE DOOR. PLEASE LET ME KNOW YOU'RE OKAY. THIS IS SCARING ME." For a moment I thought I heard a noise, but then nothing else. "HEY, I'M ALL RIGHT. OPEN THE DOOR."

Keys rattling the knob forced me to step back. My heart began racing waiting to see who was on the other side, muscles tightened in anticipation of a fight. Slowly it opened; a shadow backing away crossed the threshold. At least I know it isn't Earl. He would've come rushing in here, not play games just to watch my reaction.

"Is that really you Joyce?" Penny asked.

Relief washed over me like a cooling breeze as a few chuckles escaped. "Yes it's really me. Don't shoot. I'm coming out; okay?"

While raising my hands over my head, I slowly stepped into the main chamber. Penny had a pistol trained on me, looking slightly relieved when she saw how I'd left the room. Even though I made no threatening moves, she held her gun trained on me.

"You've got to get over it," I said. "What's going on? Was there an explosion of some sort?"

Her eyes narrowed while staring at me closely. Then she indicated with her gun for me to move toward the entrance. Fugi stood next to the door, also with a gun pointed at me. "If you don't trust me, put me back in the room," I said. "For Pete's sake would you please point those guns elsewhere? I'd hate to almost get killed a second time."

As we moved toward Fugi, Penny's gun lowered. Fugi kept hers trained on me. When we arrived, she looked at Penny and then me. "Stand ready Penny," she said; "switcher seven forty-two."

CHAPTER 23

Terror forced me to cringe. All eyes were on me, time crept by. Nothing happened. The little girl did not return. Fury rose in my mind as I glared at Fugi. Her gun remained pointed at my head, frown growing and finger gently squeezing the trigger. Penny kept her gun at her side, fearfully watching.

"Why did you say that?" I asked. "Are you *trying* to destroy me? Whose side are you on?"

Smiles grew on their faces as Fugi lowered her weapon. Her head began shaking in disbelief. Penny exhaled loudly.

"Thank God," Penny said.

"I don't know how you do it, but I'm damn glad you do," Fugi said. "Welcome back Joyce!"

"We heard you calling a short while ago," Penny said, "and decided to see what would happen when we let you out. I had to agree that if you did something, well, bad, Fugi would wound you. Fugi also said if you somehow managed to do the impossible again, recover, we had to make absolutely certain when Earl shows up, he can't turn you against us. Please try to see it from our points of view."

What she said makes complete logical sense, but it still didn't prevent me from feeling betrayed. Fugi must've read the emotions on my face as she first glanced down the hall, and then looked at me. "You can hit me later," she said, "but in about five minutes Earl is going to blast through that door. Do you feel up to a small war?"

I feel like I just fought one, albeit a mental war. A slight smile grew on my face as I calmly looked at Penny, and back toward Fugi. "As long as you give me a gun; yes. Was there an explosion of some sort?"

Fugi's expression turned grim as she looked down the hall. "Yes there was," she said. "If I'm not mistaken, the diesel-powered generator on the first basement level went up. When we destroyed the electric grids, it set up a chain reaction in that there was no place for the excess electricity to go. We still have lights and air because there's a smaller back-up generator that automatically cuts on in the event of failure. Earl had been busy trying to save the big one, which was why I wasn't so concerned about him rushing in until now. And I just know we're not lucky enough for any of them to be hurt when it went boom. I'd bet good money they're setting the explosives on the door as I speak, plus Earl is so pissed he's liable to do something stupid. Be prepared for anything. Your timing couldn't have been better, Miss Jackson."

Although I thought her last statement was debatable, I nodded my head. Penny held three guns in one hand to me, an apologetic expression on her face. "Put two of these in your holsters and hold the third in your hand," she said. "I'm really sorry about scaring you like that Joyce."

Her apology was on the verge of begging. It moved me, yet we can't afford emotional weights to interfere with quick judgments. "Though an advance warning would have been appreciated, I understand why you did it," I said. "If I were in your shoes I'd have done the same thing. Forget about it. We have far more pressing matters coming at us full-speed; keep focused and be very careful. But when this is over I want the two of you to buy me a lobster meal as repayment."

Both grinned. Fugi turned to walk between the grinder and wall, making it through faster than I thought possible. She started moving away quickly. Without looking at us she said "Remember, act like I'm in here with you. When all hell breaks loose and you speak to each other, include me in that talk. Don't let on I'm down the hall. Keep low and let me take care of any unfinished business after the big bang. Then we'll all fly to Maine and have that meal done right."

The confidence in her voice helped both Penny and me feel a little better. Even though I'd promised Penny we would be the ones walking out, my entire scheme was based on Fugi's prowess. Sure I shot great before, and Penny seemed comfortable handling guns, but neither one of us had shot another person.

Fugi entered the living room and switched off the lights. Suddenly

I remembered the integral part of our plan and checked my pockets. The remote was gone. Penny moving her hand toward me grabbed my attention. "Looking for this?" She asked. In her palm was the remote. "You'd better keep it just in case the foil gets-, well, you know."

Even though any number of things could cause the foil to tear, I understood her meaning. She's considering being shot. A compassionate smile crossed my face as I accepted. Then another question came to mind. If I'm wrong, all our planning might go up in smoke. "That wire I saw Fugi yank out of the door, was it to a microphone?"

Her head nodded as she got on the other side of the doorway and I took position where I could see the shower room. "Yes, Fugi told me about it while you were-; out. Earl had one strong microphone concealed in this door so he could listen to what was going on in this area. He only used it until abducted people no longer posed a threat. Since he felt comfortable enough to leave, it wasn't recording."

"I'm really glad to hear it," I said. "Now did Fugi tell you which way-"

An incredibly loud explosion slammed my ear drums like a hammer, followed by a rush of hot air. Serious ringing in my ears restricted my hearing, but I chanced a quick look down the hall. The door between the hall with the shower and the one with storage rooms was closed, apparently from the super-charged air pushing against it.

"HERE THEY COME," I shouted. "FUGI, PENNY, GET BEHIND THE GRINDER! MAKE EACH SHOT COUNT."

For a brief moment Penny appeared terrified, but she quickly changed to stern determination. Her eyes narrowed as she moved closer to the doorframe and dropped to use the grinder for cover. If the blast hurt her ears in any way, she hid it well.

My ears were recovering enough to make out strange sounds coming from the ceiling. Penny also heard, looking up. It sounded like a pebble rattling in a metal can.

We noticed the pipes at the same time. Several dozen open-ended tubes were spaced apart in the ceiling possibly for ventilation. The rattling got louder as I suddenly realized what it might be.

"OH DEAR GOD TAKE COVER," I shouted while scooting close to the hanging mattresses.

A small object fell from the pipe close to the door just as Penny reached her mattress protection. I covered my ears and shut my eyes.

Blinding light flashed through my eyelids in a pinkish color, followed by a hurricane of super-heated air pounding the mattress, slamming me against the wall. It felt like the floor violently tilted, sending me down in a mental maelstrom.

My head was spinning. I could only see a dark blue haze when I opened my eyes. Each time I tried moving, it felt like the Earth shifted to keep me still. Slowly objects became discernible through the dense fog, and the ringing began subsiding. Running footsteps were rapidly approaching, but when I tried to stand nausea threatened to overwhelm me. Then a shot rang out, followed by silence.

Maybe deep breaths will help clear out the cobwebs. One, two, three, and then I turned on my belly to rise on all fours. The ground stopped churning, my sight was improving dramatically. Ringing was still present, but that too was going away.

"Can you hear me?" Fugi asked. "The jig is up. Earl knows I'm in here. The good news is we're down to two. I always hated Hank and his arrogance. Hey, are you still with me?"

A quick glance toward the opposite side of the frame showed Penny slowly moving. She groaned once while trying to roll on her stomach. When my insides stopped trying to reach the outside, I took another deep breath and responded. "Yeah, we're shaken badly but still here. What was that thing they dropped on us?"

Penny managed to get on her hands and knees, rapidly shaking her head briefly before looking at me. She grimaced in pain when she tried to stand. Her hand began feeling her thigh close to where the sensor was implanted. Then her eyes opened wide as she looked at me. "Oh no," she said. "I think the foil is torn."

"Then pull back to the cell Fugi was in," I said. "If Earl comes running down the hall, I'll need to push this without looking."

As I patted the side pocket, it felt empty. Panic hit like an angry slap. Penny's expression changed to concern watching me slip my hand inside both pockets only to come out empty.

"We have a serious problem," I said. "The remote must've come out during the explosion. Do you see it anywhere?"

Our senses had returned enough for us to safely stand. Though Penny was wobbly at first, she quickly gained her balance and peeked from between the mattress and wall to look into the room. While she looked in that direction, I carefully eased my head around the frame for a check of the hall.

Hank was laying on the floor ten feet away, a pool of blood forming around his head like a macabre rose. To me that was poetic justice since he first approached me in the guise of a date. The door between halls was still closed. With Fugi in the room at the other end, and since no one was in the hall, I chanced a more thorough look. Pressure from the blast not only shook it free from my pocket but pushed it under the grinder close to Hank's right arm.

"I see it in the hall," I said. "We're going to need Fugi's help."

She stopped searching to our rear, and turned her attention toward the hall. Her eyes momentarily examined the floor before settling on the remote. Hank's body didn't seem to bother her as she nodded her head and then gently put her gun on the floor.

"Cover me," she said while making her way close to the edge.

"No don't," I said. "If Earl opens that door while you're struggling to get by the grinder, he'll shoot you before I can do anything about it. Fugi has a straight run from her door and back. Sit tight."

A look of relief washed over her face as she nodded and quickly withdrew.

"We have a slight situation Fugi," I said. "Can you hear me?"

Penny picked her gun from the floor and leaned against the wall near the frame, carefully looking down the hall. No answer came from the living room, giving me a foreboding sensation. I shifted position moving closer to the edge. "Come on Fugi," I said. "This is no time for jokes; answer me."

"WATCH OUT," Penny said as three hard thuds slammed the wall.

Dust and chunks of cinderblock flew into the hall. Two more thumps caused me to drop to my haunches. "What is that?" I asked.

Two shots fired from Penny's gun in response, and then she quickly pulled back and dropped like me. One thud against her side sent more debris flying. She quickly lifted her gun over the grinder and fired blindly down the hall, and then looked at me. "I saw the barrel aiming at you out of the living room," she said. "It's a gun with a silencer. We don't have anything like that."

My eyes closed briefly as I understood that meant one thing. They found a way to sneak up on Fugi and shoot her. Another thud against Penny's wall sent her scurrying toward the far corner.

"Hello my lovely ladies," Earl said. "I'm afraid I've got sad news. Fugi is out of the game. He, or rather she, or would that be it, whatever; she's badly wounded and needs your help. Why don't you come see what you can do?"

Panic covered Penny's face like a layer of paint, followed by a look of complete surrender. Earl's surprise announcement almost made me run, but I reached deep inside to find the strength that enabled me to hold the same appearance I had when he pointed his remote at me. So Mark is the one who dropped that thing on us and hasn't had time to get here. We have to act before he arrives. "It's no longer safe for you here," I said. "Get away from the opening, but see if you can close the air pipes in the ceiling with your gun, just in case."

"What's the use?" She asked. "Let's end this by our own doing."

If I could have run over there to grab her, I would have. Instead I glared at her briefly before returning my attention to the hall. "Just do as I say," I said. "We don't need the remote. When Earl is close enough I'll shoot the knob. That'll set off the explosives; now go!"

"My, oh my look at all the blood just pumping away," Earl said. "I'll bet Fugi has about an hour left. Oh and don't let me forget to say she's in a great deal of pain. Aw the poor thing is moaning."

My head indicated for Penny to move. Fresh hope appeared in her. She smiled slightly and quickly worked her way past the mattress.

"What have you done to her?" I asked.

"Something much more merciful than what I'm going to do to you, seven forty-two; before I'm finished you'll be insane. To hell with Doc's dissection! This is personal."

A series of shots rang out from behind me, followed by the sound of clanging metal. Then all was silent for a little while. It occurred to me Earl had no idea what Penny was shooting and could be far from the door. If the grinder wasn't in my way, I'd charge down the hall and shoot him. Since that won't work I need to goad him into blast range. "So here I am facing the most fearsome hired killer of all time, and he's cowering inside a room. Ha; you're nothing more than a wimp who shoots people from behind. Wait till I tell the world how *The Eraser* pooped his panties when he faced me."

"Step in the hall and see if that's true," he said.

There was a slight change in his voice, like he was angrier. This is good. As I carefully aimed at the knob, I spoke again. "Is that what you need; a clear shot? I'm starting to think you had others do the killing while you took credit. That explains why you sent Hank on a suicide mission. It allowed you to cowardly sneak up on Fugi without giving her a fair chance. In fact I don't think you know how to handle a gun without endangering your feet!"

Three quick thuds slammed the wall over my head, sending bits of mortar tumbling onto my scalp. It forced me to close my eyes and rub them.

"Did you really think you had a chance against me?" He asked. "I'm only making this moment last. You're going to die soon. How does that make you feel?"

Unless he thinks I can't handle a weapon, this exchange of insults will continue until Mark gets here. "We all die. I'll be sure to plant skunkweed on your grave before I do, you pervert! Oh I'm so afraid of the big bad chicken who only talks about fantasies!"

I purposely fired three wild shots nowhere near the living room. Deep chuckles came from there when the ear-ringing stopped. "Nice shooting eagle-eye," he said.

It's working. His voice seemed slightly more relaxed. Now I have to finish it with more insults. "Look who's talking. From all the bravado you spouted off I expected so much more. All this confirms my initial impression of you. Unless your victims are tied up, electrically threatened, or heavily sedated, you hide from them in the shadows and let others do the dangerous work. What a complete waste of skin. You're just a pathetic little man with delusions of Godhood. I bet you couldn't hit the ground with a stone!"

Two thuds against the wall responded, and then the rustling sounds of pants legs brushing together made me take close aim toward the knob. "In my mind I've killed you ten times and now I tire of your banter," he said. "To hell with the lovelorn; it's time to end the game. Though the other one failed this one won't. Recognize my voice only command switcher seven forty-two incinerate!"

My thoughts focused on the sound of that voice and the words spoken. Deep inside my mind a single imperative order rose forward; I am no more.

Multiple colors filled the doorway, spinning slowly at first but gaining momentum. Soon they blended into white with black dots floating in the middle.

An apparitional duplicate of me ripped away, falling into the maelstrom of light. She desperately tried to grab me, but I didn't know what to do. The light changed to fire, incinerating her as she entered, leaving nothing behind but ashes. Currents from the swirling colors blew the ashes away, and then they faded into nothing. Who am I?

"You will respond only to my voice," someone said. "Move toward my sound."

It came from outside this room, but something is blocking the way. I moved toward the center of the doorway, standing there waiting for instruction. A shadow crossed another open door further away, and a man holding something pointed at me leaned into the hall. "Drop what you're holding," he said.

His words guided every thought. My hands relaxed; something heavy hit the floor near my feet. "There is another with you," he said, "where is she?"

Foggy remnants of someone else in this room briefly rose to my thoughts. "She's hiding in the back."

A smile crossed his face as he began walking to me. When he was halfway here, sounds of running from behind drew my attention and caused him to stop. "What is it?" He asked.

"Someone is coming toward me."

He darted against the only wooden door on the opposite wall from the room he left, swinging the thing in his hand side to side. While continuing this rapid sweeping, his other hand reached inside a pocket and removed a small box that he held high in the air.

"Goodbye, six ninety-eight," he said and then jerked that hand.

The passageway immediately lit up with what appeared sunlight just before super-heated air flung me backwards at an angle. My head slammed against a soft object during my helpless flight. Everything started dimming, my thoughts returned to a former place where things were different.

Applause sounded before I'd concluded my Summa Cum Laude speech, forcing me to pause. Oh lord all of my fellow high school graduates watched me with bored attention like I was the next to the last teacher between them and freedom. Four days ago Principal Jeffries said this would get easier after I'd begun. He was wrong. I'm still a nervous wreck and it's near the end. At last the clapping is dwindling.

"This day isn't about the completion of an era. It's truly about the launching of new beginnings. No longer will we need the permission of others for our life choices. Our decisions are now completely up to us, along with the associated burdens. Do not be fearful. Grab the liberty and make the most out of it. Live your life freely, proudly, and with distinction; thank you."

Parents and guests in the audience rose from their seats in thunderous applause. Though I felt great relief at having successfully finished without fainting, their show of appreciation made me feel excited. Even my classmates were standing, which I noticed as I walked to my seat. Mary was three rows back, but remained standing long enough to give me a thumbs-up sign I could see. Then anticipation over only having to tolerate my father for a few more months overwhelmed the graduation giddiness.

Throughout the rest of the ceremony I only paid partial attention with my thoughts drifting back to last night, even though Byron Anderson was far more enthusiastic delivering his Magna Cum Laude speech than I. The highest honor that I'd achieved was uncertain until the final exams were graded. He'd been a real threat but I beat him by one point in a single course. We were notified late last night.

Dad kept watching his television after I hung up the phone and informed them, but mom sprang from her chair to hug me tightly. I'd already been accepted at Whitmore University which makes this distinction somewhat meaningless, however I still felt proud. It was a shame dad didn't think much of it. That was his problem and I didn't permit it to interfere with my delight.

My attention returned here as the ceremony drew to a conclusion. Diplomas were delivered, and then it was done. Families rushed forward to greet the new graduates while talks of great parties floated through the air. Some former students actually looked sad while most appeared absolutely thrilled. If they only knew the true meaning behind the conclusion of my speech, chances are they would've wept rather than applaud. I had tears in my eyes as I said it and know dad would get the gist of what I meant.

"JOYCE, over here," mom said. "Wait there. I'll come to you."

She was working her way toward me; dad was nowhere to be seen. Even though I really didn't expect him, I still held a faint hope he'd share my moment of glory. This is so typical, but at least it won't go on much longer. As mom drew close she said "What a wonderful speech. I had tears in my eyes listening to you. You've made me very proud!"

I was pulled into a tight embrace that was reciprocated, but I felt insulted. "So dad didn't think my speech was important enough to miss a big sales opportunity, huh?"

Her body stiffened. She slowly released me to pull back a few feet. "He called just before I left saying he couldn't get away," she said. "He really sounded upset at having to miss your shining moment. It made us both proud!"

That attempt at diverting my growing anger failed. My face developed a scowl as my head slowly shook. "No he didn't," I said. "He didn't talk about being upset over missing anything. In fact I seriously doubt he called. You don't have to be a Summa Cum Laude to figure out he never has nor ever will like me. Stop making excuses for him!"

Now that I'm almost eighteen, his vile treatment will only need to be tolerated a little longer. That means I can start speaking part of what I feel, but I'm not ready to face the world just yet. I've got to contain most of my contempt just a few more years. Once I've gotten a degree in teaching I will be ready to exact memorable revenge.

She appeared upset. Not over what I just said but what I implied in my speech. Tears lined her eyes as she glanced briefly at the ground before looking at me again. "He not only likes you, he loves you. It's just his company has him on the run all the time."

A loud chuckle escaped as I turned to walk toward the car. "You say he loves me? Why is it always you who says he loves me? Do you realize he's never once said those three little words to me? In times gone by he's made sure whatever I built was quickly torn down, but I had hoped this day would mark a new beginning. I was wrong. Do you know how hurt I am by his absence today?"

Out of the corner of my eye, I saw a tear streak down her cheek. She offered no answer while we continued walking to the vehicle. Her silence only made me madder. "Would you at least tell me why he hates me? Don't say that isn't true. You know as well as I he's despised me for as long as I remember. Please explain to me what I did."

Three more steps were taken before she briefly glanced at me and then stared ahead. "I know it may seem like he hates you, but everything he's ever done has come from his heart."

Another loud chuckle came from me as I stopped walking. She took two more steps before turning to face me. "From my vantage point he doesn't have a heart," I said. "I guess he doesn't think I'm good enough to be part of his family."

Before I could resume walking, she put her hand on my shoulder. "That's where you're wrong. Today is your beginning. Your entire life is ahead of you, and your father and I both know how far you'll go. Though you may not see it yet, someday you'll thank him for the strength he's given you."

"What a load of-"

An angry stare from her I've never seen before made me shiver, silencing me immediately. "You think I'm making this up?" She asked. "Let me tell you something Joyce. I've watched you face numerous obstacles and come out the winner when you should have lost. And look at where you are today; Summa Cum Laude out of *four hundred* students! All through your childhood when your father thought nobody was watching, he displayed true amazement at your cunning."

My face developed a sneer. Before I could speak her expression changed to one slightly more dangerous. "That's just the way he is so lose the look. You have grown from a frightened little girl into a woman strong enough to do whatever she wants. God help the person who gets in your way. Would you care to learn why you have such power? It's because your father insisted on perfection in every little thing you did. It may have seemed harsh at the time but look at you now."

That's as much as I can stand. "You couldn't be more wrong if you'd said the sun rises in the west. My strength grew because I decided he wasn't going to get the best of me, and that decision only made him try harder. Remember my sixteenth birthday party? It took *months* before I could look at any of my friends after he did his protective-father routine! You said before he acted from his heart. If that's true, his heart is filled with hatred for me!"

Her expression faltered for a moment, but she held onto that stern look that seemed so alien on her. "Your father is a hard working man who's provided for us well. It hasn't been easy for him. His time was spent between us and running a company in a very competitive industry. He didn't hate you at all and is allowing you to go away to college; remember?"

When I ignored her dismissing comment about the war I waged to attend school away from here, it all became obvious. In one sentence she cleared up a mystery plaguing me for a long time. I smiled, which made her look worried. "That's it, isn't it?" I asked. "It's about the money. He's treated you almost as badly as me, yet here you are defending him. Well I'm going to clue you in on something about me. I will never allow any man to rule me for any reason! How can you stand there telling me he did it for my own good when you tried stopping him at times? For that matter, why did you keep me within his reach? That's been bugging me for a long time and at last I understand. You're *afraid* to leave him, aren't you?"

Based on her appearance, my words stung like a wasp. That strong expression dropped into one of sadness. She looked at her feet, making me feel like a slug.

All through dad's most inventive punishments, she was always there to give comfort afterward. When he wasn't around, she allowed me to break the rules. Had it not been for her my sanity would have surely been lost. And here I am tearing into the one person who has shown true love for me. Oh how I wish I could take back what I just said.

Tears now streamed down her face as she looked at me. "You're right. I am afraid. I'm afraid to be alone, and I was afraid to leave him when you were young for more reasons than you think." She sniffed once. "He knows a lot of important people here. What would he do had he gained sole custody of you?"

I'd never considered that. Sadness crept into me thinking about the great sacrifice she made on my behalf, making my own tears form. "Mom, I-"

"Let me finish. All I said is true especially about you. He never hit either of us, but his treatment was extreme. Yet through the darkest times when I would have broken, I saw strength in you I've never had. No matter what happened I knew you'd come out okay. There's an indomitable force in your soul that can never be taken away. I assure you it didn't come from me."

When she paused to take a breath, I started to speak. Her hand went up immediately, informing me she wasn't done. "Soon you'll be on your own. And sometime down the road you'll get married. That will be a union of love and not convenience, of that I hold no doubt. Hopefully by then you'll see where your strength really comes from. All I ask is for you to forgive when you can, and know I always have and always will love you with all my heart. You are my shining beacon, and I'm so very proud of you!"

Tears were now streaming. I pulled her into an embrace. In spite of the vicious things I said, she only spoke of compassion. "I Love you mom."

"For the love of God please wake up!"

CHAPTER 24

"L-L-Love?"

Multiple colors filled my sight, spinning until they blended almost pure white. Black dots began littering the brightness moving like insects fleeing a swatter. Mom walked to them holding a transparent baby, glaring at the colors. Her free hand touched them, instantly clearing the air. Then she held the baby by its sides, kissing the infant's forehead which quickly inflated the newborn into an adult duplicate of me. She released the woman, who faced me with a smile. The copy walked to me, turned, and gently merged.

All my memories returned while mom looked on with a smile. She mouthed the words I love you, and then slowly disappeared. My eyes opened to a very worried Penny leaning over me. I smiled when I remembered Earl rushing against the shower room door and then holding up his remote.

"Are you okay?" She asked.

It felt like I'd been at the bottom of a human mound. Every part of my body ached as I slowly rose to a seated position. "I'm so over getting blown up," I said which made her smile. "Is Earl-"

"Dead," she said. "What happened? I didn't hear any shooting before the explosion."

When I tried to rise, the floor heaved underneath nearly making me vomit. Penny watched me with concern, finally helping me to my feet once the nausea passed.

"You saved us," I said. "Earl used another damned trigger phrase that;" I shuddered. "Well, let's just say it briefly worked. Then I heard you running toward me when he was halfway here, which caused him to dash against the shower room door and try killing you with his remote. Thank goodness the foil around your thigh wasn't torn after all."

She looked confused. "I wasn't running to you, just nervously pacing inside Fugi's cell until after the explosion," she said.

An astonished chuckle escaped as I stared at her. "It must've been the acoustics creating a weird echo," I said, "but I could've sworn you were rushing to the front. Had it not happened," a chill ran through my body, "I don't even want to think about it."

We exchanged glances, both with a complete understanding of what could have been. Later we can offer thanks, but Fugi needs our help.

"How long was I out?" I asked.

Her shoulders shrugged. "Long enough for me to think you weren't coming back. I guess maybe fifteen minutes, though it felt like hours."

Fifteen minutes? That means if what Earl said is true and we talked for five minutes before the blast, Fugi has forty minutes left to live.

"Did Mark put in an appearance yet?" I asked.

She shook her head twice, saying "No. And I have been keeping an eye open for him. I think he took off after Earl was killed."

My head started shaking as I removed the guns from my holsters. She observed what I was doing with absolute confusion on her face. "We can't make that assumption," I said. "If I were in his shoes, I'd wait to see who comes strolling down the hall, or at the very least check out this end to see what happened. He won't chance leaving any witnesses who could incarcerate him."

She walked to the same side of the doorframe as before and took up a position. "Then we'll send him straight to hell as soon as he shows his ugly head," she said.

This was the first opportunity I had to look closely at the grinder. Pressure from the blast packed it against the doorframe, leaving a small area underneath as our only exit. The other hall door was gone, meaning the frame was obviously designed only to withstand an explosion coming from the intended side. Plus our wooden shoe-door blocking the electric hall was reduced to small splinters on both sides of the doorway. It looked like a clear walk through the magnetic door, which scares me badly.

249

"We can't wait," I said. "Fugi will be dead in less than an hour. I have a plan to flush Mark out. It depends a lot on you."

For a moment it looked like she was going to faint. Then her expression changed to great fear. Looking toward the door I said "He's down here somewhere, I can feel it. If you get too close he might know how to use his remote against you. That makes you the person to remain hidden while I walk down the middle of the hall."

Before I could continue, she appeared shocked. "Are you insane? He will shoot you on sight!"

A smile grew on my face as I looked at her. "Not necessarily. He was, and I hate thinking about it, infatuated with me. Plus something Earl said just before springing that terrible trigger tells me he still has feelings for me. If I can convince him Earl's trick worked, he might decide to keep me alive."

She still appeared skeptical. "Earl's second trigger phrase," she said. "What in the world did it make you do?"

My eyes briefly closed at recalling the emptiness I felt. "It wiped my mind clean. I was a zombie ready to do whatever was commanded." I shuddered once before staring at her. "We don't have a choice here. Time is working against us. I'm going to walk down the hall. You stay hidden and shoot the bastard the second you see him!"

"I hate this," she said. "There has to be another way."

Oh how I wish that were true. But every other option I thought of took too much time. My head slowly shook as I looked at her solemnly. "If you can think of something that'll bring him out in the open right now, I'm all ears. Otherwise, keep a close watch on my back and be ready to shoot at any moment." I smiled at her. "See you on the other side."

Tears formed under her eyes. She opened her mouth, but closed it before nodding her head. Without saying another word, I walked to the grinder, dropped on my belly, and began sliding under it. When I was halfway out, my butt got stuck which almost made me panic. By using the palms of my hands for traction, I was able to slowly pull free.

Debris littered the hall like it had been through an earthquake. Chunks of wood, plastic, and metal covered the floor like a carpet of nails. Hank's body had been rendered into numerous pieces scattered among the litter, making me feel sick as I forced my attention to the living room. Earl was not to be seen, his body must have vaporized in the explosion.

No shots were fired from either direction, giving me the courage to stand. It took considerable strength to form that goofy smile as I got up and began walking.

The living room was my first destination. Since Earl began his assault from that location, Mark might be inside. If not I wanted to give Fugi an update on our situation. In spite of the bravado I displayed to Penny before starting, my insides were shaking as I took that first step.

Litter on the floor forced me to use my feet as brooms, making a lot of noise in the process. Oh well, I didn't want to sneak past Mark anyway. Though I didn't dare glance behind, I knew Penny was watching closely. It gave me the nerve to slowly move down the hall until I was standing in front of the dark living room.

"The one I must obey sent me looking for Mark," I said while forcing myself inside.

Every fiber of my being was screaming for me to return to Penny's field of vision and I almost caved in. A soft groan coming from the floor held me in place waiting for my eyes to adjust. Finally dim lighting entering the doorway allowed me to make out one figure lying on her side in a pool of blood. I casually walked to her and got down on my haunches. Fugi opened her eyes, a look of hopelessness in them.

"It's okay," I said. "Earl's dead. I'm going to flush out Mark. When he comes after me Penny will finish the job. One way or another, this won't take long. You hang in there. We're going to get help."

Three raspy coughs replied as she looked beyond my right leg at something on the floor. Earl's head had rolled in here, coming to rest looking at the wall. How strange the grisly sight didn't upset me.

"T-That's," she coughed, "irony. Look at where he's" another fit of coughing ended her sentence.

Nothing remarkable was noted where his head had stopped on its ear. When I looked at where his eyes were set, an opening in the wall became visible. That's how he got in here. A secret passageway was perfectly concealed behind an imitation brick panel between the halls. Earl must've told Hank we were all inside the main chamber which convinced him to charge down after the dropped bomb detonated. While Fugi was distracted shooting Hank, he snuck in here and shot her.

"L-Listen, when Mark finds you," a fit of coughing displayed blood foaming at her mouth, "t-there's something you have to know."

Her entire body contorted into spasms as she coughed violently. This was killing her fast. My head started shaking as I glanced at the doorway and then looked at her.

"Stop talking," I said. "Save your strength. I'll find out soon enough what there is to know about Mark. We will come back for you I promise. Please don't give up."

She opened her mouth; eyes rolled up, and then stopped moving. My heart began accelerating until I saw her breathing. There isn't much time left.

I quickly rose, walking out of the room. Once I reached the blasted door between halls, my adrenaline started rushing. This had the eerie feeling of a deserted house people claimed was haunted. Though Mark was nowhere to be seen, I had the sensation he was watching me closely.

All room doors on both sides were open and dark except for the one we'd armed. Of all the rotten luck, Earl must've left that one closed so light entering through the trapdoor wouldn't betray his stealth. Still the open rooms gave Mark a lot of hiding places. Using a trick I learned years ago when I had to get by dad helped me step across the threshold and casually move into the hall.

Everything was quiet as a grave. Nobody jumped at me even after I passed the next to the last doors. But when I reached the doorway between this hall and the once electrified hallway, a hand covered my mouth from behind, yanking me into a dark room. Even though my heart was racing so fast it felt in danger of exploding, I calmly allowed him to pull me away.

"Put your hands on the back of your head and turn around," Mark said.

He backed away, permitting me to comply. Lights cut on when I was facing him; his gun was pointed at my forehead. It took every ounce of inner strength not to cringe at the sight of that huge barrel aimed at me.

His gaze began roaming my body, but the pistol never wavered. I could almost feel his eyes undressing me. Suddenly his free hand grabbed the top of my suit and yanked downward, tearing it open to where my breasts were exposed. Even though I wanted to cover myself, I fought the urge and simply stood there with a zombie-like expression.

252

"Nice size D's," he said. "Think I'll partake of the pleasures of the flesh before I send you to hell. Do you have any last words before we begin?"

Penny must've seen him grab me. She'll be here any minute. I have to keep him distracted, and I know what to say. "I only wish to please, but may I please ask a question?"

The look on his face became pure fury as he pressed the barrel against my forehead, causing a great deal of pain. I called forth all power from the past to avoid wincing as he pressed harder. "Don't even THINK about trying that shit," he said. "Had Earl's little trick worked you wouldn't be out walking like you own the place. He'd have you on a leash."

His statement tells me he wasn't down here when Earl or Hank died. Plus he obviously has doubts about my recovery or I'd already be dead, but I can't be sure if that's enough to lower his guard. "I only wish to please, but are you Mark?"

A sneer grew on his face as he quickly pulled the gun back and then swung it toward me like he was going to pistol-whip my cheek. If I as much as blink, he'll shoot. The barrel gently touched, ice cold metal coming to a rest aimed at my ear.

"You know who I am," he said. "Cut the horse-shit and tell me where the others are. If you cooperate, I might keep you around a little longer."

"You are Mark?"

His left eyebrow went up, obviously considering that I may be a mindless slave. Then the gun was removed from my face. "Okay I'll play along," he said. "Yes I'm Mark. You have ten seconds to tell me why I shouldn't blow the top of your head off."

"The one I must obey sent me to find you. May I please ask a question?"

For a moment he looked confused, but that only lasted until he brought the gun to bear on my nose. "Make it a good one," he said. "It's going to be your last."

What is taking Penny so long? I focused on calm as I looked in his eyes.

"I only wish to please, but what does clean house and start fresh mean?"

He blinked fast several times while lowering the gun. Then he glanced at the door, growing nervousness becoming apparent. His attention quickly returned to me, nearly causing a startled reaction. "Did Earl say that before telling you to find me?"

My head nodded. "If you mean the one I must obey, yes. He also said things I didn't understand. May I please ask a question?"

By now he seemed impatient, but not so much in a homicidal manner. I think he's starting to believe me. "Yes and make it quick," he said. "It would please me for you to tell me everything he said."

Though it took a great deal of effort, I formed that idiotic smile he expected to follow such a statement. "What does shit now I can't hear a damn thing because of your stupidity, and you'd better pray I get better within ten seconds mean?"

His mouth dropped open, again quickly checking the door. That's not good. I've got to find a way to hold his attention away from there or Penny might inadvertently walk into his line of fire. "Earl said that?" He asked. "What was that explosion?"

"I only wish to please, I'm sorry. I don't know. I was in a room when it happened. The one named Hank let me out shortly before the one I must obey pointed something like that," I held my finger toward the gun in his hand, "at him and made quiet bright light. Then the one named Hank fell and stopped moving."

He momentarily looked away from me, stepping to the side a few feet. That movement allowed me to see three small boxes set against the wall, and a small unmarked aerosol can next to them.

"You can't be faking," he said. "No one can remain that calm with a gun pointed at them. I knew Earl was pissed at Hank and said it was up to him to fix this mess, but I never believed he would kill him."

With no warning he faced me so fast I almost jumped. "And that was when he said something about cleaning house?" He asked.

Again I nodded my head. "Yes, and then he said I would help him start over. May I please ask what auction means?"

A look of determination grew on his face as he started backing to the boxes. "I had no idea there were hidden passageways down here until today," he said. "And he wanted you to walk along like you were out for a hike in the hopes I'd give away my position. Well I have a little surprise in store. Allow me to introduce myself properly. I am Doctor Marcus Worth, PHD in Entomology. That means I study insects."

That can't be. He looks my age. Since he thinks I'm still under their thrall and terrified of bugs, I formed a horrified expression.

"Although I doubt you fully comprehend what I just said, suffice it to say I'm a genius in the field. That's why I was recruited. My latest gift to the world is a time-delayed insecticide that takes about forty minutes to work. Oh we'd planned on using the babies in those boxes a few at a time on whoever survived, but it seems none of you did. I have poisonous hunter centipedes, black widow spiders, and Sahara fat-tailed scorpions. Though only the centipedes are insects, my spray works on them all. And the scorpions already have a bad attitude, but after a shower of my stuff they go thermo-nuclear!"

If I can't find a way to stop him right now, Penny will rush into his horrors. With that in mind, I began moving toward the door just as he was turning away. The sound of my steps grabbed his attention. "Where do you think you're going?" He asked.

The gun was raised at my head as I stared blankly at him. "I must move away from you. The one I must obey said when he gets near for me to leave."

Panic gripped his face like an iron claw. The gun moved toward the door, his eyes scanning all over the room. "I didn't hear a thing. Are you saying Earl is moving in on me?"

"I only wish to please, yes I heard him out there."

My hand rose to point at the door. Rather than pull him away from the boxes, what I said caused him to rush toward them. "Take three steps into the hall and stand in front of the door," he said. "Tell me what you see."

"The one I must obey-"; I said while shaking my head.

"Is countermanded," he said. "It would please me for you to do as I say."

He was watching my every move, but what he just said shows I've completely fooled him. A big smile crossed my face as I quickly followed his instructions. Once I was in position, I looked both ways and then faced him. "I see nothing," I said.

That was true. Penny was nowhere in sight. I don't know whether that's good or bad.

"Keep looking at the shower room," he said. "It would please me for you to let me know the moment you see any movement."

At last he turned his back. Since there may be other secret openings, I don't dare close him in. He might pop out of anywhere shooting. When he lifted the can and began shaking it, I stepped to the side, pulling up my pants' leg. The steak knife was still there.

His attention was focused on what he was doing; not me as I removed the knife and held it in my hand with the blade resting against my arm. I moved back into position and held my free hand pointing at the door next to the room he was inside. "There," I said. "The noise I heard came from there. I saw someone inside."

A small smile formed on his face as he briefly looked at me before resuming his work. "Thank you, my gorgeous good luck charm. How careless of Earl to let you see him. Now I understand why he started this little business. He's slipping."

Boxes were moved, each one carefully opened. He slowly backed up, spraying the floor in his wake. Hissing sounds from compressed can air being released concealed the sound of my fabric moving while I raised the knife. As he made his way toward the door, I slowly crept up on him. Just when he reached the threshold, I brought the knife down into his back.

"SHIT one of them got me!" He said while spinning around away from me.

The knife struck a bone, not going in deep. In his terrified haste at removing what he believed to be one of his monsters, the gun slipped out of his grip landing at my feet. A smile grew on my face as I quickly picked it up and backed off pointing it at him. His expression showed total confusion.

"I only wish to please, but doesn't it just aggravate you when your gorgeous good luck charm turns into ugly bad luck?" I asked and then dropped the smile. "Give it up Mark. There's a knife stuck in you. I'll bring help-"

Absolute fury formed on his face as he ran at me. I pulled the trigger; the safety was on. Before I could release it, he was airborne heading for me like a missile. A loud explosion sounded from the doorway between halls. His head jerked away from the noise. Red mists showered my face as he struck me full force. The weight brought me down and held me pinned. Penny stepped into this hall holding her gun trained on Mark's head, his body twitching.

"Quick Penny, shut that door without turning the knob," I said.

She ran to the room I indicated with my stare and glanced inside. A horrified moan escaped her as she quickly pushed the door shut. I looked at the bottom seal of that door, and felt relief that it was a tight fit. Her attention was set on the door as she slowly backed away.

"Can you give me a hand here?" I asked.

While I struggled to get out from under Mark's weight, she eventually looked at us. Her eyes seemed far away, like none of this was real. She cautiously approached and pulled on his shoulder so I could slide out. Once free I started rising saying "Thank you. Your timing was excellent."

Her face had a mesmerized expression looking from me to Mark. "He's dead," she said. "It's really over, isn't it?"

Her tone sounded more like disbelief. I walked to her, placing my hand on her shoulder. She looked at me almost on the verge of tears, and they weren't the happy kind.

It was obviously tearing her up inside that she'd killed someone. Her conscience was raging. The same feelings I had when looking at Fred's body for the first time are now in her. Rather than feel elated, she looked miserable.

"You did what you had to do," I said. "When I killed Fred, a number of emotions went through me. Fugi helped a lot, but in all honesty, the way I got through was by recalling what he did and that I didn't ask for any of this. Had I backed off, none of us would've escaped. The same is true for you. Don't lose sight of the fact you saved my life as well as your own."

Slowly her attention returned to Mark. "When I first opened my eyes to this nightmare, he was standing over me," she said. "I was naked and tied to a bed. He did-, things, perverted things, with the others laughing and egging him on. It made me feel filthy! Each time he smirked at me I shrunk in shame." A chuckle escaped from her. "The drugs made me forget, but when I saw him grab you, it reminded me of all those horrible things he did like it happened yesterday. It terrified me. I wanted to run away but I didn't and now he's dead. They all are. They can't hurt anyone else can they?"

"No they can't," I said. "They're all dead."

Tears started running down her face as her gun dropped to the floor. She looked at me with an expression I couldn't quite make out. "Then we're really free?" She asked.

A soft smile formed on my face while I nodded my head. "Yes we're really free but we need to get moving. Fugi doesn't have much time left," I paused to glance at my torn blouse, "and I don't want to be seen in public looking like this. We have to-"

She let out a loud sob while rushing me. Her hug was so passionate I could barely breathe. Heaves from her crying were so intense it almost knocked us over, forcing me backwards several steps while she maintained her hold.

Three long years ago this nightmare began for her. Then she was returned to be killed. Now it's over. She survived; we survived. Though my mind was focused on getting help for Fugi, I thought she needed a few minutes to realize this was for real and returned her hug. After several moments passed, she released me and backed up.

"I want to check Mark's pockets for car keys," I said. "If we're lucky, he'll have them and we can drive out of here."

Those words did the trick. A light began sparkling behind her eyes as she ran to the clothes room. While she disappeared around the frame, I dropped to my haunches for a patting-search of his pockets. Nothing was in them, not even a remote.

"I think these will fit you," she said holding out a new outfit.

Disappointment was on my face as I rose accepting the clothes. "He didn't have anything other than the gun. Thanks; but it looks like we're going to have to find the hidden phone Fugi talked about."

While I began removing the torn clothes, she turned her back to afford a little privacy. "Why don't we just leave this place and send help?" She asked.

The makeshift shoes had to come off. I had hoped to avoid that. As I sat on the floor, I briefly glanced at her back. "I wish we could," I said. "But Fugi doesn't have much time left. Besides I have no idea where we are or where to go. Do you?"

Both shoes were off, and I rose to remove the clothes. Soon they were off, the new outfit was quickly put on, and I was buttoning the blouse when Penny faced me.

"No," she said. "I know what you said makes sense, but this place makes me nervous. I want out right now."

No further talk occurred while I sat on the floor to wrap the jeans around my feet. When that task was completed and I rose, I walked to her. "I want out as well," I said. "But we wouldn't be here right now if it weren't for Fugi. She shot Hank don't forget. We owe her and I intend to save her life. If you want to leave I won't blame you. I'm staying to find that phone."

At first she appeared uncertain, but then a look of determination formed. "You're right. Let's find that damned phone and finish this!"

CHAPTER 25

Death saturated this air with a copper stench. The entire section now gave me the creepy feeling of being trapped inside a mausoleum at night. My nerves were on edge, almost expecting Mark to rise off the floor and come after us. Penny's desire to leave began to seem a reasonable course of action, until I thought about all the things Fugi had done for us. We must save her.

Adding to the sense of dread was our silence. I couldn't think of a thing to say as we entered the electrified hallway. The magnetically sealed door was gone like it had been blown to pieces, the former blocking bars now like twisted claws reaching upward. On the other side, a narrow hall with steps leading up could be seen. Just before we cleared the final bent grid, Penny gasped and grabbed my arm. "I left my gun behind," she said. "Let me go grab it. We're going to need it to get by them."

Before I could ask what she meant, she turned and began working her way back. It didn't take much time for her to retrieve not only her gun, but Mark's as well. Soon she was beside me holding out one of the pistols. As I accepted it, I realized she may have been awake when they brought her here and knows what's above.

"Who do we need to get by?" I asked. "Are there more thugs in hiding?"

Her shoulders shrugged, but she looked afraid which didn't help. "It's worse than people," she said. "The guardians of the grounds are waiting for us."

"What are the guardians?" I asked. "You mean dogs are running loose?"

She shook her head as she stepped past me to look up the first set of stairs. "No dogs," she said; "snakes. Mark was their handler and now that he's dead, they'll be coming for us."

That warning brought back horrible memories of writhing snakes and how I was told they'd attack if I misbehaved. Though I don't know where those snakes are kept, I do know they aren't watching the property. "Listen to me," I said. "What they told you about trained snakes isn't true. They only said that to terrorize their captives into submission. As proof of that, right after my first drug treatment a piece of food dropped on the floor. It was still there over an hour later even though Hank said the snakes smell food and come for it. Fred took it away under the guise of protecting me, but I knew the real reason was to prevent me from seeing through their lie about snakes in the drains. Had he left it alone, it would still be there. Relax; as long as there are no more people for us to worry about, we're in the clear."

My assurances did not seem to have an effect. Her entire demeanor changed, like she reverted back to thinking we were about to die. When we began ascending the first flight, I thought of something that might change her mood. "You're going to be in the news, you know. Didn't Fugi say you were from Virginia Beach? In about fifteen minutes your name will be a household word all over that city. Do you have any plans for your future?"

For a few moments I didn't think she was going to respond. We climbed the remaining steps to a landing before she looked at me. "I wanted to go to law school before, well, before all this. Now I don't know if I'm still eligible. But more importantly, the love of my life has moved on I'm sure."

A door could be seen at the next landing once we turned the corner. Excitement started filling my thoughts as I began climbing with Penny close behind. "You don't know what, uh, Ben has done," I said. "Wait and see. As for law school, I'd bet good money you'll have your pick to choose from. Mark my words, your dreams are about to come true."

"After all we've been through you still remember his name. I'm impressed!"

That was almost as much as I could take. Rather than accept hope, she tried diverting the subject to me. I wanted to shake her and say let it go, but thought that would only aggravate the situation. Our journey up the remaining stairs was in silence.

When we reached the top, I walked to the door and opened it. Bright lighting flooded onto the landing momentarily blinding me. Once my eyes adjusted, a hallway leading in the opposite direction from the ones below came into focus, like a lengthwise continuation separated by stairs. It caused me to marvel at the enormous undertaking that went into tunneling this place, and to be thankful we were able to shut it down.

One dark entrance was halfway down the wall to the left, while two were evenly spaced apart on the right. Penny started to brush by me when I grabbed her shoulder. She looked at me in shock. "Fugi said there were no more surprises once we got past the electric hall," I said, "but she wasn't planning on touring this level I'm sure. Watch your step just in case. I doubt a phone is in there since it wouldn't be easy to hide, so look for car keys, business cards, stationary, or anything that might give us an idea where we are. Which side do you want?"

She shrugged her shoulders, which also freed her from my grip. "It doesn't matter," she said. "You've done most of the work so far. I'll take the two on the right."

"Be careful; if you see anything suspicious, leave it alone."

We parted company on my words, which I hope weren't going to be our last. If it weren't for Fugi's immediate need for help, I'd leave this floor alone.

Penny calmly walked to the closest door, reached around the frame, and turned on a light. It looked like a conference room with a large table set in the middle of the floor. She proceeded to enter as I walked to the one on the left. Once I turned on the light and peeked in, my mouth dropped open in wonder.

This must be the command and control room. One large lighted board filled the adjacent wall to the left, a computer workstation was directly in front, and many file cabinets were set against the wall to the right. Most of the lights on the board were red, which must mean trouble. A grin formed when I realized those lights came from our efforts. My destination was clear. I walked to the computer and pressed the power button.

The monitor showed standard system checks as it slowly came on. All of a sudden a command appeared on the screen that read *Auto-purge Drive C in Thirty Seconds. Abort?* With the letter Y flashing off the countdown, I pressed enter. A new screen appeared asking for the password. Several guesses were made to no avail. Before twenty seconds had passed, I reached behind the computer to pull the plug. Everything went dark, I breathed a little easier.

"I guess the authorities will have to figure this out," I said.

"No luck, huh," Penny asked from the door.

Her silent appearance nearly made me scream. As I spun around with my heart racing, she looked apologetic. "I didn't mean to spook you," she said. "Nothing other than furniture was in the first room. I'm moving to the second.

My heart was slowing as I chuckled a few times. "Yeah, there's some kind of program designed to erase the information unless a code is entered," I said. "Go ahead; I'm going to look inside the cabinets."

An expression of grave concern came over her. "Do you think that's wise? I mean if anything was booby-trapped to explode, it seems those cabinets would fit the bill."

My head began shaking as I walked to the closest one. "I don't think so. The computer is set to destroy all files, and if those cabinets hold the only back-ups, then worst case scenario says all would be lost. Earl was too conceited to believe anyone would get this far but I will be careful, thanks."

For the first time in what felt like ages, she smiled while turning to walk away. Maybe the fact we're on this floor looking through their haven unfettered has finally registered that we're almost free. Her change helped me feel less concerned about her safety as I walked to the first cabinet and placed my hand in the clasp.

Just in case, I slowly unlatched the drawer and gently pulled it out a short distance. Nothing seemed to hinder its movement, giving me a little more confidence in pulling it further. Suddenly an ear-piercing scream filled the air moments before Penny dashed by the door heading toward the steps. I ran after her, catching up just before she began climbing. It took more strength than I'd planned on stopping her panicked flight.

"What's wrong?" I asked.

Absolute horror was on her face as she slowly looked at me. Her body started trembling, her arm rising to point where she'd been. Words seemed frozen in her throat. She tried to answer but only an animalistic gurgle came out.

"Is someone in there?" I asked.

She stared at me, that expression of terror not receding at all. I grabbed both her shoulders and shook her. "Penny, pull it together.

What's in that room? Did someone or something try hurting you?"

Her mouth widened as she tried to pull free. My intensified hold must've hurt her. "You stay right here," I said. "Don't go charging off into the unknown, you *hear me*? I'll put an end to whatever is back there."

I waited until she stopped struggling before releasing her. But as I turned to leave, she tightly grabbed my arm. "D-Don't go back there," she said.

While smiling I said "We can't look ahead for a phone if we're constantly looking behind for trouble. I'll be careful. Promise you'll wait on this landing for me; okay?"

That same expression of hopelessness when the magnetic door bars dropped returned to her face. She looked on the verge of suicide. At least she nodded her head, and then released me to sit down. What she saw in that room scared her terribly and it didn't do much for my confidence when I returned to the hall.

Light from all three rooms spilled onto the carpet, but it did nothing to alleviate the sense of dread I felt slowly approaching the last door. The eerie feeling of being watched came over me when I reached the computer room, my nerves tightly strung. Once I was about ten feet from the last room, a shadow crossed the threshold prompting me to raise my gun.

Earl's head rolled out of the room glaring at me. Chills ran down my spine as I watched its mouth cast silent curses at me. My heart raced when its teeth gnashed into an ugly snarl, eyes blinking rapidly as if in great anger. The sheer horror almost sent me running hysterically toward Penny, but my legs seemed frozen in shock. As I watched it taunt me, my better senses gradually informed me this can't be.

"Go away," I said. "You're just a hallucination from the drugs they pumped into me combining with my high anxiety. Ghosts don't exist."

Silent laughter briefly moved the head's mouth. The sneer returned as it began rolling at me. My instincts were shouting to flee, but my legs found the strength to start walking toward it. We met five feet from the room, and it passed through without so much as a tingle. I spun around to an empty hall.

A few chuckles escaped while my heart slowly returned to a normal beat. Could it have been a trick of the lights that frightened her, or something similar to this? As I turned my attention to the room, confidence started returning. When I peeked around the corner, I almost ran away screaming as well.

Dozens of sleeping snakes rested on the floor spread out facing every direction. Oh dear God any loud noise might awaken them. We'd never be able to shoot them all. Hank's warning about how the trained snakes attack those who disobey threatened to overwhelm me, but then I realized the obvious. If they're sleeping, why didn't Penny wake them up when she screamed?

Slow scrutiny of the room showed open cabinets, like an explosion had rocked them. Snakes were scattered like they'd fallen from storage. It's time to see if I'm right. I said a silent prayer before lifting my pistol across the doorway and letting go.

"JOYCE WHAT ARE YOU DOING?" Penny said.

The gun seemed to fall in slow motion. Many dozens of open eyes inside the room ignored it. Shuffling sounds from Penny's location nearly drew my attention, but I remained focused. Then the gun clattered against the floor, bouncing once before landing on the back of the closest reptile. No reaction followed. "STAY COOL," I said. "THEY AREN'T REAL."

Even though all visible evidence supported what I just said, my wits were still demanding me to leave while I could. I will not give in. This is all in my mind. The fear of snakes is a hypnotic suggestion I can overcome. Mustering all of my inner strength, I leaned forward to grab the closest one.

"ARE YOU INSANE?" Penny said.

It was cold and stiff as a stick. I moved to stand in the middle of the doorway and slammed the snake against the frame. Electronic fizzing noises followed, and then it broke open. The part with the head dangled freely at the end of several wires.

Mental images of my fogged-over mind being tormented by twitching snakes returned. Those bastards had thrown phony snakes on me while I was doped up, and to me they seemed real. As I turned to hold it up for Penny to see, she was already pensively approaching. "Look," I said. "It's electronic. They all are."

Fury grew on her face while she increased her speed. When she arrived, she walked into the room, grabbed a snake, and threw it against the wall as hard as she could. An expression of shame fell on her when it exploded into pieces. "For years I've been terrified of snakes just because of what those monsters did to me," she said. "Now I see it isn't real. God I feel so foolish!"

"It's not your fault. Don't forget they used powerful drugs and hypnosis to alter our perceptions." I glanced at all the snakes scattered on the floor, a smile forming. "And now the last stranglehold those bastards had over us is finished. They can't hurt us anymore. While we're here, let's look-"

An explosion shook the floor, heated air pushing me down. Penny grabbed my arm pulling me into the room. Popping noises loud enough to be heard over the ringing in my ears followed. We exchanged worried glances as I rose.

Smoke started collecting at the ceiling. I chanced a look in the hall and noticed flickering orange light coming from the room I'd investigated. Sounds of ventilator fans kicking on replaced the crackling noises of fire.

"Oh no," I said while running out of the room.

Penny was right behind me. She nearly collided into my back as I halted just outside the computer room. It was a scene of complete devastation. The computer was cracked open and smoking; all file cabinets in flames. Some sort of booby-trap must've started when I tried powering up the computer that blew not only the hard drive, but also the tops of the file cabinets. All looked lost.

"I guess Earl wasn't that conceited after all," Penny said.

Panic over the thought of thousands of people still enthralled with no hope forced me into action. "We have to save those files," I said. "Did you see anything in that room we could use to put out the fire?"

I pointed toward the one she'd searched, and her head shook.

"Come on while there's still time!"

As soon as we turned away, three smaller explosions sent bits of metal and paper flying into the hall. One careful peek around the corner showed the cabinets gutted and empty. Depression fell over me when I thought about all those people lost forever due to my clumsiness. It must've been on my face. Penny read it and formed a compassionate smile. "That may or may not have been your fault," she said. "If it was, you had no way of knowing what would happen when you tried turning on the computer or opening a drawer. Think of it this way. If you hadn't set it off, someone else would've been working in there and probably gotten hurt or killed. You saved them. And maybe there are back-up files hidden somewhere."

Her logic makes sense. Chances are Earl kept back-ups of everything just in case. They might even be on a floppy or compact disc. Somewhere they'll turn up I'm sure. A smile grew as I turned toward the snake room. "You're going to make one heck of an attorney," I said. "Let's see if we can find anything useful back there."

As I motioned with my head toward the last room, she grinned while taking the lead. When we arrived, she went in one direction and I the other. Ten small wooden cabinets lined the wall I faced, each one holding a myriad of items. Shock collars, remote controls different than the ones I'd seen, electronic replacement parts, and various small batteries with high voltage warnings were all I found. Nothing that would help our current plight was inside any of them. "Hey check it out," she said.

Double doors the size of a large closet was open, with her standing off to the side smiling. Leaning against the back wall was a four-foot wide flat screen television monitor standing on four closed swing-set type legs on wheels. Wires ran from the left side of the screen to the floor. Fleeting images of that device being rolled toward me played in my mind as I felt drawn toward it.

"I think it's plugged in," she said. "It must have a battery charging or something. Let's see what happens when I press this."

Colors of the rainbow filled the screen, gently swirling and changing direction. Black dots appeared stationary all through the movement. This is so beautiful. I love it here. Maybe if I move closer, they'll bring me inside. "JOYCE SNAP OUT OF IT," Penny said.

The screen went blank. My balance almost gave out as I struggled against falling.

"I'm so sorry," she said. "That was stupid of me! You just went through that crap and here I am playing with this dangerous thing."

My head started throbbing which caused my hand to rub my forehead. "I'll be all right," I said. "At least now I know the face of the beast and it's as phony as everything else. Is that the last cabinet?"

"Yes; I didn't find anything we could use."

By my calculations we'd wasted about ten minutes on this floor. Fugi is down to a half-hour. "This is pointless," I said. "We have to find that phone. Let's go to the house and tear it apart!"

Urgency filled our minds as we rapidly returned to the stairs and started climbing. Fugi said this structure had three basements, but the next landing was the last, which means it ends on the first basement level. We have to find the other stairwell leading up. To make matters worse there wasn't a door. All I saw was a handle like that on a kitchen cabinet. When I touched it, my hand nearly got burned. Instinctively I yanked it off saying "Whoa, that thing's red-hot. The place must be on fire."

"I hope not," Penny said. "That's our only way out."

Had this house truly been going up in flames, why did Earl and Mark act so nonchalant about it? If serious danger exists, why didn't they put it out before entering? A fire is burning, that much is certain. Chances are it's contained to a certain degree and I think we can get past it. They obviously managed to get to us.

"Get on your hands and knees. See those rails there?" I asked while pointing at tracks on the floor. "This is a sliding panel. When I open it up, there's no telling what will happen. Be ready to drop on your belly if fire explodes in here."

Fear formed on her face while she watched me place my right hand inside the sleeve of my left arm. I got on my knees close to the panel, lifting my arm so I could touch the grip with my protected hand. She got in the recommended position, and after one last glance at her, I slid the door open.

Howling like agonized souls immediately sounded. Air rushed by me with such force it knocked me on my belly into the room. Penny fell on my ankles, preventing me from getting pulled all the way in. Thick black smoke kept me from seeing anything, and heated air in the room brought an immediate sweat. Then a loud bang sounded from somewhere below and the rushing air stopped.

"Look over there," she shouted while pointing toward the far left corner.

Smoke was flowing up a stairwell across the room. That's the way out. "I don't know how bad it's going to be," I said. "But I say we run for it. What do you think?"

"I think I'd rather be lying on the beach. Let's get this over!"

The minor clearing from the rushing air was rapidly getting lost. If we don't move now, our sight will be totally impaired. "Take a deep breath before you move and keep your eyes trained on the stairs," I said. "Let's go!"

Together we inhaled deeply and then jumped to our feet. Heat immediately prickled my skin before I started running. Eight steps into the room and I began feeling light-headed. Dense smoke now clouded my view, and my lungs felt like they were going to explode. Halfway across my foot kicked something heavy, forcing the air I held to explode outward in an exclamation of surprise.

A gulp of air brought a stinging oily taste. Suddenly the world started spinning. I began to fall. Two hands gripped my arms, pulling me across the floor, and then released me. Cooler air now reached my entire body. Penny dropped beside me, gasping. Coughing fits hit for a while. Once they began subsiding, I looked at a smiling Penny.

"Now I know what a turkey feels like at Thanksgiving," she said.

My eyebrows went up as chuckling ensued. It broke into full-blown laughter while we rested from our run. Then it happened.

The sound of a ringing phone from above reached our ears like a chorus of singing angels. Smiles grew as I started ascending the stairs on my hands and knees with Penny right behind. It stopped just when I reached the fourth from the top step. Even though it was no longer ringing, at least we know it's somewhere close to the basement.

Once we crossed over the landing, I noticed how clear the air was. Considering what we'd just run through downstairs, I found that utterly amazing. "There must be an exhaust fan somewhere," I said. "Otherwise this place would be choking with smoke. We'll look for the phone in a minute. Our first order of business is to open the outside door just in case the fan stops working. If the phone starts ringing again, we'll rush back. Oh, and try not to touch anything. There might be fingerprints the police can lift. How does that sound?"

Her shoulders shrugged. "You're the boss," she said.

Before I could respond, she patted the holster on her shoulder and grinned. What that symbolized eluded me, but she went to the left and I right.

This setting has the charm of an old farmhouse. Comfortable furniture adorned the living room, and in the dining room a large table was ready to seat a dozen. The kitchen had a refrigerator, stove, dishwasher, double sink, and a smaller table. To the unwary visitor this would seem like a nice place and not the cover for a sinister operation. One locked pantry in the kitchen drew my interest as a potential hiding place for the phone, but I kept searching for an exit. We'll come back to it.

I found a door that I assume leads outside. It's constructed of steel and locked with a double-keyed cylinder. The wall next to it has numerous windows with jail-like bars over them. There's no easy way out I could see.

"HEY JOYCE, OVER HERE," Penny said.

Lord I hope she's had better luck. The door I found would be next to impossible to open without a key and the last I knew Fugi had the key ring. Earl probably took it. We don't have time to go hunting for what may be destroyed. As I worked my way through the house, I noticed every window had bars blocking our escape. Penny was standing in front of another steel door at the end of a corridor. The gun was in her hand. "It's locked," she said holding the gun up, "but I have the universal key. Stand back."

She turned toward the door as I moved away a few feet. Her gun-hand dropped to where I couldn't see, and then four thunderous rapid explosions made me jump. For some reason the gunshots were louder up here. Then as the hand holding the gun lowered to her side, she pulled the door open with her other hand.

Late afternoon sunlight streamed through the doorway. Warm fresh air breezed in, bathing us with a scent of honeysuckle. She turned to me with tears streaming down her face. Birds singing in trees mesmerized my soul with the joy of freedom while I walked to the doorway. When I arrived, she pulled me into a hug so tight it started choking.

"Thank you for this," she said. "Oh God bless you thank you *so* much!"

"*B-Breathe*," I said.

Chuckles preceded her relaxing hug. Then she released me, looking at me with so much gratitude it brought tears to my eyes. She turned to look outside, joining my appreciation of the beauty before us.

An empty gravel lot took up a large portion of land directly in front of the house. Unfortunately trees completely surrounded the outer edges effectively concealing our location. Leaves were just starting to bud on branches, wild flowers sprouted in many spots. Loud buzzing alerted us to a large insect flying close to the door just before it zipped by. Though I'd seen nature all my life, never before has it looked so wonderful. This had the feel of a dream more than reality and I relished the moment. Suddenly the ringing of a phone abruptly reminded us this wasn't over.

CHAPTER 26

As I deduced ringing was originating near the basement door. The kitchen pantry must hold something else worth protecting. Penny and I ran as fast as the homemade denim shoes on polished floors permitted. At the end of the second ring, we were listening in front of the basement entrance. All I saw was a soot tainted wall.

The phone began ringing for the third time, bringing my ear slightly to the left. A horrifying thought became vocalized. "Oh I hope this isn't a hidden speaker announcing incoming calls."

Penny glanced at me briefly before pressing her ear against the wall, a look of concern now on her face. I moved slightly closer to her just as it stopped. "What's on the other side of this wall?" I asked.

Her shoulders shrugged; "A waiting room of some kind. There are about fifty metal seats lined up. This is only a divider wall that isn't thick enough-"

Vibrations against my face were felt the instant the phone started ringing again. This doesn't make any sense. I pulled away a little and pressed the area my face had occupied. A hidden panel clicked open; the cell phone was resting in a charger just inside. Penny gasped excitedly. Though it was a cheap model, it looked like a gigantic diamond as I snatched it out and opened the earpiece. Before I could speak an angry female voice asked "What the HELL have you been doing? It's over an hour since check-in and you didn't call! I was THIS close to initiating failsafe, you *asshole*! I've HAD it with you!"

Memories of what I found inside Fred's wallet returned, including the picture of a woman. Do I have his wife on the other end? If so this will implicate her.

"Who is this?" I asked. "What is failsafe?"

Breathing sounds came from her end for a few seconds. "Oh shit," she said and then hung up.

As I lowered the phone, Penny and I exchanged concerned expressions. "That was a woman I'd bet my first paycheck was Fred's wife," I said. "She said something about initiating failsafe. I don't know what that means but I sure don't like the way it sounds."

Anger replaced fear on Penny's face. Her teeth clenched, eyes narrowed, and frown formed. She turned from me heading back to the open door. While walking she said "I'm so SICK of this crap. Get the police out here. I'll be waiting for any unwelcome guests and send them straight to hell!"

As she turned the corner, I pressed the three magic numbers and raised the phone to my ear. Before the first ring had ended, a female answered "Willard emergency dispatch."

Chills coursed along my arms. My body began trembling. "We need help," I said. "We've been kidnapped and held prisoner. One of my friends is dying."

Clicking sounds came from her end just before she responded. "Ma'am, where are you calling from?"

"I don't know. They chloroformed me in North Carolina and kept me in a basement."

Noises like a keyboard being typed came from her end as I began walking to the front door. "Is this some kind of joke?" She asked. "There are serious penalties for falsifying a police report."

Penny briefly glanced at me as I neared, but returned her vigilance outside. "I assure you this is real," I said. "Unless you send an ambulance equipped to help someone who's lost a lot of blood, you'll have a death on your hands."

"Hold on," she said, and then a series of clicks sounded. "I can't get a fix on your location. This isn't possible."

Birds chirping in trees now sounded like they were mocking us. I covered the mouthpiece and tapped Penny's shoulder. "They can't find us," I said. "Do you know anything that'll help?"

Her head shook as that look of fear returned.

"Who are you talking to?" The dispatch asked.

"It's one of the other people who survived this nightmare. Her name is Penny Carver from Virginia Beach, Virginia. My name is Joyce Jackson from Burksdale Oklahoma. If you don't hurry," a name came to me, "Cara Ishaya will die!"

More typing was heard as I moved past Penny to step outside. Muffled talking came from their end while I moved toward the side of the house. "Ma'am, are you calling from a vehicle?"

A single sarcastic chuckle escaped. "No I'm not. We're on a farm somewhere."

"I've never seen anything like this," she said. "Your signal is bouncing all over Huron County. We can't locate you. Stay on the line while I dispatch squad cars to triangulate your signal."

Fugi will not survive the time that would take. When I walked around the side, a black van shining in the sunlight made me smile. "I think I see their van," I said. "Let me read the license plate to you."

"I've dispatched three patrol cars. Don't worry; we will find you. Just keep talking."

My heart sank when I got close enough to see the out of state tag. "I hope this helps," I said. "The license plate is from Tennessee reading BXS one four eight two. Do you have that on record?"

While I heard her typing on the computer, I walked to the front of the van and peeked at the dashboard. The vehicle identification number had been removed.

"That plate was reported stolen in Nashville a little over *ten minutes* ago," she said. "What's going on there?"

Another chuckle escaped as I searched for a big rock. A fist-sized stone was within reach. As I plucked it from the ground I said "You'll have to see it to believe it. All I know is four guys named Earl, Hank, Mark, and Fred, have been running a slave market for years. Earl claimed to have sold over two thousand people."

Silence came from her end while I raised the stone and threw it as hard as I could at the passenger window. It shattered with a terrible racket.

"What was that?" She asked.

"The VIN has been removed. I had to break a window to get inside. There might be something in the glove compartment that'll help you find us."

All things considered, it was highly doubtful Earl would be so meticulous about changing plates and then leave the true registration in the glove compartment. As helpless as I felt, I had to do something or I might cave in to hysteria. Once I had the door and glove compartment open, my concerns were justified. "There're only Tennessee road maps inside," I said while hopping out.

"Keep talking ma'am; we're working on your signal."

Her tone had a slight tinge of desperation. Something around here must be interfering with their location abilities. A check of the phone showed no phone numbers stored in memory. I continued walking around the back of the house to the other side.

"Are the cars using their sirens?" I asked.

"Yes ma'am."

Insects chirping and birds singing were all I heard while I made my way toward the front. "I don't hear them," I said.

Gravel crunched under my feet when I returned to the parking lot. Penny moving outside drew my attention while I was still far enough away to see. My lower lip trembled as I pointed at the marquee just above the front porch Penny was standing on. She ran off the steps as I spoke into the phone. "Does the name Barker Exports Annex mean anything to you?"

Again typing came from her end. Penny walked to stand beside me, looking at the sign sparkling beautifully in the early evening sun. "I have an address," she said bringing tears to my eyes. "Is that where you are?"

"A large sign over the door says so." I covered the phone and looked at Penny. "They know where we are," I said and then uncovered the mouthpiece.

Penny's mouth dropped open, tears ran down her cheeks.

"I've dispatched rescue and police to your location," the officer said. "Please stay on the line until you see them."

My eyes closed briefly before looking at Penny. "They're on the way," I said.

She started sobbing, the gun falling from her hand. I pulled her into a one-armed embrace, and we hugged each other.

"Ma'am, are you sure about the name of your companion there?"

"Yes; would you like to talk to her?"

Before she answered, I tapped Penny's back to hand her the phone. She accepted it and walked out of earshot. Just in case the bad guys got here first, I picked up the gun and moved toward the front porch. Penny stepped a little further in the front yard, paused for a moment, talked again, and then dropped the phone. I ran down the stairs to face her. She looked at me, her whole body shaking. "They're, calling my parents to make arrangements for them to come here," she said. "It's-, really over, isn't it?"

Sirens off in the distance grew louder. Penny fell to her knees, covering her face, crying and shaking her head. "Yes it is," I said while picking up the phone.

"-still there? Ma'am?"

"I'm sorry," I said. "My friend has been away from her loved ones for a long time. She accidentally dropped the phone when you said you were going to arrange for them to be here. That was very kind."

A helicopter buzzed overhead. When I looked up, a cameraman was filming us from an open doorway inside the craft. Its television emblem painted on the tail became obvious. Sirens were now screaming loudly, followed by the sound of crunching gravel. The gun fell from my grip as I knelt beside Penny.

Tears rained down her cheeks as she glanced at me. All my self-control ended, sobs of great joy now flowing freely. We hugged each other tightly even after the first police car pulled to a stop, with the helicopter circling over head. The car door opened as the cop got out with his hand on the butt of his gun. "Officer Folsom Willard Police," he said. "Move away from the weapon."

His abrupt command restored my control. One quick glance at the helicopter still taping us preceded my appreciative stare toward the officer. "Come on Penny," I said. "It would be a shame to get shot on the day of our rescue."

As we rose, dizziness hit me for a moment, forcing me to stagger slightly before regaining composure. Penny gripped my shoulder, holding me until I was steady. I looked at her and smiled, and then we walked toward the officer. More gravel crunching could be heard from a short distance as additional police vehicles pulled into view, along with a fire truck and two ambulances.

"Miss Jackson, Miss Carver," Folsom said, "please get into the backseat of my car while we sort this out."

"You need us to point out the dangers inside that house," I said. "Our friend in there has been shot and is dying. She needs immediate help."

Four firemen and two rescue squad technicians approached. Six policemen began moving to the back, while two cops headed toward us. Though they looked genuine, that angry woman left me paranoid. "Listen, I didn't tell this to dispatch," I said. "A woman called and said something about initiating failsafe. Please tell your men trouble might be coming."

The eldest firefighter arrived with the other three walking toward the porch. An ingratiating smile grew on Folsom's face as he looked at the fireman, and then me. "Don't worry about a thing," he said. "Whatever they throw at us, we'll take care of it. Please get inside the car."

That tone sounded like my father dismissing me as unimportant. It completely enraged me. "So you can handle it, huh?" I asked. "What about exploding doors, electrified hallway grids with enough juice to power a small city, poisonous insects crawling around, and mind-altering drugs so strong they turn you into a zombie? Think you can handle all that?"

Both men's eyebrows went up as they appeared to be considering me for a straightjacket. My expression softened. A black sedan pulled up within ten feet of us. Two men wearing suits stepped out flashing badges. It didn't deter from my plea. "Look, I know this sounds far-fetched but it's all true. There are dangers inside that house. My friend won't survive the time it would take for you to go it without me. I'll be your guide. Now let's move!"

"No one is entering that building until whatever fire that's burning is out," the fireman said.

Radio static sounded from behind the firemen. He reached to his back retrieving a walkie-talkie when the two men in suits arrived. "Go ahead," he said.

"Lieutenant, we have a contained fire burning in the basement; structure appears sound."

I'd been so occupied with Folsom I stopped watching the other firemen. "Tell them not to go to any of the lower basements without us," I said.

The lieutenant started to press a button, stopped for a moment to look at me, and then pressed the button. "You know the drill," he said. "Put it out and air it out."

Several more vehicles arrived, all sporting press emblems on the side. One was a van with a dish antenna attached to the roof that attempted to pull next to the black sedan. It was flagged down by a policeman and forced to move back.

"How those vultures found out about this so soon is beyond me," Folsom said. "I mean they had to gather forces and load equipment, yet here they are arriving before we can even get started. It's like someone called them before you called us."

Oh dear God now I understand failsafe. It's to notify the world Earl is gone. While moving away I said "I have to go talk to them."

One of the suited men said "No ma'am. FBI; I'm special agent Smith and this is special Agent Jones. We can't allow you to do that just yet."

"You don't understand," I said. "If word gets out about us, the monsters who've bought people from Earl will know and kill their captives!"

"Assuming what you said is true," Jones said. "What are you planning to say?"

It took great willpower for me to avoid lashing out at him. Calm reasoning permitted me to think about this from their vantage point. This must all sound like the stuff of science fiction. "You'll find out soon enough the files blew up," I said. "Chances are those intended to be warned by all the press coverage don't know that. People who've fallen victim here are now in grave peril. I want to bluff those who would do them harm into surrendering before anyone else gets killed. Please let me do this or it'll be too late!"

Stern faces remained unchanged. All four men looked at me like I'd escaped from an asylum. "Listen to her," Penny said. "By now you must know I was kidnapped three years ago. They didn't keep me here. A man by the name Arbuckle in New York held me captive. It was only a chance happening that I was returned. Let her do this or countless deaths will be on your hands."

"I'm afraid that isn't possible," Smith said. "As of this moment, we're placing you both under protective custody. Please come with us."

Notifying the press can wait. His command forced visions of Fugi lying in a pool of blood to my mind. "No," I said. "Until our friend is brought out, I'm remaining to help."

When Smith started to reach for me, Folsom stepped in front. "I don't know what I believe any more," Folsom said, "but my instincts are saying I need them. If you'd care to join the party, feel free. Otherwise leave until this is officially federal jurisdiction."

The radio in the Lieutenant's hand burst with static a second before a voice started speaking. "You won't believe this when you see it Lieutenant. There's a panel down here with stairs leading below the basement. The fire is out; as I suspected no structural damage. I believe it started when the diesel-powered generator down here overloaded from an apparent short somewhere down the line. What are your orders?"

"Let's go," I said while starting to walk toward the house.

A hand on my shoulder stopped me before I'd taken two steps. The Lieutenant was holding me back. "Lady I don't care if you just stepped off Jacob's ladder," he said. "I can't let you back inside."

This has gone far enough. I jerked my shoulder free and walked to where I was within inches of him. Though he towered over me, I glared at him with a rage that caused him to back up a step. "I've HAD it with all this testosterone crap," I said. "My friend is bleeding to death inside an extremely dangerous place, and you want to play big man protecting helpless woman? Let me tell you something *Lieutenant*. We just beat four of the vilest men you can possibly imagine, and I will not allow you or any of them to prevent me from saving a woman who saved us a number of times. As I've already said it would take you too much time working your way through when I could lead you right there. Your own man just said you won't believe it when you see it and he's right. Now either step aside or get prepared to sing soprano for the rest of your life!"

His eyebrows went up as he lifted the radio to his face. "Chavez, get out here. The rest of you return to ground level." He lowered the radio looking at my feet. "You're going to need boots. I don't have any your size, but we'll do the best we can. Is that acceptable?"

Though he was looking at me while talking, his eyes rose to the others after his question. My teeth gritted together as I snarled at all of them. No one spoke agreement or objection. Heavy footsteps sounded from inside, drawing my attention just as one of the firemen stepped through the doorway.

"I take the silence as a yes," the Lieutenant said, and then looked at the other firefighter. "Chavez, get two pairs of small boots as in yesterday!"

Chavez ran off the steps toward the truck, his actions calming me tremendously. Before we started walking, I looked at Penny. "You don't have to come with us," I said. "I know how much this place bothers you. Why don't you get in the back of Officer Folsom's car?"

Her head shook as she faced the house. "I don't want to be alone," she said. "Let's go save Fu-, Cara."

"Who is Fucara?" Folsom asked.

Fugi was one of the bad guys when I first arrived, but now I think of her as a friend. Considering all she's done I refuse to turn her in. I'm so very thankful Penny remembered the name I thought up. "It's not Fucara," I said. "It's Cara; only her closest friends call her Footy, a nickname from childhood I assume. It would offend her for you to call her that."

His shoulders shrugged like he didn't care, and then we silently walked to the porch. Penny sat on the steps waiting for Chavez to return with boots, but suddenly a nearly overwhelming dizziness caused me to stagger slightly. My hand rose to my forehead as I struggled to regain composure. When it started to subside, Folsom looked at me with concern but the Lieutenant was frowning. "You're not going in there," the Lieutenant said while motioning for the paramedics to come close.

Once the spinning stopped, I glared at him. "Oh yes I am," I said. "It was only a case of slight exhaustion. I'm fine now that I've caught my breath."

He looked at me with a frowning face. "If that was slight exhaustion, why is it only affecting you and not her?" He asked while briefly pointing at Penny. "I can't risk taking you with us unless you tell me why."

"Because just a few minutes ago she flushed out the last man left behind to make certain we didn't escape," Penny said, "You'll see for yourself what I'm about to say is true. She was nearly killed by the explosion that did kill their leader Earl when he came after us. Thank God it only knocked her out! When she came to, it was like she woke up with a plan. Since we didn't know how badly Cara was wounded we couldn't wait for this man to make his move. Years ago they put this thing in my leg that will blow up at the push of a button; yes that's right. That meant I had to keep back a safe distance or he could easily kill me. It fell on her shoulders. Her only chance at survival was to trick him into believing she was harmless, and find a way to keep him in the hall long enough for me to end it. Without hesitation she calmly walked, *unarmed*, down a long passageway with many dark, open doors. Just as she reached the exit, Mark grabbed her from behind and dragged her into a room before I could safely shoot. Joyce was completely on her own, nothing I could do that wouldn't endanger the both of us. I don't know what she did or said that convinced him to return to the hall but obviously it worked. And I have many other examples I could use but there isn't time. Does that satisfy your concern about her will to finish what she sets her mind to do?"

Birds chirping in trees answered her question. All men in our presence slowly looked at me in open-mouthed awe. My eyes fell to the ground, my face turning red. Chavez arrived with the boots, but the vibrations of heavy footsteps clomping onto the porch from the house grabbed my attention. It was obvious the two firemen had been listening just inside the doorway. "I'll watch over her Lieutenant," one of them said.

"I'm sure you will," the Lieutenant said while grinning at him, and then looked at me with seriousness returning to his expression. "Okay I'm convinced, but only on one condition. We do this my way. If I say pull back we pull back and that includes the two of you. There's no room for arguments. Is that understood?"

At this point arguing was useless and time-consuming. If they start something dangerous, I'll stop them. "Agreed; let's get Cara out of there please!"

"You're going to need something to cut through twisted metal grids," Penny said. "Otherwise you'll never get a stretcher through."

Chavez placed the boots between us, and looked at the Lieutenant. I glanced at Penny with a grim expression, and she nodded her head while we began removing our makeshift shoes. They have no idea what's waiting, and I pray they'll be able to get past the bent grate in time.

"You heard the lady," the Lieutenant said, "go get the torches and cutters."

The two paramedics walked by us, carrying a stretcher through the doorway. Chavez ran to the truck, grabbing a tank with a long hose and several long metal tools. By this time Penny and I had slipped the over-sized boots on our feet. We stood just as Chavez returned. "Remember ma'am," the Lieutenant said. "If I say stop we stop. Okay let's go!"

"Paul Backus IBC News," a man said while stepping around the side of the house. "I'm coming with you."

Another man holding a camera with a red light flashing moved to where he could film us. Folsom started moving toward him, but I jumped in front before he got past me. "To all those who did business with Earl at Barker Exports hear me," I said. "We found his extensive back-up files. You'd better believe we will come for you. Don't wait for that. Surrender your hostages now and the courts might be lenient. Ignore me or do something foolish and suffer horrible consequences."

Agent Smith nearly grabbed me by the mouth when I faced him. Folsom stepped by, motioning for two other officers to come close.

"Hostages, business; ma'am can I have a few words with you?" Backus asked.

"A statement will be released later," Folsom said. "If you don't step behind the police line, I'll have you arrested for impeding an investigation."

Smith stood between me and the reporter, Jones positioned himself between Penny and the newsman. The Lieutenant just looked at me grinning and shaking his head.

"Ma'am, hey let go," Backus said as he and the cameraman were being led away. "Ma'am what did you mean?"

Even though Smith had his hand on my shoulder in an attempt at preventing me from answering, I managed to peek around him at the cameraman who was still shooting. "Those my message was meant for know exactly what I mean."

Just before I was pushed inside, Backus looked at the cameraman who gave him a thumbs-up sign. I can only assume that meant he got all I said and will now begin whatever it is they do for validation.

"That was a risky thing you did Miss Jackson," Smith said. "I could arrest you for disclosing crucial evidence and compromise of a federal investigation."

How he knew I wasn't Penny astonished me since I never told him, but his statement made me so angry I didn't care. When I glared at him, his stern look softened into a grin. "It was also a stroke of genius," he said. "Let's see if it does any good."

Folsom stepped through the doorway, first looking at me and then the Lieutenant. Agent Jones cleared his throat loudly. "Miss Jackson, Miss Carver?" He asked. "Agent Smith and I've been on numerous case investigations that drew the attention of the press. I can accurately tell you what to expect. It's a safe bet your faces have been shown over many television stations within a hundred miles. That's why we wanted to remove you when we did, to slow this process before it got out of hand. Rest assured IBC has a parabolic dish microphone that picked up everything said. As sensational as this is becoming, what was a regional news story is probably national by now. If they follow standard procedure, they're digging up as much background as they can about this place, and desperately searching for any information they can find about you two. They heard your last names over the police-bands some time ago giving them a good head-start. It won't take long to find out nearly everything there is to know about you. Every screaming person wearing a press badge will be hounding you until this becomes old."

The way he said that makes me feel depressed, like I'm now public property. His shoulders shrugged as he looked away.

"So let them," Penny said. "Right now I really don't care what they do as long as it frees the other prisoners."

She's right. Just the tone of her voice brought me back. We have nothing to hide. The Lieutenant never stopped watching me as I recovered, his grin remained strong. "You are both remarkable women," he said. "I can't wait to read your statements. Let's go save your friend, what do you say?"

Just before the Lieutenant turned away, I tapped his shoulder. "For the sake of time let me encapsulate what's waiting," I said. "There are two basement levels below the one your men put out the fire. The first is an office complex that can wait. Nobody's left who can hurt us. It's the bottom where Cara is lying."

I paused to draw a breath and allow what I'd said to sink in. Though I had their undivided attention, it looked like they didn't know whether or not to believe me but that's okay. They'll see for themselves. "Once we reach the very bottom, the first obstacle we're going to encounter is an electric hallway we blew up. I'm assuming that's what caused the diesel generator to catch fire. It's no longer dangerous except for the twisted grates that are now like knives. The metal grids that once conducted electricity are bunched-up and will require the use of cutters. You'll understand when you see it. Now in the next hall, great danger still exists. Do not under any circumstances open the two closed doors. If you turn the knob it'll explode killing you and us. The door at the far end has a shock collar they used to keep captives under control on the inside and will have to be detonated using a remote control from a safe distance, and the other one can only be opened by turning the key while keeping the knob absolutely still. As long as you listen to me, we'll be all right. Cara is in the next hall, in the first room to the left."

With the exception of Penny, everyone was looking at me with serious doubt on their faces. I forced the rising anger back and continued with my final warning. "There are four bodies. The first you'll see is the guy Penny told you about. He came after me, Penny shot him. It was clearly self-defense. The next is Hank, who was shot by Cara when he charged our position. We moved one of the exploding doors to that hall and placed another shock collar on the inside knob. Earl ironically killed himself when he leaned against it and tried using his remote control to kill Penny, blowing up his and Hank's bodies in the process. It picked up the signal, setting off the explosion. His head is all that's left. Fred's body is out of sight in what they called the shower room. They're dead; don't waste time on them right now. Okay let's go."

Blinking eyes was the response I received. My anger threatened to overwhelm me as I glared at each of them in turn. "I SAID let's go!"

"You heard the lady," the Lieutenant said. "We'll sort this out later."

In spite of the way he acted toward me when I first saw him, I'm starting to like the Lieutenant. Folsom stepped to the side, removing his radio from his upper sleeve and speaking quiet codes, but the Lieutenant ignored Folsom while turning to walk toward the basement. The rest of us fell in line.

Our journey through the house was in silence, including our walk down the first flight of stairs. Folsom caught up before we went further. The sight of the hidden panel surprised me as well as them. This was the first chance I had to see it from this side.

Busts of waist-high dog heads lined the four cinderblock walls of the basement. The half-open panel looked like cinderblocks from this side. When closed it would be perfectly concealed. Dog heads must act like a handle, if you know which one to use.

Rattling wheels from the paramedic's stretcher was the only sound while we marched through the first basement. The Lieutenant stepped beyond the panel, glancing down the first set of stairs before looking at me.

"I have to admit I wasn't sure about you," he said. "But there's no denying something incredible happened here. Both of you are now required to remain in Willard until our investigation is completed."

A sense of hopelessness filled me. "How long will this investigation take?" I asked.

"Based on what you said," Folsom said, "about five years."

Dread became anger as I looked at him behind me. "WHAT? All of my money and possessions were stolen when I was abducted. I have no clothes or family within a thousand miles and no place to stay. There is no way I escaped one prison just to enter another!"

Chuckling came from Folsom as he first grinned at the Lieutenant, and then me. "Your part will probably be over in a couple weeks," he said. "Now before you go off on me, let me say we'll put both of you up in the finest hotel Willard has to offer, all meals on us. As for money and clothes, I'm afraid you'll need to contact someone."

His words made me realize my plans to begin a new life have gone up in flames. Here I am back at the starting point. Depression over the power that would give my father made me quietly look away.

"Relax Joyce," Penny said. "We'll survive, thanks to you."

Though her attempt at helping me didn't succeed, I managed a weak smile at her before turning toward the stairwell. Our walk down the steps was done in silence, permitting me to turn my attention to the matters at hand. Once we reached the bottom, someone behind whistled while looking at the carnage. The Lieutenant stared at me with amazement on his face.

"Is this the electric hall you mentioned?" He asked.

Footsteps descending the stairs indicated new people were arriving as I nodded. Three more uniformed officers stepped into view, followed by two men in suits.

"Yes, and it's perfectly safe. Our chat is proof. Please hurry; Cara has lost a lot of blood."

Nobody moved, like they were afraid of those grids. The Lieutenant grew impatient as he glared at the three firemen standing still. "Well what are you waiting for, the national anthem to play? I want a wide path cut through that mess ten minutes ago!"

The men silently worked their way around us, removing various tools from their backpacks in the process.

"What's in there?" Folsom asked pointing at the museum.

Penny looked sheepishly at her feet. Although our reasons were justified, I don't know how our use of crime evidence will be viewed. Oh well, it is better they find out now instead of assuming we purposely destroyed proof.

"That room will probably interest the FBI as much as you, Officer," I said. "It should solve quite a few missing persons' reports. Earl told me he was once a hit man with the nickname of The Eraser.

He not only killed for money, he removed the bodies and ground them into dog food he exported. That shiny machine blocking the last chamber was his grinder. And in that room are the names of some if not all his victims. He built display cases to house the guns used in each crime, but I'm afraid the cases are empty. We had to take some and make sure the rest couldn't be used against us."

Smith and Jones walked to stand next to Folsom, both staring at me with perplexed faces. "Are you saying this Earl killed people and then put the guns he used on display for the world to see?" Smith asked. "Assuming that's true your use of them will not be an issue. If everything pans out it's obviously a case of self defense. I'm just amazed at his carelessness. It sounds like his tree was missing all the leaves."

Folsom grinned but I stared at Smith in anger. "He'd been showing them undetected for at *least* ten years," I said. "Don't underestimate his intelligence or paranoia. If you do it might cost you dearly. The only booby-traps I know about are what I've already said. God only knows what might be waiting elsewhere."

His arrogant expression dropped, looking down the hall. Folsom stared at the museum deep in thought. Sounds of someone stepping across small debris drew my attention toward the closest wall. One of the new men dressed in a suit was studying the dark keypad Fugi tried using to set us free, and then stared at the frame.

"This looks like some sort of magna-seal doorframe," he said. "Look at that."

He pointed up at the remaining pieces of the bars jutting out of the opening like arthritic fingers. Penny grinned, glancing away. "It was," I said. "We were trapped when the wrong code-"

"Okay we can get through now," Chavez said.

I was halted in mid-sentence, slowly facing Chavez with an open mouth. All of my attention had been focused away from them, and I'd hardly paid them any mind. A path wide enough to walk the stretcher safely through had been opened. It amazed me how quietly and fast they managed to do it. The Lieutenant noticed my admiration, a smile forming. "Yep," he said, "they're Willard's finest all right. This town would be lost without them, but don't tell them I said so. They'd demand more money."

"They *deserve* it," I said.

He chuckled proudly while stepping into the hall. In less than a minute we'd gotten past the twisted metal and were standing in the next hallway. "Okay leave the knobs alone," I said. "Cara is in the next hall, through that doorway and first door on the left."

The paramedics moved to the front and began wheeling the stretcher in the direction I'd indicated. "Ainsley, Chavez, you know what to do," the Lieutenant said. "Let's go."

When I started to move, a pair of strong hands grabbed my shoulders while the others walked into the living room. Chavez held Penny in place, both of us at first surprised and then angered.

"What're you doing?" Penny asked.

"You'd better let go or your future plans for fatherhood will end right now," I said.

My struggles intensified, as did the hold against me. "Relax," Ainsley said, "this is for the best. You'd only get in the way. That might cost your friend her life. I'm sure you don't want that."

Enragement now controlled my actions. I began twisting violently while watching Ainsley's feet. First I yanked to the left, forward, and then right. Suddenly his left foot moved between my legs in an effort at maintaining balance. My left heel rose quickly and smashed down on his toes. His grip loosened enough for me to break free and run away. Quiet curses sounded when he started limping after me.

I had enough of a head start to reach the living room and dash inside. One paramedic was kneeling beside Fugi holding her limp right arm in his hand while shaking his head. Fugi was absolutely still and appeared gray in color. Tears formed as I realized we were too late. She's gone.

Why did I take the time to search the second basement and not rush to find that phone? I should have ignored the reporters, not worried over talking about what was down here, and demanded we move faster. We should have found a way to bring her with us. My stupid carelessness killed Fugi. Oh God it's all my fault!

My vision blurred, silent heaves moving my chest. Tears were streaming down my face when a hand grabbed my shoulder. That touch surprised me enough to force loud sobbing. I turned away, burying my face in Ainsley's shirt.

"How'd she get in here?" The Lieutenant asked.

"I'm sorry sir," Ainsley said. "She has more moves than a professional athlete."

"That I believe. It's alright. So what's the prognosis? Will she survive the flight or do we need to do something here?"

My weeping stopped as I slowly faced the kneeling paramedic. "Sh-She's alive?"

His head shook a few more times before looking at me. "Barely," he said. "I've never seen anything like this before in all my life. Considering the amount of blood she's lost, well frankly, I'm ast-"

All lights and sounds ended. Darkness engulfed me into oblivion.

CHAPTER 27

"Miss Jackson?"

Inky blackness was disturbed by a strange female voice. Slowly things changed to total confusion. "Miss Jackson, are you with me?"

Taking everything in was as dizzying as being spun rapidly. This strange environment was disorienting. A billowy shape took form into a curtain pulled completely around this bed with elevated rails. To my left was a small table with a lighted lamp and in front of it a pole holding a bag of liquid half drained. It was dripping into a clear narrow hose that ran from the bottom of the bag to a needle in my left hand. I must be in a hospital, but how did I get here? The last thing I remember is a man saying Fugi was alive. "Miss Jackson, welcome to Huron Memorial hospital," a nurse sitting cross-legged in a chair next to the IV pole.

My mind cleared of the sleepy fog quickly when I focused on her. Ah yes; I must've passed out and been brought in by ambulance. "I'm Nurse Foster," she said. "Try not to move just yet. You've been through a lot."

"Tell me about it," I said. "Where are Penny and Cara?"

Her legs uncrossed as she leaned close. I couldn't see her hands. "They're both doing fine," she said.

Relief washed over me as I closed my eyes and leaned back.

"Miss Jackson, I'd like to ask you a few questions if you're up to it."

My head nodded as I casually looked at her. She was not smiling, which began to bother me. "Forgive me for what I'm about to say, but there's no easy way," she said. "Your friend, the person you called

Cara, should have died but didn't. Whoever shot her knew what they were doing, hitting enough vital organs to insure a lingering death without salvation, but she's recovering at an accelerated rate. We'd like to know why."

Mental alarms sounded grave danger. Something about her doesn't feel right. As I tried sitting up, a wave of nausea forced me to remain still. "Who are you?" I asked.

"There are traces of an unknown enzyme in all three of your blood works," she said. "We don't have a clue what it is. Do you know where they kept those drugs?"

The call button for the real nurse has to be around here somewhere. While I looked at her, my right hand began a stealthy search for it. "I'm not sure I understand your question," I said. "What drugs?"

A frown grew on her face when she noticed the movement underneath my bedspread. "We'll be in touch," she said.

Then she quickly rose, lifting a hypodermic needle in her concealed hand to a port at the bottom of the liquid bag designed for speedy drug administration. It jabbed in place, her thumb emptying the contents too fast for me to do anything. "What are you-"

Wooziness forced my mouth shut, all light fading as my head relaxed on the pillow. Absolute calm made me smile.

"Miss Jackson? Your breakfast's here."

My eyes snapped open to a different nurse holding a covered tray at the foot of the bed. She was smiling kindly as she placed it on a table and began wheeling it toward me. The curtain had been pulled back showing an empty bed. Sunlight streamed through a window on the same side as the lamp table, intra-venous pole, and chair used by Nurse Foster.

"I'm Pam Auburn," she said. "The doctor wants you on solid food as soon as possible, but I let you sleep a little late. How are you feeling?"

"Totally lost," I said. "What happened to Nurse Foster?"

She looked at me like I was talking gibberish. So I had a visitor of unknown origins. I must proceed cautiously. If I make them think I'm mentally unfit, they might keep me where she can find me again.

"Who?" She asked.

Aromas of cooked eggs wafted to my nose, making my stomach rumble. It humiliated me while bringing a smile to her. "Excuse me,"

I said. "That was embarrassing. But you're saying there isn't a Nurse Foster working here?"

Her head shook as she continued staring at me.

"I guess it was a dream," I said. "Where am I?"

Maybe it was my imagination. Auburn removed the cover from the tray, showing a huge helping of scrambled eggs, sausage, toast, orange juice, and coffee. "Huron Memorial Hospital," she said which brought chills down my arms.

"Good morning sleepy-head," Penny cheerfully said from the hall.

The sound of her happy voice brought a smile to my face. Then I saw her clothing. It was a pink pantsuit with matching leather pumps.

"Wow your parents got here fast," I said.

Her left eyebrow went up as she stared at me with a puzzled expression.

"I haven't seen them," she said. "What made you say that?"

"Where'd you get the clothes?"

A large smile replaced the worried expression on her face, and Auburn joined her apparent good mood with a grin. "You tell her," Penny said while moving to a nearby seat.

Ashley rolled the table over my waist and began adjusting the bed for me to eat. "Officer Folsom paid a few visits to some of our more affluent shopkeepers after you were checked in," she said. "He explained your dilemma and asked they help out as much as they can. They were more than receptive to what he suggested. For as long as you remain in Willard," she paused while walking to a closet and opening the door, "you will be our honored guests."

She moved aside in time for me to see a light-weight lime green silk blouse fluttering in the draft created by the opening door. A dark green knee-length skirt hung next to it, and matching green flats rested on the floor. I was overcome by emotions, tears welling in my eyes. Words escaped me as I stared at her compassionate smile. "Better eat your breakfast," Auburn said. "Doctor Melton will be along shortly to determine if you're ready for discharge."

Before she turned, one question plaguing my mind needed an answer. "What about Cara? Is she all right?"

Her head nodded as she backed to the door; that smile not wavering. "I'm told it's nothing short of a miracle," she said. "Though she needs more recovery time than the two of you, she's going to be just fine. You can see her later."

Even though I thought that's what she was going to say based on the mystery woman's earlier chat, I still felt relieved to have it confirmed. She moved through the door, looking at both of us with a mysterious expression bordering on admiration.

"I'll leave the two of you alone," she said. "If you need anything, push the button on the right bed rail. I'll be back in a few minutes to collect your dishes."

Then she stepped out of sight. I lifted the fork and speared a large helping of eggs, barely able to contain my excitement over eating something other than fruit. Once it was in my mouth, Penny took the television remote control from the closest table and clicked it. "You won't believe what's happening," she said.

Another heaping forkful reached my mouth while I waited for the TV to warm up. Sound began before the picture cleared. "-like a modern-day Davie and Goliath," Paul Backus said from in front of Barker Exports, "Carolyn?"

The background immediately changed to a newsroom setting. "Thank you Paul," Carolyn said. "We now return to Huron Memorial Hospital for an update; Jim?"

Many people milling about suddenly covered the screen, with one middle-aged man in the center who was obviously Jim. "Thanks Carolyn," he said. "No word has been issued about the release of Penny Carver, Cara Ishaya, or Joyce Jackson yet, but I was told a few moments ago Ms. Jackson has awakened from her ordeal in good spirits. Police aren't permitting anyone inside the building-"

"Thank God for that," I said while lifting another forkful.

"-medical treatments. I also confirmed that Cara Ishaya, who underwent emergency surgery last night is expected to make a full recovery; Carolyn?"

We returned to the newsroom where Carolyn was smiling at the camera.

"Thanks Jim," she said. "For those of you just tuning in, an incredible drama is unfolding in northeastern Ohio. Late yesterday afternoon, a quiet, picturesque town by the name of Willard was turned upside down when a phone call from Joyce Jackson," my college graduation picture appeared, "of Burksdale Oklahoma reported an extraordinary tale of abduction, dungeon-like imprisonment, and twenty-first century slavery. Her courageous struggles against impossible odds didn't end once she was free. Investigators later found a satellite-dish antenna acting as a signal jam, making it difficult for the police to locate their whereabouts. Preliminary statements released say a crime-wave spanning over a decade and encompassing many states has ended. Cara Ishaya was gravely shot during their battle for freedom. Joyce Jackson and Penny Carver returned inside to lead rescuers to her location but only Ms. Carver walked out. No reason was given why Ms. Jackson fell unconscious while inside. A grateful nation anxiously waits-"

"Turn it off," I said.

The television went silent and dark. Penny placed the remote on the table, perplexedly looking at me. "I thought you'd be excited to see that. Is something wrong?"

During the show, I'd finished my breakfast and sipped the last of the coffee as she asked her question. After placing the cup on the tray, I stared at the blank screen. "They're playing on the messenger and not the message," I said while looking at her. "For all I know they never aired my warning and now thousands of people are dead."

Her head started shaking in disagreement while a grin formed. "That's the Joyce I've come to know and respect," she said. "Even when things were their darkest and I didn't think we'd survive, you refused to quit. They have been showing that little clip repeatedly. I've seen it. It was the talk on The Tomorrow Show this morning. The Tomorrow Show Joyce; we're being made into celebrities! Wait until they hear about your ideas that set us free. You're famous whether you like it or not. Go with it."

"We all chipped in," I said. "You did as much as I did."

Again her head shook. "Moving the only two non-exploding wooden doors across that electrified grid, using one of the exploding doors to get the guns we needed, and setting another exploding door as the booby-trap that killed Earl, not to mention you overcame their spell *three* times; that's all you Joyce. I will forever be in your debt!"

I shook my head briefly in response saying "Don't. Don't put me on a pedestal. When I think of the horrors you faced, I am in awe of how well you've recovered. You got rid of Mark, don't forget."

"Because you calmly walked down that hall where you knew he was waiting and gave me a clear shot; your plan let me remind you. You're a true heroine!"

A shadow crossed the threshold which drew my attention. Auburn entered the room. Since I didn't hear any footsteps approaching, I can only assume she'd been listening the entire time. She briefly looked at me with an open-mouthed expression of amazement before walking to the tray and lifting it. "Doctor Melton is making the rounds in this ward," she said. "He'll be here-"

"Now," an elderly grinning man said while stepping across the threshold. "So these are the people who've turned my hospital into a circus. I'm very pleased to see you awake, Miss Jackson. How are you feeling?"

He went around Auburn, taking the chair Nurse Foster had occupied. Then he lifted my arm to check my pulse. Auburn turned and left the room, shutting the door in her wake. "I'm fine," I said. "When can I leave?"

Penny started to rise, but Melton indicated with his free hand for her to remain. "Yes, yes, you're fine is what you told Fire Lieutenant Adams before passing out," he said and then released me. "You were suffering from dehydration and malnutrition, but not enough to justify seventeen hours of comatose-like sleep."

My mouth dropped open. I've been out that long? As if he could read my mind, his head nodded while a stern expression formed.

"I'm going to be candid to you both," he said. "Something is in your blood we can't identify. And your friend; to put it bluntly should be dead. Medical science can do wonders, but a ruptured kidney, spleen, liver, and punctured lung are just beyond our ability to repair without major surgery or transplant. None of the organs were on-site and most assuredly would not have arrived in time, plus she was too weak from loss of blood for us to attempt repair. Yet she's awake and asking for you. Her damaged organs didn't just heal, it's like they grew new parts to replace the wounded portions at an incredible rate which simply isn't possible. I've never seen anything like it in my life."

His eyes wandered to Penny while he rose, and then turned away from both of us to walk toward the window. This talk was making me uneasy. While clasping his hands behind his back he said "Your friend Miss Ishaya has a slightly different enzyme in her body over you two. CDC in Atlanta sent specialists to obtain samples, but they weren't the only surprise visitors we had last night. The Drug Enforcement Agency asked questions I couldn't answer. What on Earth happened to you?"

Penny's eyes were wide with fear. I must admit what he said now has me worried as he faced us with a perplexed expression.

"Are we going to die?" I asked.

"What? No, at least not anytime soon; the pathogen in your system seems to be dormant. It's not moving nor is it contagious. Before I can prescribe a treatment for removal, I must know what it is and why you were given it."

Relief washed over me. My eyes closed, and when they reopened, I glanced at a smiling Penny before looking at Melton. "What it is I can't say," I said, "but it was given to me in three doses, the first with food and the other two by injection. It's some kind of drug that works on the mind. How was it described to me? Oh yes, it assassinates personalities thus clearing the way for a person to be programmed so thoroughly, she'd be willing to kill herself at a simple command. Believe me, it works."

He looked at me with narrowing eyes indicating doubt. "And Miss Ishaya," he asked, "why is her pathogen different than yours?"

We've reached an area I couldn't discuss. If I told him what I knew it would expose Fugi. I'll let her speak for herself. "I really don't know," I said. "We were held in separate rooms."

"Miss Carver," he asked, "can you shed some light on this subject?"

Her shoulders shrugged, prompting him to move closer to us. "Only that for three years I was altered by that drug to the point I was somebody else."

While he pondered our answers, a mental alarm sounded. He has the power to commit us, or at least hold us if he deems we're a threat. "Doctor Melton," I said drawing both their attentions, "you said what was inside us was neither moving nor contagious. I take that to mean it's just sitting there harmlessly and we're free to go."

"I'm not sure about the harmless part and would like to run more tests, but there's no reason you can't do that as an outpatient. Both of your mental faculties appear to be in order. However I recommend you visit a psychiatrist, for assistance in overcoming the delusional state of being someone willing to commit suicide at a simple command."

Rising anger threatened to overpower my better reasoning. How dare he say something like that when he hasn't a clue about the drug used on us? A quick glance at Penny out of the corner of my eye showed she was also miffed but under control. I guess this is what we can expect until they've found the drug supply at that farm.

"Whatever you say," I said. "Now will you please remove this needle from my hand? I'm anxious to see Cara."

For a few moments I didn't think he was going to respond, and then he glanced at the doorway. Finally he shrugged his shoulders while gently grasping the needle. "Normally I'd send the nurse in for this," he said as he slid the needle out, "but in your case I'll make an exception." An alcohol swab was wiped over the area, and then a Band-Aid covered the spot where blood was forming. "A final word of advice is be very careful who you talk to, especially about the mind-bending part. Take this to heart. If I completely doubted your claims about that drug, at this moment I'd be transferring you to the Psyche-Ward for a full evaluation. As for what I'm writing on your medical reports, this conversation never took place."

He leaned close to me so he could speak quietly while being heard by both of us. "Some of the visitors I had made me nervous," he said. "Whatever they're looking for is big and I think you are their primary target. Keep that in mind when you speak."

This is just great. Here we escape one tyrant only to be cornered by another. As he turned to leave, Penny looked at me with concern all over her face. "Thank you for the warning doctor," I said. "One last question; is a shower in that small room?"

I pointed at a closed door just inside the room doorway. He looked at where I was pointing and nodded before continuing toward the door. "You're free to go whenever you're ready," he said. "There's no need to stop by accounting. Willard has picked up the charges. Good luck, to you both."

After he stepped out of view, I looked at Penny. She still seemed scared. "Hey relax," I said. "We just beat Earl and company. The entire United States government can't hold a candle to that."

A nervous chuckle escaped as she looked sheepishly embarrassed. I smiled at her, pushed the covers off, and rose to my feet. "I'm going to grab a quick shower," I said. "You can stay here and wait if you like."

"Oh God, after what he said I don't want to be alone! I feel like climbing in the shower with you. I guess I'll take you up on the offer and watch more television. If you hear a scream, come running."

In my opinion, her concerns may be justified. That mystery nurse lends credence that something bigger than Earl is unfolding, and this medical institution now has a menacing feeling like we're in a box and easy to take. Though I really wanted to enjoy a nice, hot, leisurely shower, I quickly entered the small bathroom and bathed in record time. A few minutes later I was dressed and watching television with Penny. Carolyn at the newsroom of IBC was accepting a document from an unseen source and then reading it. "For our continuing coverage on the amazing story of three courageous women," she said, "I've just received a report that investigators from the FBI, DEA, and National Security are converging on Barker Exports Annex. No reason has been released for this unprecedented show of multi-departmental interest-"

Penny pressed the mute button. "This keeps getting scarier by the moment," she said. "What else were they doing?"

A shoulder shrug preceded a quick glance at the TV before looking at her. "Whatever it was, it's over," I said. "Let's go check on Fugi."

When I mentioned Fugi's name, a chilling realization rose in my mind. The man responsible for the drugs as well as Fugi's new sex may still be at large. Penny picked up on my facial change, forcing me to put that worry aside for now. "You remembered something," she said; "what?"

"Just the last loose end the police need to pick up," I said. "It's no big deal. Come on; let's pay our respects to the woman who risked everything."

Before she could ask, I stepped through the doorway heading to the nurse's station. She caught up just as I found out Fugi was in Intensive Care two flights up to the left. A short ride in the elevator, followed by a brief chat with the nurse at the duty station, and we were watching a sleeping Fugi. Monitors quietly beeped behind her, two poles fed fluids to both arms. Then she slowly opened her eyes.

Memories of her lying in a pool of blood looking dead rushed into the front of my mind, bringing tears to see her awake now. I smiled, walking close to her side. "How are you feeling?" I asked.

Penny moved to her other side, also appearing close to an emotional overload. Fugi frowned, slipping the sheet aside to show how many sutures were running over her belly. "Like a quilt," she said; "next stupid question?"

My eyebrows shot up at the tone of her voice. Penny also looked astonished from the accusatory response. Then I noticed the sparkle inside her eyes as she tried to avoid grinning. I guess this is a side of Fugi we weren't able to see until now. I smiled at her, tears starting to run down my cheeks. "You're going to be just fine," I said.

"Yeah; well turn off the waterworks," she said. "I have a bone to pick with you." She raised the arm with her hospital name bracelet; "Cara Ishaya?"

Penny's hand covered her mouth in an attempt of concealing her smile. My lips pursed in a vain effort of the same thing. "It's all I could think of on short notice," I said.

"Uh *huh*," Fugi said. "Well, do you remember how I kicked you in the head after you untied me, tried taking the keys from you, and nearly killed you when I thought you were mentally gone?"

"Yes," I said.

"We're even! Shit this is outrageous! I ought to put my footy up your ass when I'm out of here!"

Snickering became laughter as Penny turned away. I tried maintaining control but failed. When I started giggling, Fugi's stern face softened into a grin. Once we'd calmed she said "I know why you did it and want to thank you. Now I want to move on to something very important to me. Soon we'll be going our separate ways, but there's one thing I want you both to do before that happens."

"We're all going to be here awhile," Penny said. "Officer Folsom said it'll take at least two weeks before our part in this investigation will be over."

Fugi appeared concerned, but then her expression changed to one of anticipation. "Good," she said. "At least you can't sneak off before I'm out of this linen prison. Now I want both of you to swear we'll never lose touch and agree to meet every year for a celebration. I'm talking wine, fine food, pleasant conversation, and general mayhem without the threat of death looming over our shoulders. How's that sound?"

Somewhere I'd heard people who fight life or death battles together become closer than family, and I now know that to be true. In just a short amount of time both of them have become important in my life. When Fugi mentioned about our parting, a wave of depression fell over me. Then her thought about getting together once a year lifted my spirits. "I think that's an excellent idea," I said. "No matter what happens, I'll be there."

"Me too," Penny said. "Where do you want to meet?"

A smile grew on Fugi's face as she looked at the wall over Penny's' head. "The Hotel Aigrette in Cleveland is a four-star joint close enough for us to thumb our noses at Barker Exports' main facility," she said. "You show up, I'll handle the bill. Shall we say the third weekend in October?"

Why that date was important to her eluded me. This is late May. But it must have some significance, and to me it really made no difference. "Sounds terrific," I said.

"Not a problem," Penny said.

Knocking on the door followed her response almost like it was on cue. It opened, and then a nurse stuck her head around the frame. "The front lobby just called," she said. "Detective Craig from the Ohio Bureau of Investigation is waiting downstairs to escort you to police headquarters."

"Fine," Fugi said. "Unhook me and I'll be right down."

"Not you Miss Ishaya," she said grinning.

Fugi's face formed a scowl as she looked at me. "Story of my life," she said.

Penny grinned and started walking away, but I glanced at the nurse without moving. "Can we have a few more moments alone?" I asked.

The nurse shrugged her shoulders while Penny looked at me in surprise. "Miss Ishaya's next check-up isn't due for another thirty minutes. As far as I'm concerned you can stay until then."

"Thanks," I said.

She stepped to the side and pulled the door shut. Fugi slowly faced me, appearing totally puzzled.

"There're a couple of things I want to say before we go," I said. "The first is I had a surprise visitor earlier today. She claimed to be a nurse asking a lot of strange questions especially about you, Fugi. Doctor Melton pretty much confirmed something weird is going on and warned us to be careful what we say. I wanted you to know."

A lopsided grin formed on Fugi's face as she nodded her head. "I appreciate the warning," she said. "Don't worry about me; you just go crack a few coconuts."

What that statement is supposed to mean escapes me, but I moved on. "That guy Earl called Doc may still be on the loose. I need his full name and address to send the police after him."

It looked like the room darkened. Fugi's pleasant demeanor instantly changed into something sinister. She frowned while answering. "If I give you his address too many questions will come up.

His name is Adolph Heidenreich out of Cleveland. There are no other people with that name in the phone book. Between you two and me, if the cops don't nab him before I'm out, in six months I'll handle it. Don't lose any sleep over that walking dead-man."

Chills coursed down my spine looking at her face. She must've noticed my rising fears, as a smile replaced the shadowy expression. "I protect my friends," she said. "If he goes to ground, I'll find him before he can hurt either of you. Relax and lose the I-think-I'm-going-to-shit look."

Slowly I started backing away. Fugi's smile left, growing concern replacing it. "Hey, forget I said anything," she said. "My friendship with you means more to me than revenge. I'll do my level best to help the authorities grab him and for the love of *God* will you stop staring at me like I have tentacles reaching out of my nose?"

"Frankly I don't care what you do to put an end to that bastard," Penny said. "Just do it."

She's right. Why am I getting so bothered over the well-being of a monster? Fugi must have contacts the police don't. If necessary I'm sure they'll come in handy. I smiled at Fugi, which caused a great expression of relief to fall over her. "I'm sorry for acting that way," I said. "Your friendship means a lot to me as well. Promise me one thing, okay?"

Her eyebrows knitted together in confusion as she nodded her head once.

"If it becomes necessary and you have to take action, please be very careful. I don't want to lose you."

Tears lined her eyes as she smiled gently at me. That show of emotions must've embarrassed her as she looked away. "Better go talk to the cops," she said. "You don't want Doc to have much more of a head start."

"I'll come back as soon as I can," I said.

CHAPTER 28

Word of our ordeal must be spreading. As Penny and I walked toward the elevators, nurses, aides, and mobile patients stopped what they were doing to gawk at us. Once we'd gone by, excited whispering floated in the air. It made me feel self-conscious like my blouse was unbuttoned, forcing me to face the wall while we waited for the elevator. People moving behind did not detract my attention from watching the slow-moving indicator light. When it informed us of arrival, I dreaded the potential occupants who may be inside.

Thankfully it was empty. We entered, but just as the doors were closing one male head looked in on us. It almost made me stick my tongue out. I refrained. At last we were on the way down. Penny glanced at me shortly after the cart jolted into action. "I guess we'd better get used to being stared at," she said.

That's a depressing thought. All I wanted was a new life starting with an anonymous vacation at the beach followed by a teaching career. It would appear the only way the first part can happen is if I go out of the country. I nodded my head as we drew closer to the ground floor without stopping.

A ding announced our arrival. Doors opened to a quiet scene in the lobby, but just beyond the glass walls utter chaos ruled. It grew in intensity once we were recognized. Cameras were pressed against glass, little red lights beneath the lenses blinking.

From our left a male voice said "Miss Jackson, Miss Carver, I'm Agent Craig, OBI." He held up a badge. "If you'll come with me, we have a car waiting."

No way will we get by that mob in one piece. They're acting like a pack of starving wolves fighting over a trapped lamb. He noticed my concern as I looked away from the front toward him. A grin formed while he turned to the left. "Local police cordoned off a side exit exclusively for our use," he said. "It's this way."

Two uniformed officers were standing like an honor guard on the inside of a narrow hallway leading to one glass door, with two more cops on the outside carefully scanning the surroundings. A squad car was parked just as he promised, the engine sounds apparent when the door opened. Officer Folsom was seated inside, looking the area over when we stepped into the warm morning sunshine.

Shouts and flashing cameras came from barricades fifty feet from both ends of the vehicle as we moved toward it. Craig casually opened the car's back door, allowing Penny to enter first, followed by me. He shut the door and climbed in the front. Slowly we pulled off. Once beyond the police blockade people started chasing us on foot.

Folsom was forced to maneuver carefully through the crowd until we were clear. "I'll give you a heads-up," he said. "Your stories all check out except for Miss Ishaya. We can't find record of her citizenship anywhere on Earth. It's like she didn't exist until yesterday. You're going to be asked about it." He glanced at me through the rearview mirror before returning his attention to the road. "Can you shed some light on that?"

His tone didn't sound threatening, yet I couldn't help but feel imperiled. Fugi's freedom is at stake and now I have to lie under oath. Maybe there's another way. "Officer Folsom," I said. "First I'd like to sincerely thank you for what you did yesterday. That was very kind to get us these clothes. I'm truly grateful for having the opportunity to thank you personally."

He briefly glanced at me through the mirror. Penny managed to remain stoic directly behind him, not giving anything away through body language.

"As for Cara," I said, "we were held prisoner in separate cells and really didn't have the chance to talk with one another, even after I got free. Our struggles kept us busy believe me, but I will personally vouch for her. She is a heroine who nearly died ending a crime spree that seems to be drawing a whole lot of attention."

"Is there any family we can notify?" Craig asked.

That was an innocent enough question, yet I can't shake the feeling they don't trust Fugi and are looking for proof to put her away. As we turned off this road onto a larger highway and accelerated, Penny shifted in her seat drawing Craig's and my attention. "I think she said something about an accident killing her family," she said. "She's an orphan. That's all I know."

Tense silence followed as we continued down the road. Craig stared at Penny, and then me before looking ahead. It's time to refocus thoughts. "I'm sorry we can't be of more help," I said. "Now I have a question. Do either of you know anything about a woman masquerading as a nurse by the name of Foster?"

Craig craned his neck briefly to look at me, while Folsom stared in the mirror for some time before returning his eyes to the road. Then the two men glanced at each other, Folsom shaking his head. "No," Craig said. "Why do you ask?"

Penny stared at me with growing concern. I ignored her to focus on Craig. "A woman claiming to be a nurse talked with me earlier today. She injected my I.V. hose with a drug that knocked me out when she was finished. I'd like to express my gratitude at being drugged-up again."

Shifting muscles on the back of Folsom's jaw indicated he was grinning. Craig looked deadly serious as he shifted in his seat to stare at me. "What did you talk about?"

The auto turned off the highway into a parking lot. Numerous squad cars were parked, along with many vehicles sporting press emblems. A vacant spot close to the front door seemed to be our destination. This must be the station. "She asked a lot of questions but I knew something was wrong. When I didn't answer, she shot me up."

His eyebrows rose by my terminology just when Folsom pulled the car into the spot. Craig turned away, opening his door to a screaming scene. Several officers approached, forming a wall with their connected arms and started moving reporters back. When Craig opened my door, many people called my name. Cameras flashed in what appeared a tremendous thunderstorm once I stepped out of the vehicle. Penny slid out amid the same stroboscopic effect. Then we were quickly led into the lobby where once again quiet replaced madness. Our pace inexplicably slowed as we looked into the waiting room. Penny seemed startled by what was in front of us, coming to a dead stop.

Three seated people, a man and woman in their forties, and a younger man our age, started facing us. A hand on my shoulder drew my attention. Folsom held his index finger to his lips, and then pointed at the turning folks. Their gasps said it all.

Penny's arms were visibly shaking. The older woman bore a striking resemblance to her; the elder man's mouth fell open. All stared at each other for a few moments, and then the younger man looked to the ceiling like he was thanking God.

"Mom, dad, Ben?" Penny asked.

Tears flowed down all of their faces. Penny's lower lip trembled as she pensively stepped toward them. The woman remained seated as if frozen in shock, but the older man rose. His eyes were red, mouth forming a slight smile as his arms opened to a waiting hug.

"H-Hello pumpkin," he said. "We've missed you."

Loud wailing came from the woman as she dropped to her knees. The younger man rose, his smile faltering between running tears. Penny took two more steps, and then rushed into her father's arms. Her mother climbed off the floor, looked at me and mouthed thank you, and then joined in a family hug. My own vision clouded from tears watching this beautiful reunion.

"I didn't think you'd want to miss this," Folsom said. "Let's give them a little privacy. An officer will escort them to a room in a few minutes. They have a lot of catching up to do. Our part with her can wait."

Warmth washed over me as I smiled at Folsom. "That was a wonderful thing to do," I said.

He smiled as we turned from them, walking down a hall. Just before we stepped where I couldn't see, I turned in time to watch Penny look at the young man, and then fall into a compassionate kiss with him.

"As much as I hate to admit it," Craig said, "what we just witnessed seldom takes place. It's times like these that make my efforts worthwhile."

Though his efforts came after we were free, I understood his meaning. This one had a happy ending. Our journey down a lonely corridor continued for a few moments in silence, until Folsom grabbed a doorknob. His expression changed to anger as he glanced at me. "They're already inside," he said. "I tried to claim jurisdiction but my superiors overruled me. Keep in mind this is only a fact-finding interrogation. No charges will be brought against you."

Being accused of any wrongdoing never crossed my mind until he said that. Now I'm becoming concerned though I don't know why. When he opened the door, a long conference table with four men and two women facing a single metal chair met my gaze. Good lord this has all the charm of a torture chamber. Two of the men I recognized; FBI Agent Smith and the fire Lieutenant Adams. Everyone else was a stranger.

Folsom stepped through the door first, indicating with his hand for me to take the lone seat in front of the table. All eyes were studying me, giving a return feeling of self-conscious embarrassment. Smith stared blankly, but Adams had a stern expression. If it hadn't been for the gleam I noticed in his eyes, I would have thought he was angry at me. Once I was seated and crossed my legs, Craig walked to a chair at the end of the table closest to the door while Folsom took a seat at the far side.

"Start the recorders," a man said. "For the record, please state your full name."

This had the feeling of a trial where I was about to be judged and hanged for witchcraft. As I looked at each face watching me closely, anger slowly replaced apprehension. "No," I said, "not until you identify yourselves."

My arms crossed over my chest as I shut my mouth and waited. Folsom started grinning, but the man who spoke appeared flustered. "You're not on trial," he said. "This is an inquisition. We're only trying to piece this puzzle together and some in attendance must remain unknown for security reasons. State your full name."

If he thinks I'm going to talk in front of people who refuse to identify their organizations, he's in for one huge surprise. I'd bet good money one of those strangers is responsible for sending Foster. Who knows what they'll do next if allowed to remain anonymous? While uncrossing my legs I said "Since I'm not on trial and no charges are filed against me, I'm free to go. Keep in mind I'm doing this voluntarily. Though I sincerely want to help, there's no way I'm talking to a group of unknown people who are staring at me like I'm a bug. I'll say this one, more, time. Unless each of you identifies yourself and who you represent, I'm leaving right now. Any answers you need can be obtained through Officer Folsom."

Adam's eyebrows rose as he slowly looked at the talking man. A sigh escaped from the man, as he faced the others at the table. No one seemed to object, so he shrugged his shoulders before returning his focus on me. "Stop the recorders," he said. "Very well, I'm Chief Wilson, Willard Police.

"Hi Miss Jackson," Adams said which made me grin.

"Charlotte Redfield, National Security Agency," the woman next to Adams said.

My eyebrows shot up as I looked at the woman seated next to her. "Operative Anderson, Central Intelligence Agency," she said.

Good heavens; what was going on at Barker Exports? "Agent Morris, Drug Enforcement Agency," the man next to Anderson said.

"Agent Givens, Interpol Attaché," the next man said.

Smith simply nodded. This group of various intelligence gathering agencies was so mind-boggling it almost felt like the room was spinning. All these people are interested in what I have to say, although I don't know how much help I'll be. They don't know that yet. Before they do I have to fix the last problem.

"Wow what a colorful audience," I said. "I haven't seen this many spooks in one place since my last trip to a carnival funhouse." Folsom chuckled, forcing me to pause until he stopped. "You obviously want something from me or you wouldn't be here. Well it comes with a price. I want this to go on record."

Anderson's eyes narrowed. Wilson sighed loudly before nodding. "Start the recorders," he said; "go ahead."

"My full name is Joyce Allison Jackson. Before I continue, there's an issue that must be resolved. I have no idea why you can't find any record of Cara Ishaya in your vast databases. It bothers me. She had no reason to lie and saved my life at the obvious risk of her own. We wouldn't be having this pleasant little chat had it not been for her selfless courage. The lady is an American who only wished to end this international slave ring that grabbed her as assuredly as it did me. Perhaps their computer-wizard Fred did something to her files. I don't know and really don't care. If you stop the recorders after my question but hear me continue talking afterwards, that'll serve as proof of complete agreement on your part and you will surrender a verified transcript copy of this meeting upon demand. I want your guarantees she will be protected as an American citizen regardless of your computer shortcomings and will not be detained for any reason. Do I have it?"

No one said a thing. They silently studied me like I'd spoken an unknown language, looking at me with narrowing eyes and frowning faces. Pressure mounted to the point blood vessels could burst. It was like they wanted me to be the one surrendering to their authority. Okay if they want to be stubborn so can I.

My arms uncrossed as I rose from my seat. Sounds of chairs scraping across the linoleum floor reached my ears when I started walking to the door. One whispered two-word comment that I think was "do it" reached my ears a second before Wilson spoke.

"Miss Jackson, your request surprised me. We have absolutely no intention of prosecuting any of you. There is no reason and besides, as popular as you're becoming it would be political suicide. You have my assurance Miss Ishaya will be treated with the utmost respect. Regardless of what happened to her records, I'll make certain she receives a full citizenship in the state of Ohio if necessary. Governor Calvin is a close friend who owes me a favor, not to mention what saving a victimized heroine of her stature will do for his popularity. Is that sufficient?"

Images of campaign ads stating how Calvin saved a poor woman wronged by computer fraud allowed me to look at him and smile. He said more than I'd hoped. As I started back to my seat, I glanced at the others before settling on him. "Yes, thank you," I said while sitting down.

Folsom was looking at me like he suspected something was amiss which no longer matters. Fugi is safe by order of his boss. None of the others seemed to care. My smile faded as I shifted in the chair to get comfortable.

"We'd like you to tell us how you became involved with," Wilson paused to pick up a piece of paper, "Earl Pinello, Henry Hank Kowslowski, Marcus Worth, and Frederick Samuelson. Please start at the beginning and tell us as much as you can."

Oh no he is still free. I had hoped they would've found something linking Doc to the rest and were at least out searching for him. As I looked away from Wilson toward Folsom, a frown formed.

"You don't know," I said. "This is what I was afraid of. Listen, there's a fifth man on the loose. I'll get to your question in a moment. You have to go find Doctor Adolph Heidenreich out of Cleveland immediately. He's the monster behind Earl's drugs, and I was told by Earl he uses live humans for experiments." My eyes took on a pleading quality toward Folsom. "Please don't wait, go now before it's too late!"

Folsom glanced at Wilson, who nodded his head. Then Folsom quickly worked his way behind all other seated inquisitors and disappeared through the door. Once it was closed, I looked at the rest and began giving testimony.

For over five hours I talked. Questions repeatedly interrupted me, seeming to focus on what I knew involving international partners. My only information was what I'd overheard about the Russian-made remote controls, a Middle Eastern Sheik, a dog food importer in Chile, and a Japanese Consortium, too vague to be of any use.

Water was wheeled in on a cart after the first hour, which I desperately needed to not only slake my dry throat but also calm my frazzling nerves. Eyes scrutinized me with growing doubt. Even though I lived through it, the entire ordeal sounded too fantastic to believe. Had there not been evidence left in the basements of that house, chances are I would have been dismissed as a sensationalist-seeking liar.

It concluded with their request I remain on-call for further questions. Of course I agreed, and then rose stretching. The room door opened before anyone reached it. Another uniformed officer stood to the side as I approached.

"Miss Jackson, I'm Officer Reilly," he said. "If you'll come with me, I'll escort you to the hotel where you'll be staying."

Exhaustion started growing making my legs feel rubbery. I nodded and followed him. Penny was no longer in the station, which I expected. Wherever she is, I'm sure her turn is coming. Reporters lingering in the parking lot were herded from Reilly's squad car, and just a few minutes later we pulled in front of The Hotel Wainscot. Before Reilly opened his door, he lifted a sealed manila envelope and handed it to me. "You might need these," he said.

As I began opening it, a kind smile formed on his face. Inside the envelope was a duplicate of my stolen Oklahoma Driver's License, several gift certificates from stores I didn't recognize, official city food vouchers, a wad of twenty dollar bills, and a credit card with my name stamped on it. My mouth dropped open as I stared at him.

"That's our way of saying welcome to Willard," he said. "Your friend has already checked in, but is probably on her way to the station by now. Let me see you to your room. If you need to go anywhere, please alert the front desk where you can be reached and call a cab. For as long as you're here that credit card will take care of everything including fare. You're now on the city payroll without the bureaucracy part."

Maybe it was the fatigue that threatened to overwhelm me with an emotional outburst, I don't know. This act of incredible kindness formed tears around the edges of my eyes as I smiled. "Thank you so much," I said.

He nodded, opened and climbed out his door, and then opened mine. As I stepped out, everything seemed oddly quiet. The parking lot only had empty vehicles without people lurking about. Not that I'm upset over it, but the screaming reporters at the police station were missing. As if he could read my thoughts, he said "This is private property. Only guests are permitted here. For the duration of your stay, trespassing violators will be vigorously prosecuted. I have a feeling some of the more aggressive news-hounds will end up paying for your stay."

A chuckle escaped from me while he grinned. We walked through the lobby doors to the front desk, where I was quickly checked-in with a signature. The clerk stared at me with professional detachment, but something about his body language told me he was excited to see me.

God that's an egotistical thought; I have got to stop believing everyone is thrilled to be in my presence. He's just doing his job. Once the key was handed over, I smiled and permitted Reilly to lead me to the elevators.

My room was on the fourth floor with a spectacular view of downtown Willard, but the bed held my undying attention. Reilly again welcomed me to town, and politely excused himself. When the door closed, I walked directly to the bed and dropped. Total relaxation flowed over me like a soothing breeze; darkness replaced afternoon light filtering through my closed eyelids.

Knocking on the door startled me awake. At first I didn't know where I was, but then remembered checking in here. Blackened windows informed me it was nighttime.

"JUST A MINUTE," I said while reaching for a bedside lamp.

My hand bumped a wide porcelain base on the table that proved to be the closest light. It clicked into stark brightness that made me squint. Once my eyes adjusted, I rolled off the mattress, stretched, and moved toward the door. "I'M COMING."

No one answered. It can't be Penny. She would've acknowledged.

Why the police didn't call first irritated me, but I guess something critical has risen. Regardless of the reason, and especially since they've agreed to give Fugi a fresh start, I want to assist them to the best of my ability. A huge yawn snuck out just when my hand grabbed the knob. I was closing my mouth as the door opened.

Both of my parents standing in the hall snapped me awake with the intensity of an ice water plunge. Mom had mascara running down her cheeks, dad looked angry. I was positively stunned, my mind unable to focus.

"May we come in?" Mom asked.

"Huh? Oh, yeah, sure," I said while moving to the side.

Penny's emotional feelings at being reunited with her parents were the exact opposite from mine. She was overjoyed while I'm apprehensive. My departure from Burksdale hadn't been under amicable terms. It was more like running away. I really had no idea what was coming next but refused to be intimidated. As they entered I prepared for the worst.

Mom came in first, taking two steps before moving to the side opposite me. Dad brushed past her, walking to the closest seat and taking it. My eyes looked at the floor. This was the most awkward moment I'd ever experienced.

"Joyce, I-;" mom said, "what I mean is we-, oh thank God you're all right!"

When I looked up, tears began running down her cheeks. My vision blurred. All anxieties melted away as I felt like a small protected child. Her arms opened. I moved to them. We lovingly hugged tightly, swaying gently from side to side. She kept repeating "Thank God" in-between sobs that had me bawling. A click from the room preceded the television sounds. It moved our attention toward dad.

"-conference scheduled for tomorrow afternoon," a newsman said. "Details are being released involving the horrendous ordeal faced by Carver, Ishaya, and Jackson, but they still remain sketchy. This is what we know."

"Joyce Jackson, who recently graduated from Whitmore University in Oklahoma, was in North Carolina when she was abducted into what can only be described as a nightmare world-"

The screen went dark. Dad glared at me as he placed the remote control on a nearby table. His visual antagonism ended my feelings of joy. "Have a seat," he said.

That wasn't a request, more like a command. Mom walked to the chair next to him, while I closed the door and moved to stand in front of them. My arms crossed over my chest as I watched his reaction.

His eyes narrowed slightly, teeth clinched for a brief moment, and then he looked at the ceiling over my head. Mom had growing fear cover her face watching him. He casually looked at me saying "You've become quite the rising star. Every news show in the country seems infatuated with you. Congratulations; you've managed to publicly embarrass me yet again."

Absolute fury threatened to overwhelm me. I closed my eyes briefly and forced myself to breathe calmly before responding. "To be blunt, as I was fighting for my life, the thought of your emotional well-being never crossed my mind."

"Brent, what are you *doing*?" Mom asked.

An icy stare from him silenced her, and then he glanced at me again. "I see," he said. "And did you ever once think about how none of this would have happened had you done what I said and stayed home?"

"Nope," I said. "But I will pass your sentiments on to the Carvers next time I see them."

Fire began burning behind his eyes. Though it appeared to be a monumental battle for him to avoid screaming, his obvious anger made me smile. "That's as much of your smart mouth as I can stand," he said. "You're coming back with us whether you like it or not."

My smile broadened to show teeth while shaking my head. The smile dropped as I asked "You really don't get it do you? Let me put it so simply even someone with your ego can understand. I left *because* of you. All those years when you thought I was under your control were nothing more than an act. I couldn't wait to get away from you, and now you're going to get away from me; good bye forever."

Mom's eyes widened out of terror watching me calmly look away. Before I could take a step toward the door, dad spoke. "Don't you turn your back on me young lady. We're not finished here."

Slowly I faced him with a gleam in my eyes, a new plan in mind. "You know what? It would be so much fun watching you placed under arrest for trespassing in my room. And I bet the news agencies would just *love* to find out why I had my own father arrested; think that'll be good for Jackson Realty?"

His expression hardened, eyes narrowed. "You wouldn't dare," he said.

Moving to the phone I said "If you leave now, you might be able to get away."

As I lifted the phone from the cradle, mom pushed the button down. "This has gone far enough," she said exchanging glances between dad and me. "Give me the phone." Her hand reached the earpiece to take it away. I was so surprised by this show of strength I released it, watching her return it to the cradle.

"Very good," dad said. "I'll take it from here."

"The hell you will," she said.

This was absolutely astonishing. In all my life she'd never stood up to him no matter the provocation. Dad stared at her in complete shock. My mouth dropped partially open into a small smile. She took a deep breath and set her sights on him. "We almost lost our baby once," she said, "and I'll be DAMNED if I'm going to let you chase her off again. What's wrong with you Brent? For *days* you asked if I'd heard from her, genuine worry in your voice. You moped around the house looking depressed. When the police called last night, you nearly ripped the phone off the wall until they said she was fine. Then you immediately made arrangements for us to be here, smiling at me saying she's okay. On the way you were giddy with excitement. And now that we're in front of her, you're acting like a total *jerk*? I don't know what your problem is but I've had enough!" Her face broke into a snarl. "You just sit there and keep QUIET!"

I was in awe. The heated anger on her face could almost melt steel. He started to say something, but closed his mouth while looking at the carpet. Then she slowly faced me, a look of loving compassion I remember so well gradually replacing enragement.

"All your life I've watched you prepare to leave," she said.

My expression changed to surprise. I'd truly believed I'd been the best actress ever. She smiled knowingly while nodding her head twice. "Yes that's right," she said. "You can fool many people, but never your mother. When the day arrived, I'd hoped you'd change your mind. That's why I shadowed your every step. As you drove into the sunrise, I prayed for your safety and forgiveness. Later that day neighbors came over to offer support in a manner that angered me, saying you were foolish and would be back. They didn't understand why you left your father's company, but I do."

"Well I don't," dad said.

"SHUT UP," Mom said. Her face immediately changed into something frightening as she glared at him. "If you say ONE more word, I'm leaving you and suing you for EVERYTHING you own. By the time I'm finished you won't have a pair of pants to wear!"

The thought of dad running around Burksdale in his boxers trying to sell homes nearly made me giggle, but it was the sheer ferocity of her threat that kept us both silent. Suddenly she slapped the armrests so viciously it made me jump. Then she raised from her chair, walking to stand less than a foot from me, a calmer appearance rapidly forming. Dad watched this development without attempting to intervene.

"As I was saying I understand why you wanted to leave," she said. "It wasn't because of anger though you might've held that for one reason. It's really about being independent. That's why you wanted to go on your own. I fully understand and expected it. Do you remember years ago when I said your father's upbringing gave you a strength I didn't have, that someday you'd understand what I meant?"

Dad's eyes started watering. As I stared at him watching me, I slowly nodded.

"What you did here proves I'm right," she said. "Reporters hounded us the moment they found out who we are, clamoring for information about you Joyce." A chuckle slipped out. "Your father went out of his way to warn them not to twist anything about you or there'd be hell to pay. We're both so proud of you and thankful you're okay. Regardless of what you might think your father loves you; I love you. Whatever you want to do with your life is all right no matter where it leads you, but I'm begging you. Please; please don't cut us out of it."

One tear streaked down dad's face catching me off-guard. This is the first time I've seen him cry. My vision started blurring as I looked at mom. She appeared worried over my answer, tears overflowing her eyes running down her cheeks. Sobs started building inside, forcing me to bite my quivering lower lip. When I started reaching for her, the phone rang.

"I- I have to get that," I said. "It's probably the police."

Proud smiles on both their faces almost made me lose control. I had to take several deep, broken breaths before answering on the third ring. "Hello?"

A moment of silence nearly made me hang up. "I'll come back as soon as I can," Fugi said in a bad imitation of me. "You know what really toasts my buns? When someone promises me something and then they don't do it."

Her voice surprised a smile. "H-How did you get this number?" I asked.

"I have my ways. Don't tell me you're blubbering again? Great galloping gophers, farmers could use you for crop irrigation. Anyway I have another bone to pick. Where do you get off telling the police I was born in Huron County Ohio when I distinctly said it was Richmond Virginia? Can't you get *anything* right?"

Several chuckles came from me as I moved the mouthpiece slightly to the side. "This is Cara, one of the women I escaped with," I said. "She's still in the hospital."

It looked like dad's chest puffed out as his smile grew. Mom backed to her seat, giving me a little privacy. "Well that's just wonderful," Fugi said. "Here you go forgetting all about me so you can throw a party. Man I am depressed."

Another snicker escaped as I moved the mouthpiece back into place. "It's my parents," I said. "We were talking."

Their proud smiles dropped as my words returned to me. Rather than say we were enjoying a glorious reunion after this terrible ordeal, I said we were just having an indifferent chat. It sounded bad. Fugi paused another moment before speaking. "Then I won't keep you. Now I know this really isn't my business, but I would like to point out they didn't have to come see you today. No matter what wrongs they did, they also did something right and people can change. Had it not been for your quick-thinking and incredible strength, none of us would be here now. In spite of what you believe it wasn't a group effort. Sure Penny and I helped out, but you made it all possible. I owe your parents much for raising you the way you are and would like to shake their hands. Visiting hours are over so it would have to be tomorrow. Do you know if they'll still be here?"

"I guess so. Let me ask."

As I moved the phone to the side, mom looked on the verge of tears. Dad appeared firm, but for the first time I could see a hint of fear under the façade. "She wants to meet you, but it's too late tonight," I said. "Are you planning on staying for a while?"

"Do you want us to stay?" Dad asked.

Six little words forming an easy question beckoning one of two opposite answers simplified everything. Here was our current issue wrapped into a nice, neat little bundle waiting to be cast out or reclaimed. Mom's hand went to her mouth, but dad remained staring at me unmoving.

The lesson I'd learned from Barker Exports is true wickedness doesn't ask your permission to stick around. It's forced upon you with an ugly sneer. Yet here is my father, the man I swore to leave, on the verge of crying asking my permission to remain.

Just like the way I feel about Fugi, everyone deserves a second chance if sincerely requested. And she's right. People can change. It's now obvious my life plans will not only be left to me without interference, but accepted as well. Tears pooled in my eyes as a large smile played on my face. "Yes," I said.

Mom wailed loudly while burying her face in her hands. Dad looked at his feet, shifted his head quickly to the left and then right, and closed his eyes while raising it. When his eyes opened looking at me, tears started running down his cheeks. "T-Then we'll be here," he said.

Heavy breathing came from Fugi's end as I moved the phone close to my mouth. "W-We'll be by tomorrow," I said.

Sniffles came from her end. "The least you could've done is cover the mouthpiece," she said. "Now *I'm* crying damn it! Go be with your folks. I'll see you when you get here."

Clicking indicated she'd hung up. I placed the phone in the cradle, holding my arms out to them. Mom rose rushing to me. As I hugged her, I looked at dad. He was hesitant in rising, but got to his feet and slowly walked to us. My closest arm pulled free from mom, reaching for him. Silent crying heaved his chest as he moved to me.

Together we stood as one. All former wrongs melted away in our tight embrace. Time seemed to stop as we relished this tender moment. A new beginning bright with promise lay on the horizon. May the past remain buried; what once was a broken family is now united through love.

CHAPTER 29: FIFTEEN YEARS LATER

ATLANTIC HIGH SCHOOL ROOM 137, SAVANNAH GEORGIA

In the silence of an empty late afternoon classroom, a soft step carries like cannon-fire. When I looked from the desk loaded with ungraded tests, no one had returned to claim a forgotten item. Even the hall seemed deserted. No shadows were falling over my doorway and it's once again quiet. Oh well, the janitors must be getting an early start. "If I let every noise interrupt me, I'll be here all night," I said.

My eyes wandered to the wall clock. Good heavens; four-fifteen all ready? I'd better let Steve know I'm going to be at least two more hours.

Wednesday's are one of his days off. Much as I try leaving at a reasonable time those days, I really have no choice today. Our annual reunion is this weekend and I want to get out of here with the students Friday. That means long days until then or I'll be swamped when I return. How would I be able to have any fun knowing a hundred papers were waiting?

Some of my fellow instructors take work home with them, but I swore never to do that. During the day I'm the professional history teacher, in the afternoon I'm mom, and at night I'm wife. If I start hauling papers out of here even for this special occasion, my entire balance will be thrown out. It's best to just get it done.

My chair rolled easily away from the desk. A loud yawn escaped before I could stop it. If any janitor is nearby, I'd be so embarrassed I'd want to crawl beneath the tiles. Good; no snickering came from the hall, giving me the confidence to rise and walk out of the room. It would seem I had the school to myself as far as I could see.

Mid-October afternoon sunshine cast an orange radiance on the shiny floor. Hall lights had been turned off, but they weren't necessary with windows facing the west. A feeling of excitement crept over me while walking to the teacher's lounge, like I was an explorer setting foot on a strange land. When I reached the door, I smiled and felt like shouting I claim this room in the name of me.

Enough foolishness; I have to make a call and get back to work. The door opened to an empty room as I expected. Without hesitation I entered walking directly to the wall phone. Seven pressed numbers later and I was seated listening to it ring. Steve answered after the second ring. "Hello?"

The sound of his voice brought a smile to my face. "Hi sweetie, it's me. I'm sorry, but it looks like I'm going to be awhile."

My youngest daughter Holly clamoring in the background made me chuckle as he said something to her before responding. "That's okay sweetheart. How much longer will you be?"

"About two hours," I said in an exhausted manner.

"*Two hours*?" He asked. "If they only knew how dedicated a teacher you are, they'd triple your salary. How's Chinese sound for dinner?"

Thoughts of food reminded me it'd been a long time since I ate lunch. "It sounds wonderful," I said. "See you around six-thirty."

"Before you go I have a question. I know this can wait, but I'm dying here. You just missed Penny's call. What's going on with Cara?"

That question caught me by surprise. It could mean any number of things, most of which Steve has no idea. In order to protect both Steve and Ben if it ever got out, Penny and I kept Fugi's criminal past a secret. Surely Penny didn't break that oath. My face formed a puzzled expression when I spoke. "Penny said something about Cara?"

"It wasn't so much what she said; it's how she said it. Cara has an announcement to make, for us to expect her call. Then she said something about a doctor and it looks like it's going to happen during our reunion. She almost sounded afraid. Do you have any idea what she meant?"

Is it possible Fugi has finally found a doctor who can perform a sex-change operation that'll completely restore his masculinity? Oh she'd found other surgeons during her fifteen year search, but none of them could do what she wanted. One time during a phone call, she said all they're proposing is like a wax banana. It looks nice but totally worthless for making grandkids. Though Penny might be scared of the consequences we'll face once Fugi's true identity is known, I'm happy for her. We'll handle whatever arises. For now Steve must be kept in the dark. "I guess we'll have to wait for the call," I said.

A sigh came from his end. "If she's globe-trotting right now, we'll have to wait until we see her Friday," he said. "Oh well, it looks like another weekend of drunken debauchery at the Aigrette!"

That tone melted my guilt away. A smile replaced the grimace I had a moment ago. "You're hopeless," I said.

"Hopelessly in love with you; hurry home okay?"

"I will; love you."

"Love you too, sweetheart."

Holly calling for his attention, followed by Jonathan shouting at Heather preceded the clicks of a disconnecting phone. It sounds like Steve has his hands full, poor guy. As I hung the phone up, thoughts about my family fell to the side, while memories of my experiences after my parents showed up in Willard so long ago rose to the front of my mind. The reunions tend to have that effect on me, and Steve's questioning finished the job.

Our loving family renewal concluded with dinner that night. For the first time I saw dad had a strong sense of humor and was quick-witted. Some of the stories he told had me laughing so hard my sides ached. Though my rising fame attempted to ruin the night with continual reporter interruptions, dad simply said she's the best now go away and kept talking like they didn't exist. I was not only surprised by this absolute reversal of treatment, I was also deeply moved.

Early the next day we met for breakfast before visiting Fugi. Again reporters and photographers hounded us, yet my growing love for dad increased each time he used his big build to force them aside. Fugi clinched it both ways once we made it to the hospital. She'd been moved to a private room in what the nurses were calling the fastest recovery they'd ever seen. Mom looked at Fugi with compassion, while dad stared at her in awe.

Fugi spent the next thirty minutes telling my folks what we'd gone through; stories not yet released to the public. She continually praised my ingenuity and bravery, threatening to rise out of bed and explain it to me each time I tried to interrupt. Dad was grinning proudly; mom had tears in her eyes. It culminated when Fugi sincerely thanked them for me and asked to shake their hands. A nurse sticking her head inside the room telling me I'm needed by the police ended our visit.

Penny and her folks were already at the station when we pulled up. Both our parents liked one another immediately. Smiles, hugs, and firm handshakes began what later turned into a lasting friendship. While Penny and I were led to the same conference room, they started talking about embarrassing things we'd done when little. That's one conversation I'm grateful to have missed.

For the next hour and a half, the same six people asked questions about some vague points made yesterday. Fugi's name of Cara was never brought up. She was safe. Then they prepped us for the upcoming press conference, saying it was inevitable and for us to relax. If we didn't want to answer their questions, just ignore it and move on. We were assured of complete crowd control should things start to get out of hand.

That press conference launched what turned into a seven month tour. Updated releases had been handed out describing the insidious nature of Barker Exports and how we'd defeated them. The locked kitchen pantry had been Mark's laboratory. So many dangerous insects living inside aquariums were discovered that all further investigation was called back until special exterminators declared the place clean. Exploding doors had been safely detonated, but no files were ever located. My accidental destruction of the computer sealed the fate of many lives. None of the victims were found.

Three days later Fugi was released from the hospital. Life of a Woman magazine held a grand buffet in our honor. National as well as international press covered the affair. Fugi was right when she said it was nothing more than a gravy-covered interview. Our meal was constantly interrupted with questions and requests for future speaking engagements. When it ended, we secretly agreed never to do that again.

Some kind of emergency rose in my father's company the next day, requiring them to leave. I never thought I'd feel that way but I hated to see them go. We'd had so much fun repairing the damaged bond. Before they headed to the airport, I promised to return to Burksdale as soon as possible.

Penny's folks left a little later that afternoon. She wanted to go with them but government officials requested she remain. Tears fell profusely when they drove off, and even Fugi looked misty-eyed.

Once Penny felt up to it, we turned our undivided attention toward Barker Exports' only villainous survivor.

Heidenreich seemed to have vanished from the Earth. Though they found his lab which looked like something from a horror movie, he'd long since left. None of his drugs were found, even at Barker Exports. Assurances were made he would be brought to justice while Fugi listened quietly. Her expression of grim hatred for the man sent shivers down my spine, but she remained calm each time a hot lead turned cold.

Ten days later our part ended. We were told if anything new comes up we'd be the first to know. Then we agreed to be on call for as long as needed.

Someone must've alerted the media our part was over. An invitation to speak in front of young girls was waiting at the hotel front desk before we could check out. It was the annual Girl Scout convention held in Savannah, Georgia. To me it was an honor being requested as the main speaker. Fugi mumbled something about jail-bait but willingly went along. My first sighting of this wonderful city occurred the next day. I fell in love with it. A quick detour to the city school board to fill out an application was made. Then we gave our talk about the only limits a girl faces are what she imposes on herself, which ended with a standing ovation.

Requests for our appearance kept us on the run. No sooner had we finished one, we had to jump a plane for another. Twice we went overseas where folks treated us like royalty. In my opinion, it culminated with an appearance on The Tomorrow Show where we found out a secret ballot had been cast. It was decided from that day forward we'd be known as The American Musketeers. Even Fugi looked moved and she always brushed sensationalistic jargon off as something that evaporated quickly.

As with all things interest faded. News about other acts of heroism at first competed with us until finally replacing our story. On Christmas Eve we said our tearful goodbyes with the assurance of never losing touch. That was one promise I knew would not be broken and I was right.

Three months after her return to Virginia Beach, Penny married Ben. Fugi and I served as maids of honor even though Fugi hated dressing that way. It was obvious she'd never be comfortable as a woman.

The following fall Penny started law school. Ben supported her as she worked very hard to achieve her goal. Her dreams became reality six years later after she passed the bar exam. Local news covered her graduation like she was still a celebrity which made all of us proud. Today she's the mother of two boys and one girl, working for one of the most prestigious law firms in all of southeastern Virginia.

For two years Fugi temporarily lived in hotels all over the world. Once she heard about a new sex change procedure, she was on a plane heading toward it. Each trip resulted in a disappointment for her yet she never stopped searching. Finally her hunts slowed enough to settle in Boston, Massachusetts. When I asked if she had any friends or family there, she said no. Her sole reason for choosing that city was because she likes beans end of discussion. The pursuits for a sex-reversal never stopped, but no matter where she was in the world she never missed our annual reunion in Cleveland.

While traveling the country for our speaking engagements I'd planted resumes in many cities. A dozen requests for interviews were waiting when I reached my parent's house. To my happy surprise, the one I'd really longed for was in the mix. Savannah wanted to speak with me at my earliest convenience. Even though mom and dad hoped I'd remain with them, my heart was set.

Burksdale welcomed me like a conquering heroine. Pictures of Penny and me kneeling in a hug captured by that first helicopter to fly over Barker Exports adorned many shop windows. Exhaustion and soot could be seen on my face while I stared at the photographer. No matter where I went folks came up asking to shake my hand. It climaxed when the town held a parade in my honor on New Year's Day. Dad looked so handsome and proud watching me accept the key to the city. Mom had tears streaming down her face. Mary joked about how I'd fooled everyone into giving me free shoes which brought back many fond childhood memories. I had a blast until Savannah asked for an official meeting in late winter. On that rainy March day, I bid farewell to my birth town. Five months later I was teaching high school history with all past adventures slipping to the background.

Ten years ago Steve literally bumped into me. I still hold a doubt about whether that was an accident or set-up. He only smiles when I ask. In little time we were dating heavily. Seven months after meeting him in the supermarket, he asked for my hand in marriage. His proposal left me speechless making my answer a tearful nod. Since then I've never been happier. He gave me three wonderful children and a beautiful life.

Okay that's enough recollecting. If I don't get back to work I'll miss out on one of my favorite meals. Besides I have all weekend to remember the past and discuss changes that occurred over the year. And this reunion promises to be extra-special with news from Fugi. Oh well all thoughts must return to the present, for now at least.

A smile was on my face as I rose from the chair. All the reminiscing made me feel twenty-two again. I was happy as I opened the door and started down the hall, but when I was about fifteen feet from my room a shadow crossed the threshold. My movements halted when a young man backed out of the doorway.

"Excuse me, can I help you?" I asked.

He turned from my voice and started running. Instincts kicked in as I set off after him. His youth combined with the wrong shoes on my feet made his getaway complete. When I reached the corner he'd turned, he was nowhere to be seen and the hall was quiet. "First I'll see what damage you did and then call the cops."

Anger built as my teeth gritted together and I stomped back to the room. Of all the timing for a vandal to strike this has to be the worst. In no way am I going to permit it to interfere with my weekend!

Enragement morphed into fear as I reached the entrance, my legs refused to advance. The test papers on the desk were now in my seat rolled out to where I could see, and on the desk rested a yellowed envelope with one line for the recipient's mailing address. No one else was in the room, giving me the fortitude to enter and slowly approach the mystery document. What I saw chilled the marrow in my bones.

The return address was Barker Exports Cleveland Ohio, addressed to BL Seven Forty-Two. My hands started shaking as I removed the single paper inside.

In simple type it read "Do you remember us? We remember you very well. Bet you thought it was over. You were wrong. That was only the preliminaries, now comes the main event fifteen years in the making. It commences with the repossession of three faulty units. See you soon, seven forty-two."

To be continued...

Acknowledgements

There are so many who've contributed to SWITCHER that if I forget someone, it's simply a testimony to my advancing age. They say the mind is the second thing to go with age. Don't ask what the first is, I forgot.

First and foremost I want to thank my wife Marcia. Her patience and assistance has been incredible. Without her input during a number of memory dreams I doubt this book would ever have been finished. Her input after reading the first draft was essential to the story.

Next would have to be Scotty for his technical and legal advice. Not once did he ever avoid me even when the chance was available. His work was and still is legendary.

This book has seen many changes due primarily to the input from many readers. Darlene, Elizabeth, Phyllis (Justme), Carlos, Patricia, Denise, Peggy, Judy (Blue Dragon), Heather, Holly, JoJo (Wildchild), Jo (Gifted Pixie), Dan, Frank, Paula, Norrin, and Cherise all played integral parts in the final draft. A few of the people listed above need to be singled out; Darlene for her assistance in making sure memory dreams and the plot were easily discernible, Elizabeth (posthumously) for suggesting a toning down of graphic parts, Phyllis for personality change suggestions, Carlos for general editing help, JoJo for so much help it would take another book to list, Patricia Denise and Peggy for final recommendations, and last but not least Cherise- my muse and guide.

Finally I'd like to acknowledge the valuable input from Norfolk Airport Security, Willard Ohio Police and Fire Departments, and the Savannah Georgia Chamber of Commerce. Of course Teri, Debbie, and Chris of E-Book Editors need to be thanked for their expeditious conversions of my manuscript into the many different formats now available today; great job guys!

www.ingramcontent.com/pod-product-compliance
Lightning Source LLC
Chambersburg PA
CBHW021309250626
47155CB00002B/455